THE WORLD LOVES
TERRY PRATCHETT . . .
AND SO WILL YOU!

"Nothing short of magical."
Chicago Tribune

"Unadulterated fun . . . witty, frequently
hilarious . . . Pratchett parodies everything in sight."
San Francisco Chronicle

"Acclaimed British author Pratchett continues to
distinguish himself from his colleagues with clever
plot lines and genuinely likable characters."
Publishers Weekly (*Starred Review*)

"Truly original . . . Discworld is more complicated
and satisfactory than Oz. . . . Brilliant."
A. S. Byatt

"Think J.R.R. Tolkien with a sharper, more satiric edge."
Houston Chronicle

"A hearty dose of comedy and genuine slapstick humor."
Library Journal

"If I were making my list of Best Books of the Twentieth
Century, Terry Pratchett's would be most of them."
Elizabeth Peters

Terry Pratchett

Small Gods

A Novel of Discworld®

HarperTorch
An Imprint of HarperCollinsPublishers

❦

HARPERTORCH
An Imprint of HarperCollins*Publishers*
10 East 53rd Street
New York, New York 10022-5299

Copyright © 1992 by Terry and Lyn Pratchett
ISBN: 0-06-109217-7

First HarperTorch paperback printing: March 2003
First HarperCollins paperback printing: November 1994
First HarperCollins hardcover printing: February 1994

HarperCollins ®, HarperTorch™, and ❦™ are trademarks of Harper-Collins Publishers Inc.

Printed in the United States of America

Visit HarperTorch on the World Wide Web at www.harpercollins.com

20   19   18

Now consider the tortoise and the eagle.

The tortoise is a ground-living creature. It is impossible to live nearer the ground without being under it. Its horizons are a few inches away. It has about as good a turn of speed as you need to hunt down a lettuce. It has survived while the rest of evolution flowed past it by being, on the whole, no threat to anyone and too much trouble to eat.

And then there is the eagle. A creature of the air and high places, whose horizons go all the way to the edge of the world. Eyesight keen enough to spot the rustle of some small and squeaky creature half a mile away. All power, all control. Lightning death on wings. Talons and claws enough to make a meal of anything smaller than it is and at least take a hurried snack out of anything bigger.

And yet the eagle will sit for hours on the crag and survey the kingdoms of the world until it spots a distant movement and then it will focus, focus, *focus* on the small shell wobbling among the bushes down there on the desert. And it will *leap* . . .

And a minute later the tortoise finds the world dropping away from it. And it sees the world for the first time, no longer one inch from the ground but five hundred feet above it, and it thinks: what a great friend I have in the eagle.

1

And then the eagle lets go.

And almost always the tortoise plunges to its death. Everyone knows why the tortoise does this. Gravity is a habit that is hard to shake off. No one knows why the eagle does this. There's good eating on a tortoise but, considering the effort involved, there's much better eating on practically anything else. It's simply the delight of eagles to torment tortoises.

But of course, what the eagle does not realize is that it is participating in a very crude form of natural selection.

One day a tortoise will learn how to fly.

The story takes place in desert lands, in shades of umber and orange. When it begins and ends is more problematical, but at least one of its beginnings took place above the snowline, thousands of miles away in the mountains around the Hub.*

One of the recurring philosophical questions is:

"Does a falling tree in the forest make a sound when there is no one to hear?"

Which says something about the nature of philosophers, because there is always someone in a forest. It may only be a badger, wondering what that cracking noise was, or a squirrel a bit puzzled by all the scenery going upwards, but *someone*. At the very least, if it was deep enough in the forest, millions of small gods would have heard it.

Things just happen, one after another. They don't care who knows. But *history* . . . ah, history is different. History has to be observed. Otherwise it's not history. It's just . . . well, things happening one after another.

---

*Or, if you are a believer in Omnianism, the Pole.

And, of course, it has to be controlled. Otherwise it might turn into anything. Because history, contrary to popular theories, *is* kings and dates and battles. And these things have to happen at the right time. This is difficult. In a chaotic universe there are too many things to go wrong. It's too easy for a general's horse to lose a shoe at the wrong time, or for someone to mishear an order, or for the carrier of the vital message to be waylaid by some men with sticks and a cash flow problem. Then there are wild stories, parasitic growths on the tree of history, trying to bend it their way.

So history has its caretakers.

They live . . . well, in the nature of things they live wherever they are sent, but their *spiritual* home is in a hidden valley in the high Ramtops of the Discworld, where the books of history are kept.

These aren't books in which the events of the past are pinned like so many butterflies to a cork. These are the books from which history is derived. There are more than twenty thousand of them; each one is ten feet high, bound in lead, and the letters are so small that they have to be read with a magnifying glass.

When people say "It is written . . ." it is written *here*.

There are fewer metaphors around than people think.

Every month the abbot and two senior monks go into the cave where the books are kept. It used to be the duty of the abbot alone, but two other reliable monks were included after the unfortunate case of the 59th Abbot, who made a million dollars in small bets before his fellow monks caught up with him.

Besides, it's dangerous to go in alone. The sheer concentratedness of History, sleeting past soundlessly out into the world, can be overwhelming. Time is a drug. Too much of it kills you.

The 493rd Abbot folded his wrinkled hands and addressed Lu-Tze, one of his most senior monks. The clear air and untroubled life of the secret valley was such that all the monks were senior; besides, when you work with Time every day, some of it tends to rub off.

"The place is Omnia," said the abbot, "on the Klatchian coast."

"I remember," said Lu-Tze. "Young fellow called Ossory, wasn't there?"

"Things must be . . . *carefully observed*," said the abbot. "There are pressures. Free will, predestination . . . the power of symbols . . . turning-point . . . you know all about this."

"Haven't been to Omnia for, oh, must be seven hundred years," said Lu-Tze. "Dry place. Shouldn't think there's a ton of good soil in the whole country, either."

"Off you go, then," said the abbot.

"I shall take my mountains," said Lu-Tze. "The climate will be good for them."

And he also took his broom and his sleeping mat. The history monks don't go in for possessions. They find most things wear out in a century or two.

It took him four years to get to Omnia. He had to watch a couple of battles and an assassination on the way, otherwise they would just have been random events.

It was the Year of the Notional Serpent, or two hundred years after the Declaration of the Prophet Abbys.

Which meant that the time of the 8th Prophet was imminent.

That was the reliable thing about the Church of the Great God Om. It had very punctual prophets. You could set your calendar by them, if you had one big enough.

And, as is generally the case around the time a prophet is expected, the Church redoubled its efforts to be holy. This was very much like the bustle you get in any large concern when the auditors are expected, but tended towards taking people suspected of being less holy and putting them to death in a hundred ingenious ways. This is considered a reliable barometer of the state of one's piety in most of the really popular religions. There's a tendency to declare that there is more backsliding around than in the national toboggan championships, that heresy must be torn out root and branch, and even arm and leg and eye and tongue, and that it's time to wipe the slate clean. Blood is generally considered very efficient for this purpose.

And it came to pass that in that time the Great God Om spake unto Brutha, the Chosen One:

"Psst!"

Brutha paused in mid-hoe and stared around the Temple garden.

"Pardon?" he said.

It was a fine day early in the lesser Spring. The prayer mills spun merrily in the breeze off the mountains. Bees loafed around in the bean blossoms, but buzzed fast in order to give the impression of hard work. High above, a lone eagle circled.

Brutha shrugged, and got back to the melons.

Yea, the Great God Om spake again unto Brutha, the Chosen One:

"Psst!"

Brutha hesitated. Someone had definitely spoken to

him from out of the air. Perhaps it was a demon. Novice master Brother Nhumrod was hot on the subject of demons. Impure thoughts and demons. One led to the other. Brutha was uncomfortably aware that he was probably overdue a demon.

The thing to do was to be resolute and repeat the Nine Fundamental Aphorisms.

Once more the Great God Om spake unto Brutha, the Chosen One:

"Are you deaf, boy?"

The hoe thudded on to the baking soil. Brutha spun around. There were the bees, the eagle and, at the far end of the garden, old Brother Lu-Tze dreamily forking over the dung heap. The prayer mills whirled reassuringly along the walls.

He made the sign with which the Prophet Ishkible had cast out spirits.

"Get thee behind me, demon," he muttered.

"I *am* behind you."

Brutha turned again, slowly. The garden was still empty.

He fled.

Many stories start long before they begin, and Brutha's story had its origins thousands of years before his birth.

There are billions of gods in the world. They swarm as thick as herring roe. Most of them are too small to see and never get worshiped, at least by anything bigger than bacteria, who never say their prayers and don't demand much in the way of miracles.

They are the small gods—the spirits of places where two ant trails cross, the gods of microclimates down between the grass roots. And most of them stay that way.

Because what they lack is *belief*.

A handful, though, go on to greater things. Anything may trigger it. A shepherd, seeking a lost lamb, finds it among the briars and takes a minute or two to build a small cairn of stones in general thanks to whatever spirits might be around the place. Or a peculiarly shaped tree becomes associated with a cure for disease. Or someone carves a spiral on an isolated stone. Because what gods need is belief, and what humans want is gods.

Often it stops there. But sometimes it goes further. More rocks are added, more stones are raised, a temple is built on the site where the tree once stood. The god grows in strength, the belief of its worshipers raising it upwards like a thousand tons of rocket fuel. For a very few, the sky's the limit.

And, sometimes, not even that.

Brother Nhumrod was wrestling with impure thoughts in the privacy of his severe cell when he heard the fervent voice from the novitiates' dormitory.

The Brutha boy was flat on his face in front of a statue of Om in His manifestation as a thunderbolt, shaking and gabbling fragments of prayer.

There was something creepy about that boy, Nhumrod thought. It was the way he looked at you when you were talking, as if he was *listening*.

He wandered out and prodded the prone youth with the end of his cane.

"Get up, boy! What do you think you're doing in the dormitory in the middle of the day? Mmm?"

Brutha managed to spin around while still flat on the floor and grasped the priest's ankles.

"Voice! A voice! It *spoke* to me!" he wailed.

Nhumrod breathed out. Ah. This was familiar ground. Voices were right up Nhumrod's cloister. He heard them all the time.

"Get up, boy," he said, slightly more kindly.

Brutha got to his feet.

He was, as Nhumrod had complained before, too old to be a proper novice. About ten years too old. Give me a boy up to the age of seven, Nhumrod had always said.

But Brutha was going to die a novice. When they made the rules, they'd never allowed for anything like Brutha.

His big red honest face stared up at the novice master.

"Sit down on your bed, Brutha," said Nhumrod.

Brutha obeyed immediately. Brutha did not know the meaning of the word disobedience. It was only one of a large number of words he didn't know the meaning of.

Nhumrod sat down beside him.

"Now, Brutha," he said, "you know what happens to people who tell falsehoods, don't you?"

Brutha nodded, blushing.

"Very well. Now tell me about these voices."

Brutha twisted the hem of his robe in his hands.

"It was more like one voice, master," he said.

"—like one voice," said Brother Nhumrod. "And what did this voice say? Mmm?"

Brutha hesitated. Now he came to think about it, the voice hadn't *said* anything very much. It had just spoken. It was, in any case, hard to talk to Brother Nhumrod, who had a nervous habit of squinting at the speaker's lips and repeating the last few words they said practically as they said them. He also touched things all the time—walls, furniture, people—as if he was afraid the universe would disappear if he didn't keep hold of it.

And he had so many nervous tics that they had to queue. Brother Nhumrod was perfectly normal for someone who had survived in the Citadel for fifty years.

"Well . . ." Brutha began.

Brother Nhumrod held up a skinny hand. Brutha could see the pale blue veins in it.

"And I am sure you know that there are *two* kinds of voice that are heard by the spiritual," said the master of novices. One eyebrow began to twitch.

"Yes, master. Brother Murduck told us that," said Brutha, meekly.

"—told us that. Yes. Sometimes, as He in His infinite wisdom sees fit, the God speaks to a chosen one and he becomes a great prophet," said Nhumrod. "Now, I am sure you wouldn't presume to consider yourself one of them? Mmm?"

"No, master."

"—master. But there are *other* voices," said Brother Nhumrod, and now his voice had a slight tremolo, "beguiling and wheedling and persuasive voices, yes? Voices that are always waiting to catch us off our guard?"

Brutha relaxed. This was more familiar ground.

All the novices knew about *those* kinds of voices. Except that usually they talked about fairly straightforward things, like the pleasures of nighttime manipulation and the general desirability of girls. Which showed that they were novices when it came to voices. Brother Nhumrod got the kind of voices that were, by comparison, a full oratorio. Some of the bolder novices liked to get Brother Nhumrod talking on the subject of voices. He was an education, they said. Especially when little bits of white spit appeared at the corners of his mouth.

Brutha listened.

*   *   *

Brother Nhumrod was the novice master, but he wasn't *the* novice master. He was only master of the group that included Brutha. There were others. Possibly someone in the Citadel knew how many there were. There was someone somewhere whose job it was to know *everything*.

The Citadel occupied the whole of the heart of the city of Kom, in the lands between the deserts of Klatch and the plains and jungles of Howondaland. It extended for miles, its temples, churches, schools, dormitories, gardens, and towers growing into and around one another in a way that suggested a million termites all trying to build their mounds at the same time.

When the sun rose the reflection of the doors of the central Temple blazed like fire. They were bronze, and a hundred feet tall. On them, in letters of gold set in lead, were the Commandments. There were five hundred and twelve so far, and doubtless the next prophet would add his share.

The sun's reflected glow shone down and across the tens of thousands of the strong-in-faith who labored below for the greater glory of the Great God Om.

Probably no one *did* know how many of them there were. Some things have a way of going critical. Certainly there was only one Cenobiarch, the Superior Iam. That was certain. And six Archpriests. And thirty lesser Iams. And hundreds of bishops, deacons, subdeacons, and priests. And novices like rats in a grain store. And craftsmen, and bull breeders, and torturers, and Vestigial Virgins . . .

No matter what your skills, there was a place for you in the Citadel.

And if your skill lay in asking the wrong kinds of

questions or losing the righteous kind of wars, the place might just be the furnaces of purity, or the Quisition's pits of justice.

A place for everyone. And everyone in their place.

The sun beat down on the temple garden.

The Great God Om tried to stay in the shade of a melon vine. He was probably safe here, here inside these walls and with the prayer towers all around, but you couldn't be too careful. He'd been lucky once, but it was asking too much to expect to be lucky again.

The trouble with being a god is that you've got no one to pray to.

He crawled forward purposefully towards the old man shoveling muck until, after much exertion, he judged himself to be within earshot.

He spake thusly: "Hey, you!"

There was no answer. There was not even any suggestion that anything had been heard.

Om lost his temper and turned Lu-Tze into a lowly worm in the deepest cesspit of hell, and then got even more angry when the old man went on peacefully shoveling.

"The devils of infinity fill your living bones with sulphur!" he screamed.

This did not make a great deal of difference.

"Deaf old bugger," muttered the Great God Om.

Or perhaps there was someone who *did* know all there was to be known about the Citadel. There's always someone who collects knowledge, not because of a love of the stuff but in the same way that a magpie collects glitter or a caddis fly collects little bits of twigs and rock.

And there's always someone who has to do all those things that need to be done but which other people would rather not do or, even, acknowledge existed.

The third thing the people noticed about Vorbis was his height. He was well over six feet tall, but stick-thin, like a normal proportioned person modeled in clay by a child and then rolled out.

The second thing that people noticed about Vorbis was his eyes. His ancestors had come from one of the deep desert tribes that had evolved the peculiar trait of having dark eyes—not just dark of pupil, but almost black of eyeball. It made it very hard to tell where he was looking. It was as if he had sunglasses on under his skin.

But the first thing they noticed was his skull.

Deacon Vorbis was bald by design. Most of the Church's ministers, as soon as they were ordained, cultivated long hair and beards that you could lose a goat in. But Vorbis shaved all over. He gleamed. And lack of hair seemed to add to his power. He didn't menace. He never threatened. He just gave everyone the feeling that his personal space radiated several meters from his body, and that anyone approaching Vorbis was intruding on something important. Superiors fifty years his senior felt apologetic about interrupting whatever it was he was thinking about.

It was almost impossible to know what he was thinking about and no one ever asked. The most obvious reason for this was that Vorbis was the head of the Quisition, whose job it was to do all those things that needed to be done and which other people would rather not do.

You do not ask people like that what they are thinking about in case they turn around very slowly and say "You."

The highest post that could be held in the Quisition was that of deacon, a rule instituted hundreds of years ago to prevent this branch of the Church becoming too big for its boots.* But with a mind like his, everyone said, he could easily be an archpriest by now, or even an Iam.

Vorbis didn't worry about that kind of trivia. Vorbis knew his destiny. Hadn't the God himself told him?

"There," said Brother Nhumrod, patting Brutha on the shoulder. "I'm sure you will see things clearer now."

Brutha felt that a specific reply was expected.

"Yes, master," he said. "I'm sure I shall."

"—shall. It is your holy duty to resist the voices at all times," said Nhumrod, still patting.

"Yes, master. I will. Especially if they tell me to do any of the things you mentioned."

"—mentioned. Good. Good. And if you hear them again, what will you do? Mmm?"

"Come and tell you," said Brutha, dutifully.

"—tell you. Good. Good. That's what I like to hear," said Nhumrod. "That's what I tell all my boys. Remember that I'm always here to deal with any little problems that may be bothering you."

"Yes, master. Shall I go back to the garden now?"

"—now. I think so. I think so. And no more voices, d'you hear?" Nhumrod waved a finger of his non-patting hand. A cheek puckered.

"Yes, master."

"What were you doing in the garden?"

"Hoeing the melons, master," said Brutha.

---

*Which were of the one-size-fits-all, tighten-the-screws variety.

"Melons? Ah. Melons," said Nhumrod slowly.

"Melons. Melons. Well, that goes some way toward explaining things, of course."

An eyelid flickered madly.

It wasn't just the Great God that spoke to Vorbis, in the confines of his head. *Everyone* spoke to an exquisitor, sooner or later. It was just a matter of stamina.

Vorbis didn't often go down to watch the inquisitors at work these days. Exquisitors didn't have to. He sent down instructions, he received reports. But special circumstances merited his special attention.

It has to be said . . . there was little to laugh at in the cellar of the Quisition. Not if you had a normal sense of humor. There were no jolly little signs saying: You Don't Have To Be Pitilessly Sadistic To Work Here But It Helps!!!

But there were things to suggest to a thinking man that the Creator of mankind had a very oblique sense of fun indeed, and to breed in his heart a rage to storm the gates of heaven.

The mugs, for example. The inquisitors stopped work twice a day for coffee. Their mugs, which each man had brought from home, were grouped around the kettle on the hearth of the central furnace which incidentally heated the irons and knives.

They had legends on them like A Present From the Holy Grotto of Ossory, or To The World's Greatest Daddy. Most of them were chipped, and no two of them were the same.

And there were the postcards on the wall. It was traditional that, when an inquisitor went on holiday, he'd send back a crudely colored woodcut of the local view with some suitably jolly and risqué message on the back. And there was the pinned-up tearful letter from Inquisitor First Class Ishmale "Pop" Quoom, thanking all the lads for collecting no fewer than seventy-eight *obols* for his retirement present and the lovely bunch of flowers for Mrs. Quoom, indicating that he'd always remember his days in No. 3 pit, and was looking forward to coming in and helping out any time they were shorthanded.

And it all meant this: that there are hardly any excesses of the most crazed psychopath that cannot easily be duplicated by a normal, kindly family man who just comes in to work every day and has a job to do.

Vorbis loved knowing that. A man who knew that, knew everything he needed to know about people.

Currently he was sitting alongside the bench on which lay what was still, technically, the trembling body of Brother Sasho, formerly his secretary.

He looked up at the duty inquisitor, who nodded. Vorbis leaned over the chained secretary.

"What were their names?" he repeated.

". . . don't know . . ."

"I know you gave them copies of my correspondence, Sasho. They are treacherous heretics who will spend eternity in the hells. Will you join them?"

". . . don't know names . . ."

"I trusted you, Sasho. You spied on me. You betrayed the Church."

". . . no names . . ."

"Truth is surcease from pain, Sasho. Tell me."

". . . truth . . ."

Vorbis sighed. And then he saw one of Sasho's fingers curling and uncurling under the manacles. Beckoning.

"Yes?"

He leaned closer over the body.

Sasho opened his one remaining eye.

". . . truth . . ."

"Yes?"

". . . The Turtle Moves . . ."

Vorbis sat back, his expression unchanged. His expression seldom changed unless he wanted it to. The inquisitor watched him in terror.

"I see," said Vorbis. He stood up, and nodded at the inquisitor.

"How long has he been down here?"

"Two days, lord."

"And you can keep him alive for—?"

"Perhaps two days more, lord."

"Do so. Do so. It is, after all," said Vorbis, "our duty to preserve life for as long as possible. Is it not?"

The inquisitor gave him the nervous smile of one in the presence of a superior whose merest word could see him manacled on a bench.

"Er . . . yes, lord."

"Heresy and lies everywhere," Vorbis sighed. "And now I shall have to find another secretary. It is too vexing."

After twenty minutes Brutha relaxed. The siren voices of sensuous evil seemed to have gone away.

He got on with the melons. He felt capable of understanding melons. Melons seemed a lot more comprehensible than most things.

"Hey, you!"

Brutha straightened up.

"I do not hear you, oh foul succubus," he said.

"Oh yes you do, boy. Now, what I want you to do is—"

"I've got my fingers in my ears!"

"Suits you. Suits you. Makes you look like a vase. Now—"

"I'm humming a tune! I'm humming a tune!"

Brother Preptil, the master of the music, had described Brutha's voice as putting him in mind of a disappointed vulture arriving too late at the dead donkey. Choral singing was compulsory for novitiates, but after much petitioning by Brother Preptil a special dispensation had been made for Brutha. The sight of his big round face screwed up in the effort to please was bad enough, but what was worse was listening to his voice, which was certainly powerful and full of intent conviction, swinging backward and forward across the tune without ever quite hitting it.

He got Extra Melons instead.

Up in the prayer towers a flock of crows took off in a hurry.

After a full chorus of *He is Trampling the Unrighteous with Hooves of Hot Iron* Brutha unplugged his ears and risked a quick listen.

Apart from the distant protests of the crows, there was silence.

It worked. Put your trust in the God, they said. And he always had. As far back as he could remember.

He picked up his hoe and turned back, in relief, to the vines.

The hoe's blade was about to hit the ground when Brutha saw the tortoise.

It was small and basically yellow and covered with dust. Its shell was badly chipped. It had one beady eye— the other had fallen to one of the thousands of dangers that attend any slow-moving creature which lives an inch from the ground.

He looked around. The gardens were well inside the temple complex, and surrounded by high walls.

"How did you get in here, little creature?" he said. "Did you fly?"

The tortoise stared monoptically at him. Brutha felt a bit homesick. There had been plenty of tortoises in the sandy hills back home.

"I could give you some lettuce," said Brutha. "But I don't think tortoises are allowed in the gardens. Aren't you vermin?"

The tortoise continued to stare. Practically nothing can stare like a tortoise.

Brutha felt obliged to do something.

"There's grapes," he said. "Probably it's not sinful to give you one grape. How would you like a grape, little tortoise?"

"How would you like to be an abomination in the nethermost pit of chaos?" said the tortoise.

The crows, who had fled to the outer walls, took off again to a rendering of *The Way of the Infidel Is A Nest Of Thorns*.

Brutha opened his eyes and took his fingers out of his ears again.

The tortoise said, "I'm still here."

Brutha hesitated. It dawned on him, very slowly, that demons and succubi didn't turn up looking like small old tortoises. There wouldn't be much point. Even Brother Nhumrod would have to agree that when it came to rampant eroticism, you could do a lot better than a one-eyed tortoise.

"I didn't know tortoises could talk," he said.

"They can't," said the tortoise. "Read my lips."

Brutha looked closer.

"You haven't got lips," he said.

"No, nor proper vocal cords," agreed the tortoise. "I'm doing it straight into your head, do you understand?"

"Gosh!"

"You *do* understand, don't you?"

"No."

The tortoise rolled its eye.

"I should have known. Well, it doesn't matter. I don't have to waste time on gardeners. Go and fetch the top man, right now."

"Top man?" said Brutha. He put his hand to his mouth. "You don't mean . . . Brother Nhumrod?"

"Who's he?" said the tortoise.

"The master of the novices!"

"Oh, *Me!*" said the tortoise. "No," it went on, in a singsong imitation of Brutha's voice, "I don't mean the master of the novices. I mean the High Priest or whatever he calls himself. I suppose there *is* one?"

Brutha nodded blankly.

"High Priest, right?" said the tortoise. "High. Priest. High Priest."

Brutha nodded again. He knew there was a High Priest. It was just that, while he could just about encompass the hierarchical structure between his own self and Brother Nhumrod, he was unable to give serious consideration to any kind of link between Brutha the novice and the Cenobiarch. He was theoretically aware that there was one, that there was a huge canonical structure with the High Priest at the top and Brutha very firmly at the bottom, but he viewed it in the same way as an amoeba might view the chain of evolution all the way between itself and, for example, a chartered accountant. It was missing links all the way to the top.

"I can't go asking the—" Brutha hesitated. Even the *thought* of talking to the Cenobiarch frightened him into silence. "I can't ask *anyone* to ask the High Cenobiarch to come and talk to a *tortoise!*"

"Turn into a mud leech and wither in the fires of retribution!" screamed the tortoise.

"There's no need to curse," said Brutha.

The tortoise bounced up and down furiously.

"That wasn't a curse! That was an order! I am the Great God Om!"

Brutha blinked.

Then he said, "No you're not. I've seen the Great God Om," he waved a hand making the shape of the holy horns, conscientiously, "and he isn't tortoise-shaped. He comes as an eagle, or a lion, or a mighty bull. There's a statue in the Great Temple. It's seven cubits high. It's got bronze on it and everything. It's trampling infidels. You can't trample infidels when you're a tortoise. I mean, all you could do is give them a meaningful look. It's got horns of real gold. Where I used to live there was a statue one cubit high in the next village and that was a bull too. So that's how I know you're not the Great God"—holy horns—"Om."

The tortoise subsided.

"How many talking tortoises have you met?" it said sarcastically.

"I don't know," said Brutha.

"What d'you mean, you don't know?"

"Well, they might all talk," said Brutha conscientiously, demonstrating the very personal kind of logic that got him Extra Melons. "They just might not say anything when I'm there."

"I am the Great God Om," said the tortoise, in a menacing and unavoidably low voice, "and before very long you are going to be a very unfortunate priest. Go and get him."

"Novice," said Brutha.

"What?"

"Novice, not priest. They won't let me—"

"Get him!"

"But I don't think the Cenobiarch ever comes into our vegetable garden," said Brutha. "I don't think he even knows what a melon *is*."

"I'm not bothered about that," said the tortoise. "Fetch him now, or there will be a shaking of the earth, the moon will be as blood, agues and boils will afflict mankind and diverse ills will befall. I really mean it," it added.

"I'll see what I can do," said Brutha, backing away.

"And I'm being very reasonable, in the circumstances!" the tortoise shouted after him.

"You don't sing badly, mind you!" it added, as an afterthought.

"I've heard worse!" as Brutha's grubby robe disappeared through the gateway.

"Puts me in mind of that time there was the affliction of plague in Pseudopolis," it said quietly, as the footsteps faded. "What a wailing and a gnashing of teeth was there, all right." It sighed. "Great days. Great days!"

Many feel they are called to the priesthood, but what they really hear is an inner voice saying, "It's indoor work with no heavy lifting, do you want to be a plowman like your father?"

Whereas Brutha didn't just believe. He really Believed. That sort of thing is usually embarrassing when it happens in a God-fearing family, but all Brutha had was his grandmother, and she Believed too. She believed like iron believes in metal. She was the kind of woman every priest dreads in a congregation, the one who knows all the chants, all the sermons. In the Omnian Church women were allowed in the temple only on sufferance, and had to keep absolutely silent and well covered-up in their own section behind the pulpit in case the sight of one half of the human race caused the male members of the congregation to hear voices not unakin to those that plagued Brother Nhumrod through every sleeping and waking hour. The problem was that Brutha's grandmother had the kind of personality that can project itself through a lead sheet and a bitter piety with the strength of a diamond-bit auger.

If she had been born a man, Omnianism would have found its 8th Prophet rather earlier than expected. As it was, she organized the temple-cleaning, statue-polishing, and stoning-of-suspected-adulteresses rotas with a terrible efficiency.

So Brutha grew up in the sure and certain knowledge of the Great God Om. Brutha grew up *knowing* that Om's eyes were on him all the time, especially in places like the privy, and that demons assailed him on all sides and were only kept at bay by the strength of his belief and the weight of grandmother's cane, which was kept behind the door on those rare occasions when it was not being used. He could recite every verse in all seven Books of the Prophets, and every single Precept. He knew all the Laws and the Songs. Especially the Laws.

The Omnians were a God-fearing people.

They had a great deal to fear.

Vorbis's room was in the upper Citadel, which was unusual for a mere deacon. He hadn't asked for it. He seldom had to ask for anything. Destiny has a way of marking her own.

He also got visited by some of the most powerful men in the Church's hierarchy.

Not, of course, the six Archpriests or the Cenobiarch himself. They weren't that important. They were merely at the top. The people who really run organizations are usually found several levels down, where it's still possible to get things done.

People liked to be friends with Vorbis, mainly because of the aforesaid mental field which suggested to them, in the subtlest of ways, that they didn't want to be his enemy.

Two of them were sitting down with him now. They were General Iam Fri'it, who whatever the official records might suggest was the man who ran most of the Divine Legion, and Bishop Drunah, secretary to the Congress of Iams. People might not think that was much of a position of power, but then they'd never been minutes secretary to a meeting of slightly deaf old men.

Neither man was in fact there. They were not talking to Vorbis. It was one of *those* kinds of meeting. Lots of people didn't talk to Vorbis, and went out of their way to not have meetings with him. Some of the abbots from the distant monasteries had recently been summoned to the Citadel, traveling secretly for up to a week across tortuous terrain, just so they definitely wouldn't join the shadowy figures visiting Vorbis's room. In the last few months, Vorbis had apparently had about as many visitors as the Man in the Iron Mask.

Nor were they talking. But if they *had* been there, and if they *had* been having a conversation, it would have gone like this:

"And now," said Vorbis, "the matter of Ephebe."

Bishop Drunah shrugged.*

"Of no consequence, they say. No threat."

The two men looked at Vorbis, a man who never raised his voice. It was very hard to tell what Vorbis was thinking, often even after he had told you.

"Really? Is this what we've come to?" he said. "No *threat*? After what they did to poor Brother Murduck? The insults to Om? This must not pass. What is proposed to be done?"

"No more fighting," said Fri'it. "They fight like madmen. No. We've lost too many already."

"They have strong gods," said Drunah.

"They have better bows," said Fri'it.

"There is no God but Om," said Vorbis. "What the Ephebians believe they worship are nothing but djinns and demons. If it can be called worship. Have you seen this?"

He pushed forward a scroll of paper.

"What is it?" said Fri'it cautiously.

"A lie. A history that does not exist and never existed . . . the . . . the things . . ." Vorbis hesitated, trying to remember a word that had long since fallen into disuse, ". . . like the . . . tales told to children, who are too young . . . words for people to say . . . the . . ."

"Oh. A play," said Fri'it. Vorbis's gaze nailed him to the wall.

"You know of these things?"

"I—when I traveled in Klatch once—" Fri'it stuttered. He visibly pulled himself together. He had commanded one hundred thousand men in battle. He didn't deserve this.

He found he didn't dare look at Vorbis's expression.

"They dance dances," he said limply. "On their holy

---

*Or would have done. If he had been there. But he wasn't. So he couldn't.

days. The women have bells on their . . . And sing songs. All about the early days of the worlds, when the gods—"

He faded. "It was disgusting," he said. He clicked his knuckles, a habit of his whenever he was worried.

"*This* one has their gods in it," said Vorbis. "*Men* in *masks*. Can you believe that? They have a god of *wine*. A drunken old man! And people say Ephebe is no threat! And this—"

He tossed another, thicker scroll on to the table.

"*This* is far worse. For while they worship false gods in error, their error is in their choice of gods, not in their worship. But this—"

Drunah gave it a cautious examination.

"I believe there are other copies, even in the Citadel," said Vorbis. "This one belonged to Sasho. I believe you recommended him to my service, Fri'it?"

"He always struck me as an intelligent and keen young man," said the general.

"But disloyal," said Vorbis, "and now receiving his just reward. It is only to be regretted that he has not been induced to give us the names of his fellow heretics."

Fri'it fought against the sudden rush of relief. His eyes met those of Vorbis.

Drunah broke the silence.

"*De Chelonian Mobile*," he said aloud. " 'The Turtle Moves.' What does that mean?"

"Even telling you could put your soul at risk of a thousand years in hell," said Vorbis. His eyes had not left Fri'it, who was now staring fixedly at the wall.

"I think it is a risk we might carefully take," said Drunah.

Vorbis shrugged. "The writer claims that the world . . . travels through the void on the back of four huge elephants," he said.

Drunah's mouth dropped open.

"On the back?" he said.

"It is claimed," said Vorbis, still watching Fri'it.

"What do they stand on?"

"The writer says they stand on the shell of an enormous turtle," said Vorbis.

Drunah grinned nervously.

"And what does that stand on?" he said.

"I see no point in speculating as to what it stands on," snapped Vorbis, "since it does not exist!"

"Of course, of course," said Drunah quickly. "It was only idle curiosity."

"Most curiosity is," said Vorbis. "It leads the mind into speculative ways. Yet the man who wrote this walks around free, in Ephebe, *now*."

Drunah glanced at the scroll.

"He says here he went on a ship that sailed to an island on the edge and he looked over and—"

"Lies," said Vorbis evenly. "And it would make no difference even if they were not lies. Truth lies within, not without. In the words of the Great God Om, as delivered through his chosen prophets. Our eyes may deceive us, but our God never will."

"But—"

Vorbis looked at Fri'it. The general was sweating.

"Yes?" he said.

"Well . . . Ephebe. A place where madmen have mad ideas. Everyone knows that. Maybe the wisest course is leave them to stew in their folly?"

Vorbis shook his head. "Unfortunately, wild and unstable ideas have a disturbing tendency to move around and take hold."

Fri'it had to admit that this was true. He knew from experience that true and obvious ideas, such as the ineffable wisdom and judgment of the Great God Om, seemed so obscure to many people that you actually had to kill them before they saw the error of their ways, whereas dangerous and nebulous and wrong-headed notions often had such an attraction for some people that they would—he rubbed a scar thoughtfully—hide up in the mountains and throw rocks at you until you starved them out. They'd prefer to die rather than see sense. Fri'it had seen sense at an early age. He'd seen it was sense not to die.

"What do you propose?" he said.

"The Council want to parley with Ephebe," said Drunah. "You know I have to organize a deputation to leave tomorrow."

"How many soldiers?" said Vorbis.

"A bodyguard only. We have been guaranteed safe passage, after all," said Fri'it.

"*We have been guaranteed safe passage,*" said Vorbis. It sounded like a lengthy curse. "And once inside . . . ?"

Fri'it wanted to say: I've spoken to the commander of the Ephebian garrison, and I think he is a man of honor, although of course he is indeed a despicable infidel and lower than the worms. But it was not the kind of thing he felt it wise to say to Vorbis.

He substituted: "We shall be on our guard."

"Can we surprise them?"

Fri'it hesitated. "We?" he said.

"I shall lead the party," said Vorbis. There was the briefest exchange of glances between himself and the secretary. "I . . . would like to be away from the Citadel for a while. A change of air. Besides, we should not let the Ephebians think they merit the attentions of a superior member of the Church. I was just musing as to the possibilities, should we be provoked—"

Fri'it's nervous click was like a whip-crack.

"We have given them our word—"

"There is no truce with unbelievers," said Vorbis.

"But there are practical considerations," said Fri'it, as sharply as he dared. "The palace of Ephebe is a labyrinth. I know. There are traps. No one gets in without a guide."

"How does the guide get in?" said Vorbis.

"I assume he guides himself," said the general.

"In my experience there is always another way," said Vorbis. "Into everything, there is always another way. Which the God will show in his own good time, we can be assured of that."

"Certainly matters would be easier if there was a lack of stability in Ephebe," said Drunah. "It does indeed harbor certain . . . elements."

"And it will be the gateway to the whole of the Turnwise coast," said Vorbis.

"Well—"

"The Djel, and then Tsort," said Vorbis.

Drunah tried to avoid seeing Fri'it's expression.

"It is our duty," said Vorbis. "Our holy duty. We must not forget poor Brother Murduck. He was unarmed and alone."

Brutha's huge sandals flip-flopped obediently along the stone-flagged corridor toward Brother Nhumrod's barren cell.

He tried composing messages in his head. Master, there's a tortoise who says—Master, this tortoise wants—Master, guess what, I heard from this tortoise in the melons that—

Brutha would never have dared to think of himself as

a prophet, but he had a shrewd idea of the outcome of any interview that began in this way.

Many people assumed that Brutha was an idiot. He looked like one, from his round open face to his splayfeet and knock-ankles. He also had the habit of moving his lips while he thought deeply, as if he was re-hearsing every sentence. And this was because that was what he was doing. Thinking was not something that came easily to Brutha. Most people think automatically, thoughts dancing through their brains like static electric-ity across a cloud. At least, that's how it seemed to him. Whereas he had to construct thoughts a bit at a time, like someone building a wall. A short lifetime of being laughed at for having a body like a barrel and feet that gave the impression that they were about to set out in opposite directions had given him a strong tendency to think very carefully about anything he said.

Brother Nhumrod was prostrate on the floor in front of a statue of Om Trampling the Ungodly, with his fin-gers in his ears. The voices were troubling him again.

Brutha coughed. He coughed again.

Brother Nhumrod raised his head.

"Brother Nhumrod?" said Brutha.

"What?"

"Er . . . Brother Nhumrod?"

"What?"

Brother Nhumrod unplugged his ears.

"Yes?" he said testily.

"Um. There's something you ought to see. In the . . . in the garden. Brother Nhumrod?"

The master of novices sat up. Brutha's face was a glowing picture of concern.

"What do you mean?" Brother Nhumrod said.

"In the garden. It's hard to explain. Um. I found out . . . where the voices were coming from, Brother Nhumrod. And you did say to be sure and tell you."

The old priest gave Brutha a sharp look. But if ever there was a person without guile or any kind of subtlety, it was Brutha.

Fear is strange soil. Mainly it grows obedience like corn, which grows in rows and makes weeding easy. But sometimes it grows the potatoes of defiance, which flourish underground.

The Citadel had a lot of underground. There were the pits and tunnels of the Quisition. There were cellars and sewers, forgotten rooms, dead ends, spaces behind ancient walls, even natural caves in the bedrock itself.

This was such a cave. Smoke from the fire in the middle of the floor found its way out through a crack in the roof and, eventually, into the maze of uncountable chimneys and light-wells above.

There were a dozen figures in the dancing shadows. They wore rough hoods over nondescript clothes—crude things made of rags, nothing that couldn't easily be burned after the meeting so that the wandering fingers of the Quisition would find nothing incriminating. Something about the way most of them moved suggested men who were used to carrying weapons. Here and there, clues. A stance. The turn of a word.

On one wall of the cave there was a drawing. It was vaguely oval, with three little extensions at the top—the middle one slightly the largest of the three—and three at the bottom, the middle one of these slightly longer and more pointed. A child's drawing of a turtle.

"Of course he'll go to Ephebe," said a mask. "He

won't dare not to. He'll have to dam the river of truth, at its source."

"We must bail out what we can, then," said another mask.

"We must kill Vorbis!"

"Not in Ephebe. When that happens, it must happen here. So that people will *know*. When we're strong enough."

"Will we ever be strong enough?" said a mask. Its owner clicked his knuckles nervously.

"Even the peasants know there's something wrong. You can't stop the truth. Dam the river of truth? Then there are leaks of great force. Didn't we find out about Murduck? Hah! '*Killed in Ephebe*,' Vorbis said."

"One of us must go to Ephebe and save the Master. If he really exists."

"He exists. His name is on the book."

"Didactylos. A strange name. It means Two-Fingered, you know."

"They must honor him in Ephebe."

"Bring him back here, if possible. And the Book."

One of the masks seemed hesitant. His knuckles clicked again.

"But will people rally behind . . . a book? People need more than a book. They're peasants. They can't read."

"But they can listen!"

"Even so . . . they need to be shown . . . they need a symbol . . ."

"We have one!"

Instinctively, every masked figure turned to look at the drawing on the wall, indistinct in the firelight but graven on their minds. They were looking at the truth, which can often impress.

"The Turtle Moves!"
"The Turtle Moves!"
"The Turtle Moves!"
The leader nodded.
"And now," he said, "we will draw lots . . ."

The Great God Om waxed wroth, or at least made a spirited attempt. There is a limit to the amount of wroth that can be waxed one inch from the ground, but he was right up against it.

He silently cursed a beetle, which is like pouring water onto a pond. It didn't seem to make any difference, anyway. The beetle plodded away.

He cursed a melon unto the eighth generation, but nothing happened. He tried a plague of boils. The melon just sat there, ripening slightly.

Just because he was temporarily embarrassed, the whole world thought it could take advantage. Well, when Om got back to his rightful shape and power, he told himself, Steps would be Taken. The tribes of Beetles and Melons would wish they'd never been created. And something really horrible would happen to all eagles. And . . . and there would be a holy commandment involving the planting of more lettuces . . .

By the time the big boy arrived back with the waxy-skinned man, the Great God Om was in no mood for pleasantries. Besides, from a tortoise-eye viewpoint even the most handsome human is only a pair of feet, a distant pointy head, and, somewhere up there, the wrong end of a pair of nostrils.

"What's this?" he snarled.

"This is Brother Nhumrod," said Brutha. "Master of the novices. He is very important."

"Didn't I tell you not to bring me some fat old pederast!" shouted the voice in his head. "Your eyeballs will be spitted on shafts of fire for this!"

Brutha knelt down.

"I can't go to the High Priest," he said, as patiently as possible. "Novices aren't even allowed in the Great Temple except on special occasions. I'd be Taught the Error of My Ways by the Quisition if I was caught. It's the Law."

"Stupid fool!" the tortoise shouted.

Nhumrod decided that it was time to speak.

"Novice Brutha," he said, "for what reason are you talking to a small tortoise?"

"Because—" Brutha paused. "Because it's talking to me . . . isn't it?"

Brother Nhumrod looked down at the small, one-eyed head poking out of the shell.

He was, by and large, a kindly man. Sometimes demons and devils did put disquieting thoughts in his head, but he saw to it that they stayed there and he did not in any literal sense deserve to be called what the tortoise called him which, in fact, if he had heard it, he would have thought was something to do with feet. And he was well aware that it was possible to hear voices attributed to demons and, sometimes, gods. Tortoises was a new one. Tortoises made him feel worried about Brutha, whom he'd always thought of as an amiable lump who did, without any sort of complaint, anything asked of him. Of course, many novices volunteered for cleaning out the cesspits and bull cages, out of a strange belief that holiness and piety had something to do with being up to your knees in dirt. Brutha never volunteered, but if he was told to do something he did it, not out of any desire to impress, but simply because he'd been told. And now he was talking to tortoises.

"I think I have to tell you, Brutha," he said, "that it is not talking."

"You can't hear it?"

"I cannot hear it, Brutha."

"It told me it was . . ." Brutha hesitated. "It told me it was the Great God."

He flinched. Grandmother would have hit him with something heavy now.

"Ah. Well, you see, Brutha," said Brother Nhumrod, twitching gently, "this sort of thing is not unknown among young men recently Called to the Church. I daresay you heard the voice of the Great God when you were Called, didn't you? Mmm?"

Metaphor was lost on Brutha. He remembered hearing the voice of his grandmother. He hadn't been Called so much as Sent. But he nodded anyway.

"And in your . . . enthusiasm, it's only natural that you should think you hear the Great God talking to you," Nhumrod went on.

The tortoise bounced up and down.

"Smite you with thunderbolts!" it screamed.

"I find healthy exercise is the thing," said Nhumrod. "And plenty of cold water."

"Writhe on the spikes of damnation!"

Nhumrod reached down and picked up the tortoise, turning it over. Its legs waggled angrily.

"How did it get here, mmm?"

"I don't know, Brother Nhumrod," said Brutha dutifully.

"Your hand to wither and drop off!" screamed the voice in his head.

"There's very good eating on one of these, you know," said the master of novices. He saw the expression on Brutha's face.

"Look at it like this," he said. "Would the Great God Om"—holy horns—"*ever* manifest Himself in such a lowly creature as this? A bull, yes, of course, an eagle, certainly, and I think on one occasion a swan . . . but a *tortoise?*"

"Your sexual organs to sprout wings and fly away!"

"After all," Nhumrod went on, oblivious to the secret chorus in Brutha's head, "what kind of miracles could a tortoise do? Mmm?"

"Your ankles to be crushed in the jaws of giants!"

"Turn lettuce into gold, perhaps?" said Brother Nhumrod, in the jovial tones of those blessed with no sense of humor. "Crush ants underfoot? Ahaha."

"Haha," said Brutha dutifully.

"I shall take it along to the kitchen, out of your way," said the master of novices. "They make *ex*cellent soup. And then you'll hear no more voices, depend upon it. Fire cures all Follies, yes?"

"*Soup?*"

"Er . . ." said Brutha.

"Your intestines to be wound around a tree until you are sorry!"

Nhumrod looked around the garden. It seemed to be full of melons and pumpkins and cucumbers. He shuddered.

"Lots of cold water, that's the thing," he said. "Lots and lots." He focused on Brutha again. "Mmm?"

He wandered off toward the kitchens.

The Great God Om was upside down in a basket in one of the kitchens, half-buried under a bunch of herbs and some carrots.

An upturned tortoise will try to right itself firstly by sticking out its neck to its fullest extent and trying to use its head as a lever. If this doesn't work it will wave its legs frantically, in case this will rock it upright.

An upturned tortoise is the ninth most pathetic thing in the entire multiverse.

An upturned tortoise *who knows what's going to happen to it next* is, well, at least up there at number four.

The quickest way to kill a tortoise for the pot is to plunge it into boiling water.

Kitchens and storerooms and craftsmen's workshops belonging to the Church's civilian population honeycombed the Citadel.* This was only one of them, a smoky-ceilinged cellar whose focal point was an arched fireplace. Flames roared up the flue. Turnspit dogs trotted in their treadmills. Cleavers rose and fell on the chopping blocks.

Off to one side of the huge hearth, among various other blackened cauldrons, a small pot of water was already beginning to seethe.

"The worms of revenge to eat your blackened nostrils!" screamed Om, twitching his legs violently. The basket rocked.

A hairy hand reached in and removed the herbs.

"Hawks to peck your liver!"

A hand reached in again and took the carrots.

"Afflict you with a thousand cuts!"

A hand reached in and took the Great God Om.

"The cannibal fungi of—!"

"Shut up!" hissed Brutha, shoving the tortoise under his robe.

He sidled toward the door, unnoticed in the general culinary chaos.

---

*It takes forty men with their feet on the ground to keep one man with his head in the air.

One of the cooks looked at him and raised an eyebrow.

"Just got to take this back," Brutha burbled, bringing out the tortoise and waving it helpfully. "Deacon's orders."

The cook scowled, and then shrugged. Novices were regarded by one and all as the lowest form of life, but orders from the hierarchy were to be obeyed without question, unless the questioner wanted to find himself faced with more important questions like whether or not it is possible to go to heaven after being roasted alive.

When they were out in the courtyard Brutha leaned against the wall and breathed out.

"Your eyeballs to—!" the tortoise began.

"One more word," said Brutha, "and it's back in the basket."

The tortoise fell silent.

"As it is, I shall probably get into trouble for missing Comparative Religion with Brother Whelk," said Brutha. "But the Great God has seen fit to make the poor man shortsighted and he probably won't notice I'm not there, only if he does I shall have to say what I've done because telling lies to a Brother is a sin and the Great God will send me to hell for a million years."

"In this one case I could be merciful," said the tortoise. "No more than a thousand years at the outside."

"My grandmother told me I shall go to hell when I die anyway," said Brutha, ignoring this. "Being alive is sinful. It stands to reason, because you have to sin every day when you're alive."

He looked down at the tortoise.

"I know you're not the Great God Om"—holy horns—"because if I was to touch the Great God Om"—holy horns—"my hands would burn away. The Great God would never become a tortoise, like Brother

Nhumrod said. But it says in the Book of the Prophet Cena that when he was wandering in the desert the spirits of the ground and the air spoke unto him, so I wondered if you were one of those."

The tortoise gave him a one-eyed stare for a while. Then it said: "Tall fellow? Full beard? Eyes wobbling all over the place?"

"What?" said Brutha.

"I think I recall him," said the tortoise. "Eyes wobbled when he talked. And he talked all the time. To himself. Walked into rocks a lot."

"He wandered in the wilderness for three months," said Brutha.

"That explains it, then," said the tortoise. "There's not a lot to eat there that isn't mushrooms."

"Perhaps you *are* a demon," said Brutha. "The Septateuch forbids us to have discourse with demons. Yet in resisting demons, says the Prophet Fruni, we may grow strong in faith—"

"Your teeth to abscess with red-hot heat!"

"Pardon?"

"I swear to *me* that I am the Great God Om, greatest of gods!"

Brutha tapped the tortoise on the shell.

"Let me show you something, demon."

He could feel his faith growing, if he listened hard.

This wasn't the greatest statue of Om, but it was the closest. It was down in the pit level reserved for prisoners and heretics. And it was made of iron plates riveted together.

The pits were deserted except for a couple of novices pushing a rough cart in the distance.

"It's a big bull," said the tortoise.

"The very likeness of the Great God Om in one of his worldly incarnations!" said Brutha proudly. "And you say you're *him*?"

"I haven't been well lately," said the tortoise.

Its scrawny neck stretched out further.

"There's a door on its back," it said. "Why's there a door on its back?"

"So that the sinful can be put in," said Brutha.

"Why's there another one in its belly?"

"So the purified ashes can be let out," said Brutha. "And the smoke issues forth from the nostrils, as a sign to the ungodly."

The tortoise craned its neck around at the rows of barred doors. It looked up at the soot-encrusted walls. It looked down at the now empty fire trench under the iron bull. It reached a conclusion. It blinked its one eye.

"People?" it said eventually. "You roast *people* in it?"

"There!" said Brutha triumphantly. "And thus you prove you are not the Great God! *He* would know that of course we do not burn people in there. Burn people in there? That would be unheard of!"

"Ah," said the tortoise. "Then what—?"

"It is for the destruction of heretical materials and other such rubbish," said Brutha.

"Very sensible," said the tortoise.

"*Sinners* and *criminals* are purified by fire in the Quisition's pits or sometimes in front of the Great Temple," said Brutha. "The Great God would know that."

"I think I must have forgotten," said the tortoise quietly.

"The Great God Om"—holy horns—"would know that He Himself said unto the Prophet Wallspur—" Brutha coughed and assumed the creased-eyebrow squint that meant serious thought was being undertaken. " 'Let the holy fire destroy utterly the unbeliever.' That's verse sixty-five."

"Did I say that?"

"In the Year of the Lenient Vegetable the Bishop Kreeblephor converted a demon by the power of reason alone," said Brutha. "It actually joined the Church and became a subdeacon. Or so it is said."

"*Fighting* I don't mind," the tortoise began.

"Your lying tongue cannot tempt me, reptile," said Brutha. "For I am strong in my faith!"

The tortoise grunted with effort.

"Smite you with thunderbolts!"

A small, a very small black cloud appeared over Brutha's head and a small, a very small bolt of lightning lightly singed an eyebrow.

It was about the same strength as the spark off a cat's fur in hot dry weather.

"Ouch!"

"*Now* do you believe me?" said the tortoise.

There was a bit of breeze on the roof of the Citadel. It also offered a good view of the high desert.

Fri'it and Drunah waited for a while to get their breath back.

Then Fri'it said, "Are we safe up here?"

Drunah looked up. An eagle circled over the dry hills. He found himself wondering how good an eagle's hearing was. It certainly was good at something. Was it hearing? It could hear a creature half a mile below in the silence of the desert. What the hells—it couldn't talk as well, could it?

"Probably," he said.

"Can I trust you?" said Fri'it.

"Can I trust *you?*"

Fri'it drummed his fingers on the parapet.

"Uh," he said.

And that was the problem. It was the problem of all really secret societies. They were *secret*. How many members did the Turtle Movement have? No one knew, exactly. What was the name of the man beside you? Two other members knew, because they would have introduced him, but who were they behind these masks? Because knowledge was dangerous. If you knew, the inquisitions could wind it slowly out of you. So you made sure you didn't know. This made conversation much easier during cell meetings, and impossible outside of them.

It was the problem of all tentative conspirators throughout history: how to conspire without actually uttering words to an untrusted possible fellow conspirator which, if reported, would point the accusing red-hot poker of guilt.

The little beads of sweat on Drunah's forehead, despite the warm breeze, suggested that the secretary was agonizing along the same lines. But it didn't *prove* it. And for Fri'it, not dying had become a habit.

He clicked his knuckles nervously.

"A holy war," he said. That was safe enough. The sentence included no verbal clue to what Fri'it thought about the prospect. He hadn't said, "Ye god, not a damn holy war, is the man insane? Some idiot missionary gets himself killed, some man writes some gibberish about the shape of the world, and we have to go to war?" If pressed, and indeed stretched and broken, he could always claim that his meaning had been "At last! A not-to-be-missed opportunity to die gloriously for Om, the one true God, who shall Trample the Unrighteous with Hooves of Iron!" It wouldn't make a lot of difference, evidence never did once you were in the deep levels where accusation had the status of proof, but at least it might leave one or two inquisitors feeling that they might just have been wrong.

"Of course, the Church has been far less militant in the last century or so," said Drunah, looking out over the desert. "Much taken up with the mundane problems of the empire."

A statement. Not a crack in it where you could insert a bone-disjointer.

"There was the crusade against the Hodgsonites," said Fri'it distantly. "And the Subjugation of the Melchiorites. And the Resolving of the false prophet Zeb. And the Correction of the Ashelians, and the Shriving of the—"

"But all that was just politics," said Drunah.

"Hmm. Yes. Of course, you are right."

"And, of course, no one could possibly doubt the wisdom of a war to further the worship and glory of the Great God."

"No. None could doubt it," said Fri'it, who had walked across many a battlefield the day after a glorious victory, when you had ample opportunity to see what winning meant. The Omnians forbade the use of all drugs. At times like that the prohibition bit hard, when you dared not go to sleep for fear of your dreams.

"Did not the Great God declare, through the Prophet Abbys, that there is no greater and more honorable sacrifice than one's own life for the God?"

"Indeed he did," said Fri'it. He couldn't help recalling that Abbys had been a bishop in the Citadel for fifty years before the Great God had Chosen him. Screaming enemies had never come at him with a sword. He'd never looked into the eyes of someone who wished him dead—no, of course he had, all the time, because of course the Church had its politics—but at least they hadn't been holding the means to that end in their hands at the time.

"To die gloriously for one's faith is a noble thing," Drunah intoned, as if reading the words off an internal notice-board.

"So the prophets tell us," said Fri'it, miserably.

The Great God moved in mysterious ways, he knew. Undoubtedly He chose His prophets, but it seemed as if He had to be helped. Perhaps He was too busy to choose for Himself. There seemed to be a lot more meetings, a lot more nodding, a lot more exchanging of glances even during the services in the Great Temple.

Certainly there was a glow about young Vorbis—how easy it was to slip from one thought to the other. There was a man touched by destiny. A tiny part of Fri'it, the part that had lived for much of its life in tents, and been shot at quite a lot, and had been in the middle of melees where you could just as easily be killed by an ally as an enemy, added: or at least by something. It was a part of him that was due to spend all the eternities in all the hells, but it had already had a lot of practice.

"You know I traveled a lot when I was much younger?" he said.

"I have often heard you talk most interestingly of your travels in heathen lands," said Drunah politely. "Often bells are mentioned."

"Did I ever tell you about the Brown Islands?"

"Out beyond the end of the world," said Drunah. "I remember. Where bread grows on trees and young women find little white balls in oysters. They dive for them, you said, while wearing not a stitc—"

"Something else I remember," said Fri'it. It was a lonely memory, out here with nothing but scrubland under a purple sky. "The sea is strong there. There are big waves, much bigger than the ones in the Circle Sea, you understand, and the men paddle out beyond them to fish. On strange planks of wood. And when they wish to return to shore, they wait for a wave, and then . . . they stand up, on the wave, and it carries them all the way to the beach."

"I like the story about the young swimming women best," said Drunah.

"Sometimes there are very big waves," said Fri'it, ignoring him. "Nothing would stop them. But if you ride them, you do not drown. This is something I learned."

Drunah caught the glint in his eye.

"Ah," he said, nodding. "How wonderful of the Great God to put such instructive examples in our path."

"The trick is to judge the strength of the wave," said Fri'it. "And ride it."

"What happens to those who don't?"

"They drown. Often. Some of the waves are very big."

"Such is often the nature of waves, I understand."

The eagle was still circling. If it had understood anything, then it wasn't showing it.

"Useful facts to bear in mind," said Drunah, with sudden brightness. "If ever one should find oneself in heathen parts."

"Indeed."

From prayer towers up and down the contours of the Citadel the deacons chanted the duties of the hour.

Brutha should have been in class. But the tutor priests weren't too strict with him. After all, he had arrived word-perfect in every Book of the Septateuch and knew all the prayers and hymns off by heart, thanks to grandmother. They probably assumed he was being useful. Usefully doing something no one else wanted to do.

He hoed the bean rows for the look of the thing. The Great God Om, although currently the small god Om, ate a lettuce leaf.

All my life, Brutha thought, I've known that the Great God Om—he made the holy horns sign in a fairly half-hearted way—was a . . . a . . . great big beard in the sky, or sometimes, when He comes down into the world, as a huge bull or a lion or . . . something big, anyway. Something you could look up to.

Somehow a tortoise isn't the same. I'm trying hard . . . but it isn't the same. And hearing him talk about the SeptArchs as if they were just . . . just some mad old men . . . it's like a dream . . .

In the rain-forests of Brutha's subconscious the butterfly of doubt emerged and flapped an experimental wing, all unaware of what chaos theory has to say about this sort of thing . . .

"I feel a lot better now," said the tortoise. "Better than I have for months."

"Months?" said Brutha. "How long have you been . . . ill?"

The tortoise put its foot on a leaf.

"What day is it?" it said.

"Tenth of Grune," said Brutha.

"Yes? What year?"

"Er . . . Notional Serpent . . . what do you mean, what *year*?"

"Then . . . three years," said the tortoise. "This is good lettuce. And it's *me* saying it. You don't get lettuce up in the hills. A bit of plantain, a thorn bush or two. Let there be another leaf."

Brutha pulled one off the nearest plant. And lo, he thought, there was another leaf.

"And you were going to be a bull?" he said.

"Opened my eyes . . . my eye . . . and I was a tortoise."

"Why?"

"How should I know? I don't know!" lied the tortoise.

"But you . . . you're omnicognisant," said Brutha.

"That doesn't mean I know everything."

Brutha bit his lip. "Um. Yes. It does."

"You sure?"

"Yes."

"Thought that was omnipotent."

"No. That means you're all-powerful. And you *are*. That's what it says in the Book of Ossory. He was one of the Great Prophets, you know. I hope," Brutha added.

"Who told him I was omnipotent?"

"You did."

"No I didn't."

"Well, he *said* you did."

"Don't even remember anyone called Ossory," the tortoise muttered.

"You spoke to him in the desert," said Brutha. "You must remember. He was eight feet tall? With a very long beard? And a huge staff? And the glow of the holy horns shining out of his head?" He hesitated. But he'd seen the statues and the holy icons. They couldn't be wrong.

"Never met anyone like that," said the small god Om.

"Maybe he was a bit shorter," Brutha conceded.

"Ossory. Ossory," said the tortoise. "No . . . no . . . can't say I—"

"He said that you spoke unto him from out of a pillar of flame," said Brutha.

"Oh, *that* Ossory," said the tortoise. "Pillar of flame. Yes."

"And you dictated to him the Book of Ossory," said Brutha. "Which contains the Directions, the Gateways, the Abjurations, and the Precepts. One hundred and ninety-three chapters."

"I don't think I did all that," said Om doubtfully. "I'm sure I would have remembered one hundred and ninety-three chapters."

"What *did* you say to him, then?"

"As far as I can remember it was 'Hey, see what I can do!' " said the tortoise.

Brutha stared at it. It looked embarrassed, insofar as that's possible for a tortoise.

"Even gods like to relax," it said.

"Hundreds of thousands of people live their lives by the Abjurations and the Precepts!" Brutha snarled.

"Well? I'm not stopping them," said Om.

"If you didn't dictate them, who did?"

"Don't ask *me*. *I'm* not omnicognisant!"

Brutha was shaking with anger.

"And the Prophet Abbys? I suppose someone just *happened* to give him the Codicils, did they?"

"It wasn't me—"

"They're written on slabs of lead ten feet tall!"

"Oh, well, it *must* have been me, yes? I always have a ton of lead slabs around in case I meet someone in the desert, yes?"

"What! If you didn't give them to him, who did?"

"I don't know. Why should I know? I can't be everywhere at once!"

"You're omnipresent!"

"What says so?"

"The Prophet Hashimi!"

"Never met the man!"

"Oh? Oh? So I suppose you didn't give him the Book of Creation, then?"

"What Book of Creation?"

"You mean you don't know?"

"No!"

"Then who gave it to him?"

"I don't know! Perhaps he wrote it himself!"

Brutha put his hand over his mouth in horror.

"Thaff blafhngf!"

"What?"

Brutha removed his hand.

"I said, that's blasphemy!"

"Blasphemy? How can I blaspheme? I'm a god!"

"I don't believe you!"

"Hah! Want another thunderbolt?"

"You call that a thunderbolt?"

Brutha was red in the face, and shaking. The tortoise hung its head sadly.

"All right. All right. Not much of one, I admit," it said. "If I was better, you'd have been just a pair of sandals with smoke coming out." It looked wretched. "I don't understand it. This sort of thing has never happened to me before. I intended to be a great big roaring white bull for a week and ended up a tortoise for three years. Why? *I* don't know, and I'm supposed to know everything. According to these prophets of yours who say they've met me, anyway. You know, no one even heard me? I tried talking to goatherds and stuff, and they never took any notice! I was beginning to think I was a tortoise dreaming about being a god. That's how bad it was getting."

"Perhaps you are," said Brutha.

"Your legs to swell to tree trunks!" snapped the tortoise.

"But—but," said Brutha, "you're saying the prophets were . . . just men who wrote things down!"

"That's what they *were!*"

"Yes, but it wasn't from you!"

"Some of it was, perhaps," said the tortoise. "I've . . . forgotten so much, the past few years."

"But if you've been down here as a tortoise, who's been listening to the prayers? Who has been accepting the sacrifices? Who has been judging the dead?"

"I don't know," said the tortoise. "Who did it before?"

"You did!"

"Did I?"

Brutha stuck his fingers in his ears and opened up with the third verse of *Lo, the infidels flee the wrath of Om.*

After a couple of minutes the tortoise stuck its head out from under its shell.

"So," it said, "before unbelievers get burned alive . . . do you sing to them first?"

"No!"

"Ah. A merciful death. Can I say something?"

"If you try to tempt my faith one more time—"

The tortoise paused. Om searched his fading memory. Then he scratched in the dust with a claw.

"I . . . remember   a   day . . . summer   day . . . you were . . . thirteen . . ."

The dry little voice droned on. Brutha's mouth formed a slowly widening O.

Finally he said, "How did you know that?"

"You believe the Great God Om watches everything you do, don't you?"

"You're a tortoise, you couldn't have—"

"When you were almost fourteen, and your grandmother had beaten you for stealing cream from the still-room, which in fact you had not done, she locked you in your room and you said, 'I wish you were—' "

There will be a sign, thought Vorbis. There was always a sign, for the man who watched for them. A wise man always put himself in the path of the God.

He strolled through the Citadel. He always made a point of taking a daily walk through some of the lower levels, although of course always at a different time, and via a different route. Insofar as Vorbis got any pleasure in life, at least in any way that could be recognized by a normal human being, it was in seeing the faces of humble members of the clergy as they rounded a corner and found themselves face-to-chin with Deacon Vorbis of the Quisition. There was always that little intake of breath that indicated a guilty conscience. Vorbis liked to see properly guilty consciences. That was what consciences were for. Guilt was the grease in which the wheels of the authority turned.

He rounded a corner and saw, scratched crudely on the wall opposite, a rough oval with four crude legs and even cruder head and tail.

He smiled. There seemed to be more of them lately. Let heresy fester, let it come to the surface like a boil. Vorbis knew how to wield the lance.

But the second or two of reflection had made him walk past a turning and, instead, he stepped out into the sunshine.

He was momentarily lost, for all his knowledge of the byways of the church. This was one of the walled gardens. Around a fine stand of tall decorative Klatchian corn, bean vines raised red and white blossoms towards the sun; in between the bean rows, melons baked gently on the dusty soil. In the normal way, Vorbis would have noted and approved of this efficient use of space, but in the normal way he wouldn't have encountered a plump young novice, rolling back and forth in the dust with his fingers in his ears.

Vorbis stared down at him. Then he prodded Brutha with his sandal.

"What ails you, my son?"

Brutha opened his eyes.

There weren't many superior members of the hierarchy he could recognize. Even the Cenobiarch was a distant blob in the crowd. But everyone recognized Vorbis the exquisitor. Something about him projected itself on your conscience within a few days of your arrival at the Citadel. The God was merely to be feared in the perfunctory ways of habit, but Vorbis was *dreaded*.

Brutha fainted.

"How very strange," said Vorbis.

A hissing noise made him look around.

There was a small tortoise near his foot. As he glared, it tried to back away, and all the time it was staring at him and hissing like a kettle.

He picked it up and examined it carefully, turning it over and over in his hands. Then he looked around the walled garden until he found a spot in full sunshine, and put the reptile down, on its back. After a moment's thought he took a couple of pebbles from one of the vegetable beds and wedged them under the shell so that the creature's movement wouldn't tip it over.

Vorbis believed that no opportunity to acquire esoteric knowledge should ever be lost, and made a mental note to come back again in a few hours to see how it was getting on, if work permitted.

Then he turned his attention to Brutha.

* * *

There was a hell for blasphemers. There was a hell for the disputers of rightful authority. There were a number of hells for liars. There was probably a hell for little boys who wished their grandmothers were dead. There were more than enough hells to go around.

This was the definition of eternity; it was the space of time devised by the Great God Om to ensure that everyone got the punishment that was due to them.

The Omnians had a great many hells.

Currently, Brutha was going through all of them.

Brother Nhumrod and Brother Vorbis looked down at him, tossing and turning on his bed like a beached whale.

"It's the sun," said Nhumrod, almost calm now after the initial shock of having the exquisitor come looking for him. "The poor lad works all day in that garden. It was bound to happen."

"Have you tried beating him?" said Brother Vorbis.

"I'm sorry to say that beating young Brutha is like trying to flog a mattress," said Nhumrod. "He says 'ow!' but I think it's only because he wants to show he's willing. Very willing lad, Brutha. He's the one I told you about."

"He doesn't *look* very sharp," said Vorbis.

"He's not," said Nhumrod.

Vorbis nodded approvingly. Undue intelligence in a novice was a mixed blessing. Sometimes it could be channeled for the greater glory of Om, but often it caused . . . well, it did not cause trouble, because Vorbis knew exactly what to do with misapplied intelligence, but it did cause unnecessary work.

"And yet you tell me his tutors speak so highly of him," he said.

Nhumrod shrugged.

"He is very obedient," he said. "And . . . well, there's his memory."

"What about his memory?"

"There's so much of it," said Nhumrod.

"He has got a good memory?"

"Good is the wrong word. It's superb. He's word-perfect on the entire Sept—"

"Hmm?" said Vorbis.

Nhumrod caught the deacon's eye.

"As perfect, that is, as anything may be in this most imperfect world," he muttered.

"A devoutly read young man," said Vorbis.

"Er," said Nhumrod, "no. He can't read. Or write."

"Ah. A *lazy* boy."

The deacon was not a man who dwelt in gray areas. Nhumrod's mouth opened and shut silently as he sought for the proper words.

"No," he said. "He tries. We're sure he tries. He just does not seem to be able to make the . . . he cannot fathom the link between the sounds and the letters."

"You have beaten him for that, at least?"

"It seems to have little effect, deacon."

"How, then, has he become such a capable pupil?"

"He listens," said Nhumrod.

No one listened quite like Brutha, he reflected. It made it very hard to teach him. It was like—it was like being in a great big cave. All your words just vanished into the unfillable depths of Brutha's head. The sheer concentrated absorption could reduce unwary tutors to stuttering silence, as every word they uttered whirled away into Brutha's ears.

"He listens to everything," said Nhumrod. "And he watches everything. He takes it all in."

Vorbis stared down at Brutha.

"And I've never heard him say an unkind word," said Nhumrod. "The other novices make fun of him, sometimes. Call him The Big Dumb Ox. You know the sort of thing?"

Vorbis's gaze took in Brutha's ham-sized hands and tree-trunk legs.

He appeared to be thinking deeply.

"Cannot read and write," said Vorbis. "But extremely loyal, you say?"

"Loyal and devout," said Nhumrod.

"And a good memory," Vorbis murmured.

"It's more than that," said Nhumrod. "It's not like memory at all."

Vorbis appeared to reach a decision.

"Send him to see me when he is recovered," he said.

Nhumrod looked panicky.

"I merely wish to talk to him," said Vorbis. "I may have a use for him."

"Yes, lord?"

"For, I suspect, the Great God Om moves in mysterious ways."

High above. No sound but the hiss of wind in feathers.

The eagle stood on the breeze, looking down at the toy buildings of the Citadel.

It had dropped it somewhere, and now it couldn't find it. Somewhere down there, in that little patch of green.

Bees buzzed in the bean blossoms. And the sun beat down on the upturned shell of Om.

There is also a hell for tortoises.

He was too tired to waggle his legs now. That was all

you could do, waggle your legs. And stick your head out as far as it would go and wave it about in the hope that you could lever yourself over.

You died if you had no believers, and that was what a small god generally worried about. But you also died if you *died*.

In the part of his mind not occupied with thoughts of heat, he could feel Brutha's terror and bewilderment. He shouldn't have done that to the boy. Of course he hadn't been watching him. What god did that? Who cared what people *did*? Belief was the thing. He'd just picked the memory out of the boy's mind, to impress, like a conjuror removing an egg from someone's ear.

I'm on my back, and getting hotter, and I'm going to *die* . . .

And yet . . . and yet . . . that bloody eagle had dropped him on a compost heap. Some kind of clown, that eagle. A whole place built of rocks on a rock in a rocky place, and he landed on the one thing that'd break his fall without breaking him as well. And really close to a believer.

Odd, that. Made you wonder if it wasn't some kind of divine providence, except that you *were* divine providence . . . and on your back, getting hotter, preparing to *die* . . .

That man who'd turned him over. That expression on that mild face. He'd remember that. That expression, not of cruelty, but of some different level of being. That expression of terrible *peace* . . .

A shadow crossed the sun. Om squinted up into the face of Lu-Tze, who gazed at him with gentle, upside-down compassion. And then turned him the right way up. And then picked up his broom and wandered off, without a second glance.

Om sagged, catching his breath. And then brightened up.

Someone up there likes me, he thought. And it's Me.

Sergeant Simony waited until he was back in his own quarters before he unfolded his own scrap of paper.

He was not at all surprised to find it marked with a small drawing of a turtle. He was the lucky one.

He'd lived for a moment like this. Someone had to bring back the writer of the Truth, to be a symbol for the movement. It had to be him. The only shame was that he couldn't kill Vorbis.

But that had to happen where it could be seen.

One day. In front of the Temple. Otherwise no one would *believe*.

Om stumped along a sandy corridor.

He'd hung around a while after Brutha's disappearance. Hanging around is another thing tortoises are very good at. They're practically world champions.

Bloody useless boy, he thought. Served himself right for trying to talk to a barely coherent novice.

Of course, the skinny old one hadn't been able to hear him. Nor had the chef. Well, the old one was probably deaf. As for the cook . . . Om made a note that, when he was restored to his full godly powers, a special fate was going to lie in wait for the cook. He wasn't sure exactly what it was going to be, but it was going to involve boiling water and probably carrots would come into it somewhere.

He enjoyed the thought of that for a moment. But where did it leave him? It left him in this wretched garden, as a tortoise. He knew how he'd got *in*—he glared in dull terror at the tiny dot in the sky that the eye of memory knew was an eagle—and he'd better find a more terrestrial way out unless he wanted to spend the next month hiding under a melon leaf.

Another thought struck him. Good eating!

When he had his power again, he was going to spend *quite some time* devising a few new hells. And a couple of fresh Precepts, too. Thou shalt not eat of the Meat of the Turtle. That was a good one. He was surprised he hadn't thought of it before. Perspective, that's what it was.

And if he'd thought of one like Thou Shalt Bloody Well Pick up Any Distressed Tortoises and Carry Them Anywhere They Want Unless, And This is Important, You're an Eagle a few years ago, he wouldn't be in this trouble now.

Nothing else for it. He'd have to find the Cenobiarch himself. Someone like a High Priest would be bound to be able to hear him.

And he'd be in this place somewhere. High Priests tended to stay put. He should be easy enough to find. And while he might currently be a tortoise, Om was still a god. How hard could it be?

He'd have to go upwards. That's what a hierarchy meant. You found the top man by going upwards.

Wobbling slightly, his shell jerking from side to side, the former Great God Om set off to explore the citadel erected to his greater glory.

He couldn't help noticing things had changed a lot in three thousand years.

"Me?" said Brutha. "But, but—"

"I don't believe he means to punish you," said Nhumrod. "Although punishment is what you richly deserve, of course. We *all* richly deserve," he added piously.

"But *why?*"

"—why? He said he just wants to talk to you."

"But there is *nothing* I could possibly say that a quisitor wants to hear!" wailed Brutha.

"—Hear. I am sure you are not questioning the deacon's wishes," said Nhumrod.

"No. No. Of course not," said Brutha. He hung his head.

"Good boy," said Nhumrod. He patted as far up Brutha's back as he could reach. "Just you trot along," he said. "I'm sure everything will be all right." And then, because he too had been brought up in habits of honesty, he added, "Probably all right."

There were few steps in the Citadel. The progress of the many processions that marked the complex rituals of Great Om demanded long, gentle slopes. Such steps as there were, were low enough to encompass the faltering steps of very old men. And there were so many very old men in the Citadel.

Sand blew in all the time from the desert. Drifts built up on the steps and in the courtyards, despite everything that an army of brush-wielding novices could do.

But a tortoise has very inefficient legs.

"Thou Shall Build Shallower Steps," he hissed, hauling himself up.

Feet thundered past him, a few inches away. This was one of the main thoroughfares of the Citadel, leading to the Place of Lamentation, and was trodden by thousands of pilgrims every day.

Once or twice an errant sandal caught his shell and spun him around.

"*Your feet to fly from your body and be buried in a termite mound!*" he screamed.

It made him feel a little better.

Another foot clipped him and slid him across the stones. He fetched up, with a clang, against a curved metal grille set low in one wall. Only a lightning grab with his jaws stopped him slipping through it. He ended up hanging by his mouth over a cellar.

A tortoise has incredibly powerful jaw muscles. He swayed a bit, legs wobbling. All right. A tortoise in a crevassed, rocky landscape was used to this sort of thing. He just had to get a leg hooked . . .

Faint sounds drew themselves to his attention. There was the clink of metal, and then a very soft whimper.

Om swiveled his eye around.

The grille was high in one wall of a very long, low room. It was brightly illuminated by the light-wells that ran everywhere through the Citadel.

Vorbis had made a point of that. The inquisitors shouldn't work in the shadows, he said, but in the light.

Where they could see, very clearly, what they were doing.

So could Om.

He hung from the grille for some time, unable to take his eye off the row of benches.

On the whole, Vorbis discouraged red-hot irons, spiked chains, and things with drills and big screws on, unless it was for a public display on an important Fast day. It was amazing what you could do, he always said, with a simple knife . . .

But many of the inquisitors liked the old ways best.

After a while, Om very slowly hauled himself up to the grille, neck muscles twitching. Like a creature with its mind on something else, the tortoise hooked first one front leg over a bar, then another. His back legs waggled for a while, and then he hooked a claw on to the rough stonework.

He strained for a moment and then pulled himself back into the light.

He walked off slowly, keeping close to the wall to avoid the feet. He had no alternative to walking slowly in any case, but now he was walking slowly because he was thinking. Most gods find it hard to walk and think at the same time.

Anyone could go to the Place of Lamentation. It was one of the great freedoms of Omnianism.

There were all sorts of ways to petition the Great God, but they depended largely on how much you could afford, which was right and proper and exactly how things should be. After all, those who had achieved success in the world clearly had done it with the approval of the Great God, because it was impossible to believe that they had managed it with His *disapproval*. In the same way, the Quisition could act without possibility of flaw. Suspicion was proof. How could it be anything else? The Great God would not have seen fit to put the suspicion in the minds of His exquisitors unless it was *right* that it should be there. Life could be very simple, if you believed in the Great God Om. And sometimes quite short, too.

But there were always the improvident, the stupid, and those who, because of some flaw or oversight in this life or a past one, were not even able to afford a pinch of incense. And the Great God, in His wisdom and mercy as filtered through His priests, had made provision for them.

Prayers and entreaties could be offered up in the Place of Lamentation. They would assuredly be heard. They might even be heeded.

Behind the Place, which was a square two hundred meters across, rose the Great Temple itself.

There, without a shadow of a doubt, the God listened. Or somewhere close, anyway . . .

Thousands of pilgrims visited the Place every day.

A heel knocked Om's shell, bouncing him off the wall. On the rebound a crutch caught the edge of his carapace and whirled him away into the crowd, spinning like a coin. He bounced up against the bedroll of an old woman who, like many others, reckoned that the efficacy of her petition was increased by the amount of time she spent in the square.

The God blinked muzzily. This was nearly as bad as eagles. It was nearly as bad as the cellar . . . no, perhaps nothing was as bad as the cellar . . .

He caught a few words before another passing foot kicked him away.

"The drought has been on our village for three years . . . a little rain, oh Lord?"

Rotating on the top of his shell, vaguely wondering if the right answer might stop people kicking him, the Great God muttered, "No problem."

Another foot bounced him, unseen by any of the pious, between the forest of legs. The world was a blur.

He caught an ancient voice, steeped in hopelessness, saying, "Lord, Lord, why must my son be taken to join your Divine Legion? Who now will tend the farm? Could you not take some other boy?"

"Don't worry about it," squeaked Om.

A sandal caught him under his tail and flicked him several yards across the square. No one was looking down. It was generally believed that staring fixedly at the golden horns on the temple roof while uttering the prayer gave it added potency. Where the presence of the tortoise was dimly registered as a bang on the ankle, it was disposed of by an automatic prod with the other foot.

". . . my wife, who is sick with the . . ."

"Right!"

Kick—

". . . make clean the well in our village, which is foul with . . ."

"You got it!"

Kick—

". . . every year the locusts come, and . . ."

"I promise, only . . . !"

Kick—

". . . lost upon the seas these five months . . ."

". . . *stop kicking me!*"

The tortoise landed, right side up, in a brief, clear space.

Visible . . .

So much of animal life is the recognition of pattern, the shapes of hunter and hunted. To the casual eye the forest is, well, just forest; to the eye of the dove it is so much unimportant fuzzy green background to the hawk which *you* did not notice on the branch of a tree. To the tiny dot of the hunting buzzard in the heights, the whole panorama of the world is just a fog compared to the scurrying prey in the grass.

From his perch on the Horns themselves, the eagle leapt into the sky.

Fortunately, the same awareness of shapes that made the tortoise so prominent in a square full of scurrying humans made the tortoise's one eye swivel upwards in dread anticipation.

Eagles are single-minded creatures. Once the idea of lunch is fixed in their mind, it tends to remain there until satisfied.

* * *

There were two Divine Legionaries outside Vorbis's quarters. They looked sideways at Brutha as he knocked timorously at the door, as if looking for a reason to assault him.

A small gray priest opened the door and ushered Brutha into a small, barely furnished room. He pointed meaningfully at a stool.

Brutha sat down. The priest vanished behind a curtain. Brutha took one glance around the room and—

Blackness engulfed him. Before he could move, and Brutha's reflexes were not well coordinated at the best of times, a voice by his ear said, "Now, brother, do not panic. I order you not to panic."

There was cloth in front of Brutha's face.

"Just nod, boy."

Brutha nodded. They put a hood over your face. All the novices knew that. Stories were told in the dormitories. They put a cloth over your face so the inquisitors didn't know who they were working on . . .

"Good. Now, we are going into the next room. Be careful where you tread."

Hands guided him upright and across the floor. Through the mists of incomprehension he felt the brush of the curtain, and then was jolted down some steps and into a sandy-floored room. The hands spun him a few times, firmly but without apparent ill-will, and then led him along a passageway. There was the swish of another curtain, and then the indefinable sense of a larger space.

Afterward, long afterward, Brutha realized: there was no terror. A hood had been slipped over his head in the room of the head of the Quisition, and it never occurred to him to be terrified. Because he had faith.

"There is a stool behind you. Be seated."

Brutha sat.

"You may remove the hood."

Brutha removed the hood.

He blinked.

Seated on stools at the far end of the room, with a Holy Legionary on either side of them, were three figures. He recognized the aquiline face of Deacon Vorbis; the other two were a short and stocky man, and a very fat one. Not heavily built, like Brutha, but a genuine lard tub. All three wore plain gray robes.

There was no sign of any branding irons, or even of scalpels.

All three were staring intently.

"Novice Brutha?" said Vorbis.

Brutha nodded.

Vorbis gave a light laugh, the kind made by very intelligent people when they think of something that probably isn't very amusing.

"And, of course, one day we shall have to call you Brother Brutha," he said. "Or even Father Brutha? Rather confusing, I think. Best to be avoided. I think we shall have to see to it that you become Subdeacon Brutha just as soon as possible; what do you think of that?"

Brutha did not think anything of it. He was vaguely aware that advancement was being discussed, but his mind had gone blank.

"Anyway, enough of this," said Vorbis, with the slight exasperation of someone who realizes that he is going to have to do a lot of work in this conversation. "Do you recognize these learned fathers on my left and right?"

Brutha shook his head.

"Good. They have some questions to ask you."

Brutha nodded.

The very fat man leaned forward.

"Do you have a tongue, boy?"

Brutha nodded. And then, feeling that perhaps this wasn't enough, presented it for inspection.

Vorbis laid a restraining hand on the fat man's arm.

"I think our young friend is a little overawed," he said mildly.

He smiled.

"Now, Brutha—please put it away—I am going to ask you some questions. Do you understand?"

Brutha nodded.

"When you first came into my apartments, you were for a few seconds in the anteroom. Please describe it to me."

Brutha stared frog-eyed at him. But the turbines of recollection ground into life without his volition, pouring their words into the forefront of his mind.

"It is a room about three meters square. With white walls. There is sand on the floor except in the corner by the door, where the flagstones are visible. There is a window on the opposite wall, about two meters up. There were three bars in the window. There is a three-legged stool. There is a holy icon of the Prophet Ossory, carved from aphacia wood and set with silver leaf. There is a scratch in the bottom left-hand corner of the frame. There is a shelf under the window. There is nothing on the shelf but a tray."

Vorbis steepled his long thin fingers in front of his nose.

"On the tray?" he said.

"I am sorry, lord?"

"What was on the tray, my son?"

Images whirled in front of Brutha's eyes.

"On the tray was a thimble. A bronze thimble. And

two needles. On the tray was a length of cord. There were knots in the cord. Three knots. And nine coins were on the tray. There was a silver cup on the tray, decorated with a pattern of aphacia leaves. There was a long dagger, I think it was steel, with a black handle with seven ridges on it. There was a small piece of black cloth on the tray. There was a stylus and a slate—"

"Tell me about the coins," murmured Vorbis.

"Three of them were Citadel cents," said Brutha promptly. "Two were showing the Horns, and one the sevenfold-crown. Four of the coins were very small and golden. There was lettering on them which . . . which I could not read, but which if you were to give me a stylus I think I could—"

"This is some sort of trick?" said the fat man.

"I assure you," said Vorbis, "the boy could have seen the entire room for no more than a second. Brutha . . . tell us about the other coins."

"The other coins were large. They were bronze. They were *derechmi* from Ephebe."

"How do you know this? They are hardly common in the Citadel."

"I have seen them once before, lord."

"When was this?"

Brutha's face screwed up with effort.

"I am not sure—" he said.

The fat man beamed at Vorbis.

"Hah," he said.

"I think . . ." said Brutha ". . . it was in the afternoon. But it may have been the morning. Around midday. On Grune 3, in the year of the Astounded Beetle. Some merchants came to our village."

"How old were you at that time?" said Vorbis.

"I was within one month of three years old, lord."

"I don't believe this," said the fat man.

Brutha's mouth opened and shut once or twice. How did the fat man know? He hadn't been there!

"You could be wrong, my son," said Vorbis. "You are a well-grown lad of . . . what . . . seventeen, eighteen years? We feel you could not really recall a chance glimpse of a foreign coin fifteen years ago."

"We think that you are making it up," said the fat man.

Brutha said nothing. Why make anything up? When it was just sitting there in his head.

"Can you remember everything that's ever happened to you?" said the stocky man, who had been watching Brutha carefully throughout the exchange. Brutha was glad of the interruption.

"No, lord. Most things."

"You forget things?"

"Uh. There are sometimes things I don't remember." Brutha had heard about forgetfulness, although he found it hard to imagine. But there were times in his life, in the first few years of his life especially, when there was . . . nothing. Not an attrition of memory, but great locked rooms in the mansion of his recollection. Not forgotten, any more than a locked room ceases to exist, but . . . locked.

"What is the first thing you can remember, my son?" said Vorbis, kindly.

"There was a bright light, and then someone hit me," said Brutha.

The three men stared at him blankly. Then they turned to one another. Brutha, through the misery of his terror, heard snatches of whispering.

". . . is there to lose? . . ." "Foolishness and probably

demonic . . ." "Stakes are high . . ." "One chance, and they will be expecting us . . ."

And so on.

He looked around the room.

Furnishing was not a priority in the Citadel. Shelves, stools, tables . . . There was a rumor among the novices that priests towards the top of the hierarchy had golden furniture, but there was no sign of it here. The room was as severe as anything in the novices' quarters although it had, perhaps, a more opulent severity; it wasn't the forced bareness of poverty, but the starkness of intent.

"My son?"

Brutha looked back hurriedly.

Vorbis glanced at his colleagues. The stocky man nodded. The fat man shrugged.

"Brutha," said Vorbis, "return to your dormitory now. Before you go, one of the servants will give you something to eat, and a drink. You will report to the Gate of Horns at dawn tomorrow, and you will come with me to Ephebe. You know about the delegation to Ephebe?"

Brutha shook his head.

"Perhaps there is no reason why you should," said Vorbis. "We are going to discuss political matters with the Tyrant. Do you understand?"

Brutha shook his head.

"Good," said Vorbis. "Very good. Oh, and—Brutha?"

"Yes, lord?"

"You will forget this meeting. You have not been in this room. You have not seen us here."

Brutha gaped at him. This was nonsense. You couldn't forget things just by wishing. Some things forgot themselves—the things in those locked rooms—but that was because of some mechanism he could not access. What did this man mean?

"Yes, lord," he said.

It seemed the simplest way.

Gods have no one to pray to.

The Great God Om scurried towards the nearest statue, neck stretched, inefficient legs pumping. The statue happened to be himself as a bull, trampling an infidel, although this was no great comfort.

It was only a matter of time before the eagle stopped circling and swooped.

Om had been a tortoise for only three years, but with the shape he had inherited a grab-bag of instincts, and a lot of them centered around a total terror of the one wild creature that had found out how to eat tortoise.

Gods have no one to pray to.

Om really wished that this was not the case.

But everyone needs *someone*.

"Brutha!"

Brutha was a little uncertain about his immediate future. Deacon Vorbis had clearly cut him loose from his chores as a novice, but he had nothing to do for the rest of the afternoon.

He gravitated towards the garden. There were beans to tie up, and he welcomed the fact. You knew where you were with beans. They didn't tell you to do impossible things, like *forget*. Besides, if he was going to be away for a while, he ought to mulch the melons and explain things to Lu-Tze.

Lu-Tze came with the gardens.

Every organization has someone like him. They might be pushing a broom in obscure corridors, or wandering among the shelves in the back of the stores (where they are the only person who knows where anything is) or have some ambiguous but essential relationship with the boiler-room. Everyone knows who they are and no one remembers a time when they weren't there, or knows where they go when they're not, well, where they usually are. Just occasionally, people who are slightly more observant than most other people, which is not on the face of it very difficult, stop and wonder about them for a while . . . and then get on with something else.

Strangely enough, given his gentle ambling from garden to garden around the Citadel, Lu-Tze never showed much interest in the plants themselves. He dealt in soil, manure, muck, compost, loam, and dust, and the means of moving it about. Generally he was pushing a broom, or turning over a heap. Once anyone put seeds in anything he lost interest.

He was raking the paths when Brutha entered. He was good at raking paths. He left scallop patterns and gentle soothing curves. Brutha always felt apologetic about walking on them.

He hardly ever spoke to Lu-Tze, because it didn't matter much what anyone ever said to Lu-Tze. The old man just nodded and smiled his single-toothed smile in any case.

"I'm going away for a little while," said Brutha, loudly and distinctly. "I expect someone else will be sent to look after the gardens, but there are some things that need doing . . ."

Nod, smile. The old man followed him patiently along the rows, while Brutha spoke beans and herbs.

"Understand?" said Brutha, after ten minutes of this.

Nod, smile. Nod, smile, beckon.

"What?"

Nod, smile, beckon. Nod, smile, *beckon*, smile.

Lu-Tze walked his little crab-monkey walk to the little area at the far end of the walled garden which contained his heaps, the flowerpot stacks, and all the other cosmetics of the garden beautiful. The old man slept there, Brutha suspected.

Nod, smile, beckon.

There was a small trestle table in the sun by a stack of bean canes. A straw mat had been spread on it, and on the mat were half a dozen pointy-shaped rocks, none of them bigger than a foot high.

A careful arrangement of sticks had been constructed around them. Bits of thin wood shadowed some parts of the rocks. Small metal mirrors directed sunlight towards other areas. Paper cones at odd angles appeared to be funneling the breeze to very precise points.

Brutha had never heard about the art of bonsai, and how it was applied to mountains.

"They're . . . very nice," he said uncertainly.

Nod, smile, pick up a small rock, smile, urge, urge.

"Oh, I really couldn't take—"

Urge, urge. Grin, nod.

Brutha took the tiny mountain. It had a strange, unreal heaviness—to his hand it felt like a pound or so, but in his head it weighed thousands of *very, very small* tons.

"Uh. Thank you. Thank you very much."

Nod, smile, push away politely.

"It's very . . . mountainous."

Nod, grin.

"That can't really be snow on the top, can—"

"Brutha!"

His head jerked up. But the voice had come from inside.

Oh, no, he thought wretchedly.

He pushed the little mountain back into Lu-Tze's hands.

"But, er, you keep it for me, yes?"

"Brutha!"

All that was a dream, wasn't it? Before I was important and talked to by deacons.

"No, it wasn't! Help me!"

The petitioners scattered as the eagle made a pass over the Place of Lamentation.

It wheeled, only a few feet above the ground, and perched on the statue of Great Om trampling the Infidel.

It was a magnificent bird, golden-brown and yellow-eyed, and it surveyed the crowds with blank disdain.

"It's a sign?" said an old man with a wooden leg.

"Yes! A sign!" said a young woman next to him.

"A sign!"

They gathered around the statue.

"It's a bugger," said a small and totally unheard voice from somewhere around their feet.

"But what's it a sign of?" said an elderly man who had been camping out in the square for three days.

"What do you mean, *of*? It's a sign!" said the wooden-legged man. "It don't have to be a sign *of* anything. That's a suspicious kind of question to ask, what's it a sign of."

"Got to be a sign of something," said the elderly man. "That's a referential wossname. A gerund. Could be a gerund."

A skinny figure appeared at the edge of the group, moving surreptitiously yet with surprising speed. It was wearing the *djeliba* of the desert tribes, but around its neck was a tray on a strap. There was an ominous suggestion of sticky sweet things covered in dust.

"It could be a messenger from the Great God himself," said the woman.

"It's a bloody eagle is what it is," said a resigned voice from somewhere among the ornamental bronze homicide at the base of the statue.

"Dates? Figs? Sherbets? Holy relics? Nice fresh indulgences? Lizards? Onna stick?" said the man with the tray hopefully.

"I thought when He appeared in the world it was as a swan or a bull," said the wooden-legged man.

"Hah!" said the unregarded voice of the tortoise.

"Always wondered about that," said a young novice at the back of the crowd. "You know . . . well . . . swans? A bit . . . lacking in machismo, yes?"

"May you be stoned to death for blasphemy!" said the woman hotly. "The Great God hears every irreverent word you utter!"

"Hah!" from under the statue. And the man with the tray oiled forward a little further, saying, "Klatchian Delight? Honeyed wasps? Get them while they're cold!"

"It's a point, though," said the elderly man, in a kind of boring, unstoppable voice. "I mean, there's something very *godly* about an eagle. King of birds, am I right?"

"It's only a better-looking turkey," said the voice from under the statue. "Brain the size of a walnut."

"Very noble bird, the eagle. Intelligent, too," said the elderly man. "Interesting fact: eagles are the only birds to work out how to eat tortoises. You know? They pick them up, flying up very high, and drop them on to the rocks. Smashes them right open. Amazing."

"One day," said a dull voice from down below, "I'm going to be back on form again and you're going to be very sorry you said that. For a very long time. I might even go so far as to make even more Time just for you to be sorry in. Or . . . no, I'll make *you* a tortoise. See how you like it, eh? That rushing wind around y'shell, the ground getting bigger the whole time. *That*'d be an interesting fact!"

"That sounds dreadful," said the woman, looking up at the eagle's glare. "I wonder what passes through the poor little creature's head when he's dropped?"

"His shell, madam," said the Great God Om, trying to squeeze himself even further under the bronze overhang.

The man with the tray was looking dejected. "Tell you what," he said. "Two bags of sugared dates for the price of one, how about it? And that's cutting my own hand off."

The woman glanced at the tray.

"Ere, there's flies all over everything!" she said.

"Currants, madam."

"Why'd they just fly away, then?" the woman demanded.

The man looked down. Then he looked back up into her face.

"A miracle!" he said, waving his hands dramatically. "The time of miracles is at hand!"

The eagle shifted uneasily.

It recognized humans only as pieces of mobile landscape which, in the lambing season in the high hills, might be associated with thrown stones when it stooped upon the newborn lamb, but which otherwise were as unimportant in the scheme of things as bushes and rocks. But it had never been so close to so many of them. Its mad eyes swiveled backward and forward uncertainly.

At that moment trumpets rang out across the Place.

The eagle looked around wildly, its tiny predatory mind trying to deal with this sudden overload.

It leapt into the air. The worshipers fought to get out of its way as it dipped across the flagstones and then rose majestically toward the turrets of the Great Temple and the hot sky.

Below it, the doors of the Great Temple, each one made of forty tons of gilded bronze, opened by the breath (it was said) of the Great God Himself, swung open ponderously and—and this was the holy part—silently.

Brutha's enormous sandals flapped and flapped on the flagstones. Brutha always put a lot of effort into running; he ran from the knees, lower legs thrashing like paddlewheels.

This was too much. There was a tortoise who said he was the God, and this couldn't be true except that it *must* be true, because of what it knew. And he'd been tried by the Quisition. Or something like that. Anyway, it hadn't been as painful as he'd been led to expect.

"*Brutha!*"

The square, normally alive with the susurration of a thousand prayers, had gone quiet. The pilgrims had all turned to face the Temple.

His mind boiling with the events of the day, Brutha shouldered his way through the suddenly silent crowd. . . .

"*Brutha!*"

People have reality-dampers.

It is a popular fact that nine-tenths of the brain is not used and, like most popular facts, it is wrong. Not even the most stupid Creator would go to the trouble of making the human head carry around several pounds of unnecessary gray goo if its only real purpose was, for example, to serve as a delicacy for certain remote tribesmen in unexplored valleys. It *is* used. And one of its functions is to make the miraculous seem ordinary and turn the unusual into the usual.

Because if this was *not* the case, then human beings, faced with the daily wondrousness of everything, would go around wearing big stupid grins, similar to those worn by certain remote tribesmen who occasionally get raided by the authorities and have the contents of their plastic greenhouses very seriously inspected. They'd say "Wow!" a lot. And no one would do much work.

Gods don't like people not doing much work. People who aren't busy all the time might start to *think*.

Part of the brain exists to stop this happening. It is very efficient. It can make people experience boredom in the middle of marvels. And Brutha's was working feverishly.

So he didn't immediately notice that he'd pushed through the last row of people and had trotted out into the middle of a wide pathway, until he turned and saw the procession approaching.

The Cenobiarch was returning to his apartments, after conducting—or at least nodding vaguely while his chaplain conducted on his behalf—the evening service.

Brutha spun around, looking for a way to escape. Then there was a cough beside him, and he stared up into the furious faces of a couple of Lesser Iams and, between them, the bemused and geriatrically good-natured expression of the Cenobiarch himself.

The old man raised his hand automatically to bless Brutha with the holy horns, and then two members of the Divine Legion picked up the novice by the elbows, on the second attempt, and marched him swiftly out of the procession's path and hurled him into the crowd.

"Brutha!"

Brutha bounded across the plaza to the statue and leaned against it, panting.

"I'm going to go to hell!" he muttered. "For all eternity!"

"Who cares? Now . . . get me away from here."

No one was paying him any attention now. They were all watching the procession. Even watching the procession was a holy act. Brutha knelt down and peered into the scrollwork around the base of the statue.

One beady eye glared back at him.

"How did you get under there?"

"It was touch and go," said the tortoise. "I tell you, when I'm back on form, there's going to be a considerable redesigning of eagles."

"What's the eagle trying to do to you?" said Brutha.

"It wants to carry me off to its nest and give me dinner," snarled the tortoise. "What do you *think* it wanted to do?" There was a short pause in which it contemplated the futility of sarcasm in the presence of Brutha; it was like throwing meringues at a castle.

"It wants to *eat* me," it said patiently.

"But you're a tortoise!"

"I am your *God!*"

"But *currently* in the shape of a tortoise. With a shell on, is what I mean."

"That doesn't worry eagles," said the tortoise darkly. "They pick you up, carry you up a few hundred feet, and then . . . drop you."

"Urrgh."

"No. More like . . . crack . . . splat. How did you think I got *in* here?"

"You were dropped? But—"

"Landed on a pile of dirt in your *garden*. That's eagles

for you. Whole place built of rock and paved with rock on a big rock and they miss."

"That was lucky. Million-to-one chance," said Brutha.

"I never had this trouble when I was a bull. The number of eagles who can pick up a bull, you can count them on the fingers of one head. Anyway," said the tortoise, "there's worse here than eagles. There's a—"

"There's good eating on one of them, you know," said a voice behind Brutha.

He stood up guiltily, the tortoise in his hand.

"Oh, hello, Mr. Dhblah," he said.

Everyone in the city knew Cut-Me-Own-Hand-Off Dhblah, purveyor of suspiciously new holy relics, suspiciously old rancid sweetmeats on a stick, gritty figs, and long-past-the-sell-by dates. He was a sort of natural force, like the wind. No one knew where he came from or where he went at night. But he was there every dawn, selling sticky things to the pilgrims. And in this the priests reckoned he was on to a good thing, because most of the pilgrims were coming for the first time and therefore lacked the essential thing you needed in dealing with Dhblah, which was the experience of having dealt with him before. The sight of someone in the Place trying to unstick their jaws with dignity was a familiar one. Many a devout pilgrim, after a thousand miles of perilous journey, was forced to make his petition in sign language.

"Fancy some sherbet for afters?" said Dhblah hopefully. "Only one cent a glass, and that's cutting me own hand off."

"Who is this fool?" said Om.

"I'm not going to eat it," said Brutha hurriedly.

"Going to teach it to do tricks, then?" said Dhblah cheerfully. "Look through hoops, that kind of thing?"

"Get rid of him," said Om. "Smite him on the head, why don't you, and push the body behind the statue."

"Shut up," said Brutha, beginning to experience once again the problems that occur when you're talking to someone no one else can hear.

"No need to be like that about it," said Dhblah.

"I wasn't talking to you," said Brutha.

"Talking to the tortoise, were you?" said Dhblah. Brutha looked guilty.

"My old mum used to talk to a gerbil," Dhblah went on. "Pets are always a great help in times of stress. And in times of starvation too, o'course."

"This man is not honest," said Om. "I can read his mind."

"Can you?"

"Can I what?" said Dhblah. He gave Brutha a lopsided look. "Anyway, it'll be company on your journey."

"What journey?"

"To Ephebe. The secret mission to talk to the infidel."

Brutha knew he shouldn't be surprised. News went around the enclosed world of the Citadel like bushfire after a drought.

"Oh," he said. "That journey."

"They say Fri'it's going," said Dhblah. "And—that other one. The *éminence grease*."

"Deacon Vorbis is a very nice person," said Brutha. "He has been very kind to me. He gave me a drink."

"What of? Never mind," said Dhblah. "Of course, I wouldn't say a word against him, myself," he added quickly.

"Why are you talking to this stupid person?" Om demanded.

"He's a . . . friend of mine," said Brutha.

"I wish he was a friend of *mine*," said Dhblah.

"Friends like that, you never have enemies. Can I press you to a candied sultana? Onna stick?"

There were twenty-three other novices in Brutha's dormitory, on the principle that sleeping alone promoted sin. This always puzzled the novices themselves, since a moment's reflection would suggest that there were whole ranges of sins only available in company. But that was because a moment's reflection was the biggest sin of all. People allowed to be by themselves overmuch might indulge in solitary cogitation. It was well known that this stunted your growth. For one thing, it could lead to your feet being chopped off.

So Brutha had to retire to the garden, with his God screaming at him from the pocket of his robe, where it was being jostled by a ball of garden twine, a pair of shears, and some loose seeds.

Finally he was fished out.

"Look, I didn't have a chance to *tell* you," said Brutha. "I've been chosen to go on a very important mission. *I'm* going to Ephebe, on a mission to the infidels. Deacon Vorbis *picked* me. He's my friend."

"Who's he?"

"He's the chief exquisitor. He . . . makes sure you're worshiped properly."

Om picked up the hesitation in Brutha's voice, and remembered the grating. And the sheer *busyness* below . . .

"He tortures people," he said coldly.

"Oh, no! The *in*quisitors do that. They work very long hours for not much money, too, Brother Nhumrod says. No, the *ex*quisitors just . . . arrange matters. Every inquisitor wants to become an exquisitor one day, Brother Nhumrod says. That's why they put up with being on duty at all hours. They go for days without sleep, sometimes."

"Torturing people," mused the God. No, a mind like that one in the garden wouldn't pick up a knife. Other people would do that. Vorbis would enjoy other methods.

"Letting out the *badness* and the *heresy* in people," said Brutha.

"But people ... perhaps ... don't survive the process?"

"But that doesn't matter," said Brutha earnestly. "What happens to us in this life is not really real. There may be a little pain, but that doesn't matter. Not if it ensures less time in the hells after death."

"But what if the exquisitors are wrong?" said the tortoise.

"They can't be wrong," said Brutha. "They are guided by the hand of ... by your hand ... your front leg ... I mean, your claw," he mumbled.

The tortoise blinked its one eye. It remembered the heat of the sun, the helplessness, and a face watching it not with any cruelty but, worse, with interest. Someone watching something die just to see how long it took. He'd remember that face anywhere. And the mind behind it—that steel ball of a mind.

"But suppose something went wrong," it insisted.

"I'm not any good at theology," said Brutha. "But the testament of Ossory is very clear on the matter. They *must* have done something, otherwise you in your wisdom would not direct the Quisition to them."

"Would I?" said Om, still thinking of that face. "It's their fault they get tortured. Did I really say that?"

" 'We are judged in life as we are in death' ... Ossory III, chapter VI, verse 56. My grandmother said that when people die they come before you, they have to cross a terrible desert and you weigh their heart in some scales," said Brutha. "And if it weighs less than a feather, they are spared the hells."

"Goodness me," said the tortoise. And it added: "Has it occurred to you, lad, that I might not be able to do that *and* be down here walking around with a shell on?"

"You could do anything you wanted to," said Brutha.

Om looked up at Brutha.

He really believes, he thought. He doesn't know how to lie.

The strength of Brutha's belief burned in him like a flame.

And then the truth hit Om like the ground hits tortoises after an attack of eagles.

"You've got to take me to this Ephebe place," he said urgently.

"I'll do whatever you want," said Brutha. "Are you going to scourge it with hoof and flame?"

"Could be, could be," said Om. "But you've got to take me." He was trying to keep his innermost thoughts calm, in case Brutha heard. *Don't leave me behind!*

"But you could get there much quicker if I left you," said Brutha. "They are very wicked in Ephebe. The sooner it is cleansed, the better. You could stop being a tortoise and fly there like a burning wind and scourge the city."

A burning wind, thought Om. And the tortoise thought of the silent wastes of the deep desert, and the chittering and sighing of the gods who had faded away to mere djinns and voices on the air.

Gods with no more believers.

Not even one. One was just enough.

Gods who had been *left behind*.

And the thing about Brutha's flame of belief was this: in all the Citadel, in all the day, it was the only one the God had found.

Fri'it was trying to pray.

He hadn't done so for a long time.

Oh, of course there had been the eight compulsory prayers every day, but in the pit of the wretched night he knew them for what they were. A habit. A time for thought, perhaps. And method of measuring time.

He wondered if he'd ever prayed, if he'd ever opened heart and mind to something out there, or up there. He must have done, mustn't he? Perhaps when he was young. He couldn't even remember that. Blood had washed away the memories.

It was his fault. It had to be his fault. He'd been to Ephebe before, and had rather liked the white marble city on its rock overlooking the blue Circle Sea. And he'd visited Djelibeybi, those madmen in their little river valley who believed in gods with funny heads and put their dead in pyramids. He'd even been to far Ankh-Morpork, across the water, where they'd worship any god at all so long as he or she had money. Yes, Ankh-Morpork—where there were streets and streets of gods, squeezed together like a deck of cards. And none of them wanted to set fire to anyone else, or at least any more than was normally the case in Ankh-Morpork. They just wanted to be left in peace, so that everyone went to heaven or hell in their own way.

And he'd drunk too much tonight, from a secret cache of wine whose discovery would deliver him into the machinery of the inquisitors within ten minutes.

Yes, you could say this for old Vorbis. Once upon a time the Quisition had been bribable, but not anymore.

The chief exquisitor had gone back to fundamentals. Now there was a democracy of sharp knives. Better than that, in fact. The search for heresy was pursued even more vigorously among the higher levels in the Church. Vorbis had made it clear: the higher up the tree, the blunter the saw.

Give me that old-time religion . . .

He squeezed his eyes shut again, and all he could see were the horns of the temple, or fragmented suggestions of the carnage to come, or . . . the face of Vorbis.

He'd liked that white city.

Even the slaves had been content. There were rules about slaves. There were things you couldn't do to slaves. Slaves had value.

He'd learned about the Turtle, there. It had all made sense. He'd thought: it sounds *right*. It makes *sense*. But sense or not, that thought was sending him to hell.

Vorbis knew about him. He must do. There were spies everywhere. Sasho had been useful. How much had Vorbis got out of him? Had he said what he knew?

Of course he'd say what he knew . . .

Something went snap inside Fri'it.

He glanced at his sword, hanging on the wall.

And why not? After all, he was going to spend all eternity in a thousand hells . . .

The knowledge was freedom, of a sort. When the least they could do to you was everything, then the most they could do to you suddenly held no terror. If he was going to be boiled for a lamb, then he might as well be roasted for a sheep.

He staggered to his feet and, after a couple of tries, got the swordbelt off the wall. Vorbis's quarters weren't far away, if he could manage the steps. One stroke, that's all it would take. He could cut Vorbis in half without trying. And maybe . . . maybe nothing would happen afterward. There were others who felt like him—somewhere. Or, anyway, he could get down to the stables, be well away by dawn, get to Ephebe, maybe, across the desert . . .

He reached the door and fumbled for the handle.

It turned of its own accord.

Fri'it staggered back as the door swung inward.

Vorbis was standing there. In the flickering light of the oil lamp, his face registered polite concern.

"Excuse the lateness of the hour, my lord," he said. "But I thought we should talk. About tomorrow."

The sword clattered out of Fri'it's hand.

Vorbis leaned forward.

"Is there something wrong, brother?" he said.

He smiled, and stepped into the room. Two hooded inquisitors slipped in behind him.

"Brother," Vorbis said again. And shut the door.

"How is it in there?" said Brutha.

"I'm going to rattle around like a pea in a pot," grumbled the tortoise.

"I could put some more straw in. And, look, I've got these."

A pile of greenstuff dropped on Om's head.

"From the kitchen," said Brutha. "Peelings and cabbage. I stole them," he added, "but then I thought it can't be stealing if I'm doing it for you."

The fetid smell of the half-rotten leaves suggested strongly that Brutha had committed his crime when the greens were halfway to the midden, but Om didn't say so. Not now.

"Right," he mumbled.

There must be others, he told himself. Sure. Out in the country. This place is too sophisticated. But . . . there had been all those pilgrims in front of the Temple. They weren't just country people, they were the devoutest ones. Whole villages clubbed together to send one person carrying the petitions of many. But there hadn't been the flame. There had been fear, and dread, and yearning, and hope. All those emotions had their flavor. But there hadn't been the flame.

The eagle had dropped him near Brutha. He'd . . . woken up. He could dimly remember all that time as a tortoise. And now he remembered being a god. How far away from Brutha would he still remember? A mile? Ten miles? How would it be . . . feeling the knowledge drain away, dwindling back to nothing but a lowly reptile? Maybe there would be a part of him that would always remember, helplessly . . .

He shuddered.

Currently Om was in a wickerwork box slung from Brutha's shoulder. It wouldn't have been comfortable at the best of times, but now it shook occasionally as Brutha stamped his feet in the pre-dawn chill.

After a while some of the Citadel grooms arrived, with horses. Brutha was the subject of a few odd looks. He smiled at everyone. It seemed the best way.

He began to feel hungry, but didn't dare leave his post. He'd been *told* to be here. But after a while sounds from around the corner made him sidle a few yards to see what was going on.

The courtyard here was U-shaped, around a wing of the Citadel buildings, and around the corner it looked as though another party was preparing to set out.

Brutha knew about camels. There had been a couple in

his grandmother's village. There seemed to be hundreds of them here, though, complaining like badly oiled pumps and smelling like a thousand damp carpets. Men in *djeliba* moved among them and occasionally hit them with sticks, which is the approved method of dealing with camels.

Brutha wandered over to the nearest creature. A man was strapping water-bottles around its hump.

"Good morning, brother," said Brutha.

"Bugger off," said the man without looking around.

"The Prophet Abbys tells us (chap. XXV, verse 6): 'Woe unto he who defiles his mouth with curses *for* his words will be *as* dust,'" said Brutha.

"Does he? Well, he can bugger off too," said the man, conversationally.

Brutha hesitated. Technically, of course, the man had bought himself vacant possession of a thousand hells and a month or two of the attentions of the Quisition, but now Brutha could see that he was a member of the Divine Legion; a sword was half-hidden under the desert robes.

And you had to make special allowances for Legionaries, just as you did for inquisitors. Their often intimate contact with the ungodly affected their minds and put their souls in mortal peril. He decided to be magnanimous.

"And where are you going to with all these camels on this fine morning, brother?"

The soldier tightened a strap.

"Probably to hell," he said, grinning nastily. "Just behind you."

"Really? According to the word of the Prophet Ishkible, a man needs no camel to ride to hell, yea, nor horse, nor mule; a man may ride into hell on his tongue," said Brutha, letting just a tremor of disapproval enter his voice.

"Does some old prophet say anything about nosy bastards being given a thump alongside the ear?" said the soldier.

" 'Woe unto him who raises *his* hand unto his brother, dealing with him as unto an Infidel,' " said Brutha. "That's Ossory, Precepts XI, verse 16."

" 'Sod off and forget you ever saw us otherwise you're going to be in real trouble, my friend.' Sergeant Aktar, chapter I, verse 1," said the soldier.

Brutha's brow wrinkled. He couldn't remember that one.

"Walk away," said the voice of the God in his head. "You don't need trouble."

"I hope your journey is a pleasant one," said Brutha politely. "Whatever the destination."

He backed away and headed toward the gate.

"A man who will have to spend some time in the hells of correction, if I am any judge," he said. The god said nothing.

The Ephebian traveling group was beginning to assemble now. Brutha stood to attention and tried to keep out of everyone's way. He saw a dozen mounted soldiers, but unlike the camel riders they were in the brightly polished fishmail and black-and-yellow cloaks that the Legionaries usually only wore on special occasions. Brutha thought they looked very impressive.

Eventually one of the stable servants came up to him.

"What are you doing here, novice?" he demanded.

"I am going to Ephebe," said Brutha.

The man glared at him and then grinned.

"You? You're not even ordained! You're going to Ephebe?"

"Yes."

"What makes you think that?"

"Because I told him so," said the voice of Vorbis, behind the man. "And here he is, most obedient to my wishes."

Brutha had a good view of the man's face. The change in his expression was like watching a grease slick cross a pond. Then the stableman turned as though his feet were nailed to a turntable.

"My Lord Vorbis," he oiled.

"And now he will require a steed," said Vorbis.

The stableman's face was yellow with dread.

"My pleasure. The very best the sta—"

"My friend Brutha is a humble man before Om," said Vorbis. "He will ask for no more than a mule, I have no doubt. Brutha?"

"I—I do not know how to ride, my lord," said Brutha.

"Any man can get on a mule," said Vorbis. "Often many times in a short distance. And now, it would appear, we are all here?"

He raised an eyebrow at the sergeant of the guard, who saluted.

"We are awaiting General Fri'it, lord," he said.

"Ah. Sergeant Simony, isn't it?"

Vorbis had a terrible memory for names. He knew every one. The sergeant paled a little, and then saluted crisply.

"Yes! Sir!"

"We will proceed without General Fri'it," said Vorbis.

The B of the word "But" framed itself on the sergeant's lips, and faded there.

"General Fri'it has other business," said Vorbis. "Most pressing and urgent business. Which only he can attend to."

* * *

Fri'it opened his eyes in grayness.

He could see the room around him, but only faintly, as a series of edges in the air.

The sword . . .

He'd dropped the sword, but maybe he could find it again. He stepped forward, feeling a tenuous resistance around his ankles, and looked down.

There was the sword. But his fingers passed through it. It was like being drunk, but he knew he wasn't drunk. He wasn't even sober. He was . . . suddenly clear in his mind.

He turned and looked at the thing that had briefly impeded his progress.

"Oh," he said.

GOOD MORNING.

"Oh."

THERE IS A LITTLE CONFUSION AT FIRST. IT IS ONLY TO BE EXPECTED.

To his horror, Fri'it saw the tall black figure stride away through the gray wall.

"Wait!"

A skull draped in a black hood poked out of the wall.

YES?

"You're Death, aren't you?"

INDEED.

Fri'it gathered what remained of his dignity.

"I know you," he said. "I have faced you many times."

Death gave him a long stare.

NO YOU HAVEN'T.

"I assure you—"

YOU HAVE FACED MEN. IF YOU HAD FACED ME, I ASSURE YOU . . . YOU WOULD HAVE KNOWN.

"But what happens to me now?"

Death shrugged.

DON'T YOU KNOW? he said, and disappeared.

"Wait!"

Fri'it ran at the wall and found to his surprise that it offered no barrier. Now he was out in the empty corridor. Death had vanished.

And then he realized that it wasn't the corridor he remembered, with its shadows and the grittiness of sand underfoot.

That corridor didn't have a glow at the end, that pulled at him like a magnet pulls at an iron filing.

You couldn't put off the inevitable. Because sooner or later, you reached the place when the inevitable just went and waited.

And this was it.

Fri'it stepped through the glow into a desert. The sky was dark and pocked with large stars, but the black sand that stretched away to the distance was nevertheless brightly lit.

A desert. After death, a desert. The desert. No hells, yet. Perhaps there was hope.

He remembered a story from his childhood. Unusually, it wasn't about smiting. No one was trampled underfoot. It wasn't about Om, dreadful in His rage. It was worse. It was about what happened when you died . . . the journey of your soul.

They said: *you must walk a desert* . . .

"Where is this place?" he said hoarsely.

THIS IS NO PLACE, said Death.

. . . *all alone* . . .

"What is at the end of the desert?"

JUDGMENT.

. . . *with your beliefs* . . .

Fri'it stared at the endless, featureless expanse.

"I have to walk it alone?" he whispered. "But . . . now, I'm not sure what I believe—"

YES?

AND NOW, IF YOU WILL EXCUSE ME . . .

Fri'it took a deep breath, purely out of habit. Perhaps he could find a couple of rocks out there. A small rock to hold and a big rock to hide behind, while he waited for Vorbis . . .

And that thought was habit, too. Revenge? *Here?*

He smiled.

Be sensible, man. You were a soldier. This is a desert. You crossed a few in your time.

And you survive by learning about them. There's whole tribes that know how to live in the worst kinds of desert. Licking water off the shady sides of dunes, that sort of thing . . . They think it's *home*. Put 'em in a vegetable garden and they'd think you were mad.

The memory stole over him: a desert is what you think it is. And now, you can think clearly . . .

There were no lies here. All fancies fled away. That's what happened in all deserts. It was just you, and what you believed.

What have I always believed?

That on the whole, and by and large, if a man lived properly, not according to what any priests said, but according to what seemed decent and honest *inside,* then it would, at the end, more or less, turn out all right.

You couldn't get that on a banner. But the desert looked better already.

Fri'it set out.

* * *

It was a small mule and Brutha had long legs; if he'd made the effort he could have remained standing and let the mule trot out from underneath.

The order of progression was not as some may have expected. Sergeant Simony and his soldiers rode ahead, on either side of the track.

They were trailed by the servants and clerks and lesser priests. Vorbis rode in the rear, where an exquisitor rode by right, like a shepherd watching over his flock.

Brutha rode with him. It was an honor he would have preferred to avoid. Brutha was one of those people who could raise a sweat on a frosty day, and the dust was settling on him like a gritty skin. But Vorbis seemed to derive some amusement from his company. Occasionally he would ask him questions:

"How many miles have we traveled, Brutha?"

"Four miles and seven *estado*, lord."

"But how do you know?"

That was a question he couldn't answer. How did he know the sky was blue? It was just something in his head. You couldn't think about how you thought. It was like opening a box with the crowbar that was inside.

"And how long has our journey taken?"

"A little over seventy-nine minutes."

Vorbis laughed. Brutha wondered why. The puzzle wasn't why he remembered, it was why everyone else seemed to forget.

"Did your fathers have this remarkable faculty?"

There was a pause.

"Could they do it as well?" said Vorbis patiently.

"I don't know. There was only my grandmother. She had—a good memory. For some things." Transgressions, certainly. "And very good eyesight and hearing."

What she could apparently see or hear through two walls had, he remembered, seemed phenomenal.

Brutha turned gingerly in the saddle. There was a cloud of dust about a mile behind them on the road.

"Here come the rest of the soldiers," he said conversationally.

This seemed to shock Vorbis. Perhaps it was the first time in years that anyone had innocently addressed a remark to him.

"The rest of the soldiers?" he said.

"Sergeant Aktar and his men, on ninety-eight camels with many water-bottles," said Brutha. "I saw them before we left."

"You did not see them," said Vorbis. "They are not coming with us. You will forget about them."

"Yes, lord." The request to do magic again.

After a few minutes the distant cloud turned off the road and started up the long slope that led to the high desert. Brutha watched them surreptitiously, and raised his eyes to the dune mountains.

There was a speck circling up there.

He put his hand to his mouth.

Vorbis heard the gasp.

"What ails you, Brutha?" he said.

"I remembered about the God," said Brutha, without thinking.

"We should always remember the God," said Vorbis, "and trust that He is with us on this journey."

"He is," said Brutha, and the absolute conviction in his voice made Vorbis smile.

He strained to hear the nagging internal voice, but there was nothing. For one horrible moment Brutha wondered if the tortoise had fallen out of the box, but there was a reassuring weight on the strap.

"And we must bear with us the certainty that He will be with us in Ephebe, among the infidel," said Vorbis.

"I am sure He will," said Brutha.

"And prepare ourselves for the coming of the prophet," said Vorbis.

The cloud had reached the top of the dunes now, and vanished in the silent wastes of the desert.

Brutha tried to put it out of his mind, which was like trying to empty a bucket underwater. No one survived in the high desert. It wasn't just the dunes and the heat. There were terrors in the burning heart, where even the mad tribes never went. An ocean without water, voices without mouths . . .

Which wasn't to say that the immediate future didn't hold terrors enough . . .

He'd seen the sea before, but the Omnians didn't encourage it. This may have been because deserts were so much harder to cross. They kept people in, though. But sometimes the desert barriers *were* a problem, and then you had to put up with the sea.

Il-drim was nothing more than a few shacks around a stone jetty, at one of which was a trireme flying the holy oriflamme. When the Church traveled, the travelers were very senior people indeed, so when the Church traveled it generally traveled in style.

The party paused on a hill and looked at it.

"Soft and corrupt," said Vorbis. "That's what we've become, Brutha."

"Yes, Lord Vorbis."

"And open to pernicious influence. The sea, Brutha. It washes unholy shores, and gives rise to dangerous ideas. Men should not travel, Brutha. At the center there is truth. As you travel, so error creeps in."

"Yes, Lord Vorbis."

Vorbis sighed.

"In Ossory's day we sailed alone in boats made of hides, and went where the winds of the God took us. That's how a holy man should travel."

A tiny spark of defiance in Brutha declared that it, personally, would risk a little corruption for the sake of traveling with two decks between its feet and the waves.

"I heard that Ossory once sailed to the island of Erebos on a millstone," he ventured by way of conversation.

"Nothing is impossible for the strong in faith," said Vorbis.

"Try striking a match on jelly, mister."

Brutha stiffened. It was impossible that Vorbis could have failed to hear the voice.

The Voice of the Turtle was heard in the land.

"Who's this bugger?"

"Forward," said Vorbis. "I can see that our friend Brutha is agog to get on board."

The horse trotted on.

"Where are we? Who's that? It's as hot as hell in here and, believe me, I know what I'm talking about."

"I can't talk now!" hissed Brutha.

"This cabbage stinks like a swamp! Let there be lettuce! Let there be slices of melon!"

The horses edged along the jetty and were led one at a time up the gangplank. By this time the box was vibrating. Brutha kept looking around guiltily, but no one else was taking any notice. Despite his size, Brutha was easy not to notice. Practically everyone had better things to do with their time than notice someone like Brutha. Even Vorbis had switched him off, and was talking to the captain.

He found a place up near the pointed end, where one

of the sticking-up bits with the sails on gave him a bit of privacy. Then, with some dread, he opened the box.

The tortoise spoke from deep within its shell.

"Any eagles about?"

Brutha scanned the sky.

"No."

The head shot out.

"You—" it began.

"I couldn't talk!" said Brutha. "People were with me all the time! Can't you . . . read the words in my mind? Can't you read my thoughts?"

"Mortal thoughts aren't like that," snapped Om. "You think it's like watching words paint themselves across the sky? Hah! It's like trying to make sense of a bundle of weeds. *Intentions,* yes. *Emotions,* yes. But not thoughts. Half the time *you* don't know what you're thinking, so why should I?"

"Because you're the God," said Brutha. "Abbys, chapter LVI, verse 17: 'All of mortal mind he knows, and there are no secrets.' "

"Was he the one with the bad teeth?"

Brutha hung his head.

"Listen," said the tortoise, "I am what I am. I can't help it if people think something else."

"But you knew about my thoughts . . . in the garden . . ." muttered Brutha.

The tortoise hesitated. "That was different," it said. "They weren't . . . thoughts. That was guilt."

"I believe that the Great God is Om, and in His Justice," said Brutha. "And I shall go on believing, whatever you say, and whatever you are."

"Good to hear it," said the tortoise fervently. "Hold that thought. Where are we?"

"On a boat," said Brutha. "On the sea. Wobbling."

"Going to Ephebe on a boat? What's wrong with the desert?"

"No one can cross the desert. No one can *live* in the heart of the desert."

"*I* did."

"It's only a couple of days' sailing." Brutha's stomach lurched, even though the boat had hardly cleared the jetty. "And they say that the God—"

"—me—"

"—is sending us a fair wind."

"I am? Oh. Yes. Trust me for a fair wind. Flat as a mill-race the whole way, don't you worry."

"I meant mill-pond! I meant mill-*pond!*"

Brutha clung to the mast.

After a while a sailor came and sat down on a coil of rope and looked at him interestedly.

"You can let go, Father," he said. "It stands up all by itself."

"The sea . . . the waves . . ." murmured Brutha carefully, although there was nothing left to throw up.

The sailor spat thoughtfully.

"Aye," he said. "They got to be that shape, see, so's to fit into the sky."

"But the boat's creaking!"

"Aye. It does that."

"You mean this isn't a storm?"

The sailor sighed, and walked away.

After a while, Brutha risked letting go. He had never felt so ill in his life.

It wasn't just the seasickness. He didn't know where

he was. And Brutha had always known where he was. Where he was, and the existence of Om, had been the only two certainties in his life.

It was something he shared with tortoises. Watch any tortoise walking, and periodically it will stop while it files away the memories of the journey so far. Not for nothing, elsewhere in the multiverse, are the little traveling devices controlled by electric thinking-engines called "turtles."

Brutha knew where he was by remembering where he had been—by the unconscious counting of footsteps and the noting of landmarks. Somewhere inside his head was a thread of memory which, if you had wired it directly to whatever controlled his feet, would cause Brutha to amble back through the little pathways of his life all the way to the place he was born.

Out of contact with the ground, on the mutable surface of the sea, the thread flapped loose.

In his box, Om tossed and shook to Brutha's motion as Brutha staggered across the moving deck and reached the rail.

To anyone except the novice, the boat was clipping through the waves on a good sailing day. Seabirds wheeled in its wake. Away to one side—port or starboard or one of those directions—a school of flying fish broke the surface in an attempt to escape the attentions of some dolphins. Brutha stared at the gray shapes as they zigzagged under the keel in a world where they never had to count at all—

"Ah, Brutha," said Vorbis. "Feeding the fishes, I see."

"No, lord," said Brutha. "I'm being sick, lord."

He turned.

There was Sergeant Simony, a muscular young man

with the deadpan expression of the truly professional soldier. He was standing next to someone Brutha vaguely recognized as the number-one salt or whatever his title was. And there was the exquisitor, smiling.

"Him! Him!" screamed the voice of the tortoise.

"Our young friend is not a good sailor," said Vorbis.

"Him! Him! I'd know him anywhere!"

"Lord, I wish I wasn't a sailor at all," said Brutha. He felt the box trembling as Om bounced around inside.

"Kill him! Find something sharp! Push him overboard!"

"Come with us to the prow, Brutha," said Vorbis. "There are many interesting things to be seen, according to the captain."

The captain gave the frozen smirk of those caught between a rock and a hard place. Vorbis could always supply both.

Brutha trailed behind the other three, and risked a whisper.

"What's the matter?"

"Him! The bald one! Push him over the side!"

Vorbis half-turned, caught Brutha's embarrassed attention, and smiled.

"We will have our minds broadened, I am sure," he said. He turned back to the captain, and pointed to a large bird gliding down the face of the waves.

"The Pointless Albatross," said the captain promptly. "Flies from the Hub to the Ri—" he faltered. But Vorbis was gazing with apparent affability at the view.

"He turned me over in the sun! *Look at his mind!*"

"From one pole of the world to the other, every year," said the captain. He was sweating slightly.

"Really?" said Vorbis. "Why?"

"No one knows."

"Excepting the God, of course," said Vorbis.

The captain's face was a sickly yellow.

"Of course. Certainly," he said.

"Brutha?" shouted the tortoise. "Are you listening to me?"

"And over there?" said Vorbis.

The sailor followed his extended arm.

"Oh. Flying fish," he said. "But they don't really fly," he added quickly. "They just build up speed in the water and glide a little way."

"One of the God's marvels," said Vorbis. "Infinite variety, eh?"

"Yes, indeed," said the captain. Relief was crossing his face now, like a friendly army.

"And the things down there?" said the exquisitor.

"Them? Porpoises," said the captain. "Sort of a fish."

"Do they always swim around ships like this?"

"Often. Certainly. Especially in the waters off Ephebe."

Vorbis leaned over the rail, and said nothing. Simony was staring at the horizon, his face absolutely immobile. This left a gap in the conversation which the captain, very stupidly, sought to fill.

"They'll follow a ship for days," he said.

"Remarkable." Another pause, a tar pit of silence ready to snare the mastodons of unthinking comment. Earlier exquisitors had shouted and ranted confessions out of people. Vorbis never did that. He just dug deep silences in front of them.

"They seem to like them," said the captain. He glanced nervously at Brutha, who was trying to shut the tortoise's voice out of his head. There was no help there.

Vorbis came to his aid instead.

"This must be very convenient on long voyages," he said.

"Uh. Yes?" said the captain.

"From the provisions point of view," said Vorbis.

"My lord, I don't quite—"

"It must be like having a traveling larder," said Vorbis.

The captain smiled. "Oh no, lord. We don't eat them."

"Surely not? They look quite wholesome to *me*."

"Oh, but you know the old saying, lord . . ."

"Saying?"

"Oh, they say that after they die, the souls of dead sailors become—"

The captain saw the abyss ahead, but the sentence had plunged on with a horrible momentum of its own.

For a while there was no sound but the zip of the waves, the distant splash of the porpoises, and the heaven-shaking thundering of the captain's heart.

Vorbis leaned back on the rail.

"But of course *we* are not prey to such superstitions," he said lazily.

"Well, of course," said the captain, clutching at this straw. "Idle sailor talk. If ever I hear it again I shall have the man flog—"

Vorbis was looking past his ear.

"I say! Yes, you there!" he said.

One of the sailors nodded.

"Fetch me a harpoon," said Vorbis.

The man looked from him to the captain and then scuttled off obediently.

"But, ah, uh, but your lordship should not, uh, ha, attempt such sport," said the captain. "Ah. Uh. A harpoon is a dangerous weapon in untrained hands, I am afraid you might do yourself an injury—"

"But *I* will not be using it," said Vorbis.

The captain hung his head and held out his hand for the harpoon.

Vorbis patted him on the shoulder.

"And then," he said, "you shall entertain us to lunch. Won't he, sergeant?"

Simony saluted. "Just as you say, sir."

"Yes."

Brutha lay on his back among sails and ropes somewhere under the decking. It was hot, and the air smelled of all air anywhere that has ever come into contact with bilges.

Brutha hadn't eaten all day. Initially he'd been too ill to. Then he just hadn't.

"But being cruel to animals doesn't mean he's a . . . bad person," he ventured, the harmonics of his tone suggesting that even he didn't believe this. It had been quite a small porpoise.

"He turned me on to my *back*," said Om.

"Yes, but humans are more important than animals," said Brutha.

"This is a point of view often expressed by humans," said Om.

"Chapter IX, verse 16 of the book of—" Brutha began.

"Who cares what any book says?" screamed the tortoise.

Brutha was shaken.

"But you never told any of the prophets that people should be kind to animals," he said. "I don't remember anything about that. Not when you were . . . bigger. You don't want people to be kind to animals because they're animals, you just want people to be kind to animals because one of them might be *you*."

"That's not a bad idea!"

"Besides, he's been kind to me. He didn't have to be."

"You think that? Is that what you think? Have you looked at the man's *mind*?"

"Of course I haven't! I don't know how to!"

"You don't?"

"No! Humans can't do—"

Brutha paused. Vorbis seemed to do it. He only had to look at someone to know what wicked thoughts they harbored. And grandmother had been the same.

"Humans can't do it, I'm sure," he said. "We can't read minds."

"I don't mean *reading* them, I mean *looking* at them," said Om. "Just seeing the shape of them. You can't *read* a mind. You might as well try and read a river. But seeing the shape's *easy*. Witches can do it, no trouble."

" 'The way of the witch shall be as a path strewn with thorns,' " said Brutha.

"Ossory?" said Om.

"Yes. But of course you'd know," said Brutha.

"Never heard it before in my life," said the tortoise bitterly. "It was what you might call an educated guess."

"Whatever you say," said Brutha, "I still know that you can't truly be Om. The God would not talk like that about His chosen ones."

"I never chose anyone," said Om. "They chose themselves."

"If you're really Om, stop being a tortoise."

"I told you, I can't. You think I haven't tried? Three years! Most of that time I thought I *was* a tortoise."

"Then perhaps you were. Maybe you're just a tortoise who *thinks* he's a god."

"Nah. Don't try philosophy again. Start thinking like

that and you end up thinking maybe you're just a butterfly dreaming it's a whelk or something. No. One day all I had on my mind was the amount of walking necessary to get to the nearest plant with decent low-growing leaves, the next . . . I had all this memory filling up my head. Three years before the shell. No, don't you tell me I'm a tortoise with big ideas."

Brutha hesitated. He knew it was wicked to ask, but he wanted to know what the memory *was*. Anyway, could it be wicked? If the God was sitting there talking to you, could you say anything truly wicked? Face to face? Somehow, that didn't seem so bad as saying something wicked when he was up on a cloud or something.

"As far as I can recall," said Om, "I'd intended to be a big white bull."

"Trampling the infidel," said Brutha.

"Not my basic intention, but no doubt some trampling could have been arranged. Or a swan, I thought. Something impressive. Three years later, I wake up and it turns out I've been a tortoise. I mean, you don't get much lower." Careful, careful . . . you need his help, but don't tell him everything. Don't tell him what you suspect.

"When did you start think— When did you remember all this?" said Brutha, who found the phenomenon of forgetting a strange and fascinating one, as other men might find the idea of flying by flapping your arms.

"About two hundred feet above your vegetable garden," said Om, "which is not a point where it's fun to become sapient, I'm here to tell you."

"But why?" said Brutha. "Gods don't have to stay tortoises unless they want to!"

"I don't know," lied Om.

If he works it out himself I'm done for, he thought.

This is a chance in a million. If I get it wrong, it's back to a life where happiness is a leaf you can reach.

Part of him screamed: I'm a god! I don't have to think like this! I don't have to put myself in the power of a human!

But another part, the part that could remember exactly what being a tortoise for three years had been like, whispered: no. You have to. If you want to be up there again. He's stupid and gormless and he's not got a drop of ambition in his big flabby body. And this is what you've got to work with . . .

The god part said: Vorbis would have been better. Be rational. A mind like that could do anything!

He turned me on my back!

No, he turned a *tortoise* on its back.

Yes. Me.

No. You're a god.

Yes, but a persistently tortoise-shaped one.

If he had known you were a god . . .

But Om remembered Vorbis's absorbed expression, in a pair of gray eyes in front of a mind as impenetrable as a steel ball. He'd never seen a mind shaped like that on anything walking upright. There was someone who probably *would* turn a god on his back, just to see what would happen. Someone who'd overturn the universe, without thought of consequence, for the sake of the knowledge of what happened when the universe was flat on its back . . .

But what *he* had to work with was Brutha, with a mind as incisive as a meringue. And if Brutha found out that . . .

Or if Brutha died . . .

"How are you feeling?" said Om.

"Ill."

"Snuggle down under the sails a bit more," said Om. "You don't want to catch a chill."

There's got to be someone else, he thought. It can't be just him who . . . the rest of the thought was so terrible he tried to block it from his mind, but he couldn't.

. . . it can't be just him who believes in me.

Really in me. Not in a pair of golden horns. Not in a great big building. Not in the dread of hot iron and knives. Not in paying your temple dues because everyone else does. Just in the fact that the Great God Om really exists.

And now he's got himself involved with the most unpleasant mind I've ever seen, someone who kills people to see if they die. An eagle kind of person if ever there was one . . .

Om was aware of a mumbling.

Brutha was lying facedown on the deck.

"What are you doing?" said Om.

Brutha turned his head.

"Praying."

"That's good. What for?"

"You don't *know*?"

"Oh."

If Brutha dies . . .

The tortoise shuddered in its shell. If Brutha died, then it could already hear in its mind's ear the soughing of the wind in the deep, hot places of the desert.

Where the small gods went.

Where do gods come from? Where do they go?

Some attempt to answer this was made by the religious philosopher Koomi of Smale in his book *Ego-Video Liber Deorum*, which translates into the vernacular roughly as *Gods: A Spotter's Guide*.

People said there had to be a Supreme Being because otherwise how could the universe exist, eh?

And of course there clearly had to be, said Koomi, a Supreme Being. But since the universe was a bit of a mess, it was obvious that the Supreme Being hadn't in fact made it. If he had made it he would, being Supreme, have made a much better job of it, with far better thought given, taking an example at random, to thinks like the design of the common nostril. Or, to put it another way, the existence of a badly put-together watch proved the existence of a blind watchmaker. You only had to look around to see that there was room for improvement practically everywhere.

This suggested that the Universe had probably been put together in a bit of a rush by an underling while the Supreme Being wasn't looking, in the same way that Boy Scouts' Association minutes are done on office photocopiers all over the country.

So, reasoned Koomi, it was not a good idea to address any prayers to a Supreme Being. It would only attract his attention and might cause trouble.

And yet there seemed to be a lot of lesser gods around the place. Koomi's theory was that gods come into being and grow and flourish *because they are believed in*. Belief itself is the food of the gods. Initially, when mankind lived in small primitive tribes, there were probably millions of gods. Now there tended to be only a few very important ones—local gods of thunder and love, for example, tended to run together like pools of mercury as the small primitive tribes joined up and became huge, powerful primitive tribes with more sophisticated weapons. But any god could join. Any god could start small. Any god could grow in stature as its believers increased. And dwindle as they decreased. It was like a great big game of ladders and snakes.

Gods liked games, provided they were winning.

Koomi's theory was largely based on the good old Gnostic heresy, which tends to turn up all over the multiverse whenever men get up off their knees and start thinking for two minutes together, although the shock of the sudden altitude tends to mean the thinking is a little whacked. But it upsets priests, who tend to vent their displeasure in traditional ways.

When the Omnian Church found out about Koomi, they displayed him in every town within the Church's empire to demonstrate the essential flaws in his argument.

There were a lot of towns, so they had to cut him up quite small.

Ragged clouds ripped across the skies. The sails creaked in the rising wind, and Om could hear the shouts of the sailors as they tried to outrun the storm.

It was going to be a big storm, even by the mariners' standards. White water crowned the waves.

Brutha snored in his nest.

Om listened to the sailors. They were not men who dealt in sophistries. Someone had killed a porpoise, and everyone knew what that meant. It meant that there was going to be a storm. It meant that the ship was going to be sunk. It was simple cause and effect. It was worse than women aboard. It was worse than albatrosses.

Om wondered if tortoises could swim. Turtles could, he was pretty sure. But those buggers had the shell for it.

It would be too much to ask (even if a god had anyone to ask) that a body designed for trundling around a dry wilderness had any hydrodynamic properties other than those necessary to sink to the bottom.

Oh, well. Nothing else for it. He was still a god. He had *rights*.

He slid down a coil of rope and crawled carefully to the edge of the swaying deck, wedging his shell against a stanchion so that he could see down into the roiling water.

Then he spoke in a voice audible to nothing that was mortal.

Nothing happened for a while. Then one wave rose higher than the rest, and changed shape as it rose. Water poured upward, filling an invisible mold; it was humanoid, but obviously only because it wanted to be. It could as easily have been a waterspout, or an undertow. The sea is always powerful. So many people believe in it. But it seldom answers prayers.

The water shape rose level with the deck and kept pace with Om.

It developed a face, and opened a mouth.

"Well?" it said.

"Greetings, oh Queen of—" Om began.

The watery eyes focused.

"But you are just a small god. And you dare to summon *me?*"

The wind howled in the rigging.

"I have believers," said Om. "So I have the right."

There was the briefest of pauses. Then the Sea Queen said, "*One* believer?"

"One or many does not matter here," said Om. "I have rights."

"And what rights do you demand, little tortoise?" said the Queen of the Sea.

"Save the ship," said Om.

The Queen was silent.

"You have to grant the request," said Om. "It's the rules."

"But I can name my price," said the Sea Queen.

"That's the rules, too."

"And it will be high."

"It will be paid."

The column of water began to collapse back into the waves.

"I will consider this."

Om stared down into the white sea. The ship rolled, sliding him back down the deck, and then rolled back. A flailing foreclaw hooked itself around the stanchion as Om's shell spun around, and for a moment both hind legs paddled helplessly over the waters.

And then Om was shaken free.

Something white swept down toward him as he see-sawed over the edge, and he bit it.

Brutha yelled and pulled his hand up, with Om trailing on the end of it.

"You didn't have to bite!"

The ship pitched into a wave and flung him to the deck. Om let go and rolled away.

When Brutha got to his feet, or at least to his hands and knees, he saw the crewmen standing around him. Two of them grabbed him by the elbows as a wave crashed over the ship.

"What are you doing?"

They were trying to avoid looking at his face. They dragged him toward the rail.

Somewhere in the scuppers Om screamed at the Sea Queen.

"It's the rules! The *rules*!"

Four sailors had got hold of Brutha now. Om could

hear, above the roaring of the storm, the silence of the desert.

"Wait," said Brutha.

"It's nothing personal," said one of the sailors. "We don't want to do this."

"I don't want you to do it either," said Brutha. "Is that any help?"

"The sea wants a life," said the oldest sailor. "Yours is nearest. Okay, get his—"

"Can I make my peace with my God?"

"What?"

"If you're going to kill me, can I pray to my God first?"

"It's not us that's killing you," said the sailor. "It's the sea."

" 'The hand that does the deed is guilty of the crime,' " said Brutha. "Ossory, chapter LVI, verse 93."

The sailors looked at one another. At a time like this, it was probably not wise to antagonize *any* god. The ship skidded down the side of a wave.

"You've got ten seconds," said the oldest sailor. "That's ten seconds more than many men get."

Brutha lay down on the deck, helped considerably by another wave that slammed into the timbers.

Om was dimly aware of the prayer, to his surprise. He couldn't make out the words, but the prayer itself was an itch at the back of his mind.

"Don't ask me," he said, trying to get upright, "I'm out of options—"

The ship smacked down . . .

. . . on to a calm sea.

The storm still raged, but only around a widening circle with the ship in the middle. The lightning, stabbing at the sea, surrounded them like the bars of a cage.

The circle lengthened ahead of them. Now the ship sped down a narrow channel of calm between gray walls of storm a mile high. Electric fire raged overhead.

And then was gone.

Behind them, a mountain of grayness squatted on the sea. They could hear the thunder dying away.

Brutha got uncertainly to his feet, swaying wildly to compensate for a motion that was no longer there.

"Now I—" he began.

He was alone. The sailors had fled.

"Om?" said Brutha.

"Over here."

Brutha fished his God out of the seaweed.

"You said you couldn't do anything!" he said accusingly.

"That wasn't m—" Om paused. There will be a price, he thought. It won't be cheap. It can't be cheap. The Sea Queen is a god. I've crushed a few towns in my time. Holy fire, that kind of thing. If the price isn't high, how can people respect you?

"I made arrangements," he said.

Tidal waves. A ship sunk. A couple of towns disappearing under the sea. It'll be something like that. If people don't respect then they won't fear, and if they don't fear, how can you get them to believe?

Seems unfair, really. One man killed a porpoise. Of course, it doesn't matter to the Queen who gets thrown overboard, just as it didn't matter to *him* which porpoise he killed. And *that's* unfair, because it was Vorbis who did it. He makes people do things they shouldn't do . . .

What am I thinking about? Before I was a tortoise, I didn't even know what *unfair* meant . . .

*   *   *

The hatches opened. People came on deck and hung on the rail. Being on deck in stormy weather always has the possibility of being washed overboard, but that takes on a rosy glow after hours below decks with frightened horses and seasick passengers.

There were no more storms. The ship plowed on in favorable winds, under a clear sky, in a sea as empty of life as the hot desert.

The days passed uneventfully. Vorbis stayed below decks for most of the time.

The crew treated Brutha with cautious respect. News like Brutha spreads quickly.

The coast here was dunes, with the occasional barren salt marsh. A heat haze hung over the land. It was the kind of coast where shipwrecked landfall is more to be dreaded than drowning. There were no seabirds. Even the birds that had been trailing the ship for scraps had vanished.

"No eagles," said Om. There was that to be said about it.

Toward the evening of the fourth day the unedifying panorama was punctuated by a glitter of light, high on the dune sea. It flashed with a sort of rhythm. The captain, whose face now looked as if sleep had not been a regular nighttime companion, called Brutha over.

"His . . . your . . . the deacon told me to watch out for this," he said. "You go and fetch him now."

Vorbis had a cabin somewhere near the bilges, where the air was as thick as thin soup. Brutha knocked.

"Enter." *

---

*Words are the litmus paper of the mind. If you find yourself in the power of someone who will use the word "commence" in cold blood, go somewhere else very quickly. But if they say "Enter," don't stop to pack.

There were no portholes down here. Vorbis was sitting in the dark.

"Yes, Brutha?"

"The captain sent me to fetch you, lord. Something's shining in the desert."

"Good. Now, Brutha. Attend. The captain has a mirror. You will ask to borrow it."

"Er . . . what is a mirror, lord?"

"An unholy and forbidden device," said Vorbis. "Which regretfully can be pressed into godly service. He will deny it, of course. But a man with such a neat beard and tiny mustache is vain, and a vain man must have his mirror. So take it. And stand in the sun and move the mirror so that it shines the sun towards the desert. Do you understand?"

"No, lord," said Brutha.

"Your ignorance is your protection, my son. And then come back and tell me what you see."

Om dozed in the sun. Brutha had found him a little space near the pointy end where he could get sun with little danger of being seen by the crew—and the crew were jittery enough at the moment not to go looking for trouble in any case.

A tortoise dreams . . .

. . . for millions of years.

It was the dreamtime. The unformed time.

The small gods chittered and whirred in the wilderness places, and the cold places, and the deep places. They swarmed in the darkness, without memory but driven by hope and lust for the one thing, the one thing a god craves—*belief*.

There are no medium-sized trees in the deep forest. There are only the towering ones, whose canopy spreads across the sky. Below, in the gloom, there's light for nothing but mosses and ferns. But when a giant falls, leaving a little space . . . *then* there's a race—between the trees on either side, who want to spread *out*, and the seedlings below, who race to grow *up*.

Sometimes, you can make your own space.

Forests were a long way from the wilderness. The nameless voice that was going to be Om drifted on the wind on the edge of the desert, trying to be heard among countless others, trying to avoid being pushed into the center. It may have whirled for millions of years—it had nothing with which to measure time. All it had was hope, and a certain sense of the presence of things. And a voice.

Then there was a day. In a sense, it was the first day.

Om had been aware of the shepherd for some ti—for a while. The flock had been wandering closer and closer. The rains had been sparse. Forage was scarce. Hungry mouths propelled hungry legs further into the rocks, searching out the hitherto scorned clumps of sun-seared grass.

They were sheep, possibly the most stupid animal in the universe with the possible exception of the duck. But even their uncomplicated minds couldn't hear the voice, because sheep don't listen.

There was a lamb, though. It had strayed a little way. Om saw to it that it strayed a little further. Around a rock. Down the slope. Into the crevice.

Its bleating drew the mother.

The crevice was well hidden and the ewe was, after all, content now that she had her lamb. She saw no reason to bleat, even when the shepherd wandered about the rocks calling, cursing, and, eventually, pleading. The shepherd had a hundred sheep, and it might have been surprising that he was prepared to spend days searching for one sheep; in fact, it was *because* he was the kind of man prepared to spend days looking for a lost sheep that he had a hundred sheep.

The voice that was going to be Om waited.

It was on the evening of the second day that he scared up a partridge that had been nesting near the crevice, just as the shepherd was wandering by.

It wasn't much of a miracle, but it was good enough for the shepherd. He made a cairn of stones at the spot and, next day, brought his whole flock into the area. And in the heat of the afternoon he lay down to sleep—and Om spoke to him, inside his head.

Three weeks later the shepherd was stoned to death by the priests of Ur-Gilash, who was at that time the chief god in the area. But they were too late. Om already had a hundred believers, and the number was growing . . .

Only a mile away from the shepherd and his flock was a goatherd and his herd. The merest accident of microgeography had meant that the first man to hear the voice of Om, and who gave Om his view of humans, was a shepherd and not a goatherd. They have quite different ways of looking at the world, and the whole of history might have been different.

For sheep are stupid, and have to be driven. But goats are intelligent, and need to be led.

Ur-Gilash, thought Om. Ah, those were the days . . . when Ossory and his followers had broken into the temple and smashed the altar and had thrown the priestesses out of the window to be torn apart by wild dogs, which was the correct way of doing things, and there had been a mighty wailing and gnashing of feet and the followers of Om had lit their campfires in the crumbled halls of Gilash just as the Prophet had said, and that counted even though he'd said it only five minutes earlier, when they were only looking for the firewood, because everyone agreed a prophecy is a prophecy and no one said you had to wait a long time for it to come true.

Great days. Great days. Every day fresh converts. The rise of Om had been unstoppable . . .

He jerked awake.

Old Ur-Gilash. Weather god, wasn't he? Yes. No. Maybe one of your basic giant spider gods? Something like that. Whatever happened to him?

What happened to me? How does it happen? You hang around the astral planes, going with the flow, enjoy the rhythms of the universe, you think that all the, you know, humans are getting on with the believing back down there, you decide to go and stir them up a bit and then . . . a tortoise. It's like going to the bank and finding the money's been leaking out through a hole. The first you know is when you stroll down looking for a handy mind, and suddenly you're a tortoise and there's no power left to get out.

Three years of looking up at practically everything . . .

Old Ur-Gilash? Perhaps he was hanging on as a lizard somewhere, with some old hermit as his only believer. More likely he had been blown out into the desert. A small god was lucky to get one chance.

There was something wrong. Om couldn't quite put his finger on it, and not only because he didn't have a finger. Gods rose and fell like bits of onion in a boiling soup, but *this* time was different. There was something wrong this time . . .

He'd forced out Ur-Gilash. Fair enough. Law of the jungle. But no one was challenging *him* . . .

Where was Brutha?

"Brutha!"

Brutha was counting the flashes of light off the desert.

"It's a good thing I had a mirror, yes?" said the captain hopefully. "I expect his lordship won't mind about the mirror because it turned out to be useful?"

"I don't think he thinks like that," said Brutha, still counting.

"No. I don't think he does either," said the captain gloomily.

"Seven, and then four."

"It'll be the Quisition for me," said the captain.

Brutha was about to say, "Then rejoice that your soul shall be purified." But he didn't. And he didn't know why he didn't.

"I'm sorry about that," he said.

A veneer of surprise overlaid the captain's grief.

"You people usually say something about how the Quisition is good for the soul," he said.

"I'm sure it is," said Brutha.

The captain was watching his face intently.

"It's flat, you know," he said quietly. "I've sailed out into the Rim Ocean. It's flat, and I've seen the Edge, and it moves. Not the Edge. I mean . . . what's down there. They can cut my head off but it will still move."

"But it will stop moving for you," said Brutha. "So I should be careful to whom you speak, captain."

The captain leaned closer.

"The Turtle Moves!" he hissed, and darted away.

"Brutha!"

Guilt jerked Brutha upright like a hooked fish. He turned around, and sagged with relief. It wasn't Vorbis, it was only God.

He padded over to the place in front of the mast. Om glared up at him.

"Yes?" said Brutha.

"You never come and see me," said the tortoise. "I know you're busy," it added sarcastically, "but a quick prayer would be nice, even."

"I checked you first thing this morning," said Brutha.

"And I'm hungry."

"You had a whole melon rind last night."

"And who had the melon, eh?"

"No, he didn't," said Brutha. "He eats stale bread and water."

"Why doesn't he eat fresh bread?"

"He waits for it to get stale."

"Yes. I expect he does," said the tortoise.

"Om?"

"What?"

"The captain just said something odd. He said the world is flat and has an edge."

"Yes? So what?"

"But, I mean, we know the world is a ball, because . . ."

The tortoise blinked.

"No, it's not," he said. "Who said it's a ball?"

"You did," said Brutha. Then he added: "According to Book One of the Septateuch, anyway."

I've never thought like this before, he thought. I'd never have said "anyway."

"Why'd the captain tell me something like that?" he said. "It's not normal conversation."

"I told you, I never made the world," said Om. "Why should I make the world? It was here already. And if I *did* make a world, I wouldn't make it a ball. People'd fall off. All the sea'd run off the bottom."

"Not if you told it to stay on."

"Hah! Will you hark at the man!"

"Besides, the sphere is a perfect shape," said Brutha. "Because in the Book of—"

"Nothing amazing about a sphere," said the tortoise. "Come to that, a turtle is a perfect shape."

"A perfect shape for what?"

"Well, the perfect shape for a turtle, to start with," said Om. "If it was shaped like a ball, it'd be bobbing to the surface the whole time."

"But it's a heresy to say the world is flat," said Brutha.

"Maybe, but it's true."

"And it's really on the back of a giant turtle?"

"That's right."

"In that case," said Brutha triumphantly, "what does the turtle stand on?"

The tortoise gave him a blank stare.

"It doesn't stand on anything," it said. "It's a *turtle*, for heaven's sake. It swims. That's what turtles are for."

"I . . . er . . . I think I'd better go and report to Vorbis," said Brutha. "He goes very calm if he's kept waiting. What did you want me for? I'll try and bring you some more food after supper."

"How are you feeling?" said the tortoise.

"I'm feeling all right, thank you."

"Eating properly, that sort of thing?"

"Yes, thank you."

"Pleased to hear it. Run along now. I mean, I'm only your *God*." Om raised its voice as Brutha hurried off. "And you might visit more often!

"And pray louder, I'm fed up with straining!" he shouted.

*   *   *

Vorbis was still sitting in his cabin when Brutha puffed along the passage and knocked on the door. There was no reply. After a while, Brutha pushed the door open.

Vorbis did not appear to read. Obviously he wrote, because of the famous Letters, but no one ever saw him do it. When he was alone he spent a lot of time staring at the wall, or prostrate in prayer. Vorbis could humble himself in prayer in a way that made the posturings of power-mad emperors look subservient.

"Um," said Brutha, and tried to pull the door shut again.

Vorbis waved one hand irritably. Then he stood up. He did not dust off his robe.

"Do you know, Brutha," he said, "I do not think there is a single person in the Citadel who would dare to interrupt me at prayer? They would fear the Quisition. *Everyone* fears the Quisition. Except you, it appears. Do you fear the Quisition?"

Brutha looked into the black-on-black eyes. Vorbis looked into a round pink face. There was a special face that people wore when they spoke to an exquisitor. It was flat and expressionless and glistened slightly, and even a half-trained exquisitor could read the barely concealed guilt like a book. Brutha just looked out of breath but then, he always did. It was fascinating.

"No, lord," he said.

"Why not?"

"The Quisition protects us, lord. It is written in Ossory, chapter VII, verse—"

Vorbis put his head on one side.

"Of course it is. But have you ever thought that the Quisition could be wrong?"

"No, lord," said Brutha.

"But why not?"

"I do not know why, Lord Vorbis. I just never have."

Vorbis sat down at a little writing table, no more than a board that folded down from the hull.

"And you are right, Brutha," he said. "Because the Quisition *cannot* be wrong. Things can only be as the God wishes them. It is impossible to think that the world could run in any other way, is this not so?"

A vision of a one-eyed tortoise flickered momentarily in Brutha's mind.

Brutha had never been any good at lying. The truth itself had always seemed so incomprehensible that complicating things even further had always been beyond him.

"So the Septateuch teaches us," he said.

"Where there is punishment, there is always a crime," said Vorbis. "Sometimes the crime follows the punishment, which only serves to prove the foresight of the Great God."

"That's what my grandmother used to say," said Brutha automatically.

"Indeed? I would like to know more about this formidable lady."

"She used to give me a thrashing every morning because I would certainly do something to deserve it during the day," said Brutha.

"A most *complete* understanding of the nature of mankind," said Vorbis, with his chin on one hand. "Were it not for the deficiency of her sex, it sounds as though she would have made an excellent inquisitor."

Brutha nodded. Oh, yes. Yes, indeed.

"And now," said Vorbis, with no change in his tone, "you will tell me what you saw in the desert."

"Uh. There were six flashes. And then a pause of about five heartbeats. And then eight flashes. And another pause. And two flashes."

Vorbis nodded thoughtfully.

"Three-quarters," he said. "All praise to the Great God. He is my staff and guide through the hard places. And you may go."

Brutha hadn't expected to be told what the flashes meant, and wasn't going to enquire. The Quisition asked the questions. They were known for it.

Next day the ship rounded a headland and the bay of Ephebe lay before it, with the city a white smudge on the horizon which time and distance turned into a spilling of blindingly white houses, all the way up a rock.

It seemed of considerable interest to Sergeant Simony. Brutha had not exchanged a word with him. Fraternization between clergy and soldiers was not encouraged; there was a certain tendency to *unholiness* about soldiers . . .

Brutha, left to his own devices again as the crew made ready for port, watched the soldier carefully. Most soldiers were a bit slovenly and generally rude to minor clergy. Simony was different. Apart from anything else, he gleamed. His breastplate hurt the eyes. His skin looked scrubbed.

The sergeant stood at the prow, staring fixedly as the city drew nearer. It was unusual to see him very far away from Vorbis. Wherever Vorbis stood there was the sergeant, hand on sword, eyes scanning the surroundings for . . . what?

And always silent, except when spoken to. Brutha tried to be friends.

"Looks very . . . white, doesn't it?" he said. "The city. Very white. Sergeant Simony?"

The sergeant turned slowly, and stared at Brutha.

Vorbis's gaze was dreadful. Vorbis looked through

your head to the sins inside, hardly interested in you except as a vehicle for your sins. But Simony's glance was pure, simple hatred.

Brutha stepped back.

"Oh. I'm sorry," he muttered. He walked back somberly to the blunt end, and tried to keep out of the soldier's way.

Anyway, there were more soldiers, soon enough . . .

The Ephebians were expecting them. Soldiers lined the quay, weapons held in a way that stopped just short of being a direct insult. And there were a lot of them.

Brutha trailed along, the voice of the tortoise insinuating itself in his head.

"So the Ephebians want peace, do they?" said Om. "Doesn't look like that. Doesn't look like we're going to lay down the law to a defeated enemy. Looks like we took a pasting and don't want to take any more. Looks like we're suing for peace. That's what it looks like to me."

"In the Citadel everyone said it was a glorious victory," said Brutha. He found he could talk now with his lips hardly moving at all; Om seemed able to pick up his words as they reached his vocal cords.

Ahead of him, Simony shadowed the deacon, staring suspiciously at each Ephebian guard.

"That's a funny thing," said Om. "Winners never talk about glorious victories. That's because they're the ones who see what the battlefield looks like afterward. It's only the losers who have glorious victories."

Brutha didn't know what to reply. "That doesn't sound like god talk," he hazarded.

"It's this tortoise brain."

"What?"

"Don't you know anything? Bodies aren't just handy things for storing your mind in. Your shape affects how you think. It's all this morphology that's all over the place."

"What?"

Om sighed. "If I don't concentrate, I think like a tortoise!"

"What? You mean slowly?"

"No! Tortoises are cynics. They always expect the worst."

"Why?"

"I don't know. Because it often happens to them, I suppose."

Brutha stared around at Ephebe. Guards with helmets crested with plumes that looked like horses' tails gone rogue marched on either side of the column. A few Ephebian citizens watched idly from the roadside. They looked surprisingly like the people at home, and not like two-legged demons at all.

"They're people," he said.

"Full marks for comparative anthropology."

"Brother Nhumrod said Ephebians eat human flesh," said Brutha. "He wouldn't tell lies."

A small boy regarded Brutha thoughtfully while excavating a nostril. If it was a demon in human form, it was an extremely good actor.

At intervals along the road from the docks were white stone statues. Brutha had never seen statues before. Apart from the statues of the SeptArchs, of course, but that wasn't the same thing.

"What are they?"

"Well, the tubby one with the toga is Tuvelpit, the God of Wine. They call him Smimto in Tsort. And the broad with the hairdo is Astoria, Goddess of Love. A complete bubblehead. The ugly one is Offler the Crocodile God. Not a local boy. He's Klatchian originally, but the Ephebians heard about him and thought he was a good idea. Note the teeth. Good teeth. *Good* teeth. Then the one with the snakepit hairdo is—"

"You talk about them as if they were real," said Brutha.

"They are."

"There is no other god but you. You told Ossory that."

"Well. You know. I exaggerated a bit. But they're not that good. There's one of 'em that sits around playing a flute most of the time and chasing milkmaids. I don't call that very divine. Call that very divine? I don't."

The road wound up steeply around the rocky hill. Most of the city seemed to be built on outcrops or was cut into the actual rock itself, so that one man's patio was another man's roof. The roads were really a series of shallow steps, accessible to a man or a donkey but sudden death to a cart. Ephebe was a pedestrian place.

More people watched them in silence. So did the statues of the gods. The Ephebians had gods in the same way that other cities had rats.

Brutha got a look at Vorbis's face. The exquisitor was staring straight ahead of himself. Brutha wondered what the man was seeing.

It was all so *new*!

And devilish, of course. Although the gods in the statues didn't look much like demons—but he could hear the voice of Nhumrod pointing out that this very fact made them even more demonic. Sin crept up on you like a wolf in a sheep's skin.

One of the goddesses had been having some very serious trouble with her dress, Brutha noticed; if Brother Nhumrod had been present, he would have had to hurry off for some very serious lying down.

"Petulia, Goddess of Negotiable Affection," said Om. "Worshiped by the ladies of the night and every other time as well, if you catch my meaning."

Brutha's mouth dropped open.

"They've got a goddess for *painted jezebels?*"

"Why not? Very religious people I understand. They're used to being on their—they spend so much time looking at the—look, belief is where you find it. Specialization. That's safe, see. Low risk, guaranteed returns. There's even a God of Lettuce somewhere. I mean, it's not as though any one else is likely to try to become a God of Lettuce. You just find a lettuce-growing community and hang on. Thunder gods come and go, but it's *you* they turn to every time when there's a bad attack of Lettuce Fly. You've got to . . . uh . . . hand it to Petulia. She spotted a gap in the market and filled it."

"There's a God of Lettuce?"

"Why not? If enough people believe, you can be god of anything . . ."

Om stopped himself and waited to see if Brutha had noticed. But Brutha seemed to have something else on his mind.

"That's not right. Not treating people like that. Ow."

He'd walked into the back of a subdeacon. The party had halted, partly because the Ephebian escort had stopped too, but mainly because a man was running down the street.

He was quite old, and in many respects resembled a frog that had been dried out for quite some time. Something about him generally made people think of the word "spry," but, at the moment, they would be much more likely to think of the words "mother naked" and possibly also "dripping wet" and would be one hundred percent accurate, too. Although there was the beard. It was a beard you could camp out in.

The man thudded down the street without any apparent self-consciousness and stopped outside a potter's shop. The potter didn't seem concerned at being addressed by a little wet naked man; in fact, none of the people in the street had given him a second glance.

"I'd like a Number Nine pot and some string, please," said the old man.

"Yes sir, Mr. Legibus." The potter reached under his counter and pulled out a towel. The naked man took it in an absent-minded way. Brutha got the feeling that this had happened to both of them before.

"And a lever of infinite length and, um, an immovable place to stand," said Legibus, drying himself off.

"What you see is what I got, sir. Pots and general household items, but a bit short on axiomatic mechanisms."

"Well, have you got a piece of chalk?"

"Got some right here from last time," said the potter.

The little naked man took the chalk and started to draw triangles on the nearest bit of wall. Then he looked down.

"Why haven't I got any clothes on?" he said.

"*We've* been having our *bath* again, haven't we?" said the potter.

"I left my clothes in the bath?"

"I think you probably had an idea while you were in the bath?" prompted the potter.

"That's right! That's right! Got this splendid idea for moving the world around!" said Legibus. "Simple lever principle. Should work perfectly. It's just a matter of getting the technical details sorted out."

"That's nice. We can move somewhere warm for the winter," said the potter.

"Can I borrow the towel?"

"It's yours anyway, Mr. Legibus."

"Is it?"

"I said, you left it here last time. Remember? When you had that idea for the lighthouse?"

"Fine. Fine," said Legibus, wrapping the towel around himself. He drew a few more lines on the wall. "Fine. Okay. I'll send someone down later to collect the wall."

He turned and appeared to see the Omnians for the first time. He peered forward and then shrugged.

"Hmm," he said, and wandered away.

Brutha tugged at the cloak of one of the Ephebian soldiers.

"Excuse me, but why did we stop?" he said.

"Philosophers have right of way," said the soldier.

"What's a philosopher?" said Brutha.

"Someone who's bright enough to find a job with no heavy lifting," said a voice in his head.

"An infidel seeking the just fate he shall surely receive," said Vorbis. "An inventor of fallacies. This cursed city attracts them like a dung heap attracts flies."

"Actually, it's the climate," said the voice of the tortoise. "Think about it. If you're inclined to leap out of your bath and run down the street every time you think you've got a bright idea, you don't want to do it somewhere cold. If you *do* do it somewhere cold, you die out. That's natural selection, that is. Ephebe's known for its philosophers. It's better than street theater."

"What, a lot of old men running around the streets with no clothes on?" said Brutha, under his breath, as they were marched onward.

"More or less. If you spend your whole time thinking about the universe, you tend to forget the less important bits of it. Like your pants. And ninety-nine out of a hundred ideas they come up with are totally useless."

"Why doesn't anyone lock them away safely, then? They don't sound much use to *me*," said Brutha.

"Because the hundredth idea," said Om, "is generally a humdinger."

"What?"

"Look up at the highest tower on the rock."

Brutha looked up. At the top of the tower, secured by metal bands, was a big disc that glittered in the morning light.

"What is it?" he whispered.

"The reason why Omnia hasn't got much of a fleet any more," said Om. "That's why it's always worth having a few philosophers around the place. One minute it's all Is Truth Beauty and Is Beauty Truth, and Does a Falling Tree in the Forest Make a Sound if There's No one There to Hear It, and then just when you think they're going to start dribbling one of 'em says, Incidentally, putting a thirty-foot parabolic reflector on a high place to shoot the rays of the sun at an enemy's ships would be a very interesting demonstration of optical principles," he added. "Always coming up with amazing new ideas, the philosophers. The one before that was some intricate device that demonstrated the principles of leverage by incidentally hurling balls of burning sulphur two miles. Then before that, I think, there was some kind of an underwater thing that shot sharpened logs into the bottom of ships."

Brutha stared at the disc again. He hadn't understood more than one-third of the words in the last statement.

"Well," he said, "does it?"

"Does what?"

"Make a sound. If it falls down when no one's there to hear it."

"Who cares?"

The party had reached a gateway in the wall that ran around the top of the rock in much the same way that a headband encircles a head. The Ephebian captain stopped, and turned.

"The . . . *visitors* . . . must be blindfolded," he said.

"That is outrageous!" said Vorbis. "We are here on a mission of diplomacy!"

"That is not my business," said the captain. "My business is to say: If you go through this gate you go blindfolded. You don't have to be blindfolded. You can stay outside. But if you want to go through, you got to wear a blindfold. This is one of them life choices."

One of the subdeacons whispered in Vorbis's ear. He held a brief *sotto voce* conversation with the leader of the Omnian guard.

"Very well," he said, "under protest."

The blindfold was quite soft, and totally opaque. But as Brutha was led . . .

. . . ten paces along a passage, and then left five paces, then diagonally forward and left three-and-a-half paces, and right one hundred and three paces, down three steps, and turned around seventeen-and-one-quarter times, and forward nine paces, and left one pace, and forward nineteen paces, and pause three seconds, and right two paces, and back two paces, and left two paces, and turned three-and-a-half times, and wait one second, and up three steps, and right twenty paces, and turned around five-and-a-quarter times, and left fifteen paces, and forward seven paces, and right eighteen paces, and up seven steps, and diagonally forward, and pause two seconds, right four paces, and down a slope that went down a meter every ten paces for thirty paces, and then turned around seven-and-a-half times, and forward six paces . . .

. . . he wondered what good it was supposed to do.

The blindfold was removed in an open courtyard, made of some white stone that turned the sunlight into a glare. Brutha blinked.

Bowmen lined the yard. Their arrows were pointing downwards, but their manner suggested that pointing horizontally could happen any minute.

Another bald man was waiting for them. Ephebe seemed to have an unlimited supply of skinny bald men wearing sheets. This one smiled, with his mouth alone.

No one likes us much, Brutha thought.

"I trust you will excuse this minor inconvenience," said the skinny man. "My name is Aristocrates. I am secretary to the Tyrant. Please ask your men to put down their weapons."

Vorbis drew himself up to his full height. He was a head taller than the Ephebian. Pale though his complexion normally was, it had gone paler.

"We are entitled to retain our arms!" he said. "We are an emissary to a foreign land!"

"But not a barbarian one," said Aristocrates mildly. "Weapons will not be required here."

"Barbarian?" said Vorbis. "You burned our ships!"

Aristocrates held up a hand.

"This is a discussion for later," he said. "My pleasant task now is to show you to your quarters. I am sure you would like to rest a little after your journey. You are, of course, at liberty to wander anywhere you wish in the palace. And if there is anywhere where *we* do not wish you to wander, the guards will be sure to inform you with speed and tact."

"And we can leave the palace?" said Vorbis coldly.

Aristocrates shrugged.

"We do not guard the gateway except in times of war," he said. "If you can remember the way, you are free to use it. But vague perambulations in the labyrinth are unwise, I must warn you. Our ancestors were sadly very suspicious and put in many traps out of distrust; we keep them well-greased and primed, of course, merely out of a respect for tradition. And now, if you would care to follow me . . ."

The Omnians kept together as they followed Aristocrates through the palace. There were fountains. There were gardens. Here and there groups of people sat around doing nothing very much except talking. The Ephebians seemed to have only a shaky grasp of the concepts of "inside" and "outside"—except for the palace's encircling labyrinth, which was very clear on the subject.

"Danger attends us at every turn," said Vorbis quietly. "Any man who breaks rank or fraternizes in any way will explain his conduct to the inquisitors. At length."

Brutha looked at a woman filling a jug from a well. It did not look like a very military act.

He was feeling that strange double feeling again. On the surface there were the thoughts of Brutha, which were exactly the thoughts that the Citadel would have approved of. This was a nest of infidels and unbelievers, its very mundanity a subtle cloak for the traps of wrong thinking and heresy. It might be bright with sunlight, but in reality it was a place of shadows.

But down below were the thoughts of the Brutha that watched Brutha from the inside . . .

Vorbis looked wrong here. Sharp and unpleasant. And any city where potters didn't worry at all when naked, dripping wet old men came and drew triangles on their walls was a place Brutha wanted to find out more about. He felt like a big empty jug. The thing to do with something empty was fill it up.

"Are you doing something to me?" he whispered.

In his box, Om looked at the shape of Brutha's mind. Then he tried to think quickly.

"No," he said, and that at least was the truth. Had this ever happened before?

Had it been like this back in the first days? It must have been. It was all so hazy now. He couldn't remember the thoughts he'd had then, just the shape of the thoughts. Everything had been highly colored, everything had been growing every day—*he* had been growing every day; thoughts and the mind that was thinking them were developing at the same speed. Easy to forget things from those times. It was like a fire trying to remember the shape of its flames. But the *feeling*—he could remember that.

He wasn't doing anything to Brutha. Brutha was doing it to himself. Brutha was beginning to think in godly ways. Brutha was starting to become a prophet.

Om wished he had someone to talk to. Someone who understood.

This *was* Ephebe, wasn't it? Where people made a *living* trying to understand?

The Omnians were to be housed in little rooms around a central courtyard. There was a fountain in the middle, in a very small grove of sweet-smelling pine trees. The soldiers nudged one another. People think that professional soldiers think a lot about fighting, but *serious* professional soldiers think a lot more about food and a warm place to sleep, because these are two things that are generally hard to get, whereas fighting tends to turn up all the time.

There was a bowl of fruit in Brutha's cell, and a plate of cold meat. But first things first. He fished the God out of the box.

"There's fruit," he said. "What're these berries?"

"Grapes," said Om. "Raw material for wine."

"You mentioned that word before. What does it mean?"

There was a cry from outside.

"Brutha!"

"That's Vorbis. I'll have to go."

Vorbis was standing in the middle of his cell.

"Have you eaten anything?" he demanded.

"No, lord."

"Fruit and meat, Brutha. And this is a fast day. They seek to insult us!"

"Um. Perhaps they don't know that it is a fast day?" Brutha hazarded.

"Ignorance is itself a sin," said Vorbis.

"Ossory VII, verse 4," said Brutha automatically.

Vorbis smiled and patted Brutha's shoulder.

"You are a walking book, Brutha. The *Septateuch perambulatus.*"

Brutha looked down at his sandals.

He's right, he thought. And I had forgotten. Or at least, not wanted to remember.

And then he heard his own thoughts echoed back to him: it's fruit and meat and bread, that's all. That's all it is. Fast days and feast days and Prophets' Days and bread days . . . who cares? A God whose only concern about food now is that it's low enough to reach?

I wish he wouldn't keep patting my shoulder.

Vorbis turned away.

"Shall I remind the others?" Brutha said.

"No. Our ordained brothers will not, of course, require reminding. As for soldiers . . . a little license, perhaps, is allowable this far from home . . ."

Brutha wandered back to his cell.

Om was still on the table, staring fixedly at the melon.

"I nearly committed a terrible sin," said Brutha. "I nearly ate fruit on a fruitless day."

"That's a terrible thing, a terrible thing," said Om. "Now cut the melon."

"But it is forbidden!" said Brutha.

"No it's not," said Om. "Cut the melon."

"But it was the eating of fruit that caused passion to invade the world," said Brutha.

"All it caused was flatulence," said Om. "Cut the melon!"

"You're tempting me!"

"No I'm not. I'm giving you permission. Special dispensation! Cut the damn melon!"

"Only a bishop or higher is allowed to giv—" Brutha began. And then he stopped.

Om glared at him.

"Yes. Exactly," he said. "And now cut the melon." His tone softened a bit. "If it makes you feel any better, I shall declare that it is bread. I happen to be the God in this immediate vicinity. I can call it what I damn well like. It's bread. Right? Now cut the damn melon."

"Loaf," corrected Brutha.

"Right. And give me a slice without any seeds in it."

Brutha did so, a bit carefully.

"And eat up quick," said Om.

"In case Vorbis finds us?"

"Because you've got to go and find a philosopher," said Om. The fact that his mouth was full didn't make any difference to his voice in Brutha's mind. "You know, melons grow wild in the wilderness. Not big ones like this. Little green jobs. Skin like leather. Can't bite through 'em. The years I've spent eating dead leaves a goat'd spit out, right next to a crop of melons. Melons should have thinner skins. Remember that."

"Find a philosopher?"

"Right. Someone who knows how to think. Someone who can help me stop being a tortoise."

"But . . . Vorbis might want me."

"You're just going for a stroll. No problem. And hurry up. There's other gods in Ephebe. I don't want to meet them right now. Not looking like this."

Brutha looked panicky.

"How do I find a philosopher?" he said.

"Around here? Throw a brick, I should think."

The labyrinth of Ephebe is ancient and full of one hundred and one amazing things you can do with hidden springs, razor-sharp knives, and falling rocks. There isn't just one guide through it. There are six, and each one knows his way through one-sixth of the labyrinth. Every year they have a special competition, when they do a little redesigning. They vie with one another to see who can make his section even more deadly than the others to the casual wanderer. There's a panel of judges, and a small prize.

The furthest anyone ever got through the labyrinth without a guide was nineteen paces. Well, more or less. His head rolled a further seven paces, but that probably doesn't count.

At each changeover point there is a small chamber without any traps at all. What it does contain is a small bronze bell. These are the little waiting-rooms where visitors are handed on to the next guide. And here and there, set high in the tunnel roof over the more ingenious traps, are observation windows, because guards like a good laugh as much as anyone else.

All of this was totally lost on Brutha, who padded amiably along the tunnels and corridors without really thinking much about it, and at last pushed open the gate into the late evening air.

It was fragrant with the scent of flowers. Moths whirred through the gloom.

"What do philosophers look like?" said Brutha, "When they're not having a bath, I mean."

"They do a lot of thinking," said Om. "Look for someone with a strained expression."

"That might just mean constipation."

"Well, so long as they're philosophical about it . . ."

The city of Ephebe surrounded them. Dogs barked. Somewhere a cat yowled. There was that general susurration of small comfortable sounds that shows that, out there, a lot of people are living their lives.

And then a door burst open down the street and there was the cracking noise of a quite large wine amphora being broken over someone's head.

A skinny old man in a toga picked himself up from the cobbles where he had landed, and glared at the doorway.

"I'm telling you, listen, a finite intellect, right, cannot by means of comparison reach the absolute truth of things, because being by nature indivisible, truth excludes the concepts of "more" or "less" so that nothing but truth itself can be the exact measure of truth. You bastards," he said.

Someone from inside the building said, "Oh yeah? Sez you."

The old man ignored Brutha but, with great difficulty, pulled a cobblestone loose and hefted it in his hand.

Then he dived back through the doorway. There was a distant scream of rage.

"Ah. Philosophy," said Om.

Brutha peered cautiously around the door.

Inside the room two groups of very nearly identical men in togas were trying to hold back two of their colleagues. It is a scene repeated a million times a day in bars around the multiverse—both would-be fighters growled and grimaced at one another and fought to escape the restraint of their friends, only of course they did not fight *too* hard, because there is nothing worse than actually *succeeding* in breaking free and suddenly finding yourself all alone in the middle of the ring with a madman who is about to hit you between the eyes with a rock.

"Yep," said Om, "that's philosophy, right enough."

"But they're fighting!"

"A full and free exchange of opinions, yes."

Now that Brutha could get a clearer view, he could see that there were one or two differences between the men. One had a shorter beard, and was very red in the face, and was waggling a finger accusingly.

"He bloody well accused me of slander!" he was shouting.

"I didn't!" shouted the other man.

"You did! You did! Tell 'em what you said!"

"Look, I merely suggested, to indicate the nature of paradox, right, that if Xeno the Ephebian said, 'All Ephebians are liars—'"

"See? See? He did it again!"

"—no, no, listen, listen . . . then, since Xeno is himself

an Ephebian, this would mean that he himself is a liar and therefore—"

Xeno made a determined effort to break free, dragging four desperate fellow philosophers across the floor.

"I'm going to lay one right *on* you, pal!"

Brutha said, "Excuse me, please?"

The philosophers froze. Then they turned to look at Brutha. They relaxed by degrees. There was a chorus of embarrassed coughs.

"Are you all philosophers?" said Brutha.

The one called Xeno stepped forward, adjusting the hang of his toga.

"That's right," he said. "We're philosophers. We think, therefore we am."

"Are," said the luckless paradox manufacturer automatically.

Xeno spun around. "I've just about had it up to *here* with you, Ibid!" he roared. He turned back to Brutha. "We *are*, therefore we am," he said confidently. "That's it."

Several of the philosophers looked at one another with interest.

"That's actually quite interesting," one said. "The evidence of our existence is the *fact* of our existence, is that what you're saying?"

"Shut up," said Xeno, without looking around.

"Have you been fighting?" said Brutha.

The assembled philosophers assumed various expressions of shock and horror.

"Fighting? Us? We're *philosophers*," said Ibid, shocked.

"My word, yes," said Xeno.

"But you were—" Brutha began.

Xeno waved a hand.

"The cut and thrust of debate," he said.

"Thesis plus antithesis equals hysteresis," said Ibid. "The stringent testing of the universe. The hammer of the intellect upon the anvil of fundamental truth—"

"Shut up," said Xeno. "And what can we do for you, young man?"

"Ask them about gods," Om prompted.

"Uh, I want to find out about gods," said Brutha.

The philosophers looked at one another.

"Gods?" said Xeno. "We don't bother with gods. Huh. Relics of an outmoded belief system, gods."

There was a rumble of thunder from the clear evening sky.

"Except for Blind Io the Thunder God," Xeno went on, his tone hardly changing.

Lightning flashed across the sky.

"And Cubal the Fire God," said Xeno.

A gust of wind rattled the windows.

"Flatulus the God of the Winds, he's all right too," said Xeno.

An arrow materialized out of the air and hit the table by Xeno's hand.

"Fedecks the Messenger of the Gods, one of the all-time greats," said Xeno.

A bird appeared in the doorway. At least, it looked vaguely like a bird. It was about a foot high, black and white, with a bent beak and an expression that suggested that whatever it was it really dreaded ever happening to it had already happened.

"What's that?" said Brutha.

"A penguin," said the voice of Om inside his head.

"Patina the Goddess of Wisdom? One of the best," said Xeno.

The penguin croaked at him and waddled off into the darkness.

The philosophers looked very embarrassed. Then Ibid said, "Foorgol the God of Avalanches? Where's the snowline?"

"Two hundred miles away," said someone.

They waited. Nothing happened.

"Relic of an outmoded belief system," said Xeno.

A wall of freezing white death did not appear anywhere in Ephebe.

"Mere unthinking personification of a natural force," said one of the philosophers, in a louder voice. They all seemed to feel a lot better about this.

"Primitive nature worship."

"Wouldn't give you tuppence for him."

"Simple rationalization of the unknown."

"Hah! A clever fiction, a bogey to frighten the weak and stupid!"

The words rose up in Brutha. He couldn't stop himself.

"Is it always this cold?" he said. "It seemed very chilly on my way here."

The philosophers all moved away from Xeno.

"Although if there's one thing you can say about Foorgal," said Xeno, "it's that he's a very understanding god. Likes a joke as much as the next . . . man."

He looked both ways, quickly. After a while the philosophers relaxed, and seemed to completely forget about Brutha.

And only now did he really have time to take in the room. He had never seen a tavern before in his life, but that was what it was. The bar ran along one side of the room. Behind it were the typical trappings of an Ephebian bar—the stacks of wine jars, racks of amphorae, and the cheery pictures of vestal virgins on cards of salted peanuts and goat jerky, pinned up in the hope that there really *were* people in the world who would slatheringly buy more and more packets of nuts they didn't want in order to look at a cardboard nipple.

"What's all this stuff?" Brutha whispered.

"How should I know?" said Om. "Let me out so's I can see."

Brutha unfastened the box and lifted the tortoise out. One rheumy eye looked around.

"Oh. Typical tavern," said Om. "Good. Mine's a saucer of whatever they were drinking."

"A tavern? A place were alcohol is drunk?"

"I very much intend this to be the case, yes."

"But . . . but . . . the Septateuch, no less than seventeen times, adjures us most emphatically to refrain from—"

"Beats the hell out of me why," said Om. "See that man cleaning the mugs? You say unto him, Give me a—"

"But it mocks the mind of Man, says the Prophet Ossory. And—"

"I'll say this one more time! I never said it! Now talk to the man!"

In fact the man talked to Brutha. He appeared magically on the other side of the bar, still wiping a mug.

"Evening, sir," he said. "What'll it be?"

"I'd like a drink of water, please," said Brutha, very deliberately.

"And something for the tortoise?"

"Wine!" said the voice of Om.

"I don't know," said Brutha. "What do tortoises usually drink?"

"The ones we have in here normally have a drop of milk with some bread in it," said the barman.

"You get a lot of tortoises?" said Brutha loudly, trying to drown out Om's outraged screams.

"Oh, a very useful philosophical animal, your average tortoise. Outrunning metaphorical arrows, beating hares in races . . . very handy."

"Uh . . . I haven't got any money," said Brutha.

The barman leaned towards him. "Tell you what," he said. "Declivities has just bought a round. He won't mind."

"Bread and milk?"

"Oh. Thank you. Thank you very much."

"Oh, we get all sorts in here," said the barman, leaning back. "Stoics. Cynics. Big drinkers, the Cynics. Epicureans. Stochastics. Anamaxandrites. Epistemologists. Peripatetics. Synoptics. All sorts. That's what I always say. What I always say is"—he picked up another mug and started to dry it—"it takes all sorts to make a world."

"Bread and milk!" shouted Om. "You'll feel my wrath for this, right? Now ask him about gods!"

"Tell me," said Brutha, sipping his mug of water, "do any of them know much about gods?"

"You'd want a priest for that sort of thing," said the barman.

"No, I mean about . . . what gods are . . . how gods came to exist . . . *that* sort of thing," said Brutha, trying to get to grips with the barman's peculiar mode of conversation.

"Gods don't like that sort of thing," said the barman. "We get that in here some nights, when someone's had a few. Cosmic speculation about whether gods really exist. Next thing, there's a bolt of lightning through the roof with a note wrapped around it saying 'Yes, we do' and a pair of sandals with smoke coming out. That sort of thing, it takes all the interest out of metaphysical speculation."

"Not even fresh bread," muttered Om, nose deep in his saucer.

"No, I know gods exist all right," said Brutha, hurriedly. "I just want to find out more about . . . them."

The barman shrugged.

"Then I'd be obliged if you don't stand next to anything valuable," he said, "Still, it'll all be the same in a hundred years." He picked up another mug and started to polish it.

"Are you a philosopher?" said Brutha.

"It kind of rubs off on you after a while," said the barman.

"This milk's off," said Om. "They say Ephebe is a democracy. This milk ought to be allowed to vote."

"I don't think," said Brutha carefully, "that I'm going to find what I want here. Um. Mr. Drink Seller?"

"Yes?"

"What was that bird that walked in when the Goddess"—he tasted the unfamiliar word—"of Wisdom was mentioned?"

"Bit of a problem there," said the barman. "Bit of an embarrassment."

"Sorry?"

"It was," said the barman, "a penguin."

"Is it a wise sort of bird, then?"

"No. Not a lot," said the barman. "Not known for its wisdom. Second most confused bird in the world. Can only fly underwater, they say."

"Then why—"

"We don't like to talk about it," said the barman. "It upsets people. Bloody sculptor," he added, under his breath.

Down the other end of the bar the philosophers had started fighting again.

The barman leaned forward. "If you haven't got any money," he said, "I don't think you're going to get much help. Talk isn't cheap around here."

"But they just—" Brutha began.

"There's the expenditure on soap and water, for a start. Towels. Flannels. Loofahs. Pumice stones. Bath salts. It all adds up."

There was a gurgling noise from the saucer. Om's milky head turned to Brutha.

"You've got no money at *all?*" he said.

"No," said Brutha.

"Well, we've got to have a philosopher," said the tortoise flatly. "I can't think and you don't know how to. We've got to find someone who does it all the time."

"Of course, you could try old Didactylos," said the barman. "He's about as cheap as they come."

"Doesn't use expensive soap?" said Brutha.

"I think it could be said without fear of contradiction," said the barman solemnly, "that he doesn't use any soap at all whatsoever in any way."

"Oh. Well. Thank you," said Brutha.

"Ask him where this man lives," Om commanded.

"Where can I find Mr. Didactylos?" said Brutha.

"In the palace courtyard. Next door to the Library. You can't miss him. Just follow your nose."

"We just came—" Brutha said, but his inner voice prompted him not to complete the sentence. "We'll just be going then."

"Don't forget your tortoise," said the barman. "There's good eating on one of them."

"May all your wine turn to water!" Om shrieked.

"Will it?" said Brutha, as they stepped out into the night.

"No."

"Tell me again. Why exactly are we looking for a philosopher?" said Brutha.

"I want to get my power back," said Om.

"But everyone believes in you!"

"If they believed in me they could talk to me. I could talk to them. I don't know what's gone wrong. No one is worshiping any other gods in Omnia, are they?"

"They wouldn't be allowed to," said Brutha. "The Quisition would see to that."

"Yeah. It's hard to kneel if you have no knees."

Brutha stopped in the empty street.

"I don't understand you!"

"You're not supposed to. The ways of gods aren't supposed to be understandable to men."

"The Quisition keeps us on the path of truth! The Quisition works for the greater glory of the Church!"

"And you believe that, do you?" said the tortoise.

Brutha looked, and found that certainty had gone missing. He opened and shut his mouth, but there were no words to be said.

"Come on," said Om, as kindly as he could manage. "Let's get back."

In the middle of the night Om awoke. There were noises from Brutha's bed.

Brutha was praying again.

Om listened curiously. He could remember prayers. There had been a lot of them, once. So many that he couldn't make out an individual prayer even if he had felt inclined to, but that didn't matter, because what mattered was the huge cosmic susurration of thousands of praying, *believing* minds. The words weren't worth listening to, anyway.

Humans! They lived in a world where the grass continued to be green and the sun rose every day and flowers regularly turned into fruit, and what impressed them? Weeping statues. And wine made out of water! A mere quantum-mechanistic tunnel effect, that'd happen anyway if you were prepared to wait zillions of years. As if the turning of sunlight into wine, by means of vines and grapes and time and enzymes, wasn't a thousand times more impressive and happened all the time . . .

Well, he couldn't even do the most basic of god tricks now. Thunderbolts with about the same effect as the spark off a cat's fur, and you could hardly smite anyone with one of those. He had smitten good and hard in his time. Now he could just about walk through water and feed the One.

Brutha's prayer was a piccolo tune in a world of silence.

Om waited until the novice was quiet again and then unfolded his legs and walked out, rocking from side to side, into the dawn.

The Ephebians walked through the palace courtyards, surrounding the Omnians almost, but not quite, in the manner of a prisoners' escort.

Brutha could see that Vorbis was boiling with fury. A small vein on the side of the exquisitor's bald temple was throbbing.

As if feeling Brutha's eyes on him, Vorbis turned his head.

"You seem ill at ease this morning, Brutha," he said.

"Sorry, lord."

"You seem to be looking into every corner. What are you expecting to find?"

"Uh. Just interested, lord. Everything's new."

"All the so-called wisdom of Ephebe is not worth one line from the least paragraph in the Septateuch," said Vorbis.

"May we not study the works of the infidel in order to be more alert to the ways of heresy?" said Brutha, surprised at himself.

"Ah. A persuasive argument, Brutha, and one that the inquisitors have heard many times, if a little indistinctly in many cases."

Vorbis glowered at the back of the head of Aristocrates, who was leading the party. "It is but a small step from listening to heresy to questioning established truth, Brutha. Heresy is often fascinating. Therein lies its danger."

"Yes, lord."

"Hah! And not only do they carve forbidden statues, but they can't even do it properly."

Brutha was no expert, but even he had to agree that this was true. Now the novelty of them had worn off, the statues that decorated every niche in the palace did have a certain badly made look. Brutha was pretty sure he'd just passed one with two left arms. Another one had one ear larger than the other. It wasn't that someone had set out to carve ugly gods. They had clearly been meant to be quite attractive statues. But the sculptor hadn't been much good at it.

"That woman there appears to be holding a penguin," said Vorbis.

"Patina, Goddess of Wisdom," said Brutha automatically, and then realized he'd said it.

"I, er, heard someone mention it," he added.

"Indeed. And what remarkably good hearing you must have," said Vorbis.

Aristocrates paused outside an impressive doorway and nodded at the party.

"Gentlemen," he said, "the Tyrant will see you now."

"You will recall everything that is said," whispered Vorbis.

Brutha nodded.

The doors swung open.

All over the world there were rulers with titles like the Exalted, the Supreme, and Lord High Something or Other. Only in one small country was the ruler elected by the people, who could remove him whenever they wanted—and they called him the Tyrant.

The Ephebians believed that every man should have the vote.* Every five years someone was elected to be Tyrant, provided he could prove that he was honest, intelligent, sensible, and trustworthy. Immediately after he was elected, of course, it was obvious to everyone that he was a criminal madman and totally out of touch with the view of the ordinary philosopher in the street looking for a towel. And then five years later they elected another one just like him, and really it was amazing how intelligent people kept on making the same mistakes.

Candidates for the Tyrantship were elected by the placing of black or white balls in various urns, thus giving rise to a well-known comment about politics.

The Tyrant was a fat little man with skinny legs, giving people the impression of an egg that was hatching upside down. He was sitting alone in the middle of the

---

*Provided that he wasn't poor, foreign, nor disqualified by reason of being mad, frivolous, or a woman.

marble floor, in a chair surrounded by scrolls and scraps of paper. His feet didn't touch the marble, and his face was pink.

Aristocrates whispered something in his ear. The Tyrant looked up from his paperwork.

"Ah, the Omnian delegation," he said, and a smile flashed across his face like something small darting across a stone. "Do be seated, all of you."

He looked down again.

"I am Deacon Vorbis of the Citadel Quisition," said Vorbis coldly.

The Tyrant looked up and gave him another lizard smile.

"Yes, I know," he said. "You torture people for a living. Please be seated, Deacon Vorbis. And your plump young friend who seems to be looking for something. And the rest of you. Some young women will be along in a moment with grapes and things. This generally happens. It's very hard to stop it, in fact."

There were benches in front of the Tyrant's chair. The Omnians sat down. Vorbis remained standing.

The Tyrant nodded. "As you wish," he said.

"This is intolerable!" snapped Vorbis. "We have been treated—"

"Much better than you would have treated us," said the Tyrant mildly. "You sit or you stand, my lord, because this is Ephebe and indeed you may stand on your head for all I care, but don't expect me to believe that if it was *I*, seeking peace in your Citadel, I would be encouraged to do anything but grovel on what was left of my stomach. Be seated or be upstanding, my lord, but be quiet. I have nearly finished."

"Finished what?" said Vorbis.

"The peace treaty," said the Tyrant.

"But that is what we are here to discuss," said Vorbis.

"No," said the Tyrant. The lizard scuttled again: "That is what you are here to sign."

Om took a deep breath and then pushed himself forward.

It was quite a steep flight of steps. He felt every one as he bumped down, but at least he was upright at the bottom.

He was lost, but being lost in Ephebe was preferable to being lost in the Citadel. At least there were no obvious cellars.

Library, library, library . . .

There was a library in the Citadel, Brutha had said. He'd described it, so Om had some idea of what he was looking for.

There would be a book in it.

Peace negotiations were not going well.

"You attacked us!" said Vorbis.

"I would call it preemptive defense," said the Tyrant. "We saw what happened to Istanzia and Betrek and Ushistan."

"They saw the truth of Om!"

"Yes," said the Tyrant. "We believe they did, eventually."

"And they are now proud members of the Empire."

"Yes," said the Tyrant. "We believe they are. But we like to remember them as they were. Before you sent them your letters, that put the minds of men in chains."

"That set the feet of men on the right road," said Vorbis.

"Chain letters," said the Tyrant. "The Chain Letter to the Ephebians. Forget Your Gods. Be Subjugated. Learn to Fear. Do not break the chain—the last people who did woke up one morning to find fifty thousand armed men on their lawn."

Vorbis sat back.

"What is it you fear?" he said. "Here in your desert, with your . . . gods? Is it not that, deep in your souls, you know that your gods are as shifting as your sand?"

"Oh, yes," said the Tyrant. "We know that. That's always been a point in their favor. We know about sand. And your God is a rock—and we know about rock."

Om stumped along a cobbled alley, keeping to the shade as much as possible.

There seemed to be a lot of courtyards. He paused at the point where the alley opened into yet another of them.

There were voices. Mainly there was one voice, petulant and reedy.

This was the philosopher Didactylos.

Although one of the most quoted and popular philosophers of all time, Didactylos the Ephebian never achieved the respect of his fellow philosophers. They felt he wasn't philosopher material. He didn't bathe often enough or, to put it another way, at all. And he philosophized about the wrong sorts of things. And he was *interested* in the wrong sorts of things. Dangerous things. Other philosophers asked questions like: Is Truth Beauty, and is Beauty Truth? and: Is Reality Created by the Observer? But Didactylos posed the famous philosophical conundrum: "Yes, But What's It *Really* All About, Then, When You Get Right Down To It, I *Mean* Really!"

His philosophy was a mixture of three famous schools—the Cynics, the Stoics, and the Epicureans—and summed up all three of them in his famous phrase,

"You can't trust any bugger further than you can throw him, and there's nothing you can do about it, so let's have a drink. Mine's a double, if you're buying. Thank *you*. And a packet of nuts. Her left bosom is nearly uncovered, eh? Two more packets, then!"

Many people have quoted from his famous *Meditations*:

"It's a rum old world all right. But you've got to laugh, haven't you? *Nil Illegitimo Carborundum* is what I say. The experts don't know everything. Still, where would we be if we were all the same?"

Om crawled closer to the voice, bringing himself around the corner of the wall so that he could see into a small courtyard.

There was a very large barrel against the far wall. Various debris around it—broken wine amphorae, gnawed bones, and a couple of lean-to shacks made out of rough boards—suggested that it was someone's home. And this impression was given some weight by the sign chalked on a board and stuck to the wall over the barrel.

It read:

DIDACTYLOS and Nephew
Practical Philosophers

No Proposition Too Large
"We Can Do Your Thinking For You"

Special Rates after 6 pm
Fresh Axioms Every Day

In front of the barrel, a short man in a toga that must have once been white, in the same way that once all continents must have been joined together, was kicking another one who was on the ground.

"You lazy bugger!"

The younger one sat up.

"Honest, Uncle—"

"I turn my back for half an hour and you go to sleep on the job!"

"What job? We haven't had anything since Mr. Piloxi the farmer last week—"

"How d'you know? How d'you know? While you were snoring dozens of people could've been goin' past, every one of 'em in need of a pers'nal philosophy!"

"—and he only paid in olives."

"I shall prob'ly get a good price for them olives!"

"They're *rotten*, Uncle."

"Nonsense! You said they were green!"

"Yes, but they're supposed to be black."

In the shadows, the tortoise's head turned back and forth like a spectator's at a tennis match.

The young man stood up.

"Mrs. Bylaxis came in this morning," he said. "She said the proverb you did for her last week has stopped working."

Didactylos scratched his head.

"Which one was that?" he said.

"You gave her 'It's always darkest before dawn.'"

"Nothing wrong with that. Damn good philosophy."

"She said she didn't feel any better. Anyway, she said she'd stayed up all night because of her bad leg and it was actually quite light just before dawn, so it wasn't true. And her leg still dropped off. So I gave her part exchange on 'Still, it does you good to laugh.'"

Didactylos brightened up a bit.

"Shifted that one, eh?"

"She said she'd give it a try. She gave me a whole dried squid for it. She said I looked like I needed feeding up."

"Right? You're learning. That's lunch sorted out at any rate. See, Urn? *Told* you it would work if we stuck at it."

"I don't call one dried squid and a box of greasy olives much of a return, master. Not for two weeks' thinking."

"We got three *obols* for doing that proverb for old Grillos the cobbler."

"No we didn't. He brought it back. His wife didn't like the color."

"And you gave him his money back?"

"Yes."

"What, all of it?"

"Yes."

"Can't do that. Not after he's put wear and tear on the words. Which one was it?"

" 'It's a wise crow that knows which way the camel points.' "

"I put a lot of work in on that one."

"He said he couldn't understand it."

"I don't understand cobbling, but I know a good pair of sandals when I wears 'em."

Om blinked his one eye. Then he looked at the shapes of the minds in front of him.

The one called Urn was presumably the nephew, and had a fairly normal sort of mind, even if it did seem to have too many circles and angles in it. But Didactylos's mind bubbled and flashed like a potful of electric eels on full boil. Om had never seen anything like it. Brutha's thoughts took eons to slide into place, it was like watching mountains colliding; Didactylos's thoughts chased after one another with a whooshing noise. No wonder he was bald. Hair would have burned off from the inside.

Om had found a thinker.

A cheap one, too, by the sound of it.

He looked up at the wall behind the barrel. Further along was an impressive set of marble steps leading up to some bronze doors, and over the doors, made of metal letters set in the stone, was the word LIBRVM.

He'd spent too much time looking. Urn's hand clamped itself on to his shell, and he heard Didactylos's voice say, "Hey . . . there's good eating on one of these things . . ."

Brutha cowered.

"You stoned our envoy!" shouted Vorbis. "An unarmed man!"

"He brought it upon himself," said the Tyrant. "Aristocrates was there. He will tell you."

The tall man nodded and stood up.

"By tradition anyone may speak in the marketplace," he began.

"And be stoned?" Vorbis demanded.

Aristocrates held up a hand.

"Ah," he said, "anyone can *say* what they like in the square. We have another tradition, though, called free listening. Unfortunately, when people dislike what they hear, they can become a little . . . testy."

"I was there too," said another advisor. "Your priest got up to speak and at first everything was fine, because people were laughing. And then he said that Om was the only real God, and everyone went quiet. And then he pushed over a statue of Tuvelpit, the God of Wine. That's when the trouble started."

"Are you proposing to tell me he was struck by lightning?" said Vorbis.

Vorbis was no longer shouting. His voice was level,

without passion. The thought rose in Brutha's mind: this is how the exquisitors speak. When the inquisitors have finished, the exquisitors speak . . .

"No. By an amphora. Tuvelpit was in the crowd, you see."

"And striking honest men is considered proper godly behavior, is it?"

"Your missionary had said that people who did not believe in Om would suffer endless punishment. I have to tell you that the crowd considered this rude."

"And so they threw stones at him . . ."

"Not many. They only hurt his pride. And only after they'd run out of vegetables."

"They threw vegetables?"

"When they couldn't find any more eggs."

"And when we came to remonstrate—"

"I am sure sixty ships intended more than remonstrating," said the Tyrant. "And we have warned you, Lord Vorbis. People find in Ephebe what they seek. There will be more raids on your coast. We will harass your ships. Unless you sign."

"And passage through Ephebe?" said Vorbis.

The Tyrant smiled.

"Across the desert? My lord, if you can cross the desert, I am sure you can go anywhere." The Tyrant looked away from Vorbis and towards the sky, visible between the pillars.

"And now I see it is nearing noon," he said. "And the day heats up. Doubtless you will wish to discuss our . . . uh . . . proposals with your colleagues. May I suggest we meet again at sunset?"

Vorbis appeared to give this some consideration.

"I think," he said eventually, "that our deliberations may take longer. Shall we say . . . tomorrow morning?"

The Tyrant nodded.

"As you wish. In the meantime, the palace is at your disposal. There are many fine temples and works of art should you wish to inspect them. When you require meals, mention the fact to the nearest slave."

"Slave is an Ephebian word. In Om we have no word for slave," said Vorbis.

"So I understand," said the Tyrant. "I imagine that fish have no word for water." He smiled the fleeting smile again. "And there are the baths and the Library, of course. Many fine sights. You are our guests."

Vorbis inclined his head.

"I pray," he said, "that one day you will be a guest of mine."

"And what sights *I* shall see," said the Tyrant.

Brutha stood up, knocking over his bench and going redder with embarrassment.

He thought: they lied about Brother Murduck. They beat him within an inch of his life, Vorbis said, and flogged him the rest of the way. And Brother Nhumrod said he saw the body, and it was really true. Just for talking! People who would do that sort of thing deserve . . . punishment. And they keep slaves. People forced to work against their will. People treated like animals. And they even *call* their ruler a Tyrant!

And why isn't any of this exactly what it seems?

Why don't I believe any of it?

Why do I know it isn't true?

And what did he mean about fish not having a word for water?

The Omnians were half-escorted, half-led back to their compound. Another bowl of fruit was waiting on the table in Brutha's cell, with some more fish and a loaf of bread.

There was also a man, sweeping the floor.

"Um," said Brutha. "Are you a slave?"

"Yes, master."

"That must be terrible."

The man leaned on his broom. "You're right. It's terrible. Really terrible. D'you know, I only get one day off a week?"

Brutha, who had never heard the words "day off" before, and who was in any case unfamiliar with the concept, nodded uncertainly.

"Why don't you run away?" he said.

"Oh, done that," said the slave. "Ran away to Tsort once. Didn't like it much. Came back. Run away for a fortnight in Djelibeybi every winter, though."

"Do you get brought back?" said Brutha.

"Huh!" said the slave. "No, I don't. Miserable skin-flint, Aristocrates. I have to come back by myself. Hitching lifts on ships, that kind of thing."

"You *come* back?"

"Yeah. Abroad's all right to visit, but you wouldn't want to live there. Anyway, I've only got another four years as a slave and then I'm free. You get the vote when you're free. *And* you get to keep slaves." His face glazed with the effort of recollection as he ticked off points on his fingers. "Slaves get three meals a day, at least one with meat. And one free day a week. And two weeks being-allowed-to-run-away every year. And I don't do ovens or heavy lifting, and worldly-wise repartee only by arrangement."

"Yes, but you're not *free*," said Brutha, intrigued despite himself.

"What's the difference?"

"Er . . . you don't get any days off." Brutha scratched his head. "And one less meal."

"Really? I think I'll give freedom a miss then, thanks."

"Er . . . have you seen a tortoise anywhere around here?" said Brutha.

"No. *And* I cleaned under the bed."

"Have you seen one anywhere else today?"

"You want one? There's good eating on a—"

"No. No. It's all right—"

"Brutha!"

It was Vorbis's voice. Brutha hurried out into the courtyard and into Vorbis's cell.

"Ah, Brutha."

"Yes, lord?"

Vorbis was sitting cross-legged on the floor, staring at the wall.

"You are a young man visiting a new place," said Vorbis. "No doubt there is much you wish to see."

"There is?" said Brutha. Vorbis was using the exquisitor voice again—a level monotone, a voice like a strip of dull steel.

"You may go where you wish. See new things, Brutha. Learn everything you can. You are my eyes and ears. And my memory. Learn about this place."

"Er. Really, lord?"

"Have I impressed you with my use of careless language, Brutha?"

"No, lord."

"Go away. Fill yourself. And be back by sunset."

"Er. Even the Library?" said Brutha.

"Ah? Yes, the Library. The Library that they have here. Of course. Crammed with useless and dangerous and evil knowledge. I can see it in my mind, Brutha. Can you imagine that?"

"No, Lord Vorbis."

"Your innocence is your shield, Brutha. No. By all

means go to the Library. I have no fear of any effect on *you*."

"Lord Vorbis?"

"Yes?"

"The Tyrant said that they hardly did anything to Brother Murduck . . ."

Silence unrolled its restless length.

Vorbis said, "He lied."

"Yes." Brutha waited. Vorbis continued to stare at the wall. Brutha wondered what he saw there. When nothing else appeared to be forthcoming, he said, "Thank you."

He stepped back a bit before he went out, so that he could squint under the deacon's bed.

He's probably in trouble, Brutha thought as he hurried through the palace. Everyone wants to eat tortoises.

He tried to look everywhere while avoiding the friezes of unclad nymphs.

Brutha was technically aware that women were a different shape from men; he hadn't left the village until he was twelve, by which time some of his contemporaries were already married. And Omnianism encouraged early marriage as a preventive against Sin, although any activity involving any part of the human anatomy between neck and knees was more or less Sinful in any case.

Brutha wished he was a better scholar so he could ask his God why this was.

Then he found himself wishing his God was a more intelligent God so it could answer.

He hasn't screamed for me, he thought. I'm sure I would have heard. So maybe no one's cooking him.

A slave polishing one of the statues directed him to the Library. Brutha pounded down an aisle of pillars.

When he reached the courtyard in front of the Library

it was crowded with philosophers, all craning to look at something. Brutha could hear the usual petulant squabbling that showed that philosophical discourse was under way.

In this case:

"I've got ten *obols* here says it can't do it again!"

"Talking money? That's something you don't hear every day, Xeno."

"Yeah. And it's about to say goodbye."

"Look, don't be stupid. It's a tortoise. It's just doing a mating dance . . ."

There was a breathless pause. Then a sort of collective sigh.

"There!"

"That's never a right angle!"

"Come *on!* I'd like to see *you* do better in the circumstances!"

"What's it doing now?"

"The hypotenuse, I think."

"Call that a hypotenuse? It's wiggly."

"It's *not* wiggly. It's drawing it straight and you're *looking* at it in a wiggly way!"

"I'll bet thirty *obols* it can't do a square!"

"Here's forty *obols* says it can."

There was another pause, and then a cheer.

"Yeah!"

"That's more of a parallelogram, if you ask me," said a petulant voice.

"Listen, I knows a square when I sees one! And *that's* a square."

"All right. Double or nothing then. Bet it can't do a dodecagon."

"Hah! You bet it couldn't do a septagon just now."

"Double or nothing. Dodecagon. Worried, eh! Feeling a bit *avis domestica*? Cluck-cluck?"

"It's a shame to take your money . . ."

There was another pause.

"Ten sides? *Ten* sides? Hah!"

"Told you it wasn't any good! Whoever heard of a tortoise doing geometry?"

"Another daft idea, Didactylos?"

"I said so all along. It's just a tortoise."

"There's good eating on one of those things . . ."

The mass of philosophers broke up, pushing past Brutha without paying him much attention. He caught a glimpse of a circle of damp sand, covered with geometrical figures. Om was sitting in the middle of them. Behind him was a very grubby pair of philosophers, counting out a pile of coins.

"How did we do, Urn?" said Didactylos.

"We're fifty-two *obols* up, master."

"See? Every day things improve. Pity it didn't know the difference between ten and twelve, though. Cut one of its legs off and we'll have a stew."

"Cut off a leg?"

"Well, a tortoise like that, you don't eat it all at once."

Didactylos turned his face towards a plump young man with splayed feet and a red face, who was staring at the tortoise.

"Yes?" he said.

"The tortoise *does* know the difference between ten and twelve," said the fat boy.

"Damn thing just lost me eighty *obols*," said Didactylos.

"Yes. But tomorrow . . ." the boy began, his eyes glazing as if he was carefully repeating something he'd just heard ". . . tomorrow . . . you should be able to get odds of at least three to one."

Didactylos's mouth dropped open.

"Give me the tortoise, Urn," he said.

The apprentice philosopher reached down and picked up Om, very carefully.

"You know, I thought right at the start there was something funny about this creature," said Didactylos. "I said to Urn, there's tomorrow's dinner, and then he says no, it's dragging its tail in the sand and doing geometry. That doesn't come natural to a tortoise, geometry."

Om's eye turned to Brutha.

"I had to," he said. "It was the only way to get his attention. Now I've got him by the curiosity. When you've got 'em by the curiosity, their hearts and minds will follow."

"He's a God," said Brutha.

"Really? What's his name?" said the philosopher.

"Don't tell him! Don't tell him! The local gods'll hear!"

"I don't know," said Brutha.

Didactylos turned Om over.

"The Turtle Moves," said Urn thoughtfully.

"What?" said Brutha.

"Master did a book," said Urn.

"Not really a book," said Didactylos modestly. "More a scroll. Just a little thing I knocked off."

"Saying that the world is flat and goes through space on the back of a giant turtle?" said Brutha.

"Have you read it?" Didactylos's gaze was unmoving. "Are you a slave?"

"No," said Brutha. "I am a—"

"Don't mention my name! Call yourself a scribe or something!"

"—scribe," said Brutha weakly.

"Yeah," said Urn. "I can see that. The telltale callus on the thumb where you hold the pen. The inkstains all over your sleeves."

Brutha glanced at his left thumb. "I haven't—"

"Yeah," said Urn, grinning. "Use your left hand, do you?"

"Er, I use both," said Brutha. "But not very well, everyone says."

"Ah," said Didactylos. "Ambi-sinister?"

"What?"

"He means incompetent with both hands," said Om.

"Oh. Yes. That's me." Brutha coughed politely. "Look . . . I'm looking for a philosopher. Um. One that knows about gods."

He waited.

Then he said, "You aren't going to say they're a relic of an outmoded belief system?"

Didactylos, still running his fingers over Om's shell, shook his head.

"Nope. I like my thunderstorms a long way off."

"Oh. Could you stop turning him over and over? He's just told me he doesn't like it."

"You can tell how old they are by cutting them in half and counting the rings," said Didactylos.

"Um. He hasn't got much of a sense of humor, either."

"You're Omnian, by the sound of it."

"Yes."

"Here to talk about the treaty?"

"I do the listening."

"And what do you want to know about gods?"

Brutha appeared to be listening.

Eventually he said: "How they start. How they grow. And what happens to them afterwards."

Didactylos put the tortoise into Brutha's hands.

"Costs money, that kind of thinking," he said.

"Let me know when we've used more than fifty-two *obols*' worth," said Brutha. Didactylos grinned.

"Looks like you can think for yourself," he said. "Got a good memory?"

"No. Not exactly a good one."

"Right? Right. Come on into the Library. It's got an earthed copper roof, you know. Gods really hate that sort of thing."

Didactylos reached down beside him and picked up a rusty iron lantern.

Brutha looked up at the big white building.

"That's the Library?" he said.

"Yes," said Didactylos. "That's why it's got LIBRVM carved over the door in such big letters. But a scribe like you'd know that, of course."

The Library of Ephebe was—before it burned down— the second biggest on the Disc.

Not as big as the library in Unseen University, of course, but *that* library had one or two advantages on account of its magical nature. No other library anywhere, for example, has a whole gallery of unwritten books—books that *would* have been written if the author hadn't been eaten by an alligator around chapter 1, and so on. Atlases of imaginary places. Dictionaries of illusory words. Spotters' guides to invisible things. Wild thesauri in the Lost Reading Room. A library so big that it distorts reality and has opened gateways to all other libraries, everywhere and everywhen . . .

And so unlike the Library at Ephebe, with its four or five hundred volumes. Many of them were scrolls, to save their readers the fatigue of having to call a slave every time they wanted a page turned. Each one lay in its own pigeonhole, though. Books shouldn't be kept too close together, otherwise they interact in strange and unforeseeable ways.

Sunbeams lanced through the shadows, as palpable as pillars in the dusty air.

Although it was the least of the wonders in the Library, Brutha couldn't help noticing a strange construction in the aisles. Wooden laths had been fixed between the rows of stone shelves about two meters from the floor, so that they supported a wider plank of no apparent use whatsoever. Its underside had been decorated with rough wooden shapes.

"The Library," announced Didactylos.

He reached up. His fingers gently brushed the plank over his head.

It dawned on Brutha.

"You're blind aren't you?" he said.

"That's right."

"But you carry a lantern?"

"It's all right," said Didactylos. "I don't put any oil in it."

"A lantern that doesn't shine for a man that doesn't see?"

"Yeah. Works perfectly. And of course it's very philosophical."

"And you live in a barrel."

"Very fashionable, living in a barrel," said Didactylos, walking forward briskly, his fingers only occasionally touching the raised patterns on the plank. "Most of the philosophers do it. It shows contempt and disdain for worldly things. Mind you, Legibus has got a sauna in his. It's amazing the kind of things you can think of in it, he says."

Brutha looked around. Scrolls protruded from their racks like cuckoos piping the hour.

"It's all so . . . I never met a philosopher before I came here," he said. "Last night, they were all . . ."

"You got to remember there's three basic approaches to philosophy in these parts," said Didactylos. "Tell him, Urn."

"There's the Xenoists," said Urn promptly. "They say the world is basically complex and random. And there's the Ibidians. They say the world is basically simple and follows certain fundamental rules."

"And there's me," said Didactylos, pulling a scroll out of its rack.

"Master says basically it's a funny old world," said Urn.

"And doesn't contain enough to drink," said Didactylos.

"And doesn't contain enough to drink."

"Gods," said Didactylos, half to himself. He pulled out another scroll. "You want to know about gods? Here's Xeno's *Reflections*, and old Aristocrates' *Platitudes*, and Ibid's bloody stupid *Discourses*, and Legibus's *Geometries* and Hierarch's *Theologies* . . ."

Didactylos's fingers danced across the racks. More dust filled the air.

"These are all books?" said Brutha.

"Oh, yes. Everyone writes 'em here. You just can't stop the buggers."

"And people can *read* them?" said Brutha.

Omnia was based on one book. And here were . . . hundreds . . .

"Well, they can if they want," said Urn. "But no one comes in here much. These aren't books for reading. They're more for writing."

"Wisdom of the ages, this," said Didactylos. "Got to write a book, see, to prove you're a philosopher. Then you get your scroll and free official philosopher's loofah."

The sunlight pooled on a big stone table in the center of the room. Urn unrolled the length of a scroll. Brilliant flowers glowed in the golden light.

"Orinjcrates' *On the Nature of Plants*," said Didactylos. "Six hundred plants and their uses . . ."

"They're beautiful," whispered Brutha.

"Yes, that is one of the uses of plants," said Didactylos. "And one which old Orinjcrates neglected to notice, too. Well done. Show him Philo's *Bestiary*, Urn."

Another scroll unrolled. There were dozens of pictures of animals, thousands of unreadable words.

"But . . . pictures of animals . . . it's wrong . . . isn't it wrong to . . ."

"Pictures of just about everything in there," said Didactylos.

Art was not permitted in Omnia.

"And this is the book Didactylos wrote," said Urn.

Brutha looked down at a picture of a turtle. There were . . . *elephants, they're elephants*, his memory supplied, from the fresh memories of the bestiary sinking indelibly into his mind . . . elephants on its back, and on them something with mountains and a waterfall of an ocean around its edge . . .

"How can this be?" said Brutha. "A world on the back of a tortoise? Why does everyone tell me this? This can't be true!"

"Tell that to the mariners," said Didactylos. "Everyone who's ever sailed the Rim Ocean knows it. Why deny the obvious?"

"But surely the world is a perfect sphere, spinning about the sphere of the sun, just as the Septateuch tells us," said Brutha. "That seems so . . . logical. That's how things ought to be."

"*Ought?*" said Didactylos. "Well, I don't know about *ought*. That's not a philosophical word."

"And . . . what is this . . ." Brutha murmured, pointing to a circle under the drawing of the turtle.

"That's a plan view," said Urn.

"Map of the world," said Didactylos.

"Map? What's a map?"

"It's a sort of picture that shows you where you are," said Didactylos.

Brutha stared in wonderment. "And how does it know?"

"Hah!"

"Gods," prompted Om again. "We're here to ask about gods!"

"But is all this *true?*" said Brutha.

Didactylos shrugged. "Could be. Could be. We are here and it is now. The way I see it is, after that, everything tends towards guesswork."

"You mean you don't *know* it's true?" said Brutha.

"I *think* it might be," said Didactylos. "I could be wrong. Not being certain is what being a philosopher is all about."

"Talk about gods," said Om.

"Gods," said Brutha weakly.

His mind was on fire. These people made all these books about things, and they weren't *sure*. But he'd been sure, and Brother Nhumrod had been sure, and Deacon Vorbis had a sureness you could bend horseshoes around. Sureness was a rock.

Now he knew why, when Vorbis spoke about Ephebe, his face was gray with hatred and his voice was tense as a wire. If there was no truth, what was there left? And

these bumbling old men spent their time kicking away
the pillars of the world, and they'd nothing to replace
them with but uncertainty. And they were *proud* of this?

Urn was standing on a small ladder, fishing among the
shelves of scrolls. Didactylos sat opposite Brutha, his
blind gaze still apparently fixed on him.

"You don't like it, do you?" said the philosopher.

Brutha had said nothing.

"You know," said Didactylos conversationally, "people'll tell you that us blind people are the real business
where the other senses are concerned. It's not true, of
course. The buggers just say it because it makes them
feel better. It gets rid of the obligation to feel sorry for us.
But when you can't see you *do* learn to listen more. The
way people breathe, the sounds their clothes make . . ."

Urn reappeared with another scroll.

"You shouldn't do this," said Brutha wretchedly. "All
this . . ." His voice trailed off.

"I know about sureness," said Didactylos. Now the
light, irascible tone had drained out of his voice. "I remember, before I was blind, I went to Omnia once. This
was before the borders were closed, when you still let
people travel. And in your Citadel I saw a crowd stoning
a man to death in a pit. Ever seen that?"

"It has to be done," Brutha mumbled. "So the soul
can be shriven and—"

"Don't know about the soul. Never been that kind of
a philosopher," said Didactylos. "All I know is, it was a
horrible sight."

"The state of the body is not—"

"Oh, I'm not talking about the poor bugger in the
pit," said the philosopher. "I'm talking about the people
throwing the stones. They were sure all right. They were
sure it wasn't them in the pit. You could see it in their

faces. So glad it wasn't them that they were throwing just as hard as they could."

Urn hovered, looking uncertain.

"I've got Abraxas's *On Religion*," he said.

"Old 'Charcoal' Abraxas," said Didactylos, suddenly cheerful again. "Struck by lightning fifteen times so far, and still not giving up. You can borrow this one overnight if you want. No scribbling comments in the margins, mind you, unless they're interesting."

"This is it!" said Om. "Come on, let's leave this idiot."

Brutha unrolled the scroll. There weren't even any pictures. Crabbed writing filled it, line after line.

"He spent years researching it," said Didactylos. "Went out into the desert, talked to the small gods. Talked to some of our gods, too. Brave man. He says gods like to see an atheist around. Gives them something to aim at."

Brutha unrolled a bit more of the scroll. Five minutes ago he would have admitted that he couldn't read. Now the best efforts of the inquisitors couldn't have forced it out of him. He held it up in what he hoped was a familiar fashion.

"Where is he now?" he said.

"Well, someone said they saw a pair of sandals with smoke coming out just outside his house a year or two back," said Didactylos. "He might have, you know, pushed his luck."

"I think," said Brutha, "that I'd better be going. I'm sorry to have intruded on your time."

"Bring it back when you've finished with it," said Didactylos.

"Is that how people read in Omnia?" said Urn.

"What?"

"Upside down."

Brutha picked up the tortoise, glared at Urn, and strode as haughtily as possible out of the Library.

"Hmm," said Didactylos. He drummed his fingers on the tables.

"It was him I saw in the tavern last night," said Urn. "I'm sure, master."

"But the Omnians are staying here in the palace."

"That's right, master."

"But the tavern is *outside*."

"Yes."

"Then he must have flown over the wall, do you think?"

"I'm sure it was him, master."

"Then . . . maybe he came later. Maybe he hadn't gone in when you saw him."

"It can only be that, master. The keepers of the labyrinth are unbribable."

Didactylos clipped Urn across the back of the head with his lantern.

"Stupid boy! I've told you about that sort of statement."

"I mean, they are not *easily* bribable, master. Not for all the gold in Omnia, for example."

"That's more like it."

"Do you think that tortoise was a god, master?"

"He's going to be in big trouble in Omnia if he is. They've got a bastard of a god there. Did you ever read old Abraxas?"

"No, master."

"Very big on gods. Big gods man. Always smelled of burnt hair. Naturally resistant."

* * *

Om crawled slowly along the length of a line.

"Stop walking up and down like that," he said, "I can't concentrate."

"How can people talk like that?" Brutha asked the empty air. "Acting as if they're *glad* they don't know things! Finding out more and more things they don't know! It's like children proudly coming to show you a full potty!"

Om marked his place with a claw.

"But they find things out," he said. "This Abraxas was a thinker and no mistake. *I* didn't know some of this stuff. Sit down!"

Brutha obeyed.

"Right," said Om. "Now . . . listen. Do you know how gods get power?"

"By people believing in them," said Brutha. "Millions of people believe in you."

Om hesitated.

All right, all right. We are here and it is now. Sooner or later he'll find out for himself . . .

"They don't believe," said Om.

"But—"

"It's happened before," said the tortoise. "Dozens of times. D'you know Abraxas found the lost city of Ee? Very strange carvings, he says. Belief, he says. Belief *shifts*. People start out believing in the god and end up believing in the structure."

"I don't understand," said Brutha.

"Let me put it another way," said the tortoise. "I am your God, right?"

"Yes."

"And you'll obey me."

"Yes."

"Good. Now take a rock and go and kill Vorbis."

Brutha didn't move.

"I'm sure you heard me," said Om.

"But he'll . . . he's . . . the Quisition would—"

"*Now* you know what I mean," said the tortoise. "You're more afraid of him than you are of me, now. Abraxas says here: 'Around the Godde there forms a Shelle of prayers and Ceremonies and Buildings and Priestes and Authority, until at Last the Godde Dies. Ande this maye notte be noticed.'"

"That can't be true!"

"I think it is. Abraxas says there's a kind of shellfish that lives in the same way. It makes a bigger and bigger shell until it can't move around any more, and so it dies."

"But . . . but . . . that means . . . the whole Church . . ."

"Yes."

Brutha tried to keep hold of the idea, but the sheer enormity of it kept wrenching it from his mental grasp.

"But you're not dead," he managed.

"Next best thing," said Om. "And you know what? No other small god is trying to usurp me. Did I ever tell you about old Ur-Gilash? No? He was the god back in what's now Omnia before me. Not much of one. Basically a weather god. Or a snake god. Something, anyway. It took years to get rid of him, though. Wars and everything. So I've been thinking . . ."

Brutha said nothing.

"Om still exists," said the tortoise. "I mean the shell. All you'd have to do is get people to understand."

Brutha still said nothing.

"You can be the next prophet," said Om.

"I can't! Everyone knows Vorbis will be the next prophet!"

"Ah, but you'll be *official*."

"No!"

"No? I am your God!"

"And I am my me. I'm not a prophet. I can't even write. I can't read. No one will listen to me."

Om looked him up and down.

"I must admit you're not the chosen one I would have chosen," he said.

"The great prophets had vision," said Brutha. "Even if they . . . even if you didn't talk to them, they had something to say. What could I say? I haven't got anything to say to anyone. What could I say?"

"Believe in the Great God Om," said the tortoise.

"And then what?"

"What do you mean, and then what?"

Brutha looked out glumly at the darkening courtyard.

"Believe in the Great God Om or be stricken with thunderbolts," he said.

"Sounds good to me."

"Is that how it always has to be?"

The last rays of the sun glinted off the statue in the center of the courtyard. It was vaguely feminine. There was a penguin perched on one shoulder.

"Patina, Goddess of Wisdom," said Brutha. "The one with a penguin. Why a penguin?"

"Can't imagine," said Om hurriedly.

"Nothing wise about penguins, is there?"

"Shouldn't think so. Unless you count the fact that you don't get them in Omnia. Pretty wise of them."

"Brutha!"

"That's Vorbis," said Brutha, standing up. "Shall I leave you here?"

"Yes. There's still some melon. I mean loaf."

Brutha wandered out into the dusk.

Vorbis was sitting on a bench under a tree, as still as a statue in the shadows.

Certainty, Brutha thought. I used to be certain. Now I'm not so sure.

"Ah, Brutha. You will accompany me on a little stroll. We will take the evening air."

"Yes, lord."

"You have enjoyed your visit to Ephebe."

Vorbis seldom asked a question if a statement would do.

"It has been . . . interesting."

Vorbis put one hand on Brutha's shoulder and used the other to haul himself up on his staff.

"And what do you think of it?" he asked.

"They have many gods, and they don't pay them much attention," said Brutha. "And they search for ignorance."

"And they find it in abundance, be sure of that," said Vorbis.

He pointed his staff into the night. "Let us walk," he said.

There was the sound of laughter, somewhere in the darkness, and the clatter of pans. The scent of evening-opening flowers hung thickly in the air. The stored heat of daytime radiating from the stones, made the night seem like a fragrant soup.

"Ephebe looks to the sea," said Vorbis after a while. "You see the way it is built? All on the slope of a hill facing the sea. But the sea is mutable. Nothing lasting comes from the sea. Whereas our dear Citadel looks towards the high desert. And what do we see there?"

Instinctively Brutha turned, and looked over the rooftops to the black bulk of the desert against the sky.

"I saw a flash of light," he said. "And again. On the slope."

"Ah. The light of truth," said Vorbis. "So let us go forth to meet it. Take me to the entrance to the labyrinth, Brutha. You know the way."

"My lord?" said Brutha.

"Yes, Brutha?"

"I would like to ask you a question."

"Do so."

"What happened to Brother Murduck?"

There was the merest suggestion of hesitation in the rhythm of Vorbis's stick on the cobbles. Then the exquisitor said, "Truth, good Brutha, is like the light. Do you know about light?"

"It . . . comes from the sun. And the moon and stars. And candles. And lamps."

"And so on," said Vorbis, nodding. "Of course. But there is another kind of light. A light that fills even the darkest of places. This has to be. For if this meta-light did not exist, how could darkness be seen?"

Brutha said nothing. This sounded too much like philosophy.

"And so it is with truth," said Vorbis. "There are some things which appear to be the truth, which have all the hallmarks of truth, but which are not the *real* truth. The real truth must sometimes be protected by a labyrinth of lies."

He turned to Brutha. "Do you understand me?"

"No, Lord Vorbis."

"I mean, that which appears to our senses is not the *fundamental* truth. Things that are seen and heard and done by the flesh are mere shadows of a deeper reality. This is what you must understand as you progress in the Church."

"But at the moment, lord, I know only the trivial

truth, the truth available on the outside," said Brutha. He felt as though he was at the edge of a pit.

"That is how we all begin," said Vorbis kindly.

"So did the Ephebians kill Brother Murduck?" Brutha persisted. Now he was inching out over the darkness.

"I am telling you that in the deepest sense of the truth they did. By their failure to embrace his words, by their intransigence, they surely killed him."

"But in the *trivial* sense of the truth," said Brutha, picking every word with the care an inquisitor might give to his patient in the depths of the Citadel, "in the trivial sense, Brother Murduck died, did he not, in Omnia, because he had *not* died in Ephebe, had been merely mocked, but it was feared that others in the Church might not understand the, the *deeper* truth, and thus it was put about that the Ephebians had killed him in, in the *trivial* sense, thus giving you, and those who saw the truth of the evil of Ephebe, due cause to launch a—a just retaliation."

They walked past a fountain. The deacon's steel-shod staff clicked in the night.

"I see a great future for you in the Church," said Vorbis, eventually. "The time of the eighth Prophet is coming. A time of expansion, and great opportunity for those true in the service of Om."

Brutha looked into the pit.

If Vorbis was right, and there was a kind of light that made darkness visible, then down there was its opposite, the darkness where no light could ever reach: darkness that blackened light. He thought of blind Didactylos and his empty lantern.

He heard himself say, "And with people like the

Ephebians, there is no truce. No treaty can be held binding, if it is between people like the Ephebians and those who follow a deeper truth?"

Vorbis nodded. "When the Great God is with us," he said, "who can stand against us? You impress me, Brutha."

There was more laughter in the darkness, and the twang of stringed instruments.

"A feast," sneered Vorbis. "The Tyrant invited us to a feast! I sent some of the party, of course. Even their generals are in there! They think themselves safe behind their labyrinth, as a tortoise thinks himself safe in his shell, not realizing it is a prison. Onward."

The inner wall of the labyrinth loomed out of the darkness. Brutha leaned against it. From far above came the chink of metal on metal as a sentry went on his rounds.

The gateway to the labyrinth was wide open. The Ephebians had never seen the point of stopping people entering. Up a short side-tunnel the guide for the first sixth of the way slumbered on a bench, a candle guttering beside him. Above his alcove hung the bronze bell that would-be traversers of the maze used to summon him. Brutha slipped past.

"Brutha?"

"Yes, lord?"

"Lead the way through the labyrinth. I know you can."

"Lord—"

"This *is* an order, Brutha," said Vorbis, pleasantly.

There is no hope for it, Brutha thought. It *is* an order.

"Then tread where I tread, lord," he whispered. "Not more than one step behind me."

"Yes, Brutha."

"If I step around a place on the floor for no reason, you step around it too."

"Yes, Brutha."

Brutha thought: perhaps I could do it wrong. No. I took vows and things. You can't just disobey. The whole world ends if you start thinking like that . . .

He let his sleeping mind take control. The way through the labyrinth unrolled in his head like a glowing wire.

. . . diagonally forward and right three-and-a-half paces, and left sixty-three paces, pause two seconds—where a steely swish in the darkness suggested that one of the guardians had devised something that won him a prize—and up three steps . . .

I could run forward, he thought. I could hide, and he'd walk into one of the pits or a deadfall or something, and then I could sneak back to my room and who would ever know?

I would.

. . . forward nine paces, and right one pace, and forward nineteen paces, and left two paces . . .

There was a light ahead. Not the occasional white glow of moonlight from the slits in the roof, but yellow lamplight, dimming and brightening as its owner came nearer.

"Someone's coming," he whispered. "It must be one of the guides!"

Vorbis had vanished.

Brutha hovered uncertainly in the passageway as the light bobbed nearer.

An elderly voice said, "That you, Number Four?"

The light came around a corner. It half-illuminated an old man, who walked up to Brutha and raised the candle to his face.

"Where's Number Four?" he said, peering around Brutha.

A figure appeared behind the man, from out of a side-passage. Brutha had the briefest glimpse of Vorbis, his face strangely peaceful, as he gripped the head of his staff, twisted and pulled. Sharp metal glittered for a moment in the candlelight.

Then the light went out.

Vorbis's voice said, "Take the lead again."

Trembling, Brutha obeyed. He felt the soft flesh of an outflung arm under his sandal for a moment.

The pit, he thought. Look into Vorbis's eyes, and there's the pit. And I'm in it with him.

I've got to remember about fundamental truth.

No more guides were patrolling the labyrinth. After a mere million years, the night air blew cool on his face, and Brutha stepped out under the stars.

"Well done. Can you remember the way to the gate?"

"Yes, Lord Vorbis."

The deacon pulled his hood over his face.

"Carry on."

There were a few torches lighting the streets, but Ephebe was not a city that stayed awake in darkness. A couple of passersby paid them no attention.

"They guard their harbor," said Vorbis, conversational. "But the way to the desert . . . everyone knows that no one can cross the desert. I am sure *you* know that, Brutha."

"But now I suspect that what I know is not the truth," said Brutha.

"Quite so. Ah. The gate. I believe it had two guards yesterday?"

"I saw two."

"And now it is night and the gate is shut. But there will be a watchman. Wait here."

Vorbis disappeared into the gloom. After a while there

was a muffled conversation. Brutha stared straight
ahead of him.

The conversation was followed by muffled silence. After a while Brutha started to count to himself.

After ten, I'll go back.

Another ten, then.

All right. Make it thirty. And *then* I'll . . .

"Ah, Brutha. Let us go."

Brutha swallowed his heart again, and turned slowly.

"I did not hear you, lord," he managed.

"I walk softly."

"Is there a watchman?"

"Not now. Come help me with the bolts."

A small wicket gate was set into the main gate.
Brutha, his mind numb with hatred, shoved the bolts
aside with the heel of his hand. The door opened with
barely a creak.

Outside there was the occasional light of a distant
farm, and crowding darkness.

Then the darkness poured in.

Hierarchy, Vorbis said later. The Ephebians didn't think
in terms of hierarchies.

No army could cross the desert. But maybe a small
army could get a quarter of the way, and leave a cache of
water. And do that several times. And another small
army could use part of that cache to go further, maybe
reach halfway, and leave a cache. And another small
army . . .

It had taken months. A third of the men had died, of
heat and dehydration and wild animals and worse
things, the worse things that the desert held . . .

You had to have a mind like Vorbis's to plan it.

And plan it early. Men were already dying in the

desert before Brother Murduck went to preach; there was already a beaten track when the Omnian fleet burned in the bay before Ephebe.

You had to have a mind like Vorbis's to plan your retaliation before your attack.

It was over in less than an hour. The fundamental truth was that the handful of Ephebian guards in the palace had no chance at all.

Vorbis sat upright in the Tyrant's chair. It was approaching midnight.

A collection of Ephebian citizens, the Tyrant among them, had been herded in front of him.

He busied himself with some paperwork and then looked up with an air of mild surprise, as if he'd been completely unaware that fifty people were waiting in front of him at crossbow point.

"Ah," he said, and flashed a little smile.

"Well," he said, "I am pleased to say that we can now dispense with the peace treaty. Quite unnecessary. Why prattle of peace when there is no more war? Ephebe is now a diocese of Omnia. There will be no argument."

He threw a paper on to the floor.

"There will be a fleet here in a few days. There will be no opposition, while we hold the palace. Your infernal mirror is even now being smashed."

He steepled his fingers and looked at the assembled Ephebians.

"Who built it?"

The Tyrant looked up.

"It was an Ephebian construction," he said.

"Ah," said Vorbis, "democracy. I forgot. Then

who"—he signaled one of the guards, who handed him a sack—"wrote this?"

A copy of *De Chelonian Mobile* was flung on to the marble floor.

Brutha stood beside the throne. It was where he had been told to stand.

He'd looked into the pit and now it was him. Everything around him was happening in some distant circle of light, surrounded by darkness. Thoughts chased one another around his head.

Did the Cenobiarch know about this? Did anyone else know about the two kinds of truth? Who else knew that Vorbis was fighting both sides of a war, like a child playing with soldiers? Was it really wrong if it was for the greater glory of . . .

. . . a god who was a tortoise. A god that only Brutha believed in?

Who did Vorbis talk to when he prayed?

Through the mental storm Brutha heard Vorbis's level tones: "If the philosopher who wrote this does not own up, the entirety of you will be put to the flame. Do not doubt that I mean it."

There was a movement in the crowd, and the sound of Didactylos's voice.

"Let go! You heard him! Anyway . . . I always wanted a chance to do this . . ."

A couple of servants were pushed aside and the philosopher stumped out of the crowd, his barren lantern held defiantly over his head.

Brutha watched the philosopher pause for a moment in the empty space, and then turn very slowly until he was directly facing Vorbis. He took a few steps forward then, and held the lantern out as he appeared to regard the deacon critically.

"Hmm," he said.

"You are the . . . perpetrator?" said Vorbis.

"Indeed. Didactylos is my name."

"You are blind?"

"Only as far as vision is concerned, my lord."

"Yet you carry a lantern," said Vorbis. "Doubtless for some catchword reason. Probably you'll tell me you're looking for an honest man?"

"I don't know, my lord. Perhaps you could tell me what he looks like?"

"I should strike you down now," said Vorbis.

"Oh, certainly."

Vorbis indicated the book.

"These *lies*. This *scandal*. This . . . this *lure* to drag the minds of men from the path of true knowledge. You dare to stand before me and declare"—he pushed the book with a toe—"that the world is flat and travels through the void on the back of a giant turtle?"

Brutha held his breath.

So did history.

Affirm your belief, Brutha thought. Just once, someone please stand up to Vorbis. I can't. But someone . . .

He found his eyes swiveling toward Simony, who stood on the other side of Vorbis's chair. The sergeant looked transfixed, fascinated.

Didactylos drew himself up to his full height. He half-turned and for a moment his blank gaze passed across Brutha. The lantern was extended at arm's length.

"No," he said.

"When every honest man knows that the world is a sphere, a perfect shape, bound to spin around the sphere of the Sun as Man orbits the central truth of Om," said Vorbis, "and the stars—"

Brutha leaned forward, heart pounding.

"My lord?" he whispered.

"What?" snapped Vorbis.

"He said 'no,'" said Brutha.

"That's right," said Didactylos.

Vorbis sat absolutely motionless for a moment. Then his jaw moved a fraction, as if he was rehearsing some words under his breath.

"You *deny* it?" he said.

"Let it be a sphere," said Didactylos. "No problem with a sphere. No doubt special arrangements are made for everything to stay on. And the Sun can be another larger sphere, a long way off. Would you like the Moon to orbit the world or the Sun? I advise the world. More hierarchical, and a splendid example to us all."

Brutha was seeing something he'd never seen before. Vorbis was looking bewildered.

"But you wrote . . . you said the world is on the back of a giant turtle! You gave the turtle a *name!*"

Didactylos shrugged. "Now I know better," he said. "Who ever heard of a turtle ten thousand miles long? Swimming through the emptiness of space? Hah. For stupidity! I am embarrassed to think of it now."

Vorbis shut his mouth. Then he opened it again.

"This is how an Ephebian philosopher behaves?" he said.

Didactylos shrugged again. "It is how any true philosopher behaves," he said. "One must always be ready to embrace new ideas, take account of new proofs. Don't you agree? And you have brought us many new points"—a gesture seemed to take in, quite by accident, the Omnian bowmen around the room—"for me to ponder. I can always be swayed by powerful argument."

"Your lies have already poisoned the world!"

"Then I shall write another book," said Didactylos

calmly. "Think how it will look—proud Didactylos swayed by the arguments of the Omnians. A full retraction. Hmm? In fact, with your permission, lord—I know you have much to do, looting and burning and so on—I will retire to my barrel right away and start work on it. A universe of spheres. Balls spinning through space. Hmm. Yes. With your permission, lord, I will write you more balls than you can imagine . . ."

The old philosopher turned and, very slowly, walked towards the exit.

Vorbis watched him go.

Brutha saw him half-raise his hand to signal the guards, and then lower it again.

Vorbis turned to the Tyrant.

"So much for your—" he began.

"*Coo-ee!*"

The lantern sailed through the doorway and shattered against Vorbis's skull.

"*Nevertheless . . . the Turtle Moves!*"

Vorbis leapt to his feet.

"I—" he screamed, and then got a grip on himself. He waved irritably at a couple of the guards. "I want him caught. Now. And . . . Brutha?"

Brutha could hardly hear him for the rush of blood in his ears. Didactylos had been a better thinker than he'd thought.

"Yes, lord?"

"You will take a party of men, and you will take them to the Library . . . and then, Brutha, you will burn the Library."

Didactylos was blind, but it was dark. The pursuing guards could see, except that there was nothing to see by.

And they hadn't spent their lives wandering the twisty, uneven and above all many-stepped lanes of Ephebe.

"—eight, nine, ten, eleven," muttered the philosopher, bounding up a pitch-dark flight of steps and haring around a corner.

"Argh, ow, that was my *knee*," muttered most of the guards, in a heap about halfway up.

One made it to the top, though. By starlight he could just make out the skinny figure, bounding madly along the street. He raised his crossbow. The old fool wasn't even dodging . . .

A perfect target.

There was a twang.

The guard looked puzzled for a moment. The bow toppled from his hands, firing itself as it hit the cobbles and sending its bolt ricocheting off a statue. He looked down at the feathered shaft sticking out of his chest, and then at the figure detaching itself from the shadows.

"Sergeant Simony?" he whispered.

"I'm sorry," said Simony. "I really am. But the Truth is important."

The soldier opened his mouth to give his opinion of the truth and then slumped forward.

He opened his eyes.

Simony was walking away. Everything looked lighter. It was still dark. But now he could see in the darkness. Everything was shades of gray. And the cobbles under his hand had somehow become a coarse black sand.

He looked up.

ON YOUR FEET, PRIVATE ICHLOS.

He stood up sheepishly. Now he was more than just a soldier, an anonymous figure to chase and be killed and be no more than a shadowy bit-player in other people's lives.

Now he was Dervi Ichlos, aged thirty-eight, comparatively blameless in the general scheme of things, and dead.

He raised a hand to his lips uncertainly.

"You're the judge?" he said.

NOT ME.

Ichlos looked at the sands stretching away. He knew instinctively what he had to do. He was far less sophisticated than General Fri'it, and took more notice of songs he'd learned in his childhood. Besides, he had an advantage. He'd had even less religion than the general.

JUDGMENT IS AT THE END OF THE DESERT.

Ichlos tried to smile.

"My mum told me about this," he said. "When you're dead, you have to walk a desert. And you see everything properly, she said. And remember everything right."

Death studiously did nothing to indicate his feelings either way.

"Might meet a few friends on the way, eh?" said the soldier.

POSSIBLY.

Ichlos set out. On the whole, he thought, it could have been worse.

Urn clambered across the shelves like a monkey, pulling books out of their racks and throwing them down to the floor.

"I can carry about twenty," he said. "But which twenty?"

"*Always* wanted to do that," murmured Didactylos happily. "Upholding truth in the face of tyranny and so on. Hah! One man, unafraid of the—"

"What to take? What to take?" shouted Urn.

"We don't need Grido's *Mechanics*," said Didactylos. "Hey, I wish I could have seen the look on his face!

Damn good shot, considering. I just hope someone wrote down what I—"

"Principles of gearing! Theory of water expansion!" shouted Urn. "But we don't need Ibid's *Civics* or Gnomon's *Ectopia*, that's for sure—"

"What? They belong to all mankind!" snapped Didactylos.

"Then if all mankind will come and help us carry them, that's fine," said Urn. "But if it's just the two of us, I prefer to carry something useful."

"Useful? Books on mechanisms?"

"Yes! They can show people how to live better!"

"And *these* show people how to be people," said Didactylos. "Which reminds me. Find me another lantern. I feel quite blind without one—"

The Library door shook to a thunderous knocking. It wasn't the knocking of people who expected the door to be opened.

"We could throw some of the others into the—"

The hinges leapt out of the walls. The door thudded down.

Soldiers scrambled over it, swords drawn.

"Ah, gentlemen," said Didactylos. "Pray don't disturb my circles."

The corporal in charge looked at him blankly, and then down at the floor.

"What circles?" he said.

"Hey, how about giving me a pair of compasses and coming back in, say, half an hour?"

"Leave him, corporal," said Brutha.

He stepped over the door.

"I said leave him."

"But I got orders to—"

"Are you deaf? If you are, the Quisition can cure

that," said Brutha, astonished at the steadiness of his own voice.

"You don't belong to the Quisition," said the corporal.

"No. But I know a man who does," said Brutha. "You are to search the palace for books. Leave him with me. He's an old man. What harm can he do?"

The corporal looked hesitantly from Brutha to his prisoners.

"Very good, corporal. I will take over."

They all turned.

"Did you hear me?" said Sergeant Simony, pushing his way forward.

"But the deacon told us—"

"Corporal?"

"Yes, sergeant?"

"The deacon is far away. I am right here."

"Yes, sergeant."

"Go!"

"Yes, sergeant."

Simony cocked an ear as the soldiers marched away.

Then he stuck his sword in the door and turned to Didactylos. He made a fist with his left hand and brought his right hand down on it, palm extended.

"The Turtle Moves," he said.

"That all depends," said the philosopher, cautiously.

"I mean I am . . . a friend," he said.

"Why should we trust you?" said Urn.

"Because you haven't got any choice," said Sergeant Simony briskly.

"Can you get us out of here?" said Brutha.

Simony glared at him. "You?" he said. "Why should I get *you* out of here? You're an inquisitor!" He grasped his sword.

Brutha backed away.

"I'm not!"

"On the ship, when the captain sounded you, you just said nothing," said Simony. "You're not one of us."

"I don't think I'm one of them, either," said Brutha. "I'm one of mine."

He gave Didactylos an imploring look, which was a wasted effort, and turned it towards Urn instead.

"I don't know about this soldier," he said. "All I know is that Vorbis means to have you killed and he *will* burn your Library. But I can help. I worked it out on the way here."

"And don't listen to him," said Simony. He dropped on one knee in front of Didactylos, like a supplicant. "Sir, there are . . . some of us . . . who know your book for what it is . . . see, I have a copy . . ."

He fumbled inside his breastplate.

"We copied it out," said Simony. "One copy! That's all we had! But it's been passed around. Some of us who could read, read it to the others! It makes so much sense!"

"Er . . ." said Didactylos. "What?"

Simony waved his hands in excitement. "Because we know it—I've been to places that—it's true! There *is* a Great Turtle. The turtle *does* move! We don't *need* gods!"

"Urn? No one's stripped the copper off the roof, have they?" said Didactylos.

"Don't think so."

"Remind me not to talk to this chap outside, then."

"You don't understand!" said Simony. "I can save you. You have friends in unexpected places. Come on. I'll just kill this priest . . ."

He gripped his sword. Brutha backed away.

"No! I can help, too! That's why I came. When I saw you in front of Vorbis I knew what I could do!"

"What can you do?" sneered Urn.

"I can save the Library."

"What? Put it on your back and run away?" sneered Simony.

"No. I don't mean that. How many scrolls are there?"

"About seven hundred," said Didactylos.

"How many of them are important?"

"All of them!" said Urn.

"Maybe a couple of hundred," said Didactylos, mildly.

"Uncle!"

"All the rest is just wind and vanity publishing," said Didactylos.

"But they're *books!*"

"I may be able to take more than that," said Brutha slowly. "Is there a way out?"

"There . . . could be," said Didactylos.

"Don't tell him!" said Simony.

"Then all your books will burn," said Brutha. He pointed to Simony. "He said you haven't got a choice. So you haven't got anything to lose, have you?"

"He's a—" Simony began.

"Everyone shut up," said Didactylos. He stared past Brutha's ear.

"There may be a way out," he said. "What do you intend?"

"I don't believe this!" said Urn. "There's Omnians here and you're telling them there's another way out!"

"There's tunnels all through this rock," said Didactylos.

"Maybe, but we don't *tell* people!"

"I'm inclined to trust this person," said Didactylos. "He's got an honest face. Speaking philosophically."

"*Why* should we trust him?"

"Anyone stupid enough to expect us to trust him in these circumstances *must* be trustworthy," said Didactylos. "He'd be too stupid to be deceitful."

"I can walk out of here right now," said Brutha. "And where will your Library be then?"

"You see?" said Simony.

"Just when things apparently look dark, suddenly we have unexpected friends everywhere," said Didactylos. "What is your plan, young man?"

"I haven't got one," said Brutha. "I just do things, one after the other."

"And how long will doing things one after another take you?"

"About ten minutes, I think."

Simony glared at Brutha.

"Now get the books," said Brutha. "And I shall need some light."

"But you can't even read!" said Urn.

"I'm not going to read them." Brutha looked blankly at the first scroll, which happened to be *De Chelonian Mobile*.

"Oh. My god," he said.

"Something wrong?" said Didactylos.

"Could someone fetch my tortoise?"

Simony trotted through the palace. No one was paying him much attention. Most of the Ephebian guard was outside the labyrinth, and Vorbis had made it clear to anyone who was thinking of venturing inside just what would happen to the palace's inhabitants. Groups of Omnian soldiers were looting in a disciplined sort of way.

Besides, he was returning to his quarters.

There *was* a tortoise in Brutha's room. It was sitting on the table, between a rolled-up scroll and a gnawed melon rind and, insofar as it was possible to tell with tortoises, was asleep. Simony grabbed it without ceremony, rammed it into his pack, and hurried back towards the Library.

He hated himself for doing it. The stupid priest had ruined everything! But Didactylos had made him promise, and Didactylos was the man who knew the Truth.

All the way there he had the impression that someone was trying to attract his attention.

"You can remember them just by looking?" said Urn.

"Yes."

"The whole scroll?"

"Yes."

"I don't believe you."

"The word LIBRVM outside this building has a chip in the top of the first letter," said Brutha. "Xeno wrote *Reflections*, and old Aristocrates wrote *Platitudes*, and Didactylos thinks Ibid's *Discourses* are bloody stupid. There are six hundred paces from the Tyrant's throne room to the Library. There is a—"

"He's got a good memory, you've got to grant him that," said Didactylos. "Show him some more scrolls."

"How will we know he's remembered them?" Urn demanded, unrolling a scroll of geometrical theorems. "He can't read! And even if he could read, he can't write!"

"We shall have to teach him."

Brutha looked at a scroll full of maps. He shut his eyes. For a moment the jagged outline glowed against the inside of his eyelids, and then he felt them settle into his mind. They were still there somewhere—he could bring them back at any time. Urn unrolled another scroll. Pictures of animals. This one, drawings of plants and lots of writing. This one, just writing. This one, triangles and things. They settled down in his memory. After a while, he wasn't even aware of the scroll unrolling. He just had to keep looking.

He wondered how much he could remember, but that was stupid. You just remembered everything you saw. A tabletop, or a scroll full of writing. There was as much information in the grain and coloring of the wood as there was in Xeno's *Reflections*.

Even so, he was conscious of a certain heaviness of mind, a feeling that if he turned his head sharply then memory would slosh out of his ears.

Urn picked up a scroll at random and unrolled it partway.

"Describe what an Ambiguous Puzuma looks like," he demanded.

"Don't know," said Brutha. He blinked.

"So much for Mr. Memory," said Urn.

"He can't *read*, boy. That's not fair," said the philosopher.

"All right. I mean—the fourth picture in the third scroll you saw," said Urn.

"A four-legged creature facing left," said Brutha. "A large head similar to a cat's and broad shoulders with the body tapering towards the hindquarters. The body is a pattern of dark and light squares. The ears are very small and laid flat against the head. There are six whiskers. The tail is stubby. Only the hind feet are clawed, three claws on each foot. The fore feet are about the same length as the head and held up against the body. A band of thick hair—"

"That was fifty scrolls ago," said Urn. "He saw the whole scroll for a second or two."

They looked at Brutha. Brutha blinked again.

"You know *everything*?" said Urn.

"I don't know."

"You've got half the Library in your head!"

"I feel . . . a . . . bit . . ."

The Library of Ephebe was a furnace. The flames burned blue where the melted copper roof dripped on to the shelves.

All libraries, everywhere, are connected by the bookworm holes in space created by the strong space-time distortions found around any large collections of books.

Only a very few librarians learn the secret, and there are inflexible rules about making *use* of the fact. Because it amounts to time travel, and time travel causes big problems.

But if a library is on fire, and down in the history books as having been on fire . . .

There was a small pop, utterly unheard among the crackling of the bookshelves, and a figure dropped out of nowhere on to a small patch of unburned floor in the middle of the Library.

It looked ape-like, but it moved in a very purposeful way. Long simian arms beat out the flames, pulled scrolls off the shelves, and stuffed them into a sack. When the sack was full, it knuckled back into the middle of the room . . . and vanished, with another pop.

This has nothing to do with the story.

Nor does the fact that, some time later, scrolls thought to have been destroyed in the Great Ephebian Library

Fire turned up in remarkably good condition in the Library of Unseen University in Ankh-Morpork.

But it's nice to know, even so.

Brutha awoke with the smell of the sea in his nostrils.

At least it was what people think of as the smell of the sea, which is the stink of antique fish and rotten seaweed.

He was in some sort of shed. Such light as managed to come through its one unglazed window was red, and flickered. One end of the shed was open to the water. The ruddy light showed a few figures clustered around something there.

Brutha gently probed the contents of his memory. Everything seemed to be there, the Library scrolls neatly arranged. The words were as meaningless to him as any other written word, but the pictures were interesting. More interesting than most things in his memory, anyway.

He sat up, carefully.

"You're awake, then," said the voice of Om, in his head. "Feel a bit full, do we? Feel a bit like a stack of shelves? Feel like we've got big notices saying 'SILENCIOS!' all over the place inside our head? What did you go and do that for?"

"I . . . don't know. It seemed like . . . the next thing to do. Where are you?"

"Your soldier friend has got me in his pack. Thanks for looking after me so carefully, by the way."

Brutha managed to get to his feet. The world revolved around him for a moment, adding a third astronomical theory to the two currently occupying the minds of local thinkers.

He peered out of the window. The red light was coming from fires all over Ephebe, but there was one huge glow over the Library.

"Guerrilla activity," said Om. "Even the slaves are fighting. Can't understand why. You think they'd jump at the chance to be revenged on their masters, eh?"

"I suppose a slave in Ephebe has the chance to be free," said Brutha.

There was a hiss from the other end of the shed, and a metallic, whirring noise. Brutha heard Urn say, "There! I told you. Just a block in the tubes. Lets get some more fuel in."

Brutha tottered towards the group.

They were clustered around a boat. As boats went, it was of normal shape—a pointed end in front, a flat end at the back. But there was no mast. What there was, was a large, copper-colored ball, hanging in a wooden framework toward the back of the boat. There was an iron basket underneath it, in which someone had already got a good fire going.

And the ball was spinning in its frame, in a cloud of steam.

"I've seen that," he said. "In *De Chelonian Mobile*. There was a drawing."

"Oh, it's the walking Library," said Didactylos. "Yes. You're right. Illustrating the principle of reaction. I never asked Urn to build a big one. This is what comes of thinking with your hands."

"I took it around the lighthouse one night last week," said Urn. "No problems at all."

"Ankh-Morpork is a lot further than that," said Simony.

"Yes, it is five times further than the distance between Ephebe and Omnia," said Brutha solemnly. "There was a scroll of maps," he added.

Steam rose in scalding clouds from the whirring ball. Now he was closer, Brutha could see that half a dozen very short oars had been joined together in a star-shaped pattern behind the copper globe, and hung over the rear of the boat. Wooden cogwheels and a couple of endless belts filled the intervening space. As the globe spun, the paddles thrashed at the air.

"How does it work?" he said.

"Very simple," said Urn. "The fire makes—"

"We haven't got time for this," said Simony.

"—*makes* the water hot and so it gets angry," said the apprentice philosopher. "So it rushes out of the globe through these four little nozzles to get away from the fire. The plumes of steam push the globe around, and the cogwheels and Legibus's screw mechanism transfer the motion to the paddles which turn, pushing the boat through the water."

"Very philosophical," said Didactylos.

Brutha felt that he ought to stand up for Omnian progress.

"The great doors of the Citadel weigh tons but are opened solely by the power of faith," he said. "One push and they swing open."

"I should very much like to see that," said Urn.

Brutha felt a faint sinful twinge of pride that Omnia still had anything he could be proud of.

"Very good balance and some hydraulics, probably."

"Oh."

Simony thoughtfully prodded the mechanism with his sword.

"Have you thought of all the possibilities?" he said.

Urn's hands began to weave through the air. "You mean mighty ships plowing the wine-dark sea with no—" he began.

"On land, I was thinking," said Simony. "Perhaps . . . on some sort of cart . . ."

"Oh, no point in putting a boat on a cart."

Simony's eyes gleamed with the gleam of a man who had seen the future and found it covered with armor plating.

"Hmm," he said.

"It's all very well, but it's not philosophy," said Didactylos.

"Where's the priest?"

"I'm here, but I'm not a—"

"How're you feeling? You went out like a candle back there."

"I'm . . . better now."

"One minute upright, next minute a draft-excluder."

"I'm much better."

"Happen a lot, does it?"

"Sometimes."

"Remembering the scrolls okay?"

"I . . . think so. Who set fire to the Library?"

Urn looked up from the mechanism.

"He did," he said.

Brutha stared at Didactylos.

"*You* set fire to your own Library?"

"I'm the only one qualified," said the philosopher. "Besides, it keeps it out of the way of Vorbis."

"What?"

"Suppose he'd read the scrolls? He's bad enough as it is. He'd be a lot worse with all that knowledge inside him."

"He wouldn't have read them," said Brutha.

"Oh, he would. I know that type," said Didactylos. "All holy piety in public, and all peeled grapes and self-indulgence in private."

"Not Vorbis," said Brutha, with absolute certainty. "He wouldn't have read them."

"Well, *anyway*," said Didactylos, "if it had to be done, I did it."

Urn turned away from the bow of the boat, where he was feeding more wood into the brazier under the globe.

"Can we all get on board?" he said.

Brutha eased his way on a rough bench seat amidships, or whatever it was called. The air smelled of hot water.

"Right," said Urn. He pulled a lever. The spinning paddles hit the water; there was a jerk and then, steam hanging in the air behind it, the boat moved forward.

"What's the name of this vessel?" said Didactylos.

Urn looked surprised.

"Name?" he said. "It's a boat. A thing, of the nature of things. It doesn't *need* a name."

"Names are more philosophical," said Didactylos, with a trace of sulkiness. "And you should have broken an amphora of wine over it."

"That would have been a waste."

The boat chugged out of the boathouse and into the dark harbor. Away to one side, an Ephebian galley was on fire. The whole of the city was a patchwork of flame.

"But you've got an amphora on board?" said Didactylos.

"Yes."

"Pass it over, then."

White water trailed behind the boat. The paddles churned.

"No wind. No rowers!" said Simony. "Do you even begin to understand what you have here, Urn?"

"Absolutely. The operating principles are amazingly simple," said Urn.

"That wasn't what I meant. I meant the things you could do with this power!"

Urn pushed another log on the fire.

"It's just the transforming of heat into work," he said. "I suppose . . . oh, the pumping of water. Mills that can grind even when the wind isn't blowing. That sort of thing? Is that what you had in mind?"

Simony the soldier hesitated.

"Yeah," he said. "Something like that."

Brutha whispered, "Om?"

"Yes?"

"Are you all right?"

"It smells like a soldier's knapsack in here. Get me out."

The copper ball spun madly over the fire. It gleamed almost as brightly as Simony's eyes.

Brutha tapped him on the shoulder.

"Can I have my tortoise?"

Simony laughed bitterly.

"There's good eating on one of these things," he said, fishing out Om.

"Everyone says so," said Brutha. He lowered his voice to a whisper.

"What sort of place is Ankh?"

"A city of a million souls," said the voice of Om, "many of them occupying bodies. And a thousand religions. There's even a temple to the small gods! Sounds like a place where people don't have trouble believing things. Not a bad place for a fresh start, I think. With my brains and your . . . with my brains, we should soon be in business again."

"You don't want to go back to Omnia?"

"No point," said the voice of Om. "It's always possible to overthrow an established god. People get fed up, they want a change. But you can't overthrow yourself, can you?"

"Who're you talking to, priest?" said Simony.

"I . . . er . . . was praying."

"Hah! To Om? You might as well pray to that tortoise."

"Yes."

"I am ashamed for Omnia," said Simony. "Look at us. Stuck in the past. Held back by repressive monotheism. Shunned by our neighbors. What good has our God been to us? Gods? Hah!"

"Steady on, steady on," said Didactylos. "We're on seawater and that's highly conductive armor you're wearing."

"Oh, I say nothing about other gods," said Simony quickly. "I have not the right. But Om? A bogeyman for the Quisition! If he exists, let him strike me down here and now!"

Simony drew his sword and held it up at arm's length.

Om sat peacefully on Brutha's lap. "I like this boy," he said. "He's almost as good as a believer. It's like love and hate, know what I mean?"

Simony sheathed his sword again.

"Thus I refute Om," he said.

"Yes, but what's the alternative?"

"Philosophy! Practical philosophy! Like Urn's engine there. It could drag Omnia kicking and screaming into the Century of the Fruitbat!"

"Kicking and screaming," said Brutha.

"By any means necessary," said Simony.

He beamed at them.

"Don't worry about him," said Om. "We'll be far

away. Just as well, too. I don't think Omnia's going to be a popular country when news of last night's work gets about."

"But it was Vorbis's fault!" said Brutha out loud. "He started the whole thing! He sent poor Brother Murduck, and then he had him killed so he could blame it on the Ephebians! He never intended any peace treaty! He just wanted to get into the palace!"

"Beats me how he managed that, too," said Urn. "No one ever got through the labyrinth without a guide. How did he do it?"

Didactylos's blind eyes sought out Brutha.

"Can't imagine," he said. Brutha hung his head.

"He really did all that?" said Simony.

"Yes."

"You idiot! You total sandhead!" screamed Om.

"And you'd tell this to other people?" said Simony, insistently.

"I suppose so."

"You'd speak out against the Quisition?"

Brutha stared miserably into the night. Behind them, the flames of Ephebe had merged into one orange spark.

"All I can say is what I remember," he said.

"We're dead," said Om. "Throw me over the side, why don't you? This bonehead will want to take us back to Omnia!"

Simony rubbed his chin thoughtfully.

"Vorbis has many enemies," he said, "in certain circumstances. Better he should be killed, but some would call that murder. Or even martyrdom. But a trial . . . if there was evidence . . . if they even *thought* there could be evidence . . ."

"I can see his mind working!" Om screamed. "We'd all be safe if you'd shut up!"

"Vorbis on trial," Simony mused.

Brutha blanched at the thought. It was the kind of thought that was almost impossible to hold in the mind. It was the kind of thought that made no sense. Vorbis on trial? Trials were things that happened to other people.

He remembered Brother Murduck. And the soldiers who had been lost in the desert. And all the things that had been done to people, even to Brutha.

"Tell him you can't remember!" Om yelled. "Tell him you can't recall!"

"And if he *was* on trial," said Simony, "he'd be found guilty. No one would dare do anything else."

Thoughts always moved slowly through Brutha's mind, like icebergs. They arrived slowly and left slowly and when they were there they occupied a lot of space, much of it below the surface.

He thought: the worst thing about Vorbis isn't that he's evil, but that he makes good people do evil. He turns people into things like himself. You can't help it. You catch it off him.

There was no sound but the slosh of water against the *Unnamed Boat*'s hull and the spinning of the philosophical engine.

"We'd be caught if we returned to Omnia," said Brutha slowly.

"We can land away from the ports," said Simony eagerly.

"Ankh-Morpork!" shouted Om.

"First we should take Mr. Didactylos to Ankh-Morpork," said Brutha. "Then—I'll come back to Omnia."

"You can damn well leave *me* there too!" said Om. "I'll soon find some believers in Ankh-Morpork, don't you worry, they believe anything there!"

"Never seen Ankh-Morpork," said Didactylos. "Still, we live and learn. That's what I always say." He turned to face the soldier. "Kicking and screaming."

"There's some exiles in Ankh," said Simony. "Don't worry. You'll be safe there."

"Amazing!" said Didactylos. "And to think, this morning, I didn't even know I was in danger."

He sat back in the boat.

"Life in this world," he said, "is, as it were, a sojourn in a cave. What can we know of reality? For all we see of the true nature of existence is, shall we say, no more than bewildering and amusing shadows cast upon the inner wall of the cave by the unseen blinding light of absolute truth, from which we may or may not deduce some glimmer of veracity, and we as troglodyte seekers of wisdom can only lift our voices to the unseen and say, humbly, 'Go on, do Deformed Rabbit . . . it's my favorite.' "

Vorbis stirred the ashes with his foot.

"No bones," he said.

The soldiers stood silently. The fluffy gray flakes collapsed and blew a little way in the dawn breeze.

"And the wrong sort of ash," said Vorbis.

The sergeant opened his mouth to say something.

"Be assured I know that of which I speak," said Vorbis.

He wandered over to the charred trapdoor, and prodded it with his toe.

"We followed the tunnel," said the sergeant, in the tones of one who hopes against experience that sounding helpful will avert the wrath to come. "It comes out near the docks."

"But if you enter it from the docks it does not come out here," Vorbis mused. The smoking ashes seemed to hold an endless fascination for him.

The sergeant's brow wrinkled.

"Understand?" said Vorbis. "The Ephebians wouldn't build a way out that was a way in. The minds that devised the labyrinth would not work like that. There would be . . . valves. Sequences of trigger-stones, perhaps. Trips that trip only one way. Whirring blades that come out of unexpected walls."

"Ah."

"Most intricate and devious, I have no doubt."

The sergeant ran a dry tongue over his lips. He could not read Vorbis like a book, because there had never been a book like Vorbis. But Vorbis had certain habits of thought that you learned, after a while.

"You wish me to take the squad and follow it up from the docks," he said hollowly.

"I was just about to suggest it," said Vorbis.

"Yes, lord."

Vorbis patted the sergeant on the shoulder.

"But do not worry!" he said cheerfully. "Om will protect the strong in faith."

"Yes, lord."

"And the last man can bring me a full report. But first . . . they are not in the city?"

"We have searched it fully, lord."

"And no one left by the gate? Then they left by sea."

"All the Ephebian war vessels are accounted for, Lord Vorbis."

"This bay is lousy with small boats."

"With nowhere to go but the open sea, sir."

Vorbis looked out at the Circle Sea. It filled the world from horizon to horizon. Beyond lay the smudge of the Sto plains and the ragged line of the Ramtops, all the way to the towering peaks that the heretics called the Hub but which was, he knew, the Pole, visible around the curve of the world only because of the way light bent in atmosphere, just as it did in water . . . and he saw a smudge of white, curling over the distant ocean.

Vorbis had very good eyesight, from a height.

He picked up a handful of gray ash, which had once been Dykeri's *Principles of Navigation*, and let it drift through his fingers.

"Om has sent us a fair wind," he said. "Let us get down to the docks."

Hope waved optimistically in the waters of the sergeant's despair.

"You won't be wanting us to explore the tunnel, lord?" he said.

"Oh, no. You can do that when we return."

Urn prodded at the copper globe with a piece of wire while the *Unnamed Boat* wallowed in the waves.

"Can't you beat it?" said Simony, who was not up to speed on the difference between machines and people.

"It's a philosophical engine," said Urn. "Beating won't help."

"But you said machines could be our slaves," said Simony.

"Not the beating sort," said Urn. "The nozzles are bunged up with salt. When the water rushes out of the globe it leaves the salt behind."

"Why?"

"I don't know. Water likes to travel light."

"We're becalmed! Can you do anything about it?"

"Yes, wait for it to cool down and then clean it out and put some more water in it."

Simony looked around distractedly.

"But we're still in sight of the coast!"

"*You* might be," said Didactylos. He was sitting in the middle of the boat with his hands crossed on the top of his walking-stick, looking like an old man who doesn't often get taken out for an airing and is quite enjoying it.

"Don't worry. No one could see us out here," said Urn. He prodded at the mechanism. "Anyway, I'm a bit worried about the screw. It was invented to move water along, not move along on water."

"You mean it's confused?" said Simony.

"Screwed up," said Didactylos happily.

Brutha lay in the pointed end, looking down at the water. A small squid siphoned past, just under the surface. He wondered what it was—

—and *knew* it was the common bottle squid, of the class Cephalopoda, phylum Mollusca, and that it had an internal cartilaginous support instead of a skeleton and a well-developed nervous system and large, image-forming eyes that were quite similar to vertebrate eyes.

The knowledge hung in the forefront of his mind for a moment, and then faded away.

"Om?" Brutha whispered.

"What?"

"What're you doing?"

"Trying to get some sleep. Tortoises need a lot of sleep, you know."

Simony and Urn were bent over the philosophical engine. Brutha stared at the globe—

—a sphere of radius r, which therefore had a volume $V = (4/3)(\pi) rrr$, and surface area $A = 4(\pi) rr$—

"Oh, my god . . ."

"What now?" said the voice of the tortoise.

Didactylos's face turned towards Brutha, who was clutching at his head.

"What's a pi?"

Didactylos reached out a hand and steadied Brutha.

"What's the matter?" said Om.

"I don't know! It's just words! I don't know what's in the books! I can't read!"

"Getting plenty of sleep is vital," said Om. "It builds a healthy shell."

Brutha sagged to his knees in the rocking boat. He felt like a householder coming back unexpectedly and finding the old place full of strangers. They were in every room, not menacing, but just filling the space with their thereness.

"The books are leaking!"

"I don't see how that can happen," said Didactylos. "You said you just looked at them. You didn't read them. You don't know what they mean."

"*They* know what they mean!"

"Listen. They're just books, of the nature of books," said Didactylos. "They're not magical. If you could know what books contained just by looking at them, Urn there would be a genius."

"What's the matter with him?" said Simony.

"He thinks he knows too much."

"No! I don't know anything! Not really *know*," said Brutha. "I just remembered that squids have an internal cartilaginous support!"

"I can see that would be a worry," said Simony. "Huh. Priests? Mad, the lot of them."

"No! I don't know what cartilaginous *means*!"

"Skeletal connective tissue," said Didactylos. "Think of bony and leathery at the same time."

Simony snorted. "Well, well," he said, "we live and learn, just like you said."

"Some of us even do it the other way around," said Didactylos.

"Is that supposed to mean something?"

"It's philosophy," said Didactylos. "And sit down, boy. You're making the boat rock. We're overloaded as it is."

"It's being buoyed upward by a force equal to the weight of the displaced fluid," muttered Brutha, sagging.

"Hmm?"

"Except that I don't know what buoyed means."

Urn looked up from the sphere. "We're ready to start again," he said. "Just bale some water in here with your helmet, mister."

"And then we shall go again?"

"Well, we can start getting up steam," said Urn. He wiped his hands on his toga.

"Y'know," said Didactylos, "there *are* different ways of learning things. I'm reminded of the time when old Prince Lasgere of Tsort asked me how he could become learned, especially since he hadn't got any time for this reading business. I said to him, 'There is no royal road to learning, sire,' and he said to me, 'Bloody well build one or I shall have your legs chopped off. Use as many slaves as you like.' A refreshingly direct approach, I always thought. Not a man to mince words. People, yes. But not words."

"Why didn't he chop your legs off?" said Urn.

"I built him his road. More or less."

"How? I thought that was just a metaphor."

"You're learning, Urn. So I found a dozen slaves who could read and they sat in his bedroom at night whispering choice passages to him while he slept."

"Did that work?"

"Don't know. The third slave stuck a six-inch dagger in his ear. Then after the revolution the new ruler let me out of prison and said I could leave the country if I promised not to think of anything on the way to the border. But I don't believe there was anything wrong with the idea in principle."

Urn blew on the fire.

"Takes a little while to heat up the water," he explained.

Brutha lay back in the bow again. If he concentrated, he could stop the knowledge flowing. The thing to do was avoid looking at things. Even a cloud—

—devised by natural philosophy as a means of occasioning shade on the surface of the world, thus preventing overheating—

—caused an intrusion. Om was fast asleep.

Knowing without learning, thought Brutha. No. The other way around. Learning without knowing . . .

Nine-tenths of Om dozed in his shell. The rest of him drifted like a fog in the real world of the gods, which is a lot less interesting than the three-dimensional world inhabited by most of humanity.

He thought: we're a little boat. She'll probably not even notice us. There's the whole of the ocean. She can't be everywhere.

Of course, she's got many believers. But we're only a little boat . . .

He felt the minds of inquisitive fishes nosing around the end of the screw. Which was odd, because in the normal course of things fishes were not known for their—

"Greetings," said the Queen of the Sea.

"Ah."

"I see you're still managing to exist, little tortoise."

"Hanging in there," said Om. "No problems."

There was a pause which, if it were taking place between two people in the human world, would have been spent in coughing and looking embarrassed. But gods are never embarrassed.

"I expect," said Om guardedly, "you are looking for your price."

"This vessel and everyone in it," said the Queen. "But your believer can be saved, as is the custom."

"What good are they to you? One of them's an atheist."

"Hah! They all believe, right at the end."

"That doesn't seem . . ." Om hesitated. "Fair?"

Now the Sea Queen paused.

"What's fair?"

"Like . . . underlying justice?" said Om. He wondered why he said it.

"Sounds a human idea to me."

"They're inventive, I'll grant you. But what I meant was . . . I mean . . . they've done nothing to deserve it."

"*Deserve?* They're *human*. What's *deserve* got to do with it?"

Om had to concede this. He wasn't thinking like a god. This bothered him.

"It's just . . ."

"You've been relying on one human for too long, little god."

"I know. I know." Om sighed. Minds leaked into one another. He was seeing too much from a human point of view. "Take the boat, then. If you must. I just wish it was—"

"Fair?" said the Sea Queen. She moved forward. Om felt her all around him.

"There's no such thing," she said. "Life's like a beach. And then you die."

Then she was gone.

Om let himself retreat into the shell of his shell.

"Brutha?"

"Yes?"

"Can you swim?"

The globe started to spin.

Brutha heard Urn say, "There. Soon be on our way."

"We'd better be." This was Simony. "There's a ship out there."

"This thing goes faster than anything with sails or oars."

Brutha looked across the bay. A sleek Omnian ship was passing the lighthouse. It was still a long way off, but Brutha stared at it with a dread and expectation that magnified better than telescopes.

"It's moving fast," said Simony. "I don't understand it—there's no wind."

Urn looked around at the flat calm.

"There can't be wind there and not here," he said.

"I said, can you swim?" The voice of the tortoise was insistent in Brutha's head.

"I don't know," said Brutha.

"Do you think you could find out quickly?"

Urn looked upwards.

"Oh," he said.

Clouds had massed over the *Unnamed Boat*. They were visibly spinning.

"You've *got* to know!" shouted Om. "I thought you had a perfect memory!"

"We used to splash around in the big cistern in the village," whispered Brutha. "I don't know if that counts!"

Mist whipped off the surface of the sea. Brutha's ears

popped. And still the Omnian ship came on, flying across the waves.

"What do you call it when you've got a dead calm surrounded by winds—" Urn began.

"Hurricane?" said Didactylos.

Lightning crackled between sky and sea. Urn yanked at the lever that lowered the screw into the water. His eyes glowed almost as brightly as the lightning.

"Now *there's* a power," he said. "Harnessing the lightning! The dream of mankind!"

The *Unnamed Boat* surged forward.

"Is it? It's not *my* dream," said Didactylos. "I always dream of a giant carrot chasing me through a field of lobsters."

"I mean *metaphorical* dream, master," said Urn.

"What's a metaphor?" said Simony.

Brutha said, "What's a dream?"

A pillar of lightning laced the mist. Secondary lightnings sparked off the spinning globe.

"You can get it from cats," said Urn, lost in a philosophical world, as the *Boat* left a white wake behind it. "You stroke them with a rod of amber, and you get tiny lightnings . . . if I could magnify that a million times, no man would ever be a slave again and we could catch it in jars and do away with the night . . ."

Lightning struck a few yards away.

"We're in a boat with a large copper ball in the middle of a body of salt water," said Didactylos. "Thanks, Urn."

"And the temples of the gods would be magnificently lit, of course," said Urn quickly.

Didactylos tapped his stick on the hull. "It's a nice idea, but you'd never get enough cats," he said. The sea surged up.

"Jump into the water!" Om shouted.

"Why?" said Brutha.

A wave almost overturned the boat. Rain hissed on the surface of the sphere, sent up a scalding spray.

"I haven't got time to explain! Jump overboard! It's for the best! *Trust* me!"

Brutha stood up, holding the sphere's framework to steady himself.

"Sit down!" said Urn.

"I'm just going out," said Brutha. "I may be some time."

The boat rocked under him as he half-jumped, half-fell into the boiling sea.

Lightning struck the sphere.

As Brutha bobbed to the surface he saw, for a moment, the globe glowing white-hot and the *Unnamed Boat*, its screw almost out of the water, skimming away through the mists like a comet. It vanished in the clouds and rain. A moment later, above the noise of the storm, there was a muffled "boom."

Brutha raised his hand. Om broke the surface, blowing seawater out of his nostrils.

"You said it would be for the best!" screamed Brutha.

"Well? *We're* still alive! And hold me out of the water! Tortoises can't swim!"

"But they might be dead!"

"Do you want to join them?"

A wave submerged Brutha. For a moment the world was a dark green curtain, ringing in his ears.

"I can't swim with one hand!" he shouted, as he broke surface again.

"We'll be saved! She wouldn't dare!"

"What do you mean?"

Another wave slapped at Brutha, and suction dragged at his robes.

"Om?"

"Yes?"

"I don't think I *can* swim . . ."

Gods are not very introspective. It has never been a survival trait. The ability to cajole, threaten, and terrify has always worked well enough. When you can flatten entire cities at a whim, a tendency toward quiet reflection and seeing-things-from-the-other-fellow's-point-of-view is seldom necessary.

Which had led, across the multiverse, to men and women of tremendous brilliance and empathy devoting their entire lives to the service of deities who couldn't beat them at a quiet game of dominoes. For example, Sister Sestina of Quirm defied the wrath of a local king and walked unharmed across a bed of coals and propounded a philosophy of sensible ethics on behalf of a goddess whose only real interest was in hairstyles, and Brother Zephilite of Klatch left his vast estates and his family and spent his life ministering to the sick and poor on behalf of the invisible god F'rum, generally considered unable, should he have a backside, to find it with both hands, should he have hands. Gods never need to be very bright when there are humans around to be it for them.

The Sea Queen was considered fairly dumb even by other gods. But there was a certain logic to her thoughts, as she moved deep below the storm-tossed waves. The little boat had been a tempting target . . . but here was a bigger one, full of people, sailing right into the storm.

This one was fair game.

The Sea Queen had the attention span of an onion *bahji*.

And, by and large, she created her own sacrifices. And she believed in quantity.

* * *

The *Fin of God* plunged from wave crest to wave trough, the gale tearing at its sails. The captain fought his way through waist-high water to the prow, where Vorbis stood clutching the rail, apparently oblivious to the fact that the ship was wallowing half-submerged.

"Sir! We *must* reef sail! We can't outrun this!"

Green fire crackled on the tops of the masts. Vorbis turned. The light was reflected in the pit of his eyes.

"It is all for the glory of Om," he said. "Trust is our sail, and glory is our destination."

The captain had had enough. He was unsteady on the subject of religion, but felt fairly confident that after thirty years he knew something about the sea.

"The ocean *floor* is our destination!" he shouted.

Vorbis shrugged. "I did not say there would not be stops along the way," he said.

The captain stared at him and then fought his way back across the heaving deck. What he knew about the sea was that storms like this didn't just happen. You didn't just sail from calm water into the midst of a raging hurricane. This wasn't the sea. This was personal.

Lightning struck the mainmast. There was a scream from the darkness as a mass of torn sail and rigging crashed on to the deck.

The captain half-swam, half-climbed up the ladder to the wheel, where the helmsman was a shadow in the spray and the eerie storm glow.

"We'll never make it alive!"

CORRECT.

"We'll have to abandon ship!"

NO. WE WILL TAKE IT WITH US. IT'S A NICE SHIP.

The captain peered closer in the murk.

"Is that you, Bosun Coplei?"

WOULD YOU LIKE ANOTHER GUESS?

The hull hit a submerged rock and ripped open. Lightning struck the remaining mast and, like a paper boat that had been too long in the water, the *Fin of God* folded up. Baulks of timber splintered and fountained up into the whirling sky . . .

And there was a sudden, velvety silence.

The captain found that he had acquired a recent memory. It involved water, and a ringing in his ears, and the sensation of cold fire in his lungs. But it was fading. He walked over to the rail, his footsteps loud in the quietness, and looked over the side. Despite the fact that the recent memory included something about the ship being totally smashed, it now seemed to be whole again. In a way.

"Uh," he said, "we appear to have run out of sea."

YES.

"And land, too."

The captain tapped the rail. It was grayish, and slightly transparent.

"Uh. Is this wood?"

MORPHIC MEMORY.

"Sorry?"

YOU WERE A SAILOR. YOU HAVE HEARD A SHIP REFERRED TO AS A LIVING THING?

"Oh, yes. You can't spend a night on a ship without feeling that it has a sou—"

YES.

The memory of *Fin of God* sailed on through the silence. There was the distant sighing of wind, or of the memory of wind. The blown-out corpses of dead gales.

"Uh," said the ghost of the captain, "did you just say 'were'?"

YES.

"I thought you did."

The captain stared down. The crew was assembling on deck, looking up at him with anxious eyes.

He looked down further. In front of the crew the ship's rats had assembled. There was a tiny robed shape in front of them.

It said, SQUEAK.

He thought: even rats have a Death . . .

Death stood aside and beckoned to the captain.

YOU HAVE THE WHEEL.

"But—but where are we going?"

WHO KNOWS?

The captain gripped the spokes helplessly. "But . . . there's no stars that I recognize! No charts! What are the winds here? Where are the currents?"

Death shrugged.

The captain turned the wheel aimlessly. The ship glided on through the ghost of a sea.

Then he brightened up. The worst had already happened. It was amazing how good it felt to know that. And if the worst had already happened . . .

"Where's Vorbis?" he growled.

HE SURVIVED.

"Did he? There's no justice!"

THERE'S JUST ME.

Death vanished.

The captain turned the wheel a bit, for the look of the thing. After all, he was still captain and this was still, in a way, a ship.

"Mr. Mate?"

The mate saluted.

"Sir!"

"Um. Where shall we go now?"

The mate scratched his head.

"Well, cap'n, I did hear as the heathen Klatch have got

this paradise place where there's drinking and singing and young women with bells on and . . . you know . . . regardless."

The mate looked hopefully at his captain.

"Regardless, eh?" said the captain thoughtfully.

"So I did hear."

The captain felt that he might be due some regardless.

"Any idea how you get there?"

"I think you get given instructions when you're alive," said the mate.

"Oh."

"And there're some barbarians up toward the Hub," said the mate, relishing the word, "who reckon they go to a big hall where there's all sorts to eat and drink."

"And women?"

"Bound to be."

The captain frowned. "It's a funny thing," he said, "but why is it that the heathens and the barbarians seem to have the best places to go when they die?"

"A bit of a poser, that," agreed the mate. "I s'pose it makes up for 'em . . . enjoying themselves all the time when they're alive, too?" He looked puzzled. Now that he was dead, the whole thing sounded suspicious.

"I suppose you've no idea of the way to that paradise either?" said the captain.

"Sorry, cap'n."

"No harm in searching, though."

The captain looked over the side. If you sailed for long enough, you were bound to strike a shore. And no harm in searching.

A movement caught his eye. He smiled. Good. A sign. Maybe it was all for the best, after all . . .

Accompanied by the ghosts of dolphins, the ghost of a ship sailed on . . .

* * *

Seagulls never ventured this far along the desert coast. Their niche was filled by the scalbie, a member of the crow family that the crow family would be the first to disown and never talked about in company. It seldom flew, but walked everywhere in a sort of lurching hop. Its distinctive call put listeners in mind of a malfunctioning digestive system. It looked like other birds looked *after* an oil slick. Nothing ate scalbies, except other scalbies. Scalbies ate things that made a vulture sick. Scalbies would *eat* vulture sick. Scalbies ate *everything*.

One of them, on this bright new morning, sidled across the flea-hopping sand, pecking aimlessly at things in case pebbles and bits of wood had become edible overnight. In the scalbie's experience, practically anything became edible if it was left for long enough. It came across a mound lying on the tideline, and gave it a tentative jab with its beak.

The mound groaned.

The scalbie backed away hurriedly and turned its attention to a small domed rock beside the mound. It was pretty certain this hadn't been there yesterday, either. It essayed an exploratory peck.

The rock extruded a head and said, "Bugger off, you evil sod."

The scalbie leapt backward and then made a kind of running jump, which was the nearest any scalbie ever bothered to come to actual flight, on to a pile of sun-bleached driftwood. Things were looking up. If this rock was alive, then eventually it would be dead.

The Great God Om staggered over to Brutha and butted him in the head with its shell until he groaned.

"Wake up, lad. Rise and shine. Huphuphup. All ashore who's going ashore."

Brutha opened an eye.

"Wha' happened?" he said.

"You're alive is what happened," said Om. Life's a beach, he remembered. And then you die.

Brutha pulled himself into a kneeling position.

There are beaches that cry out for brightly colored umbrellas.

There are beaches that speak of the majesty of the sea.

But this beach wasn't like that. It was merely a barren hem where the land met the ocean. Driftwood piled up on the high-tide line, scoured by the wind. The air buzzed with unpleasant small insects. There was a smell that suggested that something had rotted away, a long time ago, somewhere where the scalbies couldn't find it. It was not a good beach.

"Oh. God."

"Better than drowning," said Om encouragingly.

"I wouldn't know." Brutha looked along the beach. "Is there any water to drink?"

"Shouldn't think so," said Om.

"Ossory V, verse 3, says that you made living water flow from the dry desert," said Brutha.

"That was by way of being artistic license," said Om.

"You can't even do that?"

"No."

Brutha looked at the desert again. Behind the driftwood lines, and a few patches of grass that appeared to be dying even while it grew, the dunes marched away.

"Which way to Omnia?" he said.

"We don't want to go to Omnia," said Om.

Brutha stared at the tortoise. Then he picked him up.

"I think it's this way," he said.

Om's legs waggled frantically.

"What do you want to go to Omnia for?" he said.

"I don't want to," said Brutha. "But I'm going anyway."

The sun hung high above the beach.

Or possibly it didn't.

Brutha knew things about the sun now. They were leaking into his head. The Ephebians had been very interested in astronomy. Expletius had proved that the Disc was ten thousand miles across. Febrius, who'd stationed slaves with quick reactions and carrying voices all across the country at dawn, had proved that light traveled at about the same speed as sound. And Didactylos had reasoned that, in that case, in order to pass between the elephants, the sun had to travel at least thirty-five thousand miles in its orbit every day or, to put it another way, twice as fast as its own light. Which meant that mostly you could only ever see where the sun had been, except twice every day when it caught up with itself, and this meant that the whole sun was a faster-than-light particle, a tachyon or, as Didactylos put it, a bugger.

It was still hot. The lifeless sea seemed to steam.

Brutha trudged along, directly above the only piece of shadow for hundreds of miles. Even Om had stopped complaining. It was too hot.

Here and there fragments of wood rolled in the scum at the edge of the sea.

Ahead of Brutha the air shimmered over the sand. In the middle of it was a dark blob.

He regarded it dispassionately as he approached, incapable of any real thought. It was nothing more than a reference point in a world of orange heat, expanding and contracting in the vibrating haze.

Closer to, it turned out to be Vorbis.

The thought took a long time to seep through Brutha's mind.

Vorbis.

Not with a robe. All torn off. Just his singlet with. The nails sewn in. Blood all. Over one leg. Torn by. Rocks. Vorbis.

Vorbis.

Brutha slumped to his knees. On the high-tide line, a scalbie gave a croak.

"He's still . . . alive," Brutha managed.

"Pity," said Om.

"We should do something . . . for him."

"Yes? Maybe you can find a rock and stove his head in," said Om.

"We can't just leave him here."

"Watch us."

"No."

Brutha got his hand under the deacon and tried to lift him. To his dull surprise, Vorbis weighed almost nothing. The deacon's robe had concealed a body that was just skin stretched over bone. Brutha could have broken him with bare hands.

"What about me?" whined Om.

Brutha slung Vorbis over his shoulder.

"You've got four legs," he said.

"I am your God!"

"Yes. I know." Brutha trudged on along the beach.

"What are you going to *do* with him?"

"Take him to Omnia," said Brutha thickly. "People must know. What he did."

"You're mad! You're mad! You think you're going to *carry* him to Omnia?"

"Don't know. Going to try."

"You! You!" Om pounded a claw on the sand. "Millions of people in the world and it had to be *you!* Stupid! *Stupid!*"

Brutha was becoming a wavering shape in the haze.

"That's *it!*" shouted Om. "I don't need you! You think I need you? I don't need you! I can soon find another believer! No problem about that!"

Brutha disappeared.

"And I'm not chasing after you!" Om screamed.

Brutha watched his feet dragging one in front of the other.

He was past the point of thinking now. What drifted through his frying brain were disjointed images and fragments of memory.

Dreams. They were pictures in your head. Coaxes had written a whole scroll about them. The superstitious thought they were messages sent by God, but really they were created by the brain itself, thrown up as it nightly sorted and filed the experiences of the day. Brutha never dreamed. So sometimes . . . blackout, while the mind did the filing. It filed all the books. Now he knew without learning . . .

That was dreams.

God. God needed people. Belief was the food of the gods. But they also needed a shape. Gods became what people believed they ought to be. So the Goddess of Wisdom carried a penguin. It could have happened to any god. It should have been an owl. Everyone knew that. But one bad sculptor who had only ever had an owl described to him makes a mess of a statue, *belief* steps in, next thing you know the Goddess of Wisdom is lumbered with a bird that wears evening dress the whole time and smells of fish.

You gave a god its shape, like a jelly fills a mold.

Gods often became your father, said Abraxas the Agnostic. Gods became a big beard in the sky, because when you were three years old that *was* your father.

Of course Abraxas survived . . . This thought arrived sharp and cold, out of the part of his own mind that Brutha could still call his own. Gods didn't mind atheists, if they were deep, hot, fiery atheists like Simony, who spend their whole life not believing, spend their whole life hating gods for not existing. That sort of atheism was a rock. It was nearly belief . . .

Sand. It was what you found in deserts. Crystals of rock, sculpted into dunes. Gordo of Tsort said that sand was worn-down mountains *but* Irexes had found that sandstone was stone pressed out of sand, which suggested that grains were the *fathers* of mountains . . .

Every one a little crystal. And all of them getting bigger . . .

Much bigger . . .

Quietly, without realizing it, Brutha stopped falling forward and lay still.

"Bugger *off!*"

The scalbie took no notice. This was *interesting*. It was getting to see whole new stretches of sand it had never seen before and, of course, there was the prospect, even the certainty, of a good meal at the end of it all.

It had perched on Om's shell.

Om stumped along the sand, pausing occasionally to shout at his passenger.

Brutha had come this way.

But here one of the outcrops of rocks, littering the desert like islands in a sea, stretched right down to the water's edge. He'd never have been able to climb it.

The footprints in the sand turned inland, toward the deep desert.

"Idiot!"

Om struggled up the side of a dune, digging his feet in to stop himself slaloming backward.

On the far side of the dune the tracks became a long groove, where Brutha must have fallen. Om retracted his legs and tobogganed down it.

The tracks veered here. He must have thought that he could walk around the next dune and find the rock again on the other side. Om knew about deserts, and one of the things he knew was that this kind of logical thinking had been previously applied by a thousand bleached, lost skeletons.

Nevertheless, he plodded after the tracks, grateful for the brief shade of the dune now that the sun was sinking.

Around the dune and, yes, here they zigzagged awkwardly up a slope about ninety degrees away from where they should be heading. Guaranteed. That was the thing about deserts. They had their own gravity. They sucked you into the center.

Brutha crawled forward, Vorbis held unsteadily by one limp arm. He didn't dare stop. His grandmother would hit him again. And there was Master Nhumrod, too, drifting in and out of vision.

"I am really disappointed in you, Brutha. Mmm?"

"Want . . . water . . ."

"—water," said Nhumrod. "Trust in the great God."

Brutha concentrated. Nhumrod vanished.

"Great God?" he said.

Somewhere there was some shade. The desert couldn't go on forever.

* * *

The sun set fast. For a while, Om knew, heat would radiate off the sand and his own shell would store it, but that would soon go and then there would be the bitterness of a desert night.

Stars were already coming on when he found Brutha. Vorbis had been dropped a little way away.

Om pulled himself level with Brutha's ear.

"Hey!"

There was no sound, and no movement. Om butted Brutha gently in the head and then looked at the cracked lips.

There was a pecking noise behind him.

The scalbie was investigating Brutha's toes, but its explorations were interrupted when a tortoise jaw closed around its foot.

"I *old* oo, ugger *ogg!*"

The scalbie gave a burp of panic and tried to fly away, but it was hindered by a determined tortoise hanging on to one leg. Om was bounced along the sand for a few feet before he let go.

He tried to spit, but tortoise mouths aren't designed for the job.

"I hate all birds," he said, to the evening air.

The scalbie watched him reproachfully from the top of a dune. It ruffled its handful of greasy feathers with the air of one who was prepared to wait all night, if necessary. As long as it took.

Om crawled back to Brutha. Well, there was still breathing going on.

Water . . .

The god gave it some thought. Smiting the living rock. That was one way. Getting water to flow . . . no problem. It was just a matter of molecules and vectors. Water had a natural tendency to flow. You just have to see to it that it flowed *here* instead of *there*. No problem at all to a god in the peak of condition.

How did you tackle it from a tortoise perspective?

The tortoise dragged himself to the bottom of the dune and then walked up and down for a few minutes. Finally he selected a spot and began digging.

This wasn't right. It had been fiery hot. Now he was freezing.

Brutha opened his eyes. Desert stars, brilliant white, looked back at him. His tongue seemed to fill his mouth. Now, what was it . . .

Water.

He rolled over. There had been voices in his head, and now there were voices outside his head. They were faint, but they were definitely there, echoing quietly over the moonlit sands.

Brutha crawled painfully toward the foot of the dune. There was a mound there. In fact, there were several mounds. The muffled voice was coming from one of them. He pulled himself closer.

There was a hole in the mound. Somewhere far underground, someone was swearing. The words were unclear as they echoed backward and forward up the tunnel, but the general effect was unmistakable.

Brutha flopped down, and watched.

After a few minutes there was movement at the mouth of the hole and Om emerged, covered with what, if this wasn't a desert, Brutha would have called mud.

"Oh, it's you," said the tortoise. "Tear off a bit of your robe and pass it over."

Dreamlike, Brutha obeyed.

"Turnin' around down there," said Om, "is no picnic, let me tell you."

He took the rag in his jaws, backed around carefully, and disappeared down the hole. After a couple of minutes he was back, still dragging the rag.

It was soaked. Brutha let the liquid dribble into his mouth. It tasted of mud, and sand, and cheap brown dye, and slightly of tortoise, but he would have drunk a gallon of it. He could have swam in a pool of it.

He tore off another strip for Om to take down.

When Om re-emerged, Brutha was kneeling beside Vorbis.

"Sixteen feet down! Sixteen bloody feet!" shouted Om. "Don't waste it on him! Isn't he dead yet?"

"He's got a fever."

"Put him out of our misery."

"We're still taking him back to Omnia."

"You think *we'll* get there? No food? No water?"

"But you found water. Water in the desert."

"Nothing miraculous about that," said Om. "There's a rainy season near the coast. Flash floods. Wadis. Dried-up riverbeds. You get aquifers," he added.

"Sounds like a miracle to me," croaked Brutha. "Just because you can explain it doesn't mean it's not still a miracle."

"Well, there's no food down there, take it from me," said Om. "Nothing to eat. Nothing in the sea, *if* we can find the sea again. I *know* the desert. Rocky ridges you have to go around. Everything turning you out of your path. Dunes that move in the night . . . lions . . . other things . . ."

. . . *gods*.

"What do you want to do, then?" said Brutha. "You said better alive than dead. You want to go back to Ephebe? We'll be popular there, you think?"

Om was silent.

Brutha nodded.

"Fetch more water, then."

It was better traveling at night, with Vorbis over one shoulder and Om under one arm.

At this time of year—

—the glow in the sky over *there* is the Aurora Corealis, the hublights, where the magical field of the Discworld constantly discharges itself among the peaks of Cori Celesti, the central mountain. And at this time of year the sun rises over the desert in Ephebe and over the sea in Omnia, so keep the hublights on the left and the sunset glow behind you—

"Did you ever go to Cori Celesti?" said Brutha.

Om, who had been nodding off in the cold, woke up with a start.

"Huh?"

"It's where the gods live."

"Hah! I could tell you stories," said Om darkly.

"What?"

"Think they're so bloody elite!"

"You didn't live up there, then?"

"No. Got to be a thunder god or something. Got to have a whole parcel of worshipers to live on Nob Hill. Got to be an anthropomorphic personification, one of them things."

"Not just a Great God, then?"

Well, this was the desert. And Brutha was going to die.

"May as well tell you," muttered Om. "It's not as though we're going to survive . . . See, *every* god's a Great God to someone. I never wanted to be *that* great. A handful of tribes, a city or two. It's not much to ask, is it?"

"There's two million people in the empire," said Brutha.

"Yeah. Pretty good, eh? Started off with nothing but a shepherd hearing voices in his head, ended up with two million people."

"But you never *did* anything with them," said Brutha. "Like what?"

"Well . . . tell them not to kill one another, that sort of thing . . ."

"Never really given it much thought. Why should I tell them that?"

Brutha sought for something that would appeal to god psychology.

"Well, if people didn't kill one another, there'd be more people to believe in you?" he suggested.

"It's a point," Om conceded. "Interesting point. Sneaky."

Brutha walked along in silence. There was a glimmer of frost on the dunes.

"Have you ever heard," he said, "of Ethics?"

"Somewhere in Howondaland, isn't it?"

"The Ephebians were very interested in it."

"Probably thinking about invading."

"They seemed to think about it a lot."

"Long-term strategy, maybe."

"I don't think it's a place, though. It's more to do with how people live."

"What, lolling around all day while slaves do the real work? Take it from me, whenever you see a bunch of buggers puttering around talking about truth and beauty and the best way of attacking Ethics, you can bet your sandals it's because dozens of other poor buggers are doing all the real work around the place while those fellows are living like—"

"—gods?" said Brutha.

There was a terrible silence.

"I was going to say kings," said Om, reproachfully.

"They sound a bit like gods."

"Kings," said Om emphatically.

"Why do people need gods?" Brutha persisted.

"Oh, you've *got* to have gods," said Om, in a hearty, no-nonsense voice.

"But it's *gods* that need *people*," said Brutha. "To do the believing. You said."

Om hesitated. "Well, okay," he said. "But people have got to believe in something. Yes? I mean, why else does it thunder?"

"Thunder," said Brutha, his eyes glazing slightly, "I don't—"

"—is caused by clouds banging together; after the lightning stroke, there is a hole in the air, and thus the sound is engendered by the clouds rushing to fill the hole and colliding, in accordance with strict cumulodynamic principles."

"Your voice goes funny when you're quoting," said Om. "What does engendered mean?"

"I don't know. No one showed me a dictionary."

"Anyway, that's just an explanation," said Om. "It's not a *reason*."

"My grandmother said thunder was caused by the Great God Om taking his sandals off," said Brutha. "She was in a funny mood that day. Nearly smiled."

"*Metaphorically* accurate," said Om. "But I never did thundering. Demarcation, see. Bloody I've-got-a-big-hammer Blind Io up on Nob Hill does all the thundering."

"I thought you said there were hundreds of thunder gods," said Brutha.

"Yeah. And he's all of 'em. Rationalization. A couple of tribes join up, they've both got thunder gods, right?

And the gods kind of run together—you know how amoebas split?"

"No."

"Well, it's like that, only the other way."

"I still don't see how one god can be a hundred thunder gods. They all look different . . ."

"False noses."

"What?"

"And different voices. I happen to know Io's got seventy different hammers. Not common knowledge, that. And it's just the same with mother goddesses. There's only one of 'em. She just got a lot of wigs and of course it's amazing what you can do with a padded bra."

There was absolute silence in the desert. The stars, smeared slightly by high-altitude moisture, were tiny, motionless rosettes.

Away toward what the Church called the Top Pole, and which Brutha was coming to think of as the Hub, the sky flickered.

Brutha put Om down, and laid Vorbis on the sand.

Absolute silence.

Nothing for miles, except what he had brought with him. This must have been how the prophets felt, when they went into the desert to find . . . whatever it was they found, and talk to . . . whoever they talked to.

He heard Om, slightly peevish, say: "People've got to believe in something. Might as well be gods. What else is there?"

Brutha laughed.

"You know," he said, "I don't think I believe in anything any more."

"Except me!"

"Oh, I *know* you exist," said Brutha. He felt Om relax a little. "There's something about tortoises. Tortoises I can believe in. They seem to have a lot of existence in one place. It's gods in general I'm having difficulty with."

"Look, if people stop believing in gods, they'll believe in anything," said Om. "They'll believe in young Urn's steam ball. Anything at all."

"Hmm."

A green glow in the sky indicated that the light of dawn was chasing frantically after its sun.

Vorbis groaned.

"I don't know why he won't wake up," said Brutha. "I can't find any broken bones."

"How do you know?"

"One of the Ephebian scrolls was all about bones. Can't you do anything for him?"

"Why?"

"You're a god."

"Well, yes. If I was strong enough, I could probably strike him with lightning."

"I thought Io did the lightning."

"No, just the thunder. You're allowed to do as much lightning as you like but you have to contract for the thundering."

Now the horizon was a broad golden band.

"How about rain?" said Brutha. "How about something *useful*?"

A line of silver appeared at the bottom of the gold. Sunlight was racing towards Brutha.

"That was a very hurtful remark," said the tortoise. "A remark calculated to wound."

In the rapidly growing light Brutha saw one of the rock islands a little way off. Its sand-blasted pillars offered nothing but shade, but shade, always available in large quantities in the depths of the Citadel, was now in short supply here.

"Caves?" said Brutha.

"Snakes."

"But still caves?"

"In conjunction with snakes."

"Poisonous snakes?"

"Guess."

The *Unnamed Boat* clipped along gently, the wind filling Urn's robe attached to a mast made out of bits of the sphere's framework bound together with Simony's sandal thongs.

"I think I know what went wrong," said Urn. "A mere overspeed problem."

"Overspeed? We left the water!" said Simony.

"It needs some sort of governor device," said Urn, scratching a design on the side of the boat. "Something that'd open the valve if there was too much steam. I think I could do something with a pair of revolving balls."

"It's funny you should say that," said Didactylos. "When I felt us leave the water and the sphere exploded I distinctly felt my—"

"That bloody thing nearly killed us!" said Simony.

"So the next one will be better," said Urn, cheerfully. He scanned the distant coastline.

"Why don't we land somewhere along here?" he said.

"The desert coast?" said Simony. "What for? Nothing to eat, nothing to drink, easy to lose your way. Omnia's the only destination in this wind. We can land this side of the city. I know people. And those people know people. All across Omnia, there's people who know people. People who believe in the Turtle."

"You know, I never meant for people to *believe* in the Turtle," said Didactylos unhappily. "It's just a big turtle. It just exists. Things just happen that way. I don't think the Turtle gives a damn. I just thought it might be a good idea to write things down and explain things a bit."

"People sat up all night, on guard, while other people made copies," said Simony, ignoring him. "Passing them from hand to hand! Everyone making a copy and passing it on! Like a fire spreading underground!"

"Would this be *lots* of copies?" said Didactylos cautiously.

"Hundreds! Thousands!"

"I suppose it's too late to ask for, say, a five percent royalty?" said Didactylos, looking hopeful for a moment. "No. Probably out of the question, I expect. No. Forget I even asked."

A few flying fish zipped out of the waves, pursued by a dolphin.

"Can't help feeling a bit sorry for that young Brutha," said Didactylos.

"Priests are expendable," said Simony. "There's too many of them."

"He had all our books," said Urn.

"He'll probably float with all that knowledge in him," said Didactylos.

"He was mad, anyway," said Simony. "I saw him whispering to that tortoise."

"I wish we still had it. There's good eating on one of those things," said Didactylos.

It wasn't much of a cave, just a deep hollow carved by the endless desert winds and, a long time ago, even by water. But it was enough.

Brutha knelt on the stony floor and raised the rock over his head.

There was a buzzing in his ears and his eyeballs felt as though they were set in sand. No water since sunset and no food for a hundred years. He had to do it.

"I'm sorry," he said, and brought the rock down.

The snake had been watching him intently but in its early-morning torpor it was too slow to dodge. The cracking noise was a sound that Brutha knew his conscience would replay to him, over and over again.

"Good," said Om, beside him. "Now skin it, and don't waste the juice. Save the skin, too."

"I didn't want to do it," said Brutha.

"Look at it this way," said Om, "if you'd walked in the cave without me to warn you, you'd be lying on the floor now with a foot the size of a wardrobe. Do unto others before they do unto you."

"It's not even a very big snake," said Brutha.

"And then while you're writhing there in indescribable agony, you imagine all the things you would have done to that damn snake if you'd got to it first," said Om. "Well, your wish has been granted. Don't give any to Vorbis," he added.

"He's running a bad fever. He keeps muttering."

"Do you really think you'll get him back to the Citadel and they'll believe you?" said Om.

"Brother Nhumrod always said I was very truthful," said Brutha. He smashed the rock on the cave wall to create a crude cutting edge, and gingerly started dismembering the snake. "Anyway, there isn't anything else I can do. I couldn't just leave him."

"Yes you could," said Om.

"To die in the desert?"

"Yes. It's easy. Much easier than *not* leaving him to die in the desert."

"No."

"This is how they do things in Ethics, is it?" said Om sarcastically.

"I don't know. It's how I'm doing it."

The *Unnamed Boat* bobbed in a gully between the rocks. There was a low cliff beyond the beach. Simony climbed back down it, to where the philosophers were huddling out of the wind.

"I know this area," he said. "We're a few miles from the village where a friend lives. All we have to do is wait till nightfall."

"Why're you doing all this?" said Urn. "I mean, what's the point?"

"Have you ever heard of a country called Istanzia?" said Simony. "It wasn't very big. It had nothing anyone wanted. It was just a place for people to live."

"Omnia conquered it fifteen years ago," said Didactylos.

"That's right. My country," said Simony. "I was just a kid then. But I won't forget. Nor will others. There's lots of people with a reason to hate the Church."

"I saw you standing close to Vorbis," said Urn. "*I* thought you were protecting him."

"Oh, I was, I was," said Simony. "I don't want anyone to kill him before I do."

Didactylos wrapped his toga around himself and shivered.

The sun was riveted to the copper dome of the sky. Brutha dozed in the cave. In his own corner, Vorbis tossed and turned.

Om sat waiting in the cave mouth.

Waited expectantly.

Waited in dread.

And *they* came.

They came out from under scraps of stone, and from cracks in the rock. They fountained up from the sand, they distilled out of the wavering sky. The air was filled with their voices, as faint as the whispering of gnats.

Om tensed.

The language he spoke was not like the language of the high gods. It was hardly language at all. It was a mere modulation of desires and hungers, without nouns and with only a few verbs.

. . . Want . . .

Om replied, *mine*.

There were thousands of them. He was stronger, yes, he had a believer, but they filled the sky like locusts. The longing poured down on him with the weight of hot lead. The only advantage, the *only* advantage, was that the small gods had no concept of working together. That was a luxury that came with evolution.

. . . Want . . .   •

Mine!

The chittering became a whine.

But you can have the other one, said Om.

. . . Dull, hard, enclosed, shut-in . . .

I know, said Om. But this one, *mine!*

The psychic shout echoed around the desert. The small gods fled.

Except for one.

Om was aware that it had not been swarming with the others, but had been hovering gently over a piece of sun-bleached bone. It had said nothing.

He turned his attention on it.

You. *Mine!*

I know, said the small god. It knew speech, real god speech, although it talked as though every word had been winched from the pit of memory.

Who are you? said Om.

The small god stirred.

There was a city once, said the small god. Not just a city. An empire of cities. I, I, I remember there were canals, and gardens. There was a lake. They had floating gardens on the lake, I recall. I, I. And there were temples. Such temples as you may dream of. Great pyramid temples that reached to the sky. Thousands were sacrificed. To the greater glory.

Om felt sick. This wasn't just a small god. This was a small god who hadn't always been small . . .

Who were you?

And there were temples. I, I, me. Such temples as you may dream of. Great pyramid temples that reached to the sky. The glory of. Thousands were sacrificed. Me. To the greater glory.

And there were temples. Me, me, me. Greater glory. Such glory temples as you may dream of. Great pyramid dream temples that reached to the sky. Me, me. Sacrificed. Dream. Thousands were sacrificed. To me the greater sky glory.

You were their God? Om managed.

Thousands were sacrificed. To the greater glory.

Can you hear me?

Thousands sacrificed greater glory. Me, me, me.

What was your name? shouted Om.

Name?

A hot wind blew over the desert, shifting a few grains of sand. The echo of a lost god blew away, tumbling over and over, until it vanished among the rocks.

Who were you?

There was no answer.

That's what happens, Om thought. Being a small god was bad, except at the time you hardly knew that it was bad because you only barely knew anything at all, but all the time there was something which was just possibly the germ of hope, the knowledge and belief that one day you might be more than you were now.

But how much worse to have *been* a god, and to now be no more than a smoky bundle of memories, blown back and forth across the sand made from the crumbled stones of your temples . . .

Om turned around and, on stumpy legs, walked purposefully back into the cave until he came to Brutha's head, which he butted.

"Wst?"

"Just checking you're still alive."

"Fgfl."

"Right."

Om staggered back to his guard position at the mouth of the cave.

There were said to be oases in the desert, but they were never in the same place twice. The desert wasn't mappable. It ate map-makers.

So did the lions. Om could remember them. Scrawny things, not like the lions of the Howondaland veldt. More wolf than lion, more hyena than either. Not brave, but with a kind of vicious, rangy cowardice that was much more dangerous . . .

Lions.

Oh, dear . . .

He had to find lions.

Lions drank.

* * *

Brutha awoke as the afternoon light dragged across the desert. His mouth tasted of snake.

Om was butting him on the foot.

"Come on, come on, you're missing the best of the day."

"Is there any water?" Brutha murmured thickly.

"There will be. Only five miles off. Amazing luck."

Brutha pulled himself up. Every muscle ached.

"How do you know?"

"I can sense it. I *am* a god, you know."

"You said you could only sense minds."

Om cursed. Brutha didn't forget things.

"It's more complicated than that," lied Om. "Trust me. Come on, while there's some twilight. And don't forget Mister Vorbis."

Vorbis was curled up. He looked at Brutha with unfocused eyes, stood up like a man still asleep when Brutha helped him.

"I think he might have been poisoned," said Brutha. "There's sea creatures with stings. And poisonous corals. He keeps moving his lips, but I can't make out what he's trying to say."

"Bring him along," said Om. "Bring him along. Oh, yes."

"You wanted me to abandon him last night," said Brutha.

"Did I?" said Om, his very shell radiating innocence. "Well, maybe I've been to Ethics. Had a change of heart. I can see he's with us for a purpose now. Good old Vorbis. Bring him along."

Simony and the two philosophers stood on the clifftop, looking across the parched farmlands of Omnia to the distant rock of the Citadel. Two of them looking, anyway.

"Give *me* a lever and a place to stand, and I'd smash that place like an egg," said Simony, leading Didactylos down the narrow path.

"Looks big," said Urn.

"See the gleam? Those are the doors."

"Look massive."

"I was wondering," said Simony, "about the boat. The way it moved. Something like that could smash the doors, right?"

"You'd have to flood the valley," said Urn.

"I mean if it was on wheels."

"Hah, yes," said Urn, sarcastically. It had been a long day. "Yes, if I had a forge and half a dozen blacksmiths and a lot of help. Wheels? No problem. But—"

"We shall have to see," said Simony, "what we can do."

The sun was on the horizon when Brutha, his arm around Vorbis's shoulders, reached the next rock island. It was bigger than the one with the snake. The wind had carved the stones into gaunt, unlikely shapes, like fingers. There were even plants lodging in crevices in the rock.

"There's water somewhere," said Brutha.

"There's always water, even in the worst deserts," said Om. "One, oh, maybe two inches of rain a year."

"I can smell something," said Brutha, as his feet stopped treading on sand and crunched up the limestone scree around the boulders. "Something rank."

"Hold me over your head."

Om scanned the rocks.

"Right. Now bring me down again. And head for

that rock that looks like . . . that looks very unexpected, really."

Brutha stared. "It does, too," he croaked, eventually. "Amazing to think it was carved by the wind."

"The wind god has a sense of humor," said Om. "Although it's pretty basic."

Near the foot of the rock huge slabs had fallen over the years, forming a jagged pile with, here and there, shadowy openings.

"That smell—" Brutha began.

"Probably animals come to drink the water," said Om.

Brutha's foot kicked against something yellow-white, which bounced away among the rocks making a noise like a sackful of coconuts. In the stifling empty silence of the desert, it echoed loudly.

"What was that?"

"Definitely not a skull," lied Om. "Don't worry . . ."

"There's bones everywhere!"

"Well? What did you expect? This is a desert! People die here! It's a very popular occupation in this vicinity!"

Brutha picked up a bone. He was, as he well knew, stupid. But people didn't gnaw their own bones after they died.

"Om—"

"There's water here!" shouted Om. "We need it! But—there's probably one or two drawbacks!"

"What kind of drawbacks?"

"As in natural hazards!"

"Like—?"

"Well, you know lions?" said Om desperately.

"There's lions here?"

"Well . . . slightly."

"*Slightly* lions?"

"Only one lion."

"Only one—"

"—generally a solitary creature. Most to be feared are the old males, who are forced into the most inhospitable regions by their younger rivals. They are evil-tempered and cunning and in their extremity have lost all fear of man—"

The memory faded, letting go of Brutha's vocal cords.

"That kind?" Brutha finished.

"It won't take any notice of us once it's fed," said Om.

"Yes?"

"They go to sleep."

"After feeding—?"

Brutha looked around at Vorbis, who was slumped against a rock.

"Feeding?" he repeated.

"It'll be a kindness," said Om.

"To the lion, yes! You want to use him as *bait*?"

"He's not going to survive the desert. Anyway, he's done much worse to thousands of people. He'll be dying for a good cause."

"A good cause?"

"*I* like it."

There was a growl, from somewhere in the stones. It wasn't loud, but it was a sound with sinews in it. Brutha backed away.

"We don't just throw people to the lions!"

"He does."

"Yes. I don't."

"All right, we'll get on top of a slab and when the lion starts on him you can brain it with a rock. He'll probably get away with an arm or a leg. He'll never miss it."

"No! You can't do that to people just because they're helpless!"

"You know, I can't think of a better time?"

There was another growl from the rock pile. It sounded closer.

Brutha looked down desperately at the scattered bones. Among them, half-hidden by debris, was a sword. It was old, and not well-made, and scoured by sand. He picked it up gingerly by the blade.

"Other end," said Om.

"I know!"

"Can you use one?"

"I don't know!"

"I really hope you're a fast learner."

The lion emerged, slowly.

Desert lions, it has been said, are not like the lions of the veldt. They had been, when the great desert had been verdant woodland.* Then there had been time to lie around for most of the day, looking majestic, in between regular meals of goat.** But the woodland had become scrubland, the scrubland had become, well, poorer scrubland, and the goats and the people and, eventually, even the cities, went away.

The lions stayed. There's always something to eat, if you're hungry enough. People still had to cross the desert. There were lizards. There were snakes. It wasn't much of an ecological niche, but the lions were hanging on to it like grim death, which was what happened to most people who met a desert lion.

Someone had already met this one.

Its mane was matted. Ancient scars criss-crossed its

---

*i.e., before the inhabitants had let goats graze everywhere. Nothing makes a desert like a goat.

**But not enough.

pelt. It dragged itself towards Brutha, back legs trailing uselessly.

"It's hurt," said Brutha.

"Oh, good. And there's plenty of eating on one of those," said Om. "A bit stringy, but—"

The lion collapsed, its toast-rack chest heaving. A spear was protruding from its flank. Flies, which can always find something to eat in any desert, flew up in a swarm.

Brutha put down the sword. Om stuck his head in his shell.

"Oh no," he murmured. "Twenty *million* people in this world, and the only one who believes in me is a suicide—"

"We can't just leave it," said Brutha.

"We *can*. We *can*. It's a *lion*. You leave lions *alone*."

Brutha knelt down. The lion opened one crusted yellow eye, too weak even to bite him.

"You're going to die, you're going to *die*. I'm not going to find *anyone* to believe in me out here—"

Brutha's knowledge of animal anatomy was rudimentary. Although some of the inquisitors had an enviable knowledge of the insides of the human body that is denied to all those who are not allowed to open it while it's still working, medicine as such was frowned upon in Omnia. But somewhere, in every village, was someone who officially *didn't* set bones and who *didn't* know a few things about certain plants, and who stayed out of reach of the Quisition because of the fragile gratitude of their patients. And every peasant picked up a smattering of knowledge. Acute toothache can burn through all but the strongest in faith.

Brutha grasped the spear-haft. The lion growled as he moved it.

"Can't you speak to it?" said Brutha.

"It's an *animal*."

"So are you. You could try to calm it down. Because if it gets excited—"

Om snapped into concentration.

In fact the lion's mind contained nothing but pain, a spreading nebula of the stuff, overcoming even the normal background hunger. Om tried to encircle the pain, make it flow away . . . and not to think about what would happen if it went. By the feel of things, the lion had not eaten for days.

The lion grunted as Brutha withdrew the spearhead.

"Omnian," he said. "It hasn't been there long. It must have met the soldiers when they were on the way to Ephebe. They must have passed close by." He tore another strip from his robe, and tried to clean the wound.

"We want to *eat* it, not cure it!" shouted Om. "What're you thinking of? You think it's going to be grateful?"

"It wanted to be helped."

"And soon it will want to be fed, have you thought about that?"

"It's looking pathetically at me."

"Probably never seen a week's meals all walking around on one pair of legs before."

That wasn't true, Om reflected. Brutha was shedding weight like an ice-cube, out here in the desert. That kept him alive! The boy was a two-legged camel.

Brutha crunched towards the rock pile, shards and bones shifting under his feet. The boulders formed a maze of half-open tunnels and caves. By the smell, the lion had lived there for a long time, and had quite often been ill.

He stared at the nearest cave for some time.

"What's so fascinating about a lion's den?" said Om.

"The way it's got steps down into it, I think," said Brutha.

Didactylos could *feel* the crowd. It filled the barn.

"How many are there?" he said.

"Hundreds!" said Urn. "They're even sitting on the rafters! And . . . master?"

"Yes?"

"There's even one or two priests! And dozens of soldiers!"

"Don't worry," said Simony, joining them on the makeshift platform made of fig barrels. "They are Turtle believers, just like you. We have friends in unexpected places!"

"But I *don't*—" Didactylos began, helplessly.

"There isn't anyone here who doesn't hate the Church with all their soul," said Simony.

"But that's not—"

"They're just waiting for someone to lead them!"

"But I never—"

"I know you won't let us down. You're a man of reason. Urn, come over here. There's a blacksmith I want you to meet—"

Didactylos turned his face to the crowd. He could feel the hot, hushed silence of their stares.

Each drop took minutes.

It was hypnotic. Brutha found himself staring at each developing drip. It was almost impossible to see it grow, but they had been growing and dripping for thousands of years.

"How?" said Om.

"Water seeps down after the rains," said Brutha. "It lodges in the rocks. Don't gods know these things?"

"We don't need to." Om looked around. "Let's go. I hate this place."

"It's just an old temple. There's nothing here."

"That's what I mean."

Sand and rubble half-filled it. Light lanced in through the broken roof high above, on to the slope that they had climbed down. Brutha wondered how many of the wind-carved rocks in the desert had once been buildings. This one must have been huge, perhaps a mighty tower. And then the desert had come.

There were no whispering voices here. Even the small gods kept away from abandoned temples, for the same reason that people kept away from graveyards. The only sound was the occasional plink of the water.

It dripped into a shallow pool in front of what looked like an altar. From the pool it had worn a groove in the slabs of the floor all the way to a round pit, which appeared to be bottomless. There were a few statues, all of them toppled; they were heavy-proportioned, lacking any kind of detail, each one a child's clay model chiseled in granite. The distant walls had once been covered with some kind of bas-relief, but it had crumbled away except in a few places, which showed strange designs that mainly consisted of tentacles.

"Who were the people who lived here?" said Brutha.

"I don't know."

"What god did they worship?"

"I don't know."

"The statues are made of granite, but there's no granite near here."

"They were very devout, then. They dragged it all the way."

"And the altar block is covered in grooves."

"Ah. *Extremely* devout. That would be to let the blood run off."

"You really think they did human sacrifice?"

"I don't know! I want to get out of here!"

"Why? There's water and it's cool—"

"Because . . . a god lived here. A powerful god. Thousands worshiped it. I can feel it. You know? It comes out of the walls. A Great God. Mighty were his dominions and magnificent was his word. Armies went forth in his name and conquered and slew. That kind of thing. And now no one, not you, not me, no one, even knows who the god was or his name or what he looked like. Lions drink in the holy places and those little squidgy things with eight legs, there's one by your foot, what d'you call 'em, the ones with the antennae, crawl beneath the altar. Now do you understand?"

"No," said Brutha.

"Don't you fear death? You're a human!"

Brutha considered this. A few feet away. Vorbis stared mutely at the patch of sky.

"He's awake. He's just not speaking."

"Who cares? I didn't ask you about him."

"Well . . . sometimes . . . when I'm on catacomb duty . . . it's the kind of place where you can't help . . . I mean, all the skulls and things . . . and the Book says . . ."

"There you are," said Om, a note of bitter triumph in his voice. "You don't *know*. That's what stops everyone going mad, the uncertainty of it, the feeling that it might work out all right after all. But it's different for gods. We *do* know. You know that story about the sparrow flying through a room?"

"No."

"Everyone knows it."

"Not me."

"About life being like a sparrow flying through a room? Nothing but darkness outside? And it flies through the room and there's just a moment of warmth and light?"

"There are windows open?" said Brutha.

"Can't you imagine what it's like to *be* that sparrow, and know about the darkness? To know that afterward there'll be nothing to remember, ever, except that one moment of the light?"

"No."

"No. Of course you can't. But that's what it's like, being a god. And this place . . . it's a morgue."

Brutha looked around at the ancient, shadowy temple.

"Well . . . do you know what it's like, being human?"

Om's head darted into his shell for a moment, the nearest he was capable of to a shrug.

"Compared to a god? Easy. Get born. Obey a few rules. Do what you're told. Die. Forget."

Brutha stared at him.

"Is something wrong?"

Brutha shook his head. Then he stood up and walked over to Vorbis.

The deacon had drunk water from Brutha's cupped hands. But there was a switched-off quality about him. He walked, he drank, he breathed. Or something did. His body did. The dark eyes opened, but appeared to be looking at nothing that Brutha could see. There was no sense that anyone was looking out through them. Brutha was certain that if he walked away, Vorbis would sit on the cracked flagstones until he very gently fell over. Vorbis' body was present, but the whereabouts of his mind was probably not locatable on any normal atlas.

It was just that, here and now and suddenly, Brutha felt so alone that even Vorbis was good company.

"Why do you bother with him? He's had thousands of people killed!"

"Yes, but perhaps he thought you wanted it."

"I never said I wanted that."

"You didn't care," said Brutha.

"But I—"

"Shut up!"

Om's mouth opened in astonishment.

"You could have helped people," said Brutha. "But all you did was stamp around and roar and try to make people afraid. Like . . . like a man hitting a donkey with a stick. But people like Vorbis made the stick so good, that's all the donkey ends up believing in."

"That could use some work, as a parable," said Om sourly.

"This is real life I'm talking about!"

"It's not my fault if people misuse the—"

"It is! It has to be! If you muck up people's minds just because you want them to believe in you, what they do is all your fault!"

Brutha glared at the tortoise, and then stamped off toward the pile of rubble that dominated one end of the ruined temple. He rummaged around in it.

"What are you looking for?"

"We'll need to carry water," said Brutha.

"There won't be anything," said Om. "People just left. The land ran out and so did the people. They took everything with them. Why bother to look?"

Brutha ignored him. There was something under the rocks and sand.

"Why worry about Vorbis?" Om whined. "In a hundred years' time, he'll be dead anyway. We'll all be dead."

Brutha tugged at the piece of curved pottery. It came away, and turned out to be about two-thirds of a wide bowl, broken right across. It had been almost as wide as Brutha's outstretched arms, but had been too broken for anyone to loot.

It was useful for nothing. But it had once been useful for something. There were embossed figures around its rim. Brutha peered at them, for want of something to distract himself, while Om's voice droned on in his head.

The figures looked more or less human. And they were engaged in religion. You could tell by the knives (it's not murder if you do it for a god). In the center of the bowl was a larger figure, obviously important, some kind of god they were doing it for . . .

"What?" he said.

"I *said*, in a hundred years' time we'll all be dead."

Brutha stared at the figures around the bowl. No one knew who their god was, and they were gone. Lions slept in the holy places and—

—*Chilopoda aridius*, the common desert centipede, his memory resident library supplied—

—scuttled beneath the altar.

"Yes," said Brutha. "We will." He raised the bowl over his head, and turned.

Om ducked into his shell.

"But here—" Brutha gritted his teeth as he staggered under the weight. "And now—"

He threw the bowl. It landed against the altar. Fragments of ancient pottery fountained up, and clattered down again. The echoes boomed around the temple.

"—we are alive!"

He picked up Om, who had withdrawn completely into his shell.

"And we'll make it home. All of us," he said. "I know it."

"It's written, is it?" said Om, his voice muffled.

"It is *said*. And if you argue—a tortoise shell is a pretty good water container, I expect."

"You wouldn't."

"Who knows? I might. In a hundred years' time we'll all be dead, you said."

"Yes! Yes!" said Om desperately. "But here and now—"

"Right."

Didactylos smiled. It wasn't something that came easily to him. It wasn't that he was a somber man, but he could not see the smiles of others. It took several dozen muscle movements to smile, and there was no return on his investment.

He'd spoken many times to crowds in Ephebe, but they were invariably made up of other philosophers, whose shouts of "Bloody daft!," "You're making it up as you go along!" and other contributions to the debate always put him at his ease. That was because no one really paid any attention. They were just working out what *they* were going to say next.

But this crowd put him in mind of Brutha. Their listening was like a huge pit waiting for his words to fill it. The trouble was that he was talking in philosophy, but they were listening in gibberish.

"You *can't* believe in Great A'Tuin," he said. "Great A'Tuin *exists*. There's no point in believing in things that exist."

"Someone's put up their hand," said Urn.

"Yes?"

"Sir, surely only things that exist are worth believing in?" said the enquirer, who was wearing a uniform of a sergeant of the Holy Guard.

"If they exist, you don't have to believe in them," said Didactylos. "They just are." He sighed. "What can I tell you? What do you want to hear? I just wrote down what people know. Mountains rise and fall, and under them the Turtle swims onward. Men live and die, and the Turtle Moves. Empires grow and crumble, and the Turtle Moves. Gods come and go, and still the Turtle Moves. The Turtle *Moves*."

From the darkness came a voice, "And that is really true?"

Didactylos shrugged. "The Turtle *exists*. The world is a flat disc. The sun turns around it once every day, dragging its light behind it. And this will go on happening, whether you believe it is true or not. It is real. I don't know about truth. Truth is a lot more complicated than that. I don't think the Turtle gives a bugger whether it's true or not, to tell you the truth."

Simony pulled Urn to one side as the philosopher went on talking.

"This isn't what they came to hear! Can't you do anything?"

"Sorry?" said Urn.

"They don't want philosophy. They want a reason to move against the Church! Now! Vorbis is dead, the Cenobiarch is gaga, the hierarchy are busy stabbing one another in the back. The Citadel is like a big rotten plum."

"Still a few wasps in it, though," said Urn. "You said you've only got a tenth of the army."

"But they're free men," said Simony. "Free in their heads. They'll be fighting for more than fifty cents a day."

Urn looked down at his hands. He often did that when he was uncertain about anything, as if they were the only things he was sure of in all the world.

"They'll get the odds down to three to one before the rest know what's happening," said Simony grimly. "Did you talk to the blacksmith?"

"Yes."

"Can you do it?"

"I . . . think so. It wasn't what I . . ."

"They tortured his father. Just for having a horseshoe hanging up in his forge, when everyone knows that smiths have to have their little rituals. And they took his son off into the army. But he's got a lot of helpers. They'll work through the night. All you have to do is tell them what you want."

"I've made some sketches . . ."

"Good," said Simony. "*Listen*, Urn. The Church is run by people like Vorbis. That's how it all works. Millions of people have died for—for nothing but lies. We can stop all that—"

Didactylos had stopped talking.

"He's muffed it," said Simony. "He could have done *anything* with them. And he just told them a lot of facts. You can't inspire people with facts. They need a cause. They need a symbol."

They left the temple just before sundown. The lion had crawled into the shade of some rocks, but stood up unsteadily to watch them go.

"It'll track us," moaned Om. "They do that. For miles and miles."

"We'll survive."

"I wish I had your confidence."

"Ah, but I have a God to have faith in."

"There'll be no more ruined temples."

"There'll be something else."

"And not even snake to eat."

"But I walk with my God."

"Not as a snack, though. *And* you're walking the wrong way, too."

"No. I'm still heading away from the coast."

"That's what I mean."

"How far can a lion go with a spear wound like that in him?"

"What's that got to do with anything?"

"Everything."

And, half an hour later, a black shadowy line on the silver moonlit desert, there were the tracks.

"The soldiers came this way. We just have to follow the tracks back. If we head where they've come from, we'll get where we're going."

"We'll never do it!"

"We're traveling light."

"Oh, yeah. They were burdened by all the food and water they had to carry," said Om bitterly. "How lucky for us we haven't got any."

Brutha glanced at Vorbis. He was walking unaided now, provided that you gently turned him around whenever you needed to change direction.

But even Om had to admit that the tracks were some comfort. In a way they were alive, in the same way that an echo is alive. People had been this way, not long ago. There were other people in the world. Someone, somewhere, was surviving.

Or not. After an hour or so they came across a mound

beside the track. There was a helmet atop it, and a sword stuck in the sand.

"A lot of soldiers died to get here quickly," said Brutha.

Whoever had taken enough time to bury their dead had also drawn a symbol in the sand of the mound. Brutha half-expected it to be a turtle, but the desert wind had not quite eroded the crude shape of a pair of horns.

"I don't understand that," said Om. "They don't *really* believe I exist, but they go and put something like that on a grave."

"It's hard to explain. I think it's because they believe *they* exist," said Brutha. "It's because they're people, and so was he."

He pulled the sword out of the sand.

"What do you want that for?"

"Might be useful."

"Against who?"

"Might be useful."

An hour later the lion, who was limping after Brutha, also arrived at the grave. It had lived in the desert for sixteen years, and the reason it had lived so long was that it had not died, and it had not died because it never wasted handy protein. It dug.

Humans have always wasted handy protein ever since they started wondering who had lived in it.

But, on the whole, there are worse places to be buried than inside a lion.

There were snakes and lizards on the rock islands. They were probably very nourishing and every one was, in its own way, a taste explosion.

There was no more water.

But there were plants . . . more or less. They looked

like groups of stones, except where a few had put up a central flower spike that was a brilliant pink and purple in the dawn light.

"Where do they get the water from?"

"Fossil seas."

"Water that's turned to stone?"

"No. Water that sank down thousands of years ago. Right down in the bedrock."

"Can you dig down to it?"

"Don't be stupid."

Brutha glanced from the flower to the nearest rock island.

"Honey," he said.

"What?"

The bees had a nest high on the side of a spire of rock. The buzzing could be heard from ground level. There was no possible way up.

"Nice try," said Om.

The sun was up. Already the rocks were warm to the touch. "Get some rest," said Om, kindly. "I'll keep watch."

"Watch for what?"

"I'll watch and find out."

Brutha led Vorbis into the shade of a large boulder, and gently pushed him down. Then he lay down too.

The thirst wasn't too bad yet. He'd drunk from the temple pool until he squelched as he walked. Later on, they might find a snake . . . When you considered what some people in the world had, life wasn't too bad.

Vorbis lay on his side, his black-on-black eyes staring at nothing.

Brutha tried to sleep.

He had never dreamed. Didactylos had been quite excited about that. Someone who remembered everything and didn't dream would have to think slowly, he said. Imagine a heart,* he said, that was nearly all memory, and had hardly any beats to spare for the everyday purposes of thinking. That would explain why Brutha moved his lips while he thought.

So this couldn't have been a dream. It must have been the sun.

He heard Om's voice in his head. The tortoise sounded as though he was holding a conversation with people Brutha could not hear.

Mine!

Go away!

No.

Mine!

Both of them!

Mine!

Brutha turned his head.

The tortoise was in a gap between two rocks, neck extended and weaving from side to side. There was another sound, a sort of gnat-like whining, that came and went . . . and promises in his head.

They flashed past . . . faces talking to him, shapes, visions of greatness, moments of opportunity, picking him up, taking him high above the world, all this was his, he could do anything, all he had to do was believe, in *me*, in *me*, in *me*—

An image formed in front of him. There, on a stone beside him, was a roast pig surrounded by fruit, and a

---

*Like many early thinkers, the Ephebians believed that thoughts originated in the heart and that the brain was merely a device to cool the blood.

mug of beer so cold the air was frosting on the sides.

Mine!

Brutha blinked. The voices faded. So did the food.

He blinked again.

There were strange after-images, not seen but felt. Perfect though his memory was, he could not remember what the voices had said or what the other pictures had been. All that lingered was a memory of roast pork and cold beer.

"That's because they don't know what to offer you," said Om's voice, quietly. "So they try to offer you anything. Generally they start with visions of food and carnal gratification."

"They got as far as the food," said Brutha.

"Good job I overcame them, then," said Om. "No telling what they might have achieved with a young man like yourself."

Brutha raised himself on his elbows.

Vorbis had not moved.

"Were they trying to get through to him, too?"

"I suppose so. Wouldn't work. Nothing gets in, nothing gets out. Never seen a mind so turned in on itself."

"Will they be back?"

"Oh, yes. It's not as if they've got anything else to do."

"When they do," said Brutha, feeling lightheaded, "could you wait until they've shown me visions of carnal gratification?"

"Very bad for you."

"Brother Nhumrod was very down on them. But I think perhaps we should know our enemies, yes?"

Brutha's voice faded to a croak.

"I could have done with the vision of the drink," he said, wearily.

The shadows were long. He looked around in amazement.

"How long were they trying?"

"All day. Persistent devils, too. Thick as flies."

Brutha learned why at sunset.

He met St. Ungulant the anchorite, friend of all small gods. Everywhere.

"Well, well, well," said St. Ungulant. "We don't get very many visitors up here. Isn't that so, Angus?"

He addressed the air beside him.

Brutha was trying to keep his balance, because the cartwheel rocked dangerously every time he moved. They'd left Vorbis seated on the desert twenty feet below, hugging his knees and staring at nothing.

The wheel had been nailed flat on top of a slim pole. It was just wide enough for one person to lie uncomfortably. But St. Ungulant looked designed to lie uncomfortably. He was so thin that even skeletons would say, "Isn't he thin?" He was wearing some sort of minimalist loin-cloth, insofar as it was possible to tell under the beard and hair.

It had been quite hard to ignore St. Ungulant, who had been capering up and down at the top of his pole shouting "Coo-ee!" and "Over here!" There was a slightly smaller pole a few feet away, with an old-fashioned half-moon-cut-out-on-the-door privy on it. Just because you were an anchorite, St. Ungulant said, didn't mean you had to give up *everything*.

Brutha had heard of anchorites, who were a kind of one-way prophet. They went out into the desert but did not come back, preferring a hermit's life of dirt and hardship and dirt and holy contemplation and dirt.

Many of them liked to make life even more uncomfortable for themselves by being walled up in cells or living, quite appropriately, at the top of a pole. The Omnian Church encouraged them, on the basis that it was best to get madmen as far away as possible where they couldn't cause any trouble and could be cared for by the community, insofar as the community consisted of lions and buzzards and dirt.

"I was thinking of adding another wheel," said St. Ungulant, "just over there. To catch the morning sun, you know."

Brutha looked around him. Nothing but flat rock and sand stretched away on every side.

"Don't you get the sun everywhere all the time?" he said.

"But it's much more important in the morning," said St. Ungulant. "Besides, Angus says we ought to have a patio."

"He could barbecue on it," said Om, inside Brutha's head.

"Um," said Brutha. "What . . . religion . . . are you a saint of, exactly?"

An expression of embarrassment crossed the very small amount of face between St. Ungulant's eyebrows and his mustache.

"Uh. None, really. That was all rather a mistake," he said. "My parents named me Sevrian Thaddeus Ungulant, and then one day, of course, most amusing, someone drew attention to the initials. After that, it all seemed rather inevitable."

The wheel rocked slightly. St. Ungulant's skin was almost blackened by the desert sun.

"I've had to pick up herming as I went along, of

course," he said. "I taught myself. I'm entirely self-taught. You can't find a hermit to teach you herming, because of course that rather spoils the whole thing."

"Er . . . but there's . . . Angus?" said Brutha, staring at the spot where he believed Angus to be, or at least where he believed St. Ungulant believed Angus to be.

"He's over here now," said the saint sharply, pointing to a different part of the wheel. "But he doesn't do any of the herming. He's not, you know, trained. He's just company. My word, I'd have gone quite *mad* if it wasn't for Angus cheering me up all the time!"

"Yes . . . I expect you would," said Brutha. He smiled at the empty air, in order to show willing.

"Actually, it's a pretty good life. The hours are rather long but the food and drink are extremely worthwhile."

Brutha had a distinct feeling that he knew what was going to come next.

"Beer cold enough?" he said.

"Extremely frosty," said St. Ungulant, beaming.

"And the roast pig?"

St. Ungulant's smile was manic.

"All brown and crunchy round the edges, yes," he said.

"But I expect, er . . . you eat the occasional lizard or snake, too?"

"Funny you should say that. Yes. Every once in a while. Just for a bit of variety."

"And mushrooms, too?" said Om.

"Any mushrooms in these parts?" said Brutha innocently.

St. Ungulant nodded happily.

"After the annual rains, yes. Red ones with yellow spots. The desert becomes really *interesting* after the mushroom season."

"Full of giant purple singing slugs? Talking pillars of flame? Exploding giraffes? That sort of thing?" said Brutha carefully.

"Good heavens, yes," said the saint. "I don't know why. I think they're attracted by the mushrooms."

Brutha nodded.

"You're catching on, kid," said Om.

"And I expect sometimes you drink . . . water?" said Brutha.

"You know, it's odd, isn't it," said St. Ungulant. "There's all this wonderful stuff to drink but every so often I get this, well, I can only call it a *craving*, for a few sips of water. Can you explain that?"

"It must be . . . a little hard to come by," said Brutha, still talking very carefully, like someone playing a fifty-pound fish on a fifty-one-pound breaking-strain fishing-line.

"Strange, really," said St. Ungulant. "When ice-cold beer is so readily available, too."

"Where, uh, do you get it? The water?" said Brutha.

"You know the stone plants?"

"The ones with the big flowers?"

"If you cut open the fleshy part of the leaves, there's up to half a pint of water," said the saint. "It tastes like weewee, mind you."

"I think we could manage to put up with that," said Brutha, through dry lips. He backed toward the rope-ladder that was the saint's contact with the ground.

"Are you sure you won't stay?" said St. Ungulant. "It's Wednesday. We get sucking pig plus chef's selection of sun-drenched dew-fresh vegetables on Wednesdays."

"We, uh, have lots to do," said Brutha, halfway down the swaying ladder.

"Sweets from the trolley?"

"I think perhaps . . ."

St. Ungulant looked down sadly at Brutha helping Vorbis away across the wilderness.

"And afterward there's probably mints!" he shouted, through cupped hands. "No?"

Soon the figures were mere dots on the sand.

"There may be visions of sexual grati—no, I tell a lie, that's Fridays . . ." St. Ungulant murmured.

Now that the visitors had gone, the air was once again filled with the zip and whine of the small gods. There were billions of them.

St. Ungulant smiled.

He was, of course, mad. He'd occasionally suspected this. But he took the view that madness should not be wasted. He dined daily on the food of the gods, drank the rarest vintages, ate fruits that were not only out of season but out of reality. Having to drink the occasional mouthful of brackish water and chew the odd lizard leg for medicinal purposes was a small price to pay.

He turned back to the laden table that shimmered in the air. All this . . . and all the little gods wanted was someone to know about them, someone to even believe that they existed.

There was jelly and ice-cream today, too.

"All the more for us, eh, Angus?"

Yes, said Angus.

The fighting was over in Ephebe. It hadn't lasted long, especially when the slaves joined in. There were too many narrow streets, too many ambushes and, above all, too much terrible determination. It's generally held that free men will always triumph over slaves, but perhaps it all depends on your point of view.

Besides, the Ephebian garrison commander had de-

clared somewhat nervously that slavery would hence-
forth be abolished, which infuriated the slaves. What
would be the point of saving up to become free if you
couldn't own slaves afterwards? Besides, how'd they eat?

The Omnians couldn't understand, and uncertain
people fight badly. And Vorbis had gone. Certainties
seemed less certain when those eyes were elsewhere.

The Tyrant was released from his prison. He spent his
first day of freedom carefully composing messages to the
other small countries along the coast.

It was time to do something about Omnia.

Brutha sang.

His voice echoed off the rocks. Flocks of scalbies
shook off their lazy pedestrian habits and took off frantically, leaving feathers behind in their rush to get air-
borne. Snakes wriggled into cracks in the stone.

You could live in the desert. Or at least survive . . .

Getting back to Omnia could only be a matter of time.
One more day . . .

Vorbis trooped along a little behind him. He said
nothing and, when spoken to, gave no sign that he had
understood what had been said to him.

Om, bumping along in Brutha's pack, began to feel
the acute depression that steals over every realist in the
presence of an optimist.

The strained strains of *Claws of Iron shall Rend the
Ungodly* faded away. There was a small rockslide, some
way off.

"We're alive," said Brutha.

"For now."

"And we're close to home."

"Yes?"

"I saw a wild goat on the rocks back there."

"There's still a lot of 'em about."

"Goats?"

"Gods. And the ones we had back there were the puny ones, mind you."

"What do you mean?"

Om sighed. "It's *reasonable,* isn't it? Think about it. The stronger ones hang around the edge, where there's prey . . . I mean, people. The weak ones get pushed out to the sandy places, where people hardly ever go—"

"The strong gods," said Brutha, thoughtfully. "Gods that know about being strong."

"That's right."

"Not gods that know what it feels like to be weak . . ."

"What? They wouldn't last five minutes. It's a god-eat-god world."

"Perhaps that explains something about the nature of gods. Strength is hereditary. Like sin."

His face clouded.

"Except that . . . it isn't. Sin, I mean. I think, perhaps, when we get back, I shall talk to some people."

"Oh, and they'll listen, will they?"

"Wisdom comes out of the wilderness, they say."

"Only the wisdom that people want. And mushrooms."

When the sun was starting to climb Brutha milked a goat. It stood patiently while Om soothed its mind. And Om didn't suggest killing it, Brutha noticed.

Then they found shade again. There were bushes here, low-growing, spiky, every tiny leaf barricaded behind its crown of thorns.

Om watched for a while, but the small gods on the

edge of the wilderness were more cunning and less urgent. They'd be here, probably at noon, when the sun turned the landscape into a hellish glare. He'd hear them. In the meantime, he could eat.

He crawled through the bushes, their thorns scraping harmlessly along his shell. He passed another tortoise, which wasn't inhabited by a god and gave him that vague stare that tortoises employ when they're deciding whether something is there to be eaten or made love to, which are the only things on a normal tortoise mind. He avoided it, and found a couple of leaves it had missed.

Periodically he'd stomp back through the gritty soil and watch the sleepers.

And then he saw Vorbis sit up, look around him in a slow methodical way, pick up a stone, study it carefully, and then bring it down sharply on Brutha's head.

Brutha didn't even groan.

Vorbis got up and strode directly toward the bushes that hid Om. He tore the branches aside, regardless of the thorns, and pulled out the tortoise Om had just met.

For a moment it was held up, legs moving slowly, before the deacon threw it overarm into the rocks.

Then he picked up Brutha with some effort, slung him across his shoulders, and set off towards Omnia.

It happened in seconds.

Om fought to stop his head and legs retracting automatically into his shell, a tortoise's instinctive panic reaction.

Vorbis was already disappearing around some rocks.

He disappeared.

Om started to move forward and then ducked into his shell as a shadow skimmed over the ground. It was a familiar shadow, and one filled with tortoise dread.

The eagle swept down and towards the spot where the stricken tortoise was struggling and, with barely a pause in the stoop, snatched the reptile and soared back up into the sky with long, lazy sweeps of its wings.

Om watched it until it became a dot, and then looked away as a smaller dot detached itself and tumbled over and over toward the rocks below.

The eagle descended slowly, preparing to feed.

A breeze rattled the thornbushes and stirred the sand. Om thought he could hear the taunting, mocking voices of all the small gods.

St. Ungulant, on his bony knees, smashed open the hard swollen leaf of a stone plant.

Nice lad, he thought. Talked to himself a lot, but that was only to be expected. The desert took some people like that, didn't it, Angus?

Yes, said Angus.

Angus didn't want any of the brackish water. He said it gave him wind.

"Please yourself," said St. Ungulant. "Well, well! Here's a little treat."

You didn't often get *Chilopoda aridius* out here in the open desert, and here were three, all under one rock!

Funny how you felt like a little nibble, even after a good meal of *Petit porc rôti avec pommes de terre nouvelles et légumes du jour et bière glacée avec figment de l'imagination*.

He was picking the legs of the second one out of his tooth when the lion padded to the top of the nearest dune behind him.

The lion was feeling odd sensations of gratitude. It felt it should catch up with the nice food that had tended to it and, well, refrain from eating it in some symbolic way.

And now here was some more food, hardly paying it any attention. Well, it didn't owe *this* one anything . . .

It padded forward, then lumbered up into a run.

Oblivious to his fate, St. Ungulant started on the third centipede.

The lion leapt . . .

And things would have looked very bad for St. Ungulant if Angus hadn't caught it right behind the ear with a rock.

Brutha was standing in the desert, except that the sand was as black as the sky and there was no sun, although everything was brilliantly lit.

Ah, he thought. So *this* is dreaming.

There were thousands of people walking across the desert. They paid him no attention. They walked as if completely unaware that they were in the middle of a crowd.

He tried to wave at them, but he was nailed to the spot. He tried to speak, and the words evaporated in his mouth.

And then he woke up.

The first thing he saw was the light, slanting through a window. Against the light was a pair of hands, raised in the sign of the holy horns.

With some difficulty, his head screaming pain at him, Brutha followed the hands along a pair of arms to where they joined not far under the bowed head of—

"Brother Nhumrod?"

The master of novices looked up.

"Brutha?"

"Yes?"

"Om be praised!"

Brutha craned his neck to look around.

"Is he here?"

"—here? How do you feel?"

"I—"

His head ached, his back felt as though it was on fire, and there was a dull pain in his knees.

"You were very badly sunburned," said Nhumrod. "And that was a nasty knock on the head you had in the fall."

"What fall?"

"—fall. From the rocks. In the desert. You were with the *Prophet*," said Nhumrod. "You walked with the Prophet. One of *my* novices."

"I remember . . . the desert . . ." said Brutha, touching his head gingerly. "But . . . the . . . Prophet . . . ?"

"—Prophet. People are saying you could be made a bishop, or even an Iam," said Nhumrod. "There's a precedent, you know. The Most Holy St. Bobby was made a bishop because he was in the desert with the Prophet Ossory, and *he* was a donkey."

"But I don't . . . remember . . . any Prophet. There was just me and—"

Brutha stopped. Nhumrod was beaming.

"Vorbis?"

"He most graciously told me all about it," said Nhumrod. "I was privileged to be in the Place of Lamentation when he arrived. It was just after the Sestine prayers. The Cenobiarch was just departing . . . well, you know the ceremony. And there was Vorbis. Covered in dust and leading a donkey. I'm afraid you were across the back of the donkey."

"I don't remember a donkey," said Brutha.

"—donkey. He'd picked it up at one of the farms. There was quite a crowd with him!"

Nhumrod was flushed with excitement.

"And he's declared a month of Jhaddra, and double penances, and the Council has given him the Staff and the Halter, and the Cenobiarch has gone off to the hermitage in Skant!"

"Vorbis is the eighth Prophet," said Brutha.

"—Prophet. Of course."

"And . . . was there a tortoise? Has he mentioned anything about a tortoise?"

"—tortoise? What have tortoises got to do with anything?" Nhumrod's expression softened. "But, of course, the Prophet said the sun had affected you. He said you were raving—excuse me—about all sorts of strange things."

"He did?"

"He sat by your bed for three days. It was . . . inspiring."

"How long . . . since we came back?"

"—back? Almost a week."

"A week!"

"He said the journey exhausted you very much."

Brutha stared at the wall.

"And he left orders that you were to be brought to him as soon as you were fully conscious," said Nhumrod. "He was very definite about that." His tone of voice suggested that he wasn't quite sure of Brutha's state of consciousness, even now. "Do you think you can walk? I can get some novices to carry you, if you'd prefer."

"I have to go and see him now?"

"—now. Right away. I expect you'll want to thank him."

*　*　*

Brutha had known about these parts of the Citadel only by hearsay. Brother Nhumrod had never seen them, either. Although he had not been specifically included in the summons, he had come nevertheless, fussing importantly around Brutha as two sturdy novices carried him in a kind of sedan chair normally used by the more crumbling of the senior clerics.

In the center of the Citadel, behind the Temple, was a walled garden. Brutha looked at it with an expert eye. There wasn't an inch of natural soil on the bare rock—every spadeful that these shady trees grew in must have been carried up by hand.

Vorbis was there, surrounded by bishops and Iams. He looked around as Brutha approached.

"Ah, my desert companion," he said, amiably. "And Brother Nhumrod, I believe. My brothers, I should like you to know that I have it in mind to raise our Brutha to archbishophood."

There was a very faint murmur of astonishment from the clerics, and then a clearing of a throat. Vorbis looked at Bishop Treem, who was the Citadel's archivist.

"Well, technically he is not yet even ordained," said Bishop Treem, doubtfully. "But of course we all know there has been a precedent."

"Ossory's ass," said Brother Nhumrod promptly. He put his hand over his mouth and went red with shame and embarrassment.

Vorbis smiled.

"Good Brother Nhumrod is correct," he said. "Who had also not been ordained, unless the qualifications were somewhat relaxed in those days."

There was a chorus of nervous laughs, such as there always is from people who owe their jobs and possibly their lives to a whim of the person who has just cracked the not very amusing line.

"Although the donkey was only made a bishop," said Bishop "Deathwish" Treem.

"A role for which it was *highly* qualified," said Vorbis sharply. "And now, you will all leave. Including Sub-deacon Nhumrod," he added. Nhumrod went from red to white at this sudden preferment. "But Archbishop Brutha will remain. We wish to talk."

The clergy withdrew.

Vorbis sat down on a stone chair under an elder tree. It was huge and ancient, quite unlike its short-lived relatives outside the garden, and its berries were ripening.

The Prophet sat with his elbows on the stone arms of the chair, his hands interlocked in front of him, and gave Brutha a long, slow stare.

"You are . . . recovered?" he said, eventually.

"Yes, lord," said Brutha. "But, lord, I cannot be a bishop, I cannot even—"

"I assure you the job does not require much intelligence," said Vorbis. "If it did, bishops would not be able to do it."

There was another long silence.

When Vorbis next spoke, it was as if every word was being winched up from a great depth.

"We spoke once, did we not, of the nature of reality?"

"Yes."

"And about how often what is perceived is not that which is *fundamentally* true?"

"Yes."

Another pause. High overhead, an eagle circled, looking for tortoises.

"I am sure you have confused memories of our wanderings in the wilderness."

"No."

"It is only to be expected. The sun, the thirst, the hunger . . ."

"No, lord. My memory does not confuse readily."

"Oh, yes. I recall."

"So do I, lord."

Vorbis turned his head slightly, looking sidelong at Brutha as if he was trying to hide behind his own face.

"In the desert, the Great God Om spoke to me."

"Yes, lord. He did. Every day."

"You have a mighty if simple faith, Brutha. When it comes to people, I am a great judge."

"Yes, lord. Lord?"

"Yes, my Brutha?"

"Nhumrod said *you* led *me* through the desert, lord."

"Remember what I said about fundamental truth, Brutha? Of course you do. There was a physical desert, indeed, but also a desert of the soul. My God led me, and I led you."

"Ah. Yes. I see."

Overhead, the spiraling dot that was the eagle appeared to hang motionless in the air for a moment. Then it folded its wings and fell—

"Much was given to me in the desert, Brutha. Much was learned. Now I must tell the world. That is the duty of a prophet. To go where others have not been, and bring back the truth of it."

—faster than the wind, its whole brain and body existing only as a mist around the sheer intensity of its purpose—

"I did not expect it to be this soon. But Om guided my

steps. And now that we have the Cenobiarchy, we shall . . . make use of it."

Somewhere out on the hillsides the eagle swooped, picked something up, and strove for height . . .

"I'm just a novice, Lord Vorbis! I am not a bishop, even if everyone calls me one."

"You will get used to it."

It sometimes took a long time for an idea to form in Brutha's mind, but one was forming now. It was something about the way Vorbis was sitting, something about the edge in his voice.

Vorbis was afraid of him.

Why me? Because of the desert? Who would care? For all I know, it was always like this—probably it was Ossory's ass that carried him in the wilderness, who found the water, who kicked a lion to death.

Because of Ephebe? Who would listen? Who would care? He is the Prophet and the Cenobiarch. He could have me killed just like that. Anything he does is right. Anything he says is true.

Fundamentally true.

"I have something to show you that may amuse you," said Vorbis, standing up. "Can you walk?"

"Oh, yes. Nhumrod was just being kind. It's mainly sunburn."

As they moved away, Brutha saw something he hadn't noticed before. There were members of the Holy Guard, armed with bows, in the garden. They were in the shade of trees, or amongst bushes—not too obvious, but not exactly hidden.

Steps led from the garden to the maze of underground tunnels and rooms that underlay the Temple and, indeed, the whole of the Citadel. Noiselessly, a couple of guards fell in behind them at a respectful distance.

Brutha followed Vorbis through the tunnels to the artificers' quarter, where forges and workshops clustered around one wide, deep light-well. Smoke and fumes billowed up around the hewn rock walls.

Vorbis walked directly to a large alcove that glowed red with the light of forge fires. Several workers were clustered around something wide and curved.

"There," said Vorbis. "What do you think?"

It was a turtle.

The iron-founders had done a pretty good job, even down to the patterning on the shell and the scales on the legs. It was about eight feet long.

Brutha heard a rushing noise in his ears as Vorbis spoke.

"They speak poisonous gibberish about turtles, do they not? They think they live on the back of a Great Turtle. Well, let them die on one."

Now Brutha could see the shackles attached to each iron leg. A man, or a woman, could with great discomfort lie spread-eagled on the back of the turtle and be chained firmly at the wrists and ankles.

He bent down. Yes, there was the firebox underneath. Some aspects of Quisition thinking never changed.

That much iron would take ages to heat up to the point of pain. Much time, therefore, to reflect on things . . .

"What do you think?" said Vorbis.

A vision of the future flashed across Brutha's mind.

"Ingenious," he said.

"And it will be a salutary lesson for all others tempted to stray from the path of true knowledge," said Vorbis.

"When do you intend to, uh, demonstrate it?"

"I am sure an occasion will present itself," said Vorbis.

When Brutha straightened up, Vorbis was staring at

him so intently that it was as if he was reading Brutha's thoughts off the back of his head.

"And now, please leave," said Vorbis. "Rest as much as you can . . . my son."

Brutha walked slowly across the Place, deep in unaccustomed thought.

"Afternoon, Your Reverence."

"You know already?"

Cut-Me-Own-Hand-Off Dhblah beamed over the top of his lukewarm ice-cold sherbet stand.

"Heard it on the grapevine," he said. "Here, have a slab of Klatchian Delight. Free. Onna stick."

The Place was more crowded than usual. Even Dhblah's hot cakes were selling like hot cakes.

"Busy today," said Brutha, hardly thinking about it.

"Time of the Prophet, see," said Dhblah, "when the Great God is manifest in the world. And if you think it's busy now, you won't be able to swing a goat here in a few days' time."

"What happens then?"

"You all right? You look a bit peaky."

"What happens then?"

"The Laws. *You* know. The Book of Vorbis? I suppose—" Dhblah leaned toward Brutha—"you wouldn't have a hint, would you? I suppose the Great God didn't happen to say anything of benefit to the convenience food industry?"

"I don't know. I think he'd like people to grow more lettuce."

"Really?"

"It's only a guess."

Dhblah grinned evilly. "Ah, yes, but it's *your* guess. A nod's as good as a poke with a sharp stick to a deaf camel, as they say. I know where I can get my hands on a few acres of well-irrigated land, funnily enough. Perhaps I ought to buy now, ahead of the crowd?"

"Can't see any harm in it, Mr. Dhblah."

Dhblah sidled closer. This was not hard. Dhblah sidled everywhere. *Crabs* thought he walked sideways.

"Funny thing," he said. "I mean . . . Vorbis?"

"Funny?" said Brutha.

"Makes you think. Even Ossory must have been a man who walked around, just like you and me. Got wax in his ears, just like ordinary people. Funny thing."

"What is?"

"The whole thing."

Dhblah gave Brutha another conspiratorial grin and then sold a footsore pilgrim a bowl of hummus that he would come to regret.

Brutha wandered down to his dormitory. It was empty at this time of day, hanging around dormitories being discouraged in case the presence of the rock-hard mattresses engendered thoughts of sin. His few possessions were gone from the shelf by his bunk. Probably he had a room of his own somewhere, although no one had told him.

Brutha felt totally lost.

He lay down on the bunk, just in case, and offered up a prayer to Om. There was no reply. There had been no reply for almost all of his life, and that hadn't been too bad, because he'd never expected one. And before, there'd always been the comfort that perhaps Om was listening and simply not deigning to say anything.

Now, there was nothing to hear.

He might as well be talking to himself, and listening to himself.

Like Vorbis.

That thought wouldn't go away. Mind like a steel ball, Om had said. Nothing got in or out. So all Vorbis could hear were the distant echoes of his own soul. And out of the distant echoes he would forge a Book of Vorbis, and Brutha suspected he knew what the commandments would be. There would be talk of holy wars and blood and crusades and blood and piety and blood.

Brutha got up, feeling like a fool. But the thoughts wouldn't go away.

He was a bishop, but he didn't know what bishops did. He'd only seen them in the distance, drifting along like earthbound clouds. There was only one thing he felt he knew how to do.

Some spotty boy was hoeing the vegetable garden. He looked at Brutha in amazement when he took the hoe, and was stupid enough to try to hang on to it for a moment.

"I am a *bishop*, you know," said Brutha. "Anyway, you aren't doing it right. Go and do something else."

Brutha jabbed viciously at the weeds around the seedlings. Only away a few weeks and already there was a haze of green on the soil.

You're a bishop. For being good. And here's the iron turtle. In case you're bad. Because . . .

. . . there were two people in the desert, and Om spoke to one of them.

It had never occurred to Brutha like that before.

Om had spoken to him. Admittedly, he hadn't said the things that the Great Prophets said he said. Perhaps he'd never said things like that . . .

He worked his way along to the end of the row. Then he tidied up the bean vines.

Lu-Tze watched Brutha carefully from his little shed by the soil heaps.

* * *

It was another barn. Urn was seeing a lot of barns.

They'd started with a cart, and invested a lot of time in reducing its weight as much as possible. Gearing had been a problem. He'd been doing a lot of thinking about gears. The ball wanted to spin much faster than the wheels wanted to turn. That was probably a metaphor for something or other.

"And I can't get it to go backward," he said.

"Don't worry," said Simony. "It won't have to go backward. What about armor?"

Urn waved a distracted hand around his workshop.

"This is a village forge!" he said. "This thing is twenty feet long! Zacharos can't make plates bigger than a few feet across. I've tried nailing them on a framework, but it just collapses under the weight."

Simony looked at the skeleton of the steam car and the pile of plates stacked beside it.

"Ever been in a battle, Urn?" he said.

"No. I've got flat feet. And I'm not very strong."

"Do you know what a tortoise is?"

Urn scratched his head. "Okay. The answer isn't a little reptile in a shell, is it? Because you *know* I know that."

"I mean a shield tortoise. When you're attacking a fortress or a wall, and the enemy is dropping everything he's got on you, every man holds his shield overhead so that it . . . kind of . . . slots into all the shields around it. Can take a lot of weight."

"Overlapping," murmured Urn.

"Like scales," said Simony.

Urn looked reflectively at the cart.

"A tortoise," he said.

"And the battering-ram?" said Simony.

"Oh, that's no problem," said Urn, not paying much attention. "Tree-trunk bolted to the frame. Big iron rammer. They're only bronze doors, you say?"

"Yes. But very big."

"Then they're probably hollow. Or cast bronze plates on wood. That's what I'd do."

"Not solid bronze? Everyone says they're solid bronze."

"That's what I'd say, too."

"Excuse me, sirs."

A burly man stepped forward. He wore the uniform of the palace guards.

"This is Sergeant Fergmen," said Simony. "Yes, sergeant?"

"The doors is reinforced with Klatchian steel. Because of all the fighting in the time of the False Prophet Zog. And they opens outwards only. Like lock gates on a canal, you understand? If you push on 'em, they only locks more firmly together."

"How are they opened, then?" said Urn.

"The Cenobiarch raises his hand and the breath of God blows them open," said the sergeant.

"In a *logical* sense, I meant."

"Oh. Well, one of the deacons goes behind a curtain and pulls a lever. But . . . when I was on guard down in the crypts, sometimes, there was a room . . . there was gratings and things . . . well, you could hear water gushing . . ."

"Hydraulics," said Urn. "Thought it would be hydraulics."

"Can you get in?" said Simony.

"To the room? Why not? No one bothers with it."

"Could he make the doors open?" said Simony.

"Hmm?" said Urn.

Urn was rubbing his chin reflectively with a hammer. He seemed to be lost in a world of his own.

"I said, could Fergmen make these hydra haulics work?"

"Hmm? Oh. Shouldn't think so," said Urn, vaguely.

"Could you?"

"What?"

"Could you make them work?"

"Oh. Probably. It's just pipes and pressures, after all. Um."

Urn was still staring thoughtfully at the steam cart. Simony nodded meaningfully at the sergeant, indicating that he should go away, and then tried the mental interplanetary journey necessary to get to whatever world Urn was in.

He tried looking at the cart, too.

"How soon can you have it all finished?"

"Hmm?"

"I said—"

"Late tomorrow night. If we work through tonight."

"But we'll need it for the next dawn! We won't have time to see if it works!"

"It'll work first time," said Urn.

"Really?"

"I built it. I know about it. You know about swords and spears and things. I know about things that go round and round. It will work first time."

"Good. Well, there are other things I've got to do—"

"Right."

Urn was left alone in the barn. He looked reflectively at his hammer, and then at the iron cart.

They didn't know how to cast bronze properly here. Their iron was pathetic, just pathetic. Their copper? It was terrible. They seemed to be able to make steel that shattered at a blow. Over the years the Quisition had weeded out all the good smiths.

He'd done the best he could, but . . .

"Just don't ask me about the second or third time," he said quietly to himself.

Vorbis sat in the stone chair in his garden, papers strewn around him.

"Well?"

The kneeling figure did not look up. Two guards stood over it, with drawn swords.

"The Turtle people . . . the people are plotting something," it said, the voice shrill with terror.

"Of course they are. Of course they are," said Vorbis. "And what is this plot?"

"There is some kind of . . . when you are confirmed as Cenobiarch . . . some kind of device, some machine that goes by itself . . . it will smash down the doors of the Temple . . ."

The voice faded away.

"And where is this device now?" said Vorbis.

"I don't know. They've bought iron from me. That's all I know."

"An iron device."

"Yes." The man took a deep breath—half-breath, half-gulp. "People say . . . the guards said . . . you have my father in prison and you might . . . I plead . . ."

Vorbis looked down at the man.

"But you *fear*," he said, "that I might have you thrown into the cells as well. You think I am that sort of person. You fear that I may think, this man has associated with heretics and blasphemers in familiar circumstances . . ."

The man continued to stare fixedly at the ground.

Vorbis's fingers curled gently around his chin and raised his head until they were eye to eye.

"What you have done is a *good* thing," he said. He looked at one of the guards. "Is this man's father still alive?"

"Yes, lord."

"Still capable of walking?"

The inquisitor shrugged. "Ye-es, lord."

"Then release him this instant, put him in the charge of his dutiful son here, and send them both back home."

The armies of hope and fear fought in the informant's eyes.

"Thank you, lord," he said.

"Go in peace."

Vorbis watched one of the guards escort the man from the garden. Then he waved a hand vaguely at one of the head inquisitors.

"Do we know where he lives?"

"Yes, lord."

"Good."

The inquisitor hesitated.

"And this . . . device, lord?"

"Om has spoken to me. A machine that goes by itself? Such a thing is against all reason. Where are its muscles? Where is its mind?"

"Yes, lord."

The inquisitor, whose name was Deacon Cusp, had got where he was today, which was a place he wasn't sure right now that he wanted to be, because he liked hurting people. It was a simple desire, and one that was satisfied in abundance within the Quisition. And he was one of those who were terrified in a very particular way by Vorbis. Hurting people because you enjoyed it . . .

that was understandable. Vorbis just hurt people because he'd decided that they should be hurt, without passion, even with a kind of hard love.

In Cusp's experience, people didn't make things up, ultimately, not in front of an exquisitor. Of course there were no such things as devices that moved by themselves, but he made a mental note to increase the guard—

"However," said Vorbis, "there will be a disturbance during the ceremony tomorrow."

"Lord?"

"I have . . . special knowledge," said Vorbis.

"Of course, lord."

"You know the breaking strain of sinews and muscles, Deacon Cusp."

Cusp had formed an opinion that Vorbis was somewhere on the other side of madness. Ordinary madness he could deal with. In his experience there were quite a lot of mad people in the world, and many of them became even more insane in the tunnels of the Quisition. But Vorbis had passed right through that red barrier and had built some kind of logical structure on the other side. Rational thoughts made out of insane components . . .

"Yes, lord," he said.

"I know the breaking strain of people."

It was night, and cold for the time of year.

Lu-Tze crept through the gloom of the barn, sweeping industriously. Sometimes he took a rag from the recesses of his robe and polished things.

He polished the outside of the Moving Turtle, which loomed low and menacing in the shadows.

And he swept his way toward the forge, where he watched for a while.

It takes extreme concentration to pour good steel. No wonder gods have always clustered around isolated smithies. There are so many things that can go wrong. A slight mis-mix of ingredients, a moment's lapse—

Urn, who was almost asleep on his feet, grunted as he was nudged awake and something was put in his hands.

It was a cup of tea. He looked into the little round face of Lu-Tze.

"Oh," he said. "Thank you. Thank you very much."

Nod, smile.

"Nearly done," said Urn, more or less to himself. "Just got to let it cool now. Got to let it cool really *slowly*. Otherwise it crystallizes, you see."

Nod, smile, nod.

It was *good* tea.

"S'not 'n important cast anyway," said Urn, swaying. "Jus' the control levers—"

Lu-Tze caught him carefully and steered him to a seat on a heap of charcoal. Then he went and watched the forge for a while. The bar of steel was glowing in the mold.

He poured a bucket of cold water over it, watched the great cloud of steam spread and disperse, and then put his broom over his shoulder and ran away hurriedly.

People to whom Lu-Tze was a vaguely glimpsed figure behind a very slow broom would have been surprised at his turn of speed, especially in a man six thousand years old who ate nothing but brown rice and drank only green tea with a knob of rancid butter in it.

A little way away from the Citadel's main gates he stopped running and started sweeping. He swept up to the gates, swept around the gates themselves, nodded and smiled at a soldier who glared at him and then realized that it was only the daft old sweeper, polished one of the handles of the gates, and swept his way by passages and cloisters to Brutha's vegetable garden.

He could see a figure crouched among the melons.

Lu-Tze found a rug and padded back out into the garden, where Brutha was sitting hunched up with his hoe over his knees.

Lu-Tze had seen many agonized faces in his time, which was a longer time than most whole civilizations managed to see. Brutha's was the worst. He tugged the rug over the bishop's shoulders.

"I can't hear him," said Brutha hoarsely. "It may mean that he's too far away. I keep on thinking that. He might be out there somewhere. Miles away!"

Lu-Tze smiled and nodded.

"It'll happen all over again. *He* never told anyone to do anything. Or not to do anything. He didn't care!"

Lu-Tze nodded and smiled again. His teeth were yellow. They were in fact his two-hundredth set.

"He should have cared."

Lu-Tze disappeared into his corner again and returned with a shallow bowl full of some kind of tea. He nodded and smiled and proffered it until Brutha took it and had a sip. It tasted like hot water with a lavender bag in it.

"You don't understand anything I'm talking about, do you?" said Brutha.

"Not much," said Lu-Tze.

"You *can* talk?"

Lu-Tze put a wisened finger to his lips.

"Big secret," he said.

Brutha looked at the little man. How much did he

know about him? How much did anyone know about him?

"You talk to God," said Lu-Tze.

"How do you know that?"

"Signs. Man who talk to God have difficult life."

"You're right!" Brutha stared at Lu-Tze over the cup. "Why are you here?" he said. "You're not Omnian. Or Ephebian."

"Grew up near Hub. Long time ago. Now Lu-Tze a stranger everywhere he goes. Best way. Learned religion in temple at home. Now go where job is."

"Carting soil and pruning plants?"

"Sure. Never been bishop or high panjandrum. Dangerous life. Always be man who cleans pews or sweeps up behind altar. No one bother useful man. No one bother small man. No one remember name."

"That's what I was going to do! But it doesn't work for me."

"Then find other way. I learn in temple. Taught by ancient master. When trouble, always remember wise words of ancient and venerable master."

"What were they?"

"Ancient master say: 'That boy there! What you eating? Hope you brought enough for everybody!' Ancient master say: 'You bad boy! Why you no do homework?' Ancient master say: 'What boy laughing? No tell what boy laughing, whole dojo stay in after school!' When remember these wise words, nothing seems so bad."

"What shall I do? I can't hear *him!*"

"You do what you must. I learn anything, it you have to walk it all alone."

Brutha hugged his knees.

"But he told me nothing! Where's all this wisdom? All the other prophets came back with commandments!"

"Where they get them?"

"I . . . suppose they made them up."

"You get them from same place."

"You call this philosophy?" roared Didactylos, waving his stick.

Urn cleaned pieces of the sand mold from the lever.

"Well . . . *natural* philosophy," he said.

The stick whanged down on the Moving Turtle's flanks.

"I never taught you this sort of thing!" shouted the philosopher. "Philosophy is supposed to make life *better!*"

"This *will* make it better for a lot of people," said Urn, calmly. "It will help overthrow a tyrant."

"And then?" said Didactylos.

"And then what?"

"And then you'll take it to bits, will you?" said the old man. "Smash it up? Take the wheels off? Get rid of all those spikes? Burn the plans? Yes? When it's served its purpose, yes?"

"Well—" Urn began.

"Aha!"

"Aha what? What if we do keep it? It'll be a . . . a deterrent to other tyrants!"

"You think tyrants won't build 'em too?"

"Well . . . I can build bigger ones!" Urn shouted.

Didactylos sagged. "Yes," he said. "No doubt you can. So that's all right, then. My word. And to think I was worrying. And now . . . I think I'll go and have a rest somewhere . . ."

He looked hunched up, and suddenly old.

"Master?" said Urn.

"Don't 'master' me," said Didactylos, feeling his way along the barn walls to the door. "I can see you know every bloody thing there is to know about human nature now. Hah!"

The Great God Om slid down the side of an irrigation ditch and landed on his back in the weeds at the bottom. He righted himself by gripping a root with his mouth and hauling himself over.

The shape of Brutha's thoughts flickered back and forth in his mind. He couldn't make out any actual words, but he didn't need to, any more than you needed to see the ripples to know which way the river flowed.

Occasionally, when he could see the Citadel as a gleaming dot in the twilight, he'd try shouting his own mind back as loudly as he could:

"Wait! Wait! You don't want to do that! We can go to Ankh-Morpork! Land of opportunity! With my brains and your . . . with you, the world is our mollusk! Why throw it all away . . ."

And then he'd slide into another furrow. Once or twice he saw the eagle, forever circling.

"Why put your hand into a grinder? This place *deserves* Vorbis! Sheep *deserve* to be led!"

It had been like this when his very first believer had been stoned to death. Of course, by then he had dozens of other believers. But it had been a wrench. It had been upsetting. You never forgot your first believer. They gave you shape.

Tortoises are not well equipped for cross-country navigation. They need longer legs or shallower ditches.

Om estimated that he was doing less than a fifth of a mile an hour in a direct line, and the Citadel was at least twenty miles away. Occasionally he made good time between the trees in an olive grove, but that was more than pulled back by rocky ground and field walls.

All the time, as his legs whirred, Brutha's thoughts buzzed in his head like a distant bee.

He tried shouting in his mind again.

"What've you got? He's got an army! You've got an army? How many divisions have you got?"

But thoughts like that needed energy, and there was a limit to the amount of energy available in one tortoise. He found a bunch of fallen grapes and gobbled them until the juice covered his head, but it didn't make a lot of difference.

And then there was nightfall. Nights here weren't as cold as the desert, but they weren't as warm as the day. He'd slow down at night as his blood cooled. He wouldn't be able to think as fast. Or walk as fast.

He was losing heat already. Heat meant speed.

He pulled himself up on to an anthill—

"You're going to die! You're going to die!"

—and slid down the other side.

Preparations for the inauguration of the Cenobiarch Prophet began many hours before the dawn. Firstly, and not according to ancient tradition, there was a very careful search of the temple by Deacon Cusp and some of his colleagues. There was a prowling for tripwires and a poking of odd corners for hidden archers. Although it was against the thread, Deacon Cusp had his head screwed on. He also sent a few squads into the town to round up the usual suspects. The Quisition always found it advisable to leave a few suspects at large. Then you knew where to find them when you needed them.

After that a dozen lesser priests arrived to shrive the

premises and drive out all afreets, djinns, and devils. Deacon Cusp watched them without comment. He'd never had any personal dealings with supernatural entities, but he knew what a well-placed arrow would do to an unexpecting stomach.

Someone tapped him on the rib-cage. He gasped at the sudden linkage of real life into the chain of thought, and reached instinctively for his dagger.

"Oh," he said.

Lu-Tze nodded and smiled and indicated with his broom that Deacon Cusp was standing on a patch of floor that he, Lu-Tze, wished to sweep.

"Hello, you ghastly little yellow fool," said Deacon Cusp.

Nod, smile.

"Never say a bloody word, do you?" said Deacon Cusp.

Smile, smile.

"Idiot."

Smile. Smile. Watch.

Urn stood back.

"Now," he said, "you sure you've got it all?"

"Easy," said Simony, who was sitting in the Turtle's saddle.

"Tell me again," said Urn.

"We-stoke-up-the-firebox," said Simony. "Then-when-the-red-needle-points-to-XXVI, turn-the-brass-tap; when-the-bronze-whistle-blows, pull-the-big-lever. And steer by pulling the ropes."

"Right," said Urn. But he still looked doubtful. "It's a precision device," he said.

"And I am a professional soldier," said Simony. "I'm not a superstitious peasant."

"Fine, fine. Well . . . if you're *sure* . . ."

They'd had time to put a few finishing touches to the Moving Turtle. There were serrated edges to the shell and spikes on the wheels. And of course the waste steam pipe . . . he was a little uncertain about the waste steam pipe . . .

"It's merely a device," said Simony. "It does not present a problem."

"Give us an hour, then. You should just get to the Temple by the time we get the doors open."

"Right. Understood. Off you go. Sergeant Fergmen knows the way."

Urn looked at the steam pipe and bit his lip. I don't know what effect it's going to have on the enemy, he thought, but it scares the hells out of me.

Brutha woke up, or at least ceased trying to sleep. Lu-Tze had gone. Probably sweeping somewhere.

He wandered through the deserted corridors of the novice section. It would be hours before the new Cenobiarch was crowned. There were dozens of ceremonies to be undertaken first. Everyone who was anyone would be in the Place and the surrounding piazzas, and so would the even greater number of people who were no one very much. The sestinas were empty, the endless prayers left unsung. The Citadel might have been dead, were it not for the huge indefinable background roar of tens of thousands of people being silent. Sunlight filtered down through the light-wells.

Brutha had never felt more alone. The wilderness had been a feast of fun compared to this. Last night . . . last night, with Lu-Tze, it had all seemed so clear. Last night he had been in a mood to confront Vorbis there and then. Last night there seemed to be a chance. Anything was possible last night. That was the trouble with last nights. They were always followed by this mornings.

He wandered out into the kitchen level, and then into the outside world. There were one or two cooks around, preparing the ceremonial meal of meat, bread, and salt, but they paid him no attention at all.

He sat down outside one of the slaughterhouses. There was, he knew, a back gate somewhere around. Probably no one would stop him, today, if he walked out. Today they would be looking for unwanted people walking in.

He could just walk away. The wilderness had seemed quite pleasant, apart from the thirst and hunger. St. Ungulant with his madness and his mushrooms seemed to have life exactly right. It didn't matter if you fooled yourself provided you didn't let yourself know it, and did it well. Life was so much simpler, in the desert.

But there were a dozen guards by the gate. They had an unsympathetic look. He went back to his seat, which was tucked away in a corner, and stared gloomily at the ground.

If Om was alive, surely he could send a sign?

A grating by Brutha's sandals lifted itself up a few inches and slid aside. He stared at the hole.

A hooded head appeared, stared back, and disappeared again. There was a subterranean whispering. The head reappeared, and was followed by a body. It pulled itself on to the cobbles. The hood was pushed back. The man grinned conspiratorially at Brutha, put his finger to his lips and then, without warning, launched himself at him with violent intent.

Brutha rolled across the cobbles and raised his hands

frantically as he saw the gleam of metal. One filthy hand clamped against his mouth. A knifeblade made a dramatic and very final silhouette against the light—

"No!"

"Why not? We said the first thing we'll do, we'll kill all the priests!"

"Not that one!"

Brutha dared to swivel his eyes sideways. Although the second figure rising from the hole was also wearing a filthy robe, there was no mistaking the paintbrush hairstyle.

He tried to say "Urn?"

"Shut up, you," said the other man, pressing the knife to his throat.

"Brutha?" said Urn. "You're alive?"

Brutha moved his eyes from his captor to Urn in a way which he hoped would indicate that it was too soon to make any commitment on this point.

"He's all right," said Urn.

"All right? He's a priest!"

"But he's on our side. Aren't you, Brutha?"

Brutha tried to nod, and thought: I'm on everyone's side. It'd be nice if, just for once, someone was on mine.

The hand was unclamped from his mouth, but the knife remained resting on his throat. Brutha's normally careful thought processes ran like quicksilver.

"The Turtle Moves?" he ventured.

The knife was withdrawn, with obvious reluctance.

"I don't trust him," said the man. "We should shove him down the hole at least."

"Brutha's one of us," said Urn.

"That's right. That's *right*," said Brutha. "Which ones are you?"

Urn leaned closer.

"How's your memory?"

"Unfortunately, it is fine."

"Good. Good. Uh. It would be a good idea to stay out of trouble, d'you hear . . . if anything happens. Remember the Turtle. Well, of course you would."

"What things?"

Urn patted him on the shoulder, making Brutha think for a moment of Vorbis. Vorbis, who never touched another person inside his head, was a great toucher with his hands.

"Best if you don't know what's happening," said Urn.

"But I don't know what's happening," said Brutha.

"Good. That's the way."

The burly man gestured with his knife towards the tunnels that led into the rock.

"Are we going, or what?" he demanded.

Urn ran after him and then stopped briefly and turned.

"Be careful," he said. "We need what's in your head!"

Brutha watched them go.

"So do I," he murmured.

And then he was alone again.

But he thought: Hold on. I don't have to be. I'm a bishop. At least I can watch. Om's gone and soon the world will end, so at least I might as well watch it happen.

Sandals flapping, Brutha set off towards the Place.

Bishops move diagonally. That's why they often turn up where the kings don't expect them to be.

"You godawful idiot! Don't go *that* way!"

The sun was well up now. In fact it was probably setting, if Didactylos's theories about the speed of light were correct, but in matters of relativity the point of view of the observer is very important, and from Om's point of view the sun was a golden ball in a flaming orange sky.

He pulled himself up another slope, and stared blearily at the distant Citadel. In his mind's eye, he could hear the mocking voices of all small gods.

They didn't like a god who had failed. They didn't like that at all. It let them all down. It reminded them of mortality. He'd be thrust out into the deep desert, where no one would ever come. Ever. Until the end of the world.

He shivered in his shell.

Urn and Fergmen walked nonchalantly through the tunnels of the Citadel, using the kind of nonchalant walk which, had there been anyone to take an interest in it, would have drawn detailed and arrow-sharp attention to them within seconds. But the only people around were those with vital jobs to do. Besides, it was not a good idea to stare too hard at the guards, in case they stared back.

Simony had told Urn he'd agreed to this. He couldn't quite remember doing so. The sergeant knew a way into the Citadel, that was sensible. And Urn knew about hydraulics. Fine. Now he was walking through these dry tunnels with his toolbelt clinking. There was a logical connection, but it had been made by someone else.

Fergmen turned a corner and stopped by a large grille, which stretched from floor to ceiling. It was very rusty. It might once have been a door—there was a suggestion of hinges, rusted into the stone. Urn peered through the bars. Beyond, in the gloom, there were pipes.

"Eureka," he said.

"Going to have a bath, then?" said Fergmen.

"Just keep watch."

Urn selected a short crowbar from his belt and inserted it between the grille and the stonework. Give me a foot of good steel and a wall to brace . . . my . . . foot . . . against—the grille ground forward and then popped out with a leaden sound—and I can change the world . . .

He stepped inside the long, dark, damp room, and gave a whistle of admiration.

No one had done any maintenance for—well, for as long as it took iron hinges to become a mass of crumbling rust—but all this still worked?

He looked up at lead and iron buckets bigger than he was, and a tangle of man-sized pipes.

This was the breath of God.

Probably the last man who knew how it worked had been tortured to death years before. Or as soon as it was installed. Killing the creator was a traditional method of patent-protection.

There were the levers and *there*, hanging over pits in the rock floor, were the two sets of counterweights. Probably it'd only take a few hundred gallons of water to swing the balance either way. Of course, the water'd have to be pumped up—

"Sergeant?"

Fergmen peered around the door. He looked nervous, like an atheist in a thunderstorm.

"What?"

Urn pointed.

"There's a big shaft through the wall there, see? At the bottom of the gear-chain?"

"The what?"

"The big knobbly wheels?"

"Oh. Yeah."

"Where does the shaft go to?"

"Don't know. There's the big Treadmill of Correction through there."

Ah.

The breath of God was ultimately the sweat of men. Didactylos would have appreciated the joke, Urn thought.

He was aware of a sound that had been there all the time but was only now penetrating through his concentration. It was tinny and faint and full of echoes, but it was voices. From the pipes.

The sergeant, to judge by his expression, had heard them too.

Urn put his ear to the metal. There was no possibility of making out words, but the general religious rhythm was familiar enough.

"It's just the service going on in the Temple," he said. "It's probably resonating off the doors and the sound's being carried down the pipes."

Fergmen did not look reassured.

"No gods are involved in any way," Urn translated. He turned his attention to the pipes again.

"Simple principle," said Urn, more to himself than to Fergmen. "Water pours into the reservoirs on the weights, disturbing the equilibrium. One lot of weights descends and the other rises up the shaft in the wall. The weight of the door is immaterial. As the bottom weights descend, these buckets *here* tip over, pouring the water out. Probably quite a smooth action. Perfect equilibrium at either end of the movement, too. Nicely thought out."

He caught Fergmen's expression.

"Water goes in and out and the doors swing open," he translated. "So all we've got to do is wait for . . . what did he say the sign would be?"

"They'll blow a trumpet when they're through the main gate," said Fergmen, pleased to be of service.

"Right." Urn eyed the weights and the reservoirs overhead. The bronze pipes dripped with corrosion.

"But perhaps we'd better just check that we know what we're doing," he said. "It probably takes a minute or two before the doors start moving." He fumbled under his robe and produced something that looked, to Fergmen's eye, very much like a torture instrument. This must have communicated itself to Urn, who said very slowly and kindly: "This is an ad-just-ab-ble span-ner."

"Yes?"

"It's for twisting nuts off."

Fergmen nodded miserably.

"Yes?" he said.

"And this is a bottle of penetrating oil."

"Oh, good."

"Just give me a leg up, will you? It'll take time to unhook the linkage to the valve, so we might as well make a start." Urn heaved himself into the ancient machinery while, above, the ceremony droned on.

Cut-Me-Own-Hand-Off Dhblah was all for new prophets. He was even in favor of the end of the world, if he could get the concession to sell religious statues, cut-price icons, rancid sweetmeats, fermenting dates, and putrescent olives on a stick to any watching crowds.

Subsequently, this was his testament. There never was a Book of the Prophet Brutha, but an enterprising scribe, during what came to be called the Renovation, did assemble some notes, and Dhblah had this to say:

"I. I was standing right by the statue of Ossory, right, when I noticed Brutha just beside me. Everyone was keeping away from him because of him being a bishop and they do things to you if you jostle bishops.

"II. I said to him, hello, Your Graciousness, and offered him a yogurt practically free.

"III. He responded, no.

"IV. I said, it's very healthy, it's a *live* yogurt.

"V. He said, yes, he could see.

"VI. He was staring at the doors. This was about the time of the third gong, right, so we all knew we'd got hours to wait. He was looking a bit down and it's not as if he even ate the yogurt, which I admit was on the hum a bit, what with the heat. I mean, it was more alive than usual. I mean, I had to keep hitting it with a spoon to stop it getting out of the . . . all right. I was just explaining about the yogurt. All *right*. I mean, you want to put a bit of color in, don't you? People like a bit of color. It was green.

"VII. He just stood there, staring. So I said, got a problem, Your Reverence? Upon which he vouchsafed, I cannot hear him. I said, what is this he to whom what you refer? He said, if he was here, he would send me a sign.

"VIII. There is no truth whatsoever in the rumor that I ran away at this juncture. It was just the pressure of the crowd. I have never been a friend of the Quisition. I might have sold them food, but I always charged them extra.

"IX. Anyway, right, then he pushed through the line of guards what was holding the crowd back and stood right in front of the doors, and they weren't sure what to do about bishops, and I heard him say something like, I carried you in the desert, I believed all my life, just give me this one thing.

"X. Something like that, anyway. How about some yogurt? Bargain offer. Onna stick."

* * *

Om lifted himself over a creeper-clad wall by grasping tendrils in his beak and hauling himself up by the neck muscles. Then he fell down the other side. The Citadel was as far away as ever.

Brutha's mind was flaming like a beacon in Om's senses. There's a streak of madness in everyone who spends quality time with gods, and it was driving the boy now.

"It's too soon!" Om yelled. "You need followers! It can't be just *you!* You can't do it by *yourself!* You have to get disciples first!"

Simony turned to look down the length of the Turtle. Thirty men were crouched under the shell, looking very apprehensive.

A corporal saluted.

"The needle's there, sergeant."

The brass whistle whistled.

Simony picked up the steering ropes. This was what war should be, he thought. No uncertainty. A few more Turtles like this, and no one would ever fight again.

"Stand by," he said.

He pulled the big lever hard.

The brittle metal snapped in his hand.

Give anyone a lever long enough and they can change the world. It's unreliable levers that are the problem.

In the depths of the Temple's hidden plumbing, Urn grasped a bronze pipe firmly with his spanner and gave the nut a cautious turn. It resisted. He changed position, and grunted as he used more pressure.

With a sad little metal sound, the pipe twisted—and broke . . .

Water gushed out, hitting him in the face. He dropped the tool and tried to block the flow with his fingers, but it spurted around his hands and gurgled down the channel towards one of the weights.

"Stop it! Stop it!" he shouted.

"What?" said Fergmen, several feet below him.

"Stop the water!"

"How?"

"The pipe's broken!"

"I thought that's what we wanted to do?"

"Not yet!"

"Stop shouting, mister! There's guards around!"

Urn let the water gush for a moment as he struggled out of his robe, and then he rammed the sodden material into the pipe. It shot out again with some force and slapped wetly against the lead funnel, sliding down until it blocked the tube that led to the weights. The water piled up behind it and then spilled over on to the floor.

Urn glanced at the weight. It hadn't begun to move. He relaxed slightly. Now, provided there was still enough water to make the weight drop . . .

"Both of you—stand still."

He looked around, his mind going numb.

There was a heavy-set man in a black robe standing in the stricken doorway. Behind him, a guard held a sword in a meaningful manner.

"Who are you? Why are you here?"

Urn hesitated for only a moment.

He gestured with his spanner.

"Well, it's the seating, innit," he said. "You've got shocking seepage around the seating. Amazing it holds together."

The man stepped into the room. He glared uncertainly

at Urn for a moment and then turned his attention to the gushing pipe. And then back to Urn.

"But you're not—" he began.

He spun around as Fergmen hit the guard hard with a length of broken pipe. When he turned back, Urn's spanner caught him full in the stomach. Urn wasn't strong, but it was a long spanner, and the well-known principles of leverage did the rest. He doubled up and then sagged backwards against one of the weights.

What happened next happened in frozen time. Deacon Cusp grabbed at the weight for support. It sank down, ponderously, his extra poundage adding to the weight of the water. He clawed higher. It sank further, dropping below the lip of the pit. He sought for balance again, but this time it was against fresh air, and he tumbled on top of the falling weight.

Urn saw his face staring up at him as the weight fell into the gloom.

With a lever, he could change the world. It had certainly changed it for Deacon Cusp. It had made it stop existing.

Fergmen was standing over the guard, his pipe raised.

"I know this one," he said. "I'm going to give him a—"

"Never mind about that!"

"But—"

Above them linkage clanked into action. There was a distant creaking of bronze against bronze.

"Let's get out of here," said Urn. "Only the gods know what's happening up there."

And blows rained on the unmoving Moving Turtle's carapace.

"Damn! Damn! Damn!" shouted Simony, thumping it

again. "Move! I command you to move! Can you understand plain Ephebian! Move!"

The unmoving machine leaked steam and sat there.

And Om pulled himself up the slope of a small hill. So it
came to this, then. There was only one way to get to the
Citadel now.

It was a million-to-one chance, with any luck.

And Brutha stood in front of the huge doors, oblivious
to the crowd and the muttering guards. The Quisition
could arrest anyone, but the guards weren't certain what
happened to you if you apprehended an archbishop, especially one so recently favored by the Prophet.

Just a sign, Brutha thought, in the loneliness of his
head.

The doors trembled, and swung slowly outwards.

Brutha stepped forward. He wasn't fully conscious
now, not in any coherent way as understood by normal
people. Just one part of him was still capable of looking
at the state of his own mind and thinking: perhaps the
Great Prophets felt like this *all the time*.

The thousands inside the temple were looking around
in confusion. The choirs of lesser Iams paused in their
chant. Brutha walked on up the aisle, the only one with
a purpose in the suddenly bewildered throng.

Vorbis was standing in the center of the temple, under
the vault of the dome. Guards hurried toward Brutha,
but Vorbis raised a hand in a gentle but very positive
movement.

Now Brutha could take in the scene. There was the
staff of Ossory, and Abbys's cloak, and the sandals of
Cena. And, supporting the dome, the massive statues of

the first four prophets. He'd never seen them. He'd heard about them every day of his childhood.

And what did they mean now? They didn't mean anything. Nothing meant anything, if Vorbis was Prophet. Nothing meant anything, if the Cenobiarch was a man who'd heard nothing in the inner spaces of his own head but his own thoughts.

He was aware that Vorbis's gesture had not only halted the guards, although they surrounded him like a hedge. It had also filled the temple with silence. Into which Vorbis spoke.

"Ah. My Brutha. We had looked for you in vain. And now even you are here . . ."

Brutha stopped a few feet away. The moment of . . . whatever it had been . . . that had propelled him through the doors had drained away.

Now all there was, was Vorbis.

Smiling.

The part of him still capable of thought was thinking: there is nothing you can say. No one will listen. No one will care. It doesn't matter what you tell people about Ephebe, and Brother Murduck, and the desert. It won't be *fundamentally* true.

Fundamentally true. That's what the world is, with Vorbis in it.

Vorbis said, "There is something wrong? Something you wish to say?"

The black-on-black eyes filled the world, like two pits.

Brutha's mind gave up, and Brutha's body took over. It brought his hand back and raised it, oblivious to the sudden rush forward of the guards.

He saw Vorbis turn his cheek, and smile.

Brutha stopped, and lowered his hand.

He said, "No, I won't."

Then, for the first and only time, he saw Vorbis really enraged. There had been times before when the deacon had been angry, but it had been something driven by the brain, switched on and off as the need arose. This was something else, something out of control. And it flashed across his face only for a moment.

As the hands of the guards closed on him, Vorbis stepped forward and patted him on the shoulder. He looked Brutha in the eye for a moment and then said softly:

"Thrash him within an inch of his life and burn him the rest of the way."

An Iam began to speak, but stopped when he saw Vorbis's expression.

"Do it *now*."

A world of silence. No sound up here, except the rush of wind through the feathers.

Up here the world is round, bordered by a band of sea. The viewpoint is from horizon to horizon, the sun is closer.

And yet, looking down, looking for shapes . . .

. . . down in the farmland on the edge of the wilderness . . .

. . . on a small hill . . .

. . . a tiny moving dome, ridiculously exposed . . .

No sound but the rush of wind through feathers as the eagle pulls in its wings and drops like an arrow, the world spinning around the little moving shape that is the focus of all the eagle's attention.

Closer and . . .

. . . talons down . . .

. . . grip . . .
. . . and rise . . .

Brutha opened his eyes.

His back was merely agonizing. He'd long ago got used to switching off pain.

But he was spread-eagled on a surface, his arms and legs chained to something he couldn't see. Sky above. The towering frontage of the temple to one side.

By turning his head a little he could see the silent crowd. And the brown metal of the iron turtle. He could smell smoke.

Someone was just tightening the shackles on his hand. Brutha looked over at the inquisitor. Now, what was it he had to say? Oh, yes.

"The Turtle Moves?" he mumbled.

The man sighed.

"Not this one, friend," he said.

The world spun under Om as the eagle sought for shell-cracking height, and his mind was besieged by the tortoise's existential dread of being off the ground. And Brutha's thoughts, bright and clear this close to death . . .

I'm on my back and getting hotter and I'm going to die . . .

Careful, careful. Concentrate, *concentrate*. It'll let go any second . . .

Om stuck out his long scrawny neck, stared at the body just above him, picked what he hoped was about the right spot, plunged his beak through the brown feathers between the talons, and *gripped*.

The eagle blinked. No tortoise had ever done that to an eagle, anywhere else in history.

Om's thoughts arrived in the little silvery world of its mind:

"We don't want to hurt one another, now do we?"

The eagle blinked again.

Eagles have never evolved much imagination or forethought, beyond that necessary to know that a turtle smashes when you drop it on the rocks. But it was forming a mental picture of what happened when you let go of a heavy tortoise that was still intimately gripping an essential bit of you.

Its eyes watered.

Another thought crept into its mind.

"Now. You play, uh, ball with me, I'll play . . . ball with you. Understand? This is important. This is what I want you to do . . ."

The eagle soared on a thermal off the hot rocks, and sped towards the distant gleam of the Citadel.

No tortoise had ever done this before. No tortoise in the whole universe. But no tortoise had ever been a god, and knew the unwritten motto of the Quisition: *Cuius testiculos habes, habeas cardia et cerebellum.*

When you have their full attention in your grip, their hearts and minds will follow.

Urn pushed his way through the crowds, with Fergmen trailing behind. That was the best and the worst of civil war, at least at the start—everyone wore the same uniform. It was much easier when you picked enemies who were a different color or at least spoke with a funny accent. You could call them "gooks" or something. It made things easier.

Hey, Urn thought. This is nearly philosophy. Pity I probably won't live to tell anyone.

The big doors were ajar. The crowd was silent, and

very attentive. He craned forward to see, and then looked up at the soldier beside him.

It was Simony.

"I thought—"

"It didn't work," said Simony, bitterly.

"Did you—?"

"We did everything! Something broke!"

"It must be the steel they make here," said Urn. "The link pins on—"

"That doesn't matter now," said Simony.

The flat tones of his voice made Urn follow the eyes of the crowd.

There was another iron turtle there—a proper model of a turtle, mounted on a sort of open gridwork of metal bars in which a couple of inquisitors were even now lighting a fire. And chained to the back of the turtle—

"Who's that?"

"Brutha."

"*What?*"

"I don't know what happened. He hit Vorbis, or didn't hit him. Or something. Enraged him anyway. Vorbis stopped the ceremony, right there and then."

Urn glanced at the deacon. Not Cenobiarch yet, so uncrowned. Among the Iams and bishops standing uncertainly in the open doorway, his bald head gleamed in the morning light.

"Come on, then," said Urn.

"Come on what?"

"We can rush the steps and save him!"

"There's more of them than there are of us," said Simony.

"Well, haven't there always been? There's not magically more of them than there are of us just because they've got Brutha, are there?"

Simony grabbed his arm.

"Think logically, will you?" he said. "You're a philosopher, aren't you? Look at the crowd!"

Urn looked at the crowd.

"Well?"

"They don't like it." Simon turned. "Look, Brutha's going to die anyway. But this way it'll mean something. People don't understand, really understand, about the shape of the universe and all that stuff, but they'll remember what Vorbis did to a man. Right? We can make Brutha's death a symbol for people, don't you see?"

Urn stared at the distant figure of Brutha. It was naked, except for a loin-cloth.

"A symbol?" he said. His throat was dry.

"It has to be."

He remembered Didactylos saying the world was a funny place. And, he thought distantly, it really was. Here people were about to roast someone to death, but they'd left his loin-cloth on, out of respectability. You had to laugh. Otherwise you'd go mad.

"You know," he said, turning to Simony. "Now I *know* Vorbis is evil. He burned my city. Well, the Tsorteans do it sometimes, and we burn theirs. It's just war. It's all part of history. And he lies and cheats and claws power for himself, and lots of people do that, too. But do you know what's special? Do you know what it is?"

"Of course," said Simony. "It's what he's doing to—"

"It's what he's done to *you*."

"What?"

"He turns other people into copies of himself."

Simony's grip was like a vice. "You're saying *I'm* like *him*?"

"Once you said you'd cut him down," said Urn. "Now you're thinking like him . . ."

"So we rush them, then?" said Simony. "I'm sure of— maybe four hundred on our side. So I give the signal and a few hundred of us attack thousands of them? And he dies anyway and we die too? What difference does that make?"

Urn's face was gray with horror now.

"You mean you don't know?" he said.

Some of the crowd looked around curiously at him.

"You don't *know?*" he said.

The sky was blue. The sun wasn't high enough yet to turn it into Omnia's normal copper bowl.

Brutha turned his head again, towards the sun. It was about a width above the horizon, although if Didactylos's theories about the speed of light were correct, it was really setting, thousands of years in the future.

It was eclipsed by the head of Vorbis.

"Hot yet, Brutha?" said the deacon.

"Warm."

"It will get warmer."

There was a disturbance in the crowd. Someone was shouting. Vorbis ignored it.

"Nothing you want to say?" he said. "Can't you manage even a curse? Not even a curse?"

"You never heard Om," said Brutha. "You never believed. You never, ever heard his voice. All you heard were the echoes inside your own mind."

"Really? But I am the Cenobiarch and you are going to burn for treachery and heresy," said Vorbis. "So much for Om, perhaps?"

"There will be justice," said Brutha. "If there is no justice, there is nothing."

He was aware of a small voice in his head, too faint yet to distinguish words.

"Justice?" said Vorbis. The idea seemed to enrage him. He spun around to the crowd of bishops. "Did you hear him? There will be justice? Om *has* judged! Through *me!* This *is* justice!"

There was a speck in the sun now, speeding toward the Citadel. And the little voice was saying *left left left up up left right a bit up left*—The mass of metal under him was getting uncomfortably hot.

"He comes now," said Brutha.

Vorbis waved his hand to the great facade of the temple. "Men built this. We built this," he said. "And what did Om do? Om comes? Let him come! Let him judge between us!"

"He comes now," Brutha repeated. "The God."

People looked apprehensively upward. There was that moment, just one moment, when the world holds its breath and against all experience waits for a miracle.

—*up left now, when I say three, one, two, THREE*—

"Vorbis?" croaked Brutha.

"What?" snapped the deacon.

"You're going to die."

It was hardly a whisper, but it bounced off the bronze doors and carried across the Place . . .

It made people uneasy, although they couldn't quite say why.

The eagle sped across the square, so low that people ducked. Then it cleared the roof of the temple and curved away towards the mountains. The watchers relaxed. It was only an eagle. For a moment there, just for a moment . . .

No one saw the tiny speck, tumbling down from the sky.

Don't put your faith in gods. But you can believe in turtles.

A feeling of rushing wind in Brutha's mind, and a voice . . .

—obuggerbuggerbuggerhelpaarghnoNoNoAargh-BuggerNONOAARGH—

Even Vorbis got a grip of himself. There had been just a moment, when he'd seen the eagle—but, no . . .

He extended his arms and smiled beatifically at the sky.

"I'm sorry," said Brutha.

One or two people, who had been watching Vorbis closely, said later that there was just time for his expression to change before two pounds of tortoise, traveling at three meters a second, hit him between the eyes.

It was a revelation.

And that does something to people watching. For a start, they believe with all their heart.

Brutha was aware of feet running up the steps, and hands pulling at the chains.

And then a voice:

I. He is Mine.

The Great God rose over the Temple, billowing and changing as the belief of thousands of people flowed into him. There were shapes there, of eagle-headed men, and bulls, and golden horns, but they tangled and flamed and fused into one another.

Four bolts of fire whirred out of the cloud and burst the chains holding Brutha.

II. He Is Cenobiarch And Prophet of Prophets.

The voice of theophany rumbled off the distant mountains.

III. Do I Hear Any Objections? No? Good.

The cloud had by now condensed into a shimmering golden figure, as tall as the Temple. It leaned down until its face was a few feet away from Brutha, and in a whisper that boomed across the Place said:

IV. Don't Worry. This Is Just The Start. You and Me, Kid! People Are Going To Find Out What Wailing and Gnashing Of Teeth Really Is.

Another shaft of flame shot out and struck the Temple doors. They slammed shut, and then the white-hot bronze melted, erasing the commandments of the centuries.

V. What Shall It Be, Prophet?

Brutha stood up, unsteadily. Urn supported him by one arm, and Simony by the other.

"Mm?" he said, muzzily.

VI. Your Commandments?

"I thought they were supposed to come from you," said Brutha. "I don't know if I can think of any . . ."

The world waited.

"How about 'Think for Yourself'?" said Urn, staring in horrified fascination at the manifestation.

"No," said Simony. "Try something like 'Social Cohesiveness is the Key to Progress.'"

"Can't say it rolls off the tongue," said Urn.

"If I can be of any help," said Cut-Me-Own-Hand-Off Dhblah, from the crowd, "something of benefit to the convenience food industry would be very welcome."

"Not killing people. We could do with one like that," said someone else.

"It'd be a good start," said Urn.

They looked at the Chosen One. He shook himself free of their grip and stood alone, swaying a little.

"No-oo," said Brutha. "No. I thought like that once, but it wouldn't. Not really."

Now, he said. Only now. Just one point in history. Not tomorrow, not next month, it'll always be too late unless it's *now*.

They stared at him.

"Come *on*," said Simony. "What's wrong with it? You can't argue with it."

"It's hard to explain," said Brutha. "But I think it's got something to do with how people should behave. I think . . . you should do things because they're right. Not because gods say so. They might say something different another time."

VII. I Like One About Not Killing, said Om, from far above.

VIII. It's Got A Good Ring To It. Hurry Up, I've Got Some Smiting To Do.

"You see?" said Brutha. "No. No smiting. No commandments unless you obey them too."

Om thumped on the roof of the Temple.

IX. You Order Me? Here? NOW? ME?

"No. I ask."

X. That's Worse Than Ordering!

"Everything works both ways."

Om thumped his Temple again. A wall caved in. That part of the crowd that hadn't managed to stampede from the Place redoubled its efforts.

XI. There Must Be Punishment! Otherwise There Will Be No Order!

"No."

XII. I Do Not Need You! I Have Believers Enough Now!

"But only through me. And, perhaps, not for long. It

will all happen again. It's happened before. It happens all the time. That's why gods die. They never believe in people. But you have a chance. All you need to do is . . . believe."

XIII. What? Listen To Stupid Prayers? Watch Over Small Children? Make It Rain?

"Sometimes. Not always. It could be a bargain."

XIV. BARGAIN! I don't Bargain! Not With Humans!

"Bargain now," said Brutha. "While you have the chance. Or one day you'll have to bargain with Simony, or someone like him. Or Urn, or someone like *him*."

XV. I Could Destroy You Utterly.

"Yes. I am entirely in your power."

XVI. I Could Crush You Like An Egg!

"Yes."

Om paused.

Then he said: *XVII. You Can't Use Weakness As A Weapon.*

"It's the only one I've got."

XVIII. Why Should I Yield, Then?

"Not yield. Bargain. Deal with me in weakness. Or one day you'll have to bargain with someone in a position of strength. The world changes."

XIX. Hah! You Want A Constitutional Religion?

"Why not? The other sort didn't work."

Om leaned on the Temple, his temper subsiding.

Chap. II v.I. Very Well, Then. But Only For A Time. A grin spread across the enormous, smoking face. *For One Hundred Years, Yes?*

"And after a hundred years?"

II. We Shall See.

"Agreed."

A finger the length of a tree unfolded, descended, touched Brutha.

III. You Have A Persuasive Way. You Will Need It. A Fleet Approaches.

"Ephebians?" said Simony.

IV. And Tsorteans. And Djelibeybians. And Klatchians. Every Free Country Along The Coast. To Stamp Out Omnia For Good. Or Bad.

"You don't have many friends, do you?" said Urn.

"Even I don't like us much, and I *am* us," said Simony. He looked up at the god.

"Will you help?"

V. You Don't Even Believe In Me!

"Yes, but I'm a practical man."

VI. And Brave, Too, To Declare Atheism Before Your God.

"This doesn't change anything, you know!" said Simony. "Don't think you can get around me by existing!"

"No help," said Brutha, firmly.

"What?" said Simony. "We'll need a mighty army against that lot!"

"Yes. And we haven't got one. So we'll do it another way."

"You're crazy!"

Brutha's calmness was like a desert.

"This may be the case."

"We have to fight!"

"Not yet."

Simony clenched his fists in anger.

"Look . . . *listen* . . . We died for lies, for *centuries* we died for lies." He waved a hand towards the god. "Now we've got a truth to die for!"

"No. Men should die for lies. But the truth is too precious to die for."

Simony's mouth opened and shut soundlessly as he

sought for words. Finally, he found some from the dawn
of his education.

"I was told it was the finest thing to die for a god," he
mumbled.

"Vorbis said that. And he was . . . stupid. You can die
for your country or your people or your family, but for a
god you should live fully and busily, every day of a long
life."

"And how long is that going to be?"

"We shall see."

Brutha looked up at Om.

"You will not show yourself like this again?"

Chap. III v.I. No. Once Is Enough.

"Remember the desert."

II. I Will Remember.

"Walk with me."

Brutha went over to the body of Vorbis and picked it
up.

"I think," he said, "that they will land on the beach
on the Ephebian side of the forts. They won't use the
rock shore and they can't use the cliffs. I'll meet them
there." He glanced down at Vorbis. "Someone should."

"You can't mean you want to go by yourself?"

"Ten thousand won't be sufficient. One might be
enough."

He walked down the steps.

Urn and Simony watched him go.

"He's going to die," said Simony. "He won't even be a
patch of grease on the sand." He turned to Om. "Can
you stop him?"

III. It May Be That I Cannot.

Brutha was already halfway across the Place.

"Well, we're not deserting him," said Simony.

IV. Good.

Om watched them go, too. And then he was alone, except for the thousands watching him, crammed around the edges of the great square. He wished he knew what to say to them. That's why he needed people like Brutha. That's why all gods needed people like Brutha.

"Excuse me?"

The god looked down.

V. Yes?

"Um. I can't sell you anything, can I?"

VI. What Is Your Name?

"Dhblah, god."

VII. Ah, Yes. And What Is It You Wish?

The merchant hopped anxiously from one foot to the other.

"You couldn't manage just a small commandment? Something about eating yogurt on Wednesdays, say? It's always very difficult to shift, midweek."

VIII. You Stand Before Your God And Look For Business Opportunities?

"We-ell," said Dhblah, "we could come to an arrangement. Strike while the iron is hot, as the inquisitors say. Haha. Twenty percent? How about it? After expenses, of course—"

The Great God Om smiled.

IX. I Think You Will Make A Little Prophet, Dhblah, he said.

"Right. Right. That's all I'm looking for. Just trying to make both ends hummus."

X. Tortoises Are To Be Left Alone.

Dhblah put his head on one side.

"Doesn't *sing*, does it?" he said. "But . . . tortoise

necklaces . . . hmm . . . brooches, of course. Tortoise-shel—"

XI. NO!

"Sorry, sorry. See what you mean. All right. Tortoise statues. Ye-ess. I thought about them. Nice shape. Incidentally, you couldn't make a statue wobble every now and again, could you? Very good for business, wobbling statues. The statue of Ossory wobbles every Fast of Ossory, reg'lar. By means of a small piston device operated in the basement, it is said. But very good for the prophets, all the same."

XII. You Make me Laugh, Little Prophet. Sell Your Tortoises, By All Means.

"Tell you the truth," said Dhblah, "I've already drawn a few designs just now . . ."

Om vanished. There was a brief thunderclap. Dhblah looked reflectively at his sketches.

". . . but I suppose I'll have to take the little figure off them," he said, more or less to himself.

The shade of Vorbis looked around.

"Ah. The desert," he said. The black sand was absolutely still under the starlit sky. It looked cold.

He hadn't planned on dying yet. In fact . . . he couldn't quite remember how he'd died . . .

"The desert," he repeated, and this time there was a hint of uncertainty. He'd never been uncertain about anything in his . . . life. The feeling was unfamiliar and terrifying. Did ordinary people feel like this?

He got a grip on himself.

Death was impressed. Very few people managed this, managed to hold on to the shape of their old thinking after death.

Death took no pleasure in his job. It was an emotion he found hard to grasp. But there was such a thing as satisfaction.

"So," said Vorbis. "The desert. And at the end of the desert—?"

JUDGMENT.

"Yes, yes, of course."

Vorbis tried to concentrate. He couldn't. He could feel certainty draining away. And he'd always *been* certain.

He hesitated, like a man opening a door to a familiar room and finding nothing there but a bottomless pit. The memories were still there. He could feel them. They had the right shape. It was just that he couldn't remember what they *were*. There had been a voice. . . . Surely, there had been a voice? But all he could remember was the sound of his own thoughts, bouncing off the inside of his own head.

Now he had to cross the desert. What could there be to fear—

The desert was what you believed.

Vorbis looked inside himself.

And went on looking.

He sagged to his knees.

I CAN SEE THAT YOU ARE BUSY, said Death.

"Don't leave me! It's so *empty!*"

Death looked around at the endless desert. He snapped his fingers and a large white horse trotted up.

I SEE A HUNDRED THOUSAND PEOPLE, he said, swinging himself into the saddle.

"Where? Where?"

HERE. WITH YOU.

"I can't see them!"

Death gathered up the reins.

NEVERTHELESS, he said. His horse trotted forward a few steps.

"I don't understand!" screamed Vorbis.

Death paused. "YOU HAVE PERHAPS HEARD THE PHRASE, he said, THAT HELL IS OTHER PEOPLE?

"Yes. Yes, of course."

Death nodded. IN TIME, he said, YOU WILL LEARN THAT IT IS WRONG.

The first boats grounded in the shallows, and the troops leapt into shoulder-high surf.

No one was quite sure who was leading the fleet. Most of the countries along the coast hated one another, not in any personal sense, but simply on a kind of historical basis. On the other hand, how much leadership was necessary? Everyone knew where Omnia was. None of the countries in the fleet hated the others worse than they did Omnia. Now it was necessary for it . . . not to exist.

General Argavisti of Ephebe considered that he was in charge, because although he didn't have the most ships he was avenging the attack on Ephebe. But Imperiator Borvorius of Tsort knew that *he* was in charge, because there were more Tsortean ships than any others. And Admiral Rham-ap-Efan of Djelibeybi knew that *he* was in charge, because he was the kind of person who always thought he was in charge of anything. The only captain who did not, in fact, think that he was commanding the fleet was Fasta Benj, a fisherman from a very small nation of marsh-dwelling nomads of whose existence all the other countries were in complete ignorance, and whose small reed boat had been in the path of the fleet and had got swept along. Since his tribe believed that there were only fifty-one people in the world, worshiped a giant newt, spoke a very personal language which no one else understood, and had never seen metal or fire before, he was spending a lot of time wearing a puzzled grin.

Clearly they had reached a shore, not of proper mud and reeds, but of very small gritty bits. He lugged his little reed boat up the sand, and sat down with interest to see what the men in the feathery hats and shiny fish-scale vests were going to do next.

General Argavisti scanned the beach.

"They must have seen us coming," he said. "So why would they let us establish a beachhead?"

Heat haze wavered over the dunes. A dot appeared, growing and contracting in the shimmering air.

More troops poured ashore.

General Argavisti shaded his eyes against the sun.

"Fella's just standing there," he said.

"Could be a spy," said Borvorius.

"Don't see how he could be a spy in his own country," said Argavisti. "Anyway, if he was a spy he'd be creepin' around. That's how you can tell."

The figure had stopped at the foot of the dunes. There was something about it that drew the eye. Argavisti had faced many an opposing army, and this was normal. One patiently waiting figure was not. He found he kept turning to look at it.

"S'carrying something," he said eventually. "Sergeant? Go and bring that man here."

A few minutes later the sergeant returned.

"Says he'll meet you in the middle of the beach, sir," he reported.

"Didn't I tell you to bring him here?"

"He didn't want to come, sir."

"You've got a sword, haven't you?"

"Yessir. Prodded him a bit, but he dint want to move, sir. And he's carrying a dead body, sir."

"On a battlefield? It's not bring-your-own, you know."

"And . . . sir?"

"What?"

"Says he's probably the Cenobiarch, sir. Wants to talk about a peace treaty."

"Oh, he does? Peace treaty? We know about peace treaties with Omnia. Go and tell . . . no. Take a couple of men and bring him here."

Brutha walked back between the soldiers, through the organized pandemonium of the camp. I ought to feel afraid, he thought. I was always afraid in the Citadel. But not now. This is through fear and out the other side.

Occasionally one of the soldiers would give him a push. It's not allowed for an enemy to walk freely into a camp, even if he wants to.

He was brought before a trestle table, behind which sat half a dozen large men in various military styles, and one small olive-skinned man who was gutting a fish and grinning hopefully at everyone.

"Well, now," said Argavisti, "Cenobiarch of Omnia, eh?"

Brutha dropped Vorbis's body on to the sand. Their gaze followed it.

"I know him—" said Borvorius. "Vorbis! Someone killed him at last, eh? And will you stop trying to sell me fish? Does anyone know who this man is?" he added, indicating Fasta Benj.

"It was a tortoise," said Brutha.

"Was it? Not surprised. Never did trust them, always creeping around. *Look*, I said no fish! He's not one of mine, I know that. Is he one of yours?"

Argavisti waved a hand irritably. "Who sent you, boy?"

"No one. I came by myself. But you could say I come from the future."

"Are you a philosopher? Where's your sponge?"

"You've come to wage war on Omnia. This would not be a good idea."

"From Omnia's point of view, yes."

"From everyone's. You will probably defeat us. But not all of us. And then what will you do? Leave a garrison? Forever? And eventually a new generation will retaliate. Why you did this won't mean anything to them. You'll be the oppressors. They'll fight. They might even win. And there'll be another war. And one day people will say: why didn't they sort it all out, back then? On the beach. Before it all started. Before all those people died. Now we have that chance. Aren't we lucky?"

Argavisti stared at him. Then he nudged Borvorius.

"What did he say?"

Borvorius, who was better at thinking than the others, said, "Are you talking about surrender?"

"Yes. If that's the word."

Argavisti exploded.

"You can't do that!"

"Someone will have to. Please listen to me. Vorbis is dead. He's paid."

"Not enough. What about your soldiers? They tried to sack our city!"

"Do your soldiers obey your orders?"

"Certainly!"

"And they'd cut me down here and now if you commanded it?"

"I should say so!"

"And I'm unarmed," said Brutha.

The sun beat down on an awkward pause.

"When I say they'd obey—" Argavisti began.

"We were not sent here to parley," said Borvorius abruptly. "Vorbis's death changes nothing fundamental. We are here to see that Omnia is no longer a threat."

"It is not. We will send materials and people to help rebuild Ephebe. And gold, if you like. We will reduce the size of our army. And so on. Consider us beaten. We will even open Omnia to whatever other religions wish to build holy places here."

A voice echoed in his head, like the person behind you who says, "Put the red Queen on the black King," when you think you have been playing all by yourself . . .

I. What?

"This will encourage . . . local effort," said Brutha.

II. Other Gods? Here?

"There will be free trade along the coast. I wish to see Omnia take its place among its fellow nations."

III. I heard You Mention Other Gods.

"Its place is at the bottom," said Borvorius.

"No. That won't work."

IV. Could We Please Get Back To The Matter Of Other Gods?

"Will you please excuse me a moment?" said Brutha, brightly. "I need to pray."

Even Argavisti raised no objection as Brutha walked

off a little way up the beach. As St. Ungulant preached to any who would listen, there were plus points in being a madman. People hesitated to stop you, in case it made things worse.

"Yes?" said Brutha, under his breath.

V. I Don't Seem To Recall Any Discussion About Other Gods Being Worshiped In Omnia?

"Ah, but it'll work for you," said Brutha. "People will soon see that those other ones are no good at all, won't they?" He crossed his fingers behind his back.

VI. This Is Religion, Boy. Not Comparison Bloody Shopping! You Shall Not Subject Your God To Market Forces!

"I'm sorry. I can see that you would be worried about—"

VII. Worried? Me? By A Bunch Of Primping Women And Muscle-bound Posers In Curly Beards?

"Fine. Is that settled, then?"

VIII. They Won't Last Five Minutes! . . . what?

"And now I'd better go and talk to these men one more time."

His eye was caught by a movement among the dunes.

"Oh, no," he said. "The idiots . . ."

He turned and ran desperately toward the beached fleet.

"No! It's not like that! Listen! *Listen!*"

But they had seen the army, too.

It looked impressive, perhaps more impressive than it really was. When news gets through that a huge enemy fleet has beached with the intent of seriously looting, pillaging, and—because they are from civilized countries—whistling and making catcalls at the women and impressing them with their flash bloody uniforms and wooing them away with their flash bloody consumer goods, I don't know, show them a polished bronze mirror and it goes right to their heads, you'd think there was something wrong with the local lads ... *then* people either head for the hills or pick up some handy, swingable object, get Granny to hide the family treasures in her drawers, and prepare to make a fight of it.

And, in the lead, the iron cart. Steam poured out of its funnel. Urn must have got it working again.

"Stupid! Stupid!" Brutha shouted, to the world in general, and carried on running.

The fleet was already forming battle-lines, and its commander, whichever he was, was amazed to see an apparent attack by one man.

Borvorius caught him as he plunged towards a line of spears.

"I *see*," he said. "Keep us talking while your soldiers got into position, eh?"

"No! I didn't want that!"

Borvorius's eyes narrowed. He had not survived the many wars of his life by being a stupid man.

"No," he said, "maybe you didn't. But it doesn't matter. Listen to me, my innocent little priest. Sometimes there has to be a war. Things go too far for words. There's ... other forces. Now ... go back to your people. Maybe we'll both be alive when all this is over and *then* we can talk. Fight first, talk after. That's how it works, boy. That's *history*. Now, go back."

Brutha turned away.

I. *Shall I Smite Them?*

"No!"

II. *I Could Make Them As Dust. Just Say The Word.*

"No. That's worse than war."

III. But You Said A God Must Protect His People—

"What would we be if I told you to crush honest men?"

IV. Not Stuck Full Of Arrows?

"No."

The Omnians were assembling among the dunes. A lot of them had clustered around the iron-shielded cart. Brutha looked at it through a mist of despair.

"Didn't I say I'd go down there alone?" he said.

Simony, who was leaning against the Turtle, gave him a grim smile.

"Did it work?" he said.

"I think . . . it didn't."

"I knew it. Sorry you had to find out. Things have a way of wanting to happen, see? Sometimes you get people facing off and . . . that's it."

"But if only people would—"

"Yeah. You could use *that* as a commandment."

There was a clanging noise, and a hatch opened on the side of the Turtle. Urn emerged, backward, holding a spanner.

"What is this thing?" said Brutha.

"It's a machine for fighting," said Simony. "The Turtle Moves, eh?"

"For fighting Ephebians?" said Brutha.

Urn turned around.

"What?" he said.

"You've built this . . . this thing . . . to fight Ephebians?"

"Well . . . no . . . no," said Urn, looking bewildered. "We're fighting Ephebians?"

"Everyone," said Simony.

"But I never . . . *I'm* an . . . I never—"

Brutha looked at the spiked wheels and the saw-edged plates around the edge of the Turtle.

"It's a device that goes by itself," said Urn. "We were going to use it for . . . I mean . . . look, I never wanted it to . . ."

"We need it now," said Simony.

"Which we?"

"What comes out of the big long spout thing at the front?" said Brutha.

"Steam," said Urn dully. "It's connected to the safety valve."

"Oh."

"It comes out very hot," said Urn, sagging even more.

"Oh?"

"Scalding, in fact."

Brutha's gaze drifted from the steam funnel to the rotating knives.

"Very philosophical," he said.

"We were going to use it against Vorbis," said Urn.

"And now you're not. It's going to be used against Ephebians. You know, I used to think *I* was stupid, and then I met philosophers."

Simony broke the silence by patting Brutha on the shoulder.

"It will all work out," he said. "We won't lose. After all," he smiled encouragingly, "*we* have God on our side."

Brutha turned. His fist shot out. It wasn't a scientific blow, but it was hard enough to spin Simony around. He clutched his chin.

"What was *that* for? Isn't this what you wanted?"

"We get the gods we deserve," said Brutha, "and I think we don't deserve any. Stupid. Stupid. The sanest man I've met this year lives up a pole in the desert. Stupid. I think I ought to join him."

I. Why?

"Gods and men, men and gods," said Brutha. "Everything happens because things have happened before. Stupid."

II. But You Are The Chosen One.

"Choose someone else."

Brutha strode off through the ragged army. No one tried to stop him. He reached the path that led up to the cliffs, and did not even turn to look at the battle-lines.

"Aren't you going to watch the battle? I need someone to watch the battle."

Didactylos was sitting on a rock, his hands folded on his stick.

"Oh, hello," said Brutha, bitterly. "Welcome to Omnia."

"It helps if you're philosophical about it," said Didactylos.

"But there's no reason to fight!"

"Yes there is. Honor and revenge and duty and things like that."

"Do you really think so? I thought philosophers were supposed to be logical?"

Didactylos shrugged.

"Well, the way I see it, logic is only a way of being ignorant by numbers."

"I thought it would all be over when Vorbis was dead."

Didactylos stared into his inner world.

"It takes a long time for people like Vorbis to die. They leave echoes in history."

"I know what you mean."

"How's Urn's steam machine?" said Didactylos.

"I think he's a bit upset about it," said Brutha.

Didactylos cackled and banged his stick on the ground.

"Hah! He's learning! Everything works both ways!"

"It should do," said Brutha.

Something like a golden comet sped across the sky of the Discworld. Om soared like an eagle, buoyed up by the freshness, by the *strength* of the belief. For as long as it lasted, anyway. Belief this hot, this desperate, never lasted long. Human minds could not sustain it. But while it did last, he was *strong*.

The central spire of Cori Celesti rises up from the mountains at the Hub, ten vertical miles of green ice and snow, topped by the turrets and domes of Dunmanifestin.

There the gods of the Discworld live.

At the least, any god who is anybody. And it is strange that, although it takes years of effort and work and scheming for a god to get there, once there they never seem to do a lot apart from drink too much and indulge in a little mild corruption. Many systems of government follow the same broad lines.

They play games. They tend to be very simple games, because gods are easily bored by complicated things. It is strange that, while small gods can have one aim in mind for millions of years, *are* in fact one aim, large gods seem to have the attention span of the common mosquito.

And style? If the gods of the Discworld were people they would think that three plaster ducks is a bit avant-garde.

There was a double door at the end of the main hall.

It rocked to a thunderous knocking.

The gods looked up vaguely from their various preoccupations, shrugged and turned away.

The doors burst inward.

Om strode through the debris, looking around with the air of one who has a search to complete and not a lot of time to do it in.

"Right," he said.

Io, God of Thunder, looked up from his throne and waved his hammer threateningly.

"Who are you?"

Om strode toward the throne, picked up Io by his toga, and gave a quick jab with his forehead.

Hardly anyone really believes in thunder gods any more . . .

"Ow!"

"Listen, friend. I've got no time for talking to some pantywaister in a sheet. Where's the gods of Ephebe and Tsort?"

Io, clutching at his nose, waved vaguely towards the center of the hall.

"You nidn't naf to ndo dat!" he said reproachfully.

Om strode across the hall.

In the center of the room was what at first looked like a round table, and then looked like a model of the Discworld, Turtle, elephants and all, and then in some undefinable way looked like the *real* Discworld, seen from far off yet brought up close to. There was something subtly wrong about the distances, a feeling of vast space curled up small. But possibly the real Discworld wasn't covered with a network of glowing lines, hovering just above the surface. Or perhaps miles above the surface?

Om hadn't seen this before, but he knew what it was.

Both a wave and a particle; both a map and the place mapped. If he focused on the tiny glittering dome on top of the tiny Cori Celesti, he would undoubtedly see himself, looking down on an even smaller model . . . and so on, down to the point where the universe coiled up like the tail of an ammonite, a kind of creature that lived millions of years ago and never believed in any gods at all . . .

The gods clustered around it, watching intently.

Om elbowed aside a minor Goddess of Plenty.

There were dice floating just above the world, and a mess of little clay figures and gaming counters. You didn't need to be even slightly omnipotent to know what was going on.

"He hid by nose!"

Om turned around.

"I never forget a face, friend. Just take yours away, right? While you still have some left?"

He turned back to the game.

"S'cuse me," said a voice by his waist. He looked down at a very large newt.

"Yes?"

"You not supposed do that here. No Smiting. Not up *here*. It the rules. You want fight, you get your humans fight his humans."

"Who're you?"

"P'Tang-P'Tang, me."

"*You're* a god?"

"Definite."

"Yeah? How many worshipers have you got?"

"Fifty-one!"

The newt looked at him hopefully, and added, "Is that lots? Can't count."

It pointed at a rather crudely molded figure on the beach in Omnia and said, "But got a stake!"

Om looked at the figure of the little fisherman.

"When he dies, you'll have fifty worshipers," he said.

"That more or less than fifty-one?"

"A lot less."

"Definite?"

"Yes."

"No one tell me that."

There were several dozen gods watching the beach. Om vaguely remembered the Ephebian statues. There was the goddess with the badly carved owl. Yes.

Om rubbed his head. This wasn't god-like thinking. It seemed simpler when you were up here. It was all a game. You forgot that it wasn't a game down there. People died. Bits got chopped off. We're like eagles up here, he thought. Sometimes we show a tortoise how to fly.

Then we let go.

He said, to the occult world in general, "There's people going to die down there."

A Tsortean God of the Sun did not even bother to look around.

"That's what they're for," he said. In his hand he was holding a dice box that looked very much like a human skull with rubies in the eye-sockets.

"Ah, yes," said Om. "I forgot that, for a moment." He looked at the skull, and then turned to the little Goddess of Plenty.

"What's this, love? A cornucopia? Can I have a look? Thanks."

Om emptied some of the fruit out. Then he nudged the Newt God.

"If I was you, friend, I'd find something long and hefty," he said.

"Is one less than fifty-one?" said P'Tang-P'Tang.

"It's the same," said Om, firmly. He eyed the back of the Tsortean God's head.

"But you have thousands," said the Newt God. "You fight for thousands."

Om rubbed his forehead. I spent too long down there, he thought. I can't stop thinking at ground level.

"I think," he said, "I think, if you want thousands, you have to fight for one." He tapped the Solar God on the shoulder. "Hey, sunshine?"

When the God looked around, Om broke the cornucopia over his head.

It wasn't a normal thunderclap. It stuttered like the shyness of supernovas, great ripping billows of sound that tore up the sky. Sand fountained up and whirled across the recumbent bodies lying facedown on the beach. Lightning stabbed down, and sympathetic fire leapt from spear-tip and sword-point.

Simony looked up at the booming darkness.

"What the hell's happening?" He nudged the body next to him.

It was Argavisti. They stared at one another.

More thunder smashed across the sky. Waves climbed up one another to rip into the fleet. Hull drifted with awful grace into hull, giving the bass line of the thunder a counterpoint of groaning wood.

A broken spar thudded into the sand by Simony's head.

"We're dead if we stay here," he said. "Come on."

They staggered through the spray and sand, amidst

groups of cowering and praying soldiers, fetching up against something hard, half-covered.

They crawled into the calm under the Turtle.

Other people had already had the same idea. Shadowy figures sat or sprawled in the darkness. Urn sat dejectedly on his toolbox. There was a hint of gutted fish.

"The gods are angry," said Borvorius.

"Bloody furious," said Argavisti.

"I'm not that happy myself," said Simony. "Gods? Huh!"

"This is no time for impiety," said Rham-ap-Efan.

There was a shower of grapes outside.

"Can't think of a better one," said Simony.

A piece of cornucopia shrapnel bounced off the roof of the Turtle, which rocked on its spiked wheels.

"But why be angry with us?" said Argavisti. "We're doing what they want."

Borvorius tried to smile. "Gods, eh?" he said. "Can't live with 'em, can't live without 'em."

Someone nudged Simony, and passed him a soggy cigarette. It was a Tsortean soldier. Despite himself, he took a puff.

"It's good tobacco," he said. "The stuff we grow tastes like camel's droppings."

He passed it along to the next hunched figure.

THANK YOU.

Borvorius produced a flask from somewhere.

"Will you go to hell if you have a drop of spirit?" he said.

"So it seems," said Simony, absently. Then he noticed the flask. "Oh, you mean alcohol? Probably. But who cares? I won't be able to get near the fire for priests. Thanks."

"Pass it around."

THANK YOU.

The Turtle rocked to a thunderbolt.

"G'n y'himbe bo?"

They all looked at the pieces of raw fish, and Fasta Benj's hopeful expression.

"I could rake some of the coals out of the firebox from here," said Urn, after a while.

Someone tapped Simony on the shoulder, creating a strange tingling sensation.

THANK YOU. I HAVE TO GO.

As he took it he was aware of the rush of air, a sudden breath in the universe. He looked around in time to see a wave lift a ship out of the water and smash it against the dunes.

A distant scream colored the wind.

The soldiers stared.

"There were people under there," said Argavisti.

Simony dropped the flask.

"Come on," he said.

And no one, as they hauled on timbers in the teeth of the gale, as Urn applied everything he knew about levers, as they used their helmets as shovels to dig under the wreckage, asked who it was they were digging for, or what kind of uniform they'd been wearing.

Fog rolled in on the wind, hot and flashing with electricity, and still the sea pounded down.

Simony hauled on a spar, and then found the weight lessen as someone grasped the other end. He looked up into Brutha's eyes.

"Don't say anything," said Brutha.

"Gods are doing this to us?"

"Don't say anything!"

"I've got to know!"

"It's better than *us* doing this to us, isn't it?"

"There's still people who never got off the ships!"

"No one ever said it was going to be nice!"

Simony pulled aside some planking. There was a man there, armor and leathers so stained as to be unrecognizable, but alive.

"Listen," said Simony, as the wind whipped at him, "I'm not giving in! You've haven't won! I'm not doing this for any sort of god, whether they exist or not! I'm doing it for other people! *And stop smiling like that!*"

A couple of dice dropped on to the sand. They sparkled and crackled for a while and then evaporated.

The sea calmed. The fog went ragged and curled into nothingness. There was still a haze in the air, but the sun was at least visible again, if only as a brighter area in the dome of the sky.

Once again, there was the sensation of the universe drawing breath.

The gods appeared, transparent and shimmering in and out of focus. The sun glinted off a hint of golden curls, and wings, and lyres.

When they spoke, they spoke in unison, their voices drifting ahead or trailing behind the others, as always happens when a group of people are trying to faithfully repeat something they've been told to say.

Om was in the throng, standing right behind the Tsortean God of Thunder with a faraway expression on his face. It was noticeable, if only to Brutha, that the Thunder God's right arm disappeared up behind his own back in a way that, if such a thing could be imagined, would suggest that someone was twisting it to the edge of pain.

What the gods said was heard by each combatant in his own language, and according to his own understanding. It boiled down to:

I. This is Not a Game.

II. Here and Now, You are Alive.

And then it was over.

"You'd make a good bishop," said Brutha.

"Me?" said Didactylos. "I'm a philosopher!"

"Good. It's about time we had one."

"And an Ephebian!"

"Good. You can think up a better way of ruling the country. Priests shouldn't do it. They can't think about it properly. Nor can soldiers."

"Thank you," said Simony.

They were sitting in the Cenobiarch's garden. Far overhead an eagle circled, looking for anything that wasn't a tortoise.

"I like the idea of democracy. You have to have someone everyone distrusts," said Brutha. "That way, everyone's happy. Think about it. Simony?"

"Yes?"

"I'm making you head of the Quisition."

"*What?*"

"I want it stopped. And I want it stopped the hard way."

"You want me to kill all the inquisitors? Right!"

"No. That's the easy way. I want as few deaths as possible. Those who enjoyed it, perhaps. But only those. Now . . . where's Urn?"

The Moving Turtle was still on the beach, wheels buried in the sand blown about by the storm. Urn had been too embarrassed to try to unearth it.

"The last I saw, he was tinkering with the door mechanism," said Didactylos. "Never happier than when he's tinkering with things."

"Yes. We shall have to find things to keep him occupied. Irrigation. Architecture. That sort of thing."

"And what are *you* going to do?" said Simony.

"I've got to copy out the Library," said Brutha.

"But you can't read and write," said Didactylos.

"No. But I can see and draw. Two copies. One to keep here."

"Plenty of room when we burn the Septateuch," said Simony.

"No burning of anything. You have to take a step at a time," said Brutha. He looked out at the shimmering line of the desert. Funny. He'd been as happy as he'd ever been in the desert.

"And then . . ." he began.

"Yes?"

Brutha lowered his eyes, to the farmlands and villages around the Citadel. He sighed.

"And then we'd better get on with things," he said. "Every day."

Fasta Benj rowed home, in a thoughtful frame of mind.

It had been a very good few days. He'd met a lot of new people and sold quite a lot of fish. P'Tang-P'Tang, with his lesser servants, had talked personally to him, making him promise not to wage war on some place he'd never heard of. He'd agreed.*

---

*Fasta Benj's people had no word for war, since they had no one to fight and life was quite tough enough as it was. P'Tang-P'Tang's words had arrived as: "remember when Pacha Moj hit his uncle with big rock? Like that, only more worse."

Some of the new people had shown him this amazing way of making lightning. You hit this rock with this piece of hard stuff and you got little bits of lightning which dropped on to dry stuff which got red and hot like the sun. If you put more wood on it got bigger and if you put a fish on it got black but if you were quick it didn't get black but got brown and tasted better than anything he'd ever tasted, although this was not difficult. And he'd been given some knives not made out of rock and cloth not made out of reeds and, all in all, life was looking up for Fasta Benj and his people.

He wasn't sure why *lots* of people would want to hit Pacha Moj's uncle with a big rock, but it definitely escalated the pace of technological progress.

No one, not even Brutha, noticed that old Lu-Tze wasn't around any more. Not being noticed, either as being present or absent, is part of a history monk's stock in trade.

In fact he'd packed his broom and his bonsai mountains and had gone by secret tunnels and devious means to the hidden valley in the central peaks, where the abbot was waiting for him. The abbot was playing chess in the long gallery that overlooked the valley. Fountains bubbled in the gardens, and swallows flew in and out of the windows.

"All went well?" said the abbot, without looking up.

"Very well, lord," said Lu-Tze. "I had to *nudge* things a little, though."

"I wish you wouldn't do that sort of thing," said the abbot, fingering a pawn. "You'll overstep the mark one day."

"It's the history we've got these days," said Lu-Tze. "Very shoddy stuff, lord. I have to patch it up all the time—"

"Yes, yes—"

"We used to get much better history in the old days."

"Things were always better than they are now. It's in the nature of things."

"Yes, lord. Lord?"

The abbot looked up in mild exasperation.

"Er . . . you know the books say that Brutha died and there was a century of terrible warfare?"

"You know my eyesight isn't what it was, Lu-Tze."

"Well . . . it's not entirely like that now."

"Just so long as it all turns out all right in the end," said the abbot.

"Yes, lord," said the history monk.

"There are a few weeks before your next assignment. Why don't you have a little rest?"

"Thank you, lord. I thought I might go down to the forest and watch a few falling trees."

"Good practice. Good practice. Mind always on the job, eh?"

As Lu-Tze left, the abbot glanced up at his opponent.

"Good man, that," he said. "Your move."

The opponent looked long and hard at the board.

The abbot waited to see what long-term, devious strategies were being evolved. Then his opponent tapped a piece with a bony finger.

REMIND ME AGAIN, he said. HOW THE LITTLE HORSE-SHAPED ONES MOVE.

Eventually Brutha died, in unusual circumstances.

He had reached a great age, but this at least was not

unusual in the Church. As he said, you had to keep busy, every day.

He rose at dawn, and wandered over to the window. He liked to watch the sunrise.

They hadn't got around to replacing the Temple doors. Apart from anything else, even Urn hadn't been able to think of a way of removing the weirdly contorted heap of molten metal. So they'd just built steps over them. And after a year or two people had quite accepted it, and said it was probably a symbol. Not *of* anything, exactly, but still a symbol. Definitely symbolic.

But the sun did shine off the copper dome of the Library. Brutha made a mental note to enquire about the progress of the new wing. There were too many complaints about overcrowding these days.

People came from everywhere to visit the Library. It was the biggest non-magical library in the world. Half the philosophers of Ephebe seemed to live there now, and Omnia was even producing one or two of its own. And even priests were coming to spend some time in it, because of the collection of religious books. There were one thousand, two hundred and eighty-three religious books in there now, each one—according to itself—the only book any man need ever read. It was sort of nice to see them all together. As Didactylos used to say, you had to laugh.

It was while Brutha was eating his breakfast that the subdeacon whose job it was to read him his appointments for the day, and tactfully make sure he wasn't wearing his underpants on the outside, shyly offered him congratulations.

"Mmm?" said Brutha, his gruel dripping off the spoon.

"One hundred years," said the subdeacon. "Since you walked in the desert, sir."

"Really? I thought it was, mm, fifty years? Can't be more than sixty years, boy."

"Uh, one hundred years, lord. We had a look in the records."

"Really. One hundred years? One hundred years' time?" Brutha laid down his spoon very carefully, and stared at the plain white wall opposite him. The subdeacon found himself turning to see what it was the Cenobiarch was looking at, but there was nothing, only the whiteness of the wall.

"One hundred years," mused Brutha. "Mmm. Good lord. I forgot." He laughed. "I *forgot*. One hundred years, eh? But here and now, we—"

The subdeacon turned around.

"Cenobiarch?"

He stepped closer, the blood draining from his face.

"Lord?"

He turned and ran for help.

Brutha's body toppled forward almost gracefully, smacking into the table. The bowl overturned, and gruel dripped down on to the floor.

And then Brutha stood up, without a second glance at his corpse.

"Hah. I wasn't expecting you," he said.

Death stopped leaning against the wall.

How fortunate you were.

"But there's still such a lot to be done . . ."

Yes. There always is.

Brutha followed the gaunt figure through the wall where, instead of the privy that occupied the far side in normal space, there was . . .

. . . black sand.

The light was brilliant, crystalline, in a black sky filled with stars.

"Ah. There really *is* a desert. Does everyone get this?" said Brutha.

WHO KNOWS?

"And what is at the end of the desert?"

JUDGMENT.

Brutha considered this.

"*Which* end?"

Death grinned and stepped aside.

What Brutha had thought was a rock in the sand was a hunched figure, sitting clutching its knees. It looked paralyzed with fear.

He stared.

"Vorbis?" he said.

He looked at Death.

"But Vorbis died a hundred years ago!"

YES. HE HAD TO WALK IT ALL ALONE. ALL ALONE WITH HIMSELF. IF HE DARED.

"He's been here for a hundred years?"

POSSIBLY NOT. TIME IS DIFFERENT HERE. IT IS . . . MORE PERSONAL.

"Ah. You mean a hundred years can pass like a few seconds?"

A HUNDRED YEARS CAN PASS LIKE INFINITY.

The black-on-black eyes stared imploringly at Brutha, who reached out automatically, without thinking . . . and then hesitated.

HE WAS A MURDERER, said Death. AND A CREATOR OF MURDERERS. A TORTURER. WITHOUT PASSION. CRUEL. CALLOUS. COMPASSIONLESS.

"Yes. I know. He's Vorbis," said Brutha. Vorbis changed people. Sometimes he changed them into dead people. But he always changed them. That was his triumph.

He sighed.

"But I'm me," he said.

Vorbis stood up, uncertainly, and followed Brutha across the desert.

Death watched them walk away.

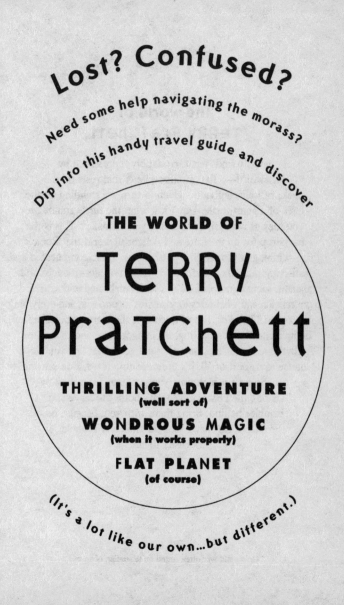

Lost? Confused?

Need some help navigating the morass?

Dip into this handy travel guide and discover

THE WORLD OF

TERRY PRATCHETT

THRILLING ADVENTURE
(well sort of)

WONDROUS MAGIC
(when it works properly)

FLAT PLANET
(of course)

(It's a lot like our own...but different.)

The world of
TeRRY PraTChett

usually finds itself irresistibly represented by
Discworld—a flat, circular planet that rests on the
backs of four elephants, which in turn are standing on the
back of a giant turtle. Don't ask what the turtle stands on;
you may as well ask what sound yellow makes. This is the
backdrop for an intricate and delightful world that Booker
Prize–winning author A. S. Byatt hails as "more complicated and
satisfying than Oz," where every aspect of life—modern and
ancient, sacred and profane—is both celebrated and satirized,
from religion and Christmas to vampires, opera, war, and everything
in between.* Reading Terry Pratchett is the literary equivalent of
doing a cha-cha. It's exciting, it's invigorating, and those more
rhythmically inclined say it's got a good beat and you can
dance to it. Best of all, it's pure unadulterated, sidesplitting
fun. So isn't it high time you got away from it all by
visiting the Discworld? Don't bother to leave your
troubles behind. Bring them with you, because on
Discworld they'll look different and a whole
lot easier to cure.

---

* Opera and war often sound quite similar, of course...

A Brief Musing on **DISCWORLD**
(in theory and in practice)

DISCWORLD novels are, appropriately enough, about things on Discworld, but they have a tendency to reflect events or ideas from our world. In each case, subjects are covered in a distinctly "Discworld" way, but some of what's seen and heard seems to comment pointedly and very humorously on the lives lived in what we are pleased to call "the Real World." Discworld is definitely not our world but eerily resembles it, and the sheer contrary humanity of all the characters on this extremely flat planet is as challenging and hilarious as our own at its best and worst.

TERRY Pratchett himself sums it up best:

"The world rides through space on the back of a turtle. This is one of the great ancient world myths, found wherever men and turtles were gathered together; the four elephants were an Indo-European sophistication. The idea has been lying in the lumber rooms of legend for centuries. All I had to do was grab it and run away before the alarms went off.

There are no maps. You can't map a sense of humor. Anyway, what is a fantasy map but a space beyond which There Be Dragons? On the Discworld we know There Be Dragons Everywhere. They might not all have scales and forked tongues, but they Be Here all right, grinning and jostling and trying to sell you souvenirs.

Enjoy. **"** *

---

* He's also been known to describe it in *The Discworld Companion* as "like a geological pizza but without the anchovies."

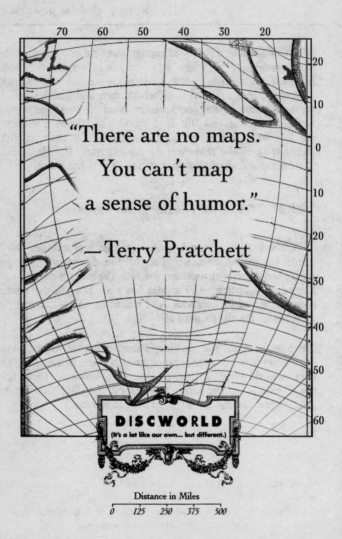

"There are no maps.
You can't map
a sense of humor."

— Terry Pratchett

Some characters show up all the time in the novels of Discworld; others you may be hard-pressed at times to find. Any way you slice it, Discworld would be much more akin to a drab, uninteresting sitting room without this cast of heroes, villains, and assorted none-of-the-aboves.

So without any further ado, here's a taste of some of Discworld's finest whom you may run into from time to time. . . .

DEATH . . . An obvious sort of fellow: tall, thin (skeletal, as a matter of fact), and ALWAYS SPEAKS IN CAPITAL LETTERS. Generally shows up when you're dead, or just when he thinks you ought to be. Not a bad chap when you get to know him (and sooner or later, everyone gets to know him).

CARROT IRONFOUNDERSSON . . . Captain of Ankh-Morpork's City Watch police force. Bulging with muscles, this six-foot-six-inch dwarf (he was adopted) remains honest, good-natured, and honorable despite the city's best efforts. Carrot may also be the true heir to Ankh-Morpork's throne (a subject filed under "I wouldn't ask if I were you").

COMMANDER SAMUEL VIMES . . . Head of Ankh-Morpork's City Watch, despite his best efforts to the contrary. A slightly tarnished walker along mean streets, and like all good cops knows exactly when it's time to be a bad cop.

CORPORAL C. W. ST. J. NOBBS . . . Call him "Nobby"—everyone else does. Looking sufficiently like a monkey to have to bear a written testimonial as to his actual species, this City Watch member has a known affinity for thievery—namely, anything that isn't nailed down is his (and anything that can be pried loose is not considered nailed down). But honest about the big things (i.e., the ones too heavy to lift).

ANGUA . . . Now a sergeant in Ankh-Morpork's City Watch (which has a very good affirmative-action policy; they'll take anyone except vampires). She is a werewolf at full moon, a vegetarian for the rest of the month. Her ability to smell colors and rip out a man's throat if she so chooses serve as useful job skills, and have done wonders for her arrest record if not for her social life. A definite K-9 cop.

The **GANG**'s all there!

ESMERELDA "GRANNY" WEATHERWAX . . . The greatest witch on all of Discworld, at least in her opinion. Lives in the village of Bad Ass in the kingdom of Lancre (the village was named after a legendarily disobedient donkey, since you ask). A bad witch by inclination but a good witch by instinct, Granny prefers to achieve by psychology, trickery, and guile what others prefer to achieve by simple spells. She's someone to have on your side, because believe us, it's better than the alternative. Owner of a rather temperamental broom now made up entirely of spare parts. Any questions?

GYTHA "NANNY" OGG . . . The broad-minded, understanding, and grandmotherly matriarch of a somewhat extensive family, with fifteen children and countless grandchildren. She's had many husbands (and was married to three of them). Very knowledgeable on matters of the heart and associated organs. Likes a drink. Likes another drink. Likes a third drink. Make that a double, will you? She is the second member of the coven, which has included:

MAGRAT GARLICK . . . Once a witch, now the Queen of the kingdom of Lancre, this young witch doesn't adhere to the "old school" of witchcraft. She believes in crystals and candles and being nice to people—but she is a witch, so in a tight corner will fight like a cat...

and AGNES NITT . . . and while you're at it, why not meet Perdita as well? A witch with a split personality, the rather overweight Agnes Nitt walks the Discworld while Perdita (the "thin" person said to be within every fat one) whiles away her time daydreaming and offering unwanted advice and criticism. Gifted with an incredibly beautiful singing voice capable of any pitch or sound (comes in handy for belting out an aria in perfect harmony with herself).

MUSTRUM RIDCULLY . . . The Archchancellor of Unseen University. The longest-standing head of the University, Ridcully is notorious for his ironclad decision-making, the incredible lapse of time it takes to explain something to him, and his all-purpose wizarding hat (suitable for emergency shelter and the storage of alcohol). Is now ever more terrifying since he read a book on how to be a dynamic manager in one minute.

RINCEWIND . . . Simply put, the most inept wizard to ever exist in any universe. Rincewind possesses a survival instinct that far outweighs his spellcasting, and is such a coward that (if Einstein is right) he's coming back from the other direction as a hero. Guaranteed to solve every minor problem by turning it into a major disaster.

THE LIBRARIAN . . . It's the primary function of the Librarian of Unseen University to keep people from using the books, lest they wear out from all that reading. It also happens to be a primate function, given the fact that he's also a 300-lb. orangutan (transformed by a magic spell, but he prefers it so much he refuses to be re-transformed). Don't ever call him a monkey. *Ever.*

LORD HAVELOCK VETINARI . . . The supreme ruler of Ankh-Morpork. A keen believer in the principle of One Man, One Vote; he is the Man, so he's got the vote. Always in complete control of every situation he finds himself in, Lord Vetinari's sense of leadership and stability keep the city up and running...and you'd better believe that this is at the forefront of his mind at all times.

CUT-ME-OWN-THROAT DIBBLER . . . Not really a criminal, more of an entrepreneur who fits the needs of the times. Usually seen selling some kind of food in a bun (no matter how questionable its origins), C.M.O.T. Dibbler is always on the lookout for Discworld's latest business opportunity (again, no matter how questionable its origins). Not a man who asks questions, in fact, and he would prefer if you would also keep off ones like "what's in this sausage?"

COHEN THE BARBARIAN . . . The greatest hero in the history of Discworld. He's an old man now, but hasn't let that stop him. Don't laugh at him. In one of the most dangerous professions in the world, he has survived to be very, very old. Get the point?

THE LUGGAGE . . . Know it. Love it. Fear it. Constructed of magical sapient pearwood, the Luggage is a suitcase with lots of little legs, completely faithful to its owner, and completely homicidal to anyone it perceives as a threat to said owner. Baggage with a nasty overbite. Definitely *not* your standard carry-on.

THE GREAT A'TUIN . . . The gigantic space turtle upon which the entire Discworld rests (with four elephants sandwiched in between, of course). What is it really? How did it get there? Where is it going? (Actually, it is the only creature in the universe that knows *exactly* where it is going).

DISCWORLD on $30 a Day

This is quite easy to do, provided you don't eat and like sleeping out of doors. There are about four continents on Discworld:*

THE (UNNAMED) CONTINENT
Includes Ankh-Morpork, the Ramtops region, the witches' haven of Lancre, and the mysterious vampire-ridden domain of Überwald, whose fragmentation into smaller states after the breakup of the Evil Empire is occupying a lot of politicians' minds (anything strike you as familiar?).

THE COUNTERWEIGHT CONTINENT
Home to the fruitful, multiplying, and extremely rich Agatean Empire. Has a certain "Far East" flavor, with a side order of Hot and Sour soup.

KLATCH
Not loosely based on Africa at all. Honestly.

XXXX
A mysterious place to be certain, but some of its secrets have since spilled forth in the novel *The Last Continent* (by the way, "XXXX" is the manner in which it's written on the maps, since no one knew what it was supposed to be called). A vast dry red continent, where water is so scarce everyone has to drink beer. Still, no worries, eh?

---

* According to Terry Pratchett in *The Discworld Companion*, "there have been other continents, which have sunk, blown up, or simply disappeared. This sort of thing happens all the time, even on the best-regulated planets."

ANKH-MORPORK

"There's a saying that all roads lead to Ankh-Morpork.
And it's wrong. All roads lead away from Ankh-Morpork,
but sometimes people just walk along them the wrong way.**"**
—Terry Pratchett

Welcome to Ankh-Morpork, Discworld's most happening city and so carefully described it could be considered a character in its own right. Divided in two by the River Ankh—a waterway so thick with silt that it should really be considered a walkway instead,* Ankh-Morpork is one of those rather large cosmopolitan burgs that, like a lot of others with a similar claim to fame, always seems on the move but never really goes anywhere.

TAVERNS
Some of the many watering holes you can frequent on Discworld, where revelers can go in as men, and come out still men but with fewer teeth:

The Mended Drum
Originally known as The Broken Drum ("you can't beat it") before the fire, The Mended Drum ("you can get beaten") is hailed as the most reputable disreputable tavern on Discworld, where the beer is, well, supposedly beer (more colorful metaphors may apply). It's also here that you'll find some of the best in live entertainment that Ankh-Morpork has to offer . . . if getting slammed over the head with something heavy or a single serving of knuckle sandwich is your idea of fun.

Other pubs of (dis)interest: The Bucket; Bunch of Grapes; Crimson Leech; Stab in the Back; King's Head; Quene's Head; Duke's Head; Troll's Head (perfect for those with a death wish because it's still attached to the troll).

---

* "They say that it is hard to drown in the Ankh, but easy to suffocate."
—Terry Pratchett, *The Discworld Companion*

THE SHADES
Choose your path around Ankh-Morpork carefully, as you do *not* want to end up in the Shades. The oldest part of the city and about a ten-minute walk from Unseen University, the Shades is a yawning black pit with buildings and streets, an urban canker sore festering with criminal activity, immorality, and other similarly nasty habits. Every city has one. Need help? Don't expect any bleeding hearts around these parts, with the exception of your own. Multiple stab wounds can *hurt*.

THE PATRICIAN'S PALACE
Lord Vetinari's pleasure dome, complete with dungeons, scorpion pits, and other various forms of entertainment. The Palace Grounds are a must-see. Besides the obligatory bird garden, zoo, and racehorse stable, the Gardens, designed by the blissfully incompetent landscaper Bergholt Stuttley ("Bloody Stupid") Johnson, highlight a garden maze so minuscule that visitors lose their way looking for it, a trout lake 150 yards long and 1 inch wide (perfect for the dieting fish), and a chiming sundial best avoided at noon (it tends to explode).

UNSEEN UNIVERSITY
Welcome to Discworld's most prestigious (i.e. only) school of higher learning and the heart of Ankh-Morpork. Think of it as a wizard's college and chief learning center of the occult on Discworld, dedicated to serious drinking and really big dinners.

The wizards don't so much use magic as not use it, but in a dynamic way (a bit like the atomic bomb) and the time not spent eating is mostly taken up by interdepartmental squabbles (which of course never happen in *real* universities).

Be sure to visit the Library, if the Librarian allows you in, that is (hint: bananas will get you everywhere). Once inside, gaze in wild wonder at its violation of physics with seemingly endless rows and shelves of tomes magical and otherwise—theoretically all of the books in existence, as well as those that were never written. Remember: no talking, no reading, no kidding.

School motto:

NVNC ID VIDES, NVNC NE VIDES

("Now you see it, now you don't.")

TeRRY PRaTCheTT's **DISCWORLD** TRivia Quiz

1. Which book told us about the history of Roundworld through the model universe created in the Unseen University's High Energy Magic Building?

A. *Maskerade*
B. *The Science of Discworld*
C. *Hogfather*
D. *Feet of Clay*

2. In *Small Gods,* Brutha finds himself to be the Chosen One for which Great God?

A. Auditors
B. Om
C. The Great A'tuin
D. Tobrun

3. Ysabell grew up to marry Mort, Death's apprentice, and they had a child. Who is the child?

A. Carrot
B. Mustrum Ridcully
C. Susan
D. Lord Havelock Vetinari
E. Corporal C. W. St. J. Nobbs

4. Ankh-Morpork's most brilliant genius, he just doesn't know when to stop creating . . . is?

A. Leonard of Quirm
B. Rincewind
C. Ned Simnel
D. Corporal C. W. St. J. Nobbs

5. Which character in Discworld speaks only in capital letters?

A. Lord Havelock Vetinari
B. Death
C. Rincewind
D. Granny Weatherwax

6. Which dwarven member of the Watch has a proclivity toward wearing items of clothing and makeup (here's a hint, it's female)?

A. Miss Cheery Littlebottom
B. Miss Angua von Überwald
C. Miss Magrat Garlick
D. Miss Agnes Nitt
E. Corporal C. W. St. J. Nobbs

7. In *The Truth*, Mr. Pin snorts which items?

A. Mr. Dibbler's "hot dogs"
B. Powdered moth balls
C. Dog worming tablets
D. Sugar
E. Probably any of the above except maybe the hot dogs.

If you're stuck for answers (or would rather just cheat instead), turn to the last page.

THE PRAISE! THE ACCOLADES! THE KUDOS!

Oh, why not just skip the formalities and hoist Terry Pratchett on our shoulders for a job well done?

"Nothing short of magical.... Pratchett's Monty Python-like plots are almost impossible to describe. His talent for characterization and dialogue and his pop-culture allusions steal the show."
—*Chicago Tribune*

"Pratchett has now moved beyond the limits of humorous fantasy, and should be recognized as one of the more significant contemporary English language satirists."
—*Publishers Weekly*

"Offers more entertainment per page than anything this side of Wodehouse."
—*Washington Post Book World*

"Gloriously uproarious.... Pratchett's humor is international, satirical, devious, knowing, irreverent, unsparing and, above all, funny."
—*Kirkus Reviews*

"If Terry Pratchett is not yet an institution he should be."
—*Fantasy and Science Fiction*

"Think J.R.R. Tolkien with a sharper, more satiric edge."
—*Houston Chronicle*

"Discworld takes the classic fantasy universe through its logical, and comic evolution."
—*Cleveland Plain Dealer*

"Truly original.... Discworld is more complicated and satisfactory than Oz.... Has the energy of *The Hitchhiker's Guide to the Galaxy* and the inventiveness of *Alice in Wonderland*.... Brilliant!"
—A. S. BYATT

TEMPTED YET? How about enticed? Maybe pleasantly coaxed? Go on—but remember, once you read one Discworld novel you'll want to read them all. Here they are, then, conveniently listed in chronological order of events—and you don't even have to start at the beginning to get in on all the fun...

THE COLOR OF MAGIC
Introducing the wild and wonderful Discworld—witnessed through the four eyes of the tourist Twoflower and his inept wizard guide Rincewind.
ISBN 0-06-102071-0

THE LIGHT FANTASTIC
Here's encouraging news: A red star finds itself in Discworld's way, and it would appear that one incompetent and forgetful wizard is all that stands between the world and Doomsday.
ISBN 0-06-102070-2

EQUAL RITES
A dying wizard's powers were supposed to be bequeathed to the eighth son of an eighth son, but he never bothered to check the baby's sex. Now who says there can't be a female wizard?
ISBN 0-06-102069-9

MORT
Death comes to us all. When he came to Mort, he offered him a job. After being assured that being dead was not compulsory, Mort accepted.
ISBN 0-06-102068-0

SOURCERY
There was an eighth son of an eighth son. He was, quite naturally, a wizard. He had seven sons. And then he had an eighth son...a wizard squared...a source of magic...a Sourceror.
ISBN 0-06-102067-2

WYRD SISTERS
Granny Weatherwax was the most highly regarded witch of the witches' coven. But even she found that meddling in royal politics was a lot more difficult than certain playwrights would have you believe...
ISBN 0-06-102066-4

PYRAMIDS

Being trained by the Assassin's Guild in Ankh-Morpork did not fit
Teppic for the task assigned to him by fate. He inherited the throne of
Djelibeybi rather earlier than he expected (his father wasn't too happy
about it either)...but that was only the beginning of his problems.
ISBN 0-06-102065-6

GUARDS! GUARDS!

Terror stalks the denizens of Ankh-Morpork. A huge dragon has
appeared in the greatest city on Discworld, swooping from the sky at
any time, day or night, charbroiling everything in its path. To the rescue
arrives the Night Watch....
ISBN 0-06-102064-8

SMALL GODS

What do you do when your cup runneth over with little intelligence and a
lot of faith, and your small but bossy god proclaims you the Chosen One?
ISBN 0-06-109217-7

SOUL MUSIC

Sure, there are skeletons in every family's closet. Just ask Susan Sto
Helit, who is about to mind the family store a while for dear old
Grandpa Death.
ISBN 0-06-105489-5

INTERESTING TIMES

The Counterweight Continent is in urgent need of a Great Wizard. They
get the incapable wizard Rincewind instead. See him run away from war,
revolution, and fortune cookies.
ISBN 0-06-105690-1

MASKERADE

Ankh-Morpork's newest diva (and wannabe witch) must flush out a
Ghost in the Opera House who insists on terrorizing the entire company.
Hint: that chandelier looks like an accident just *waiting* to happen...
ISBN 0-06-105691-X

FEET OF CLAY
A killer with fiery eyes is stalking Ankh-Morpork, leaving behind lots of corpses and a major headache for City Watch Captain Sam Vimes.
ISBN 0-06-105764-9

HOGFATHER
The jolly Hogfather vanishes on the eve of Hogswatchnight, and it's up to the grim specter of Death to act as a not-so-ideal stand-in to deliver goodies to all the children of Discworld.
ISBN 0-06-105905-6

JINGO
A nasty little case of war breaks out when rival cities Ankh-Morpork and Al-Khali both stake a claim to the same island. Not like anything that happens on Earth at all.
ISBN 0-06-105906-4

THE LAST CONTINENT
A professor is missing from Unseen University, and a bevy of senior wizards must follow the trail to the other side of Discworld, where the Last Continent is currently under construction. No worries, mate.
ISBN 0-06-105907-2

CARPE JUGULUM
The vampires of Überwald have come out of the casket, and this time they don't plan to be back indoors by dawn. They *love* garlic.
ISBN 0-06-102039-7

THE FIFTH ELEPHANT
Captain Vimes is Überwald's newest ambassador. His mission: to find the Scone of Stone and rectify the dwarves' succession problem.
ISBN 0-06-102040-0

THE TRUTH
Starting Ankh-Morpork's first newspaper is a bit harder than it seems. First your biggest supporter gets jailed, then there's the competition, but nothing is mightier than the pen in this satire on, well, the pen.
ISBN 0-380-97895-4 (hc) ISBN 0-380-81819-1 (mm)

COLLECT THEM ALL and watch your bookshelf jump up and down with uninhibited glee. Well, not *exactly*, because it's a bookshelf. But *you* will.

DISCWORLD Trivia Quiz Answers

1. B
2. B
3. C
4. A
5. B
6. A
7. E